CIRCLE

of

SHADOWS

Also by Marisa Linton:

The Binding Spell

CIRCLE

of

SHADOWS

MARISA
LINTON

HODDERSCAPE

First published in Great Britain in 2025 by Hodderscape
An imprint of Hodder & Stoughton Limited
An Hachette UK company

The authorised representative in the EEA is Hachette Ireland, 8 Castlecourt
Centre, Dublin 15, D15 XTP3, Ireland (email: info@hbgi.ie)

1

A CIP catalogue record for this title is available from the British Library

Hardback ISBN 978 1 399 74018 0
Trade Paperback ISBN 978 1 399 74019 7
ebook ISBN 978 1 399 74020 3

Typeset in TYPEFACE by [t/setter to insert t/face and own
imprint here for newly set titles and re-runs]

Printed and bound in Great Britain by Clays Ltd, Elcograf S.p.A.

Hodder & Stoughton policy is to use papers that are natural, renewable and recyclable
products and made from wood grown in sustainable forests. The logging and manufacturing
processes are expected to conform to the environmental regulations of the country of origin.

Hodder & Stoughton Limited
Carmelite House
50 Victoria Embankment
London EC4Y 0DZ

www.hodderscape.co.uk

To Sarah Garrett,
Who loved this story from the beginning,
And has been with me – and Evie – every step of the way.

CIRCLE
of
SHADOWS

'I am borne darkly, fearfully, afar . . .'

Percy Bysshe Shelley, *Adonais*

8 March 1904

S HE CIRCLES THE chamber, leaving bloody handprints on the damp stone walls, looking for a way out. There isn't one. Her chest heaves. Her screams ricochet off the walls.

'Why are you doing this?'

Her tormentors seize her and begin a ritual chant that drowns out her voice as they drag her towards the waiting man – the one they call the Magister. He holds the bloodstained dagger with which he has slashed marks into her forearms and thighs.

The gloom of the underground chamber is relieved only by oil lamps and lanterns. Her captors' faces are concealed by hoods, their bodies enshrouded in long red robes. One is the man who betrayed her.

'Why?' Her voice fractures into ragged moans.

Reason tells her it's hopeless. There are too many of them. Yet she thrashes wildly; her flailing hands clutch at their robes, the rough material catching and tearing her nails. The Magister awaits, standing by a square opening in the flagstoned floor.

Her captors form a crescent, pinning her at the edge of the opening. They fall silent. She glimpses an expanse of water, like a giant's well. The lamplight reflects its surface, showing nothing of what lies beneath. She has the impression of unseen depth, an unknown world far below the surface.

The Magister speaks. '*Obsecro vos ut venias et epulemur in oblatione nostra*,' he says as he grabs her bleeding left arm, holds it above the water. She writhes helplessly. Beads of scarlet hang as if suspended in the air. With a succession of small plinks, they shatter the dark mirror surface and vanish into the depths.

'Why?' she sobs.

The Magister's eyes smile through slits in his hood. 'There's nothing to fear.' He speaks as though to a child who is needlessly scared of the dark.

'Let me go!' she cries. 'Please.'

'If we free you, won't you go straight to the police, and tell stories about us?'

'I won't tell anyone,' she assures him abjectly. 'I promise. I just want to go home. Back to my family.'

He nods. 'Of course. We are gentlemen, not monsters.'

He gestures. The others release her, as though loath now to touch her. She slumps forwards, shaking with terror, anger and shame at having to give her promise. She squints disbelievingly at the four symbols cut into her arms, her legs – wounds deep enough to leave scars for the rest of her life.

'You've hurt me.' Her mind is numb with shock.

'It was a game,' he says. 'Nothing more. You're free to go.'

The men fall back.

Her heart gives a great leap. They're not going to kill her. She's going to live.

Rage courses through her. She darts forward, grabs one of the retreating figures – recognising him by the smell of his fancy cologne, the way he holds himself – swings him round and punches him. He crumples, swearing. She pulls the hood off, seeing with satisfaction the blood pouring from his nose. She spits in his face.

'You bitch!' he yells. He doesn't touch her. He stanches the bleeding. He's shaking. She realises, bewildered, that he's afraid of her.

'We'll leave a light,' says the Magister, seeming not to have noticed her retaliation. 'You can follow when you're ready. Take the time you need to recover your spirits.'

He climbs the long ladder that leads through a trapdoor set in the high vaulted ceiling. One by one, the others follow, bearing their lanterns. Circles of light pass upwards and out of her sight.

Within moments she's alone in the semi-darkness of the lower chamber. The single lamp left burning gives a meagre light. Her ragged breathing echoes in the shadowy space.

She crouches, arms round her knees, trying to slow her racing heart. She'll give them time to get right away before she follows. *Damn them to hell.* Once she gets out of here, she's going straight to the police.

She becomes conscious of searing pain from her wounds and realises then how cold she is. Her captors had torn off her coat and her dress to make the cuts on her arms and legs. Somewhere in her struggles, she has lost her shoes. Stale air fills her nostrils, along with the smell of her own blood. She stirs. She'll have to climb the ladder; there's no other way out. High above her head the sound of footsteps dies away. She grits her teeth, heads for the ladder.

Ice-cold water surges over her bare feet, making her gasp. She looks down. Water is bubbling out of the square pool, rippling in small waves across the stone floor. With it comes a rank smell.

Through the open trapdoor above her she catches a sound, like the shuffling of boots. Whatever lies beyond the trapdoor, she has to get away from the rising water filling the underground chamber.

The lamp reflects the water lapping around it and it teeters. She starts to climb the ladder. Her wounds burn as she moves. She barely notices.

With a crash, the lamp topples and goes out. Now the only light comes from the square of illumination visible through the trapdoor.

Sounds: a wet thud, a dragging. Somewhere in the invisible depths below, something is emerging out of the water. She cranes to look downwards, but the space below her feet is shrouded in darkness.

She climbs faster, heart hammering.

If her tormentors are still up there, waiting to finish their game, at least they're human.

'There's something down here!' she screams.

Under her hands, the ladder shudders violently. She twists round to make out what's moving beneath her. She can't see it. But she can smell it, hear it. It's coming for her.

With shaking hands made slippery with her own blood, she struggles to grip the ladder rungs.

A sharp tug at her torn petticoat. She clutches the ladder with one hand, yanks her petticoat with the other. It rips.

She gasps as something seizes her ankles. She wraps her arms around the ladder, clinging on. She's ripped away from the ladder, shaken like a rag doll. Her hands clutch, close on empty air.

Her screams cut off as she is pulled into the bitter-cold water. There's a frenzied splashing. The water churns and convulses. She gets to the surface, fills her lungs with her last breath. She is yanked under. The dark water closes over her head, leaving a trail of bubbles.

Eventually the water grows still again.

The Mansion on the Moors

One

R AIN SPLATTERED AGAINST the high windows of the Round
Reading Room. In the great circular space beneath the
domed roof of the British Museum, rows of desks radiated out
like spokes on a wheel. Most of the seats were occupied by men:
some young, some old, some very old – learned professionals,
students and gentlemen scholars.

Women were a rare sight in this temple of knowledge, but one
young woman ignored that convention. Evelyn Winstanley sat at
the outer end of a row, making notes on sheets of paper from the
leather book propped open before her. The ancient gentleman at
the seat adjoining hers, dressed in a shiny black suit that creaked
when he moved and sporting muttonchop whiskers from a bygone
era, caught sight of the title of her book, discovered it was a history
of Egyptian magic and frowned. *Hardly a suitable subject for a
woman. Especially such a young one.* Faint tuts of disapproval came
from his direction.

Evelyn leant towards him and whispered, 'Did you know that
Hapi, god of the Nile, was depicted as androgynous, possessing
both male and female sexual attributes? Fascinating, isn't it?'

Words seemed to fail him. He goggled at her.

Evelyn gave him a beaming smile, calculated to infuriate him
further, and returned to her task.

She read on, apparently absorbed, yet today it was hard to
concentrate. Something troubled her – a growing conviction that
somewhere in that vast room a pair of eyes were fixed on her with
purpose and intent. Someone was watching her. The sensation
made her twitch as though at any moment a dagger might be

thrust between her shoulder blades. She shot a glance around her. No one was looking her way.

You're imagining things.

Evelyn glanced at her wristwatch and made a face. She would be late home, and for the second time that week; she could predict her mother's likely reaction. Springing to her feet, she knocked her papers, scattering them across the desk and over the floor. *Like an awkward schoolgirl.* She flushed, mortified, as her neighbour loudly clicked his tongue. Scooping up the papers, she bore the book back to the librarians at the central desk and hurried for the exit.

Outside the rain had stopped, yet the wind blew cold around her, nipping at her exposed face and hands, and Evelyn pulled her round felt hat lower to protect her ears. Dodging puddles, she darted along the narrow passageway towards Charing Cross. Suddenly she stopped short. She'd glimpsed something out of the corner of her eye.

The hairs on the nape of her neck stirred and lifted. It felt like a warning.

In the wan light of late afternoon, she faced a stationery shop, its windows grimy with soot. A wooden rack, still damp from the recent downpour, was propped beside the doorway. Postcards were slotted into it: sepia photographs of busy London streets; prominent buildings; scenic views; Edward VII and his family, stiff as pokers.

One postcard stood out in contrast to the rest, drawing her attention: a monochrome photograph of a lake encircled by steep hills, like a circle of colossal teeth. A lonely and mysterious place, with something about it, both oddly familiar and profoundly strange, that made her uneasy. Had she seen it before? Somewhere she'd visited in her childhood, perhaps, or in a dream. She fixed on the dark water of the lake, wondering what lay beneath its surface, how it would feel to swim in its embrace, to move through the inky blackness, so cold it might stop her heart. A feeling that was alien, desolate, yet somehow irresistible ran through her, a compulsion to sink into the watery depths, to give herself up and be lost.

Where could it be? As if in answer to her question, she made out words in a curling black script on the white margin beneath the photograph:

Sithwater, Wastdale, North Yorkshire.

Almost without knowing what she was doing, she reached out to touch the card, noticing as she did so that she wasn't wearing gloves. With a flicker of annoyance at her own absent-mindedness, she realised she'd left them on the desk in the museum.

The postcard felt damp, wet from the rain.

She drew it out of the display stand to see it more closely.

At that moment she felt warm breath stir her hair. Someone was standing behind her, looking over her shoulder at what she held. Very close – uncomfortably close.

'That's the one,' whispered a soft voice encouragingly.

She spun round.

A few stragglers moved along the passageway. No one she recognised. Had it been one of them?

You're tired, that's all. Too much time spent at a desk, reading, making notes, forgetting to eat or to stretch her cramped body. She was astonished at her own momentary weakness. She wasn't the type of person to fall prey to sinister imaginings. *Not me. Not Evie Winstanley.*

Evie pulled herself together and opened the shop door. A bell chimed. The small interior was crammed with goods: reams of paper, guidebooks to London, artists' brushes, pens, inkbottles, notebooks, a few cheap novels. A musty smell lingered. No one was in sight.

As Evie went to press the countertop bell, she realised that her left hand, clutching the postcard, felt unpleasantly moist. The card was positively *wet*, wetter by the moment. Drops of liquid fell from her fingertips, splashing on the linoleum floor.

Dash it!

The postcard was saturated, as though it had been floating in a river.

No. Not water. The liquid sensation was too thick for that, viscous . . . and sticky.

Her eyes travelled to her hand – and saw it stained with crimson. With a jerk of disgust, she flung the card away. It spiralled downwards, scattering flecks of glistening red.

She must have cried out, for a moment later the shopkeeper emerged from a doorway and began to polish the wooden counter with a dust rag, his curious eyes on Evie.

'Are you all right, miss?'

She bent to retrieve the card. It was perfectly dry. She stood, staring at her hand, at the floor. No water. No blood.

'I . . . yes. What's this?' She held out the card.

His gaze fell on it, then lifted to her face, as though she were deranged. 'A scenic postcard, miss.'

'But it's not a scene from London.'

His smile was perfunctory. 'Doesn't look like it, does it? I didn't know we carried this one.'

'It's in North Yorkshire.'

'Yorkshire?' He sounded incredulous. 'Somewhere on the South Downs more like.'

Evie pulled her scattered wits together, conscious that the shopkeeper's mouth twitched with suppressed smirks. She passed along the counter, selecting a few inexpensive objects almost at random – pencils, an India rubber – and handed them to the man.

As he gathered brown paper and a length of string to make the items up into a small parcel, she laid the postcard on top of her purchases, as though it was an afterthought. It lay there innocuously, awaiting wrapping. She bent closer, gripped almost in spite of herself. The photograph was unchanged, but the white border was plain and unmarked.

The words had vanished.

CHAPTER

Two

E VIE TURNED HER key in the lock and slipped into the hall, shutting the front door quietly behind her. Not quietly enough. A white-and-brown spaniel came scampering to meet her uttering joyous staccato barks, his claws scratching on the parquet. He flung himself at her feet, rolled over and, in his ecstasy, peed slightly on the hall rug.

'Evie? *C'est toi, chérie?*'

'D'Artagnan, you traitor,' Evie murmured to the dog. He whined, tail thumping. She bent to stroke the softness of his rounded tummy and called out, 'Yes, Maman.' There being nothing else for it, she hid the package she had brought behind the umbrella stand, tossed her hat onto a hook, took off her coat and went into the drawing room, where her mother, Leonie Winstanley, sat surrounded by the afternoon post.

Leonie had been what was popularly called a stunner in her youth, and even now, as a respectable matron, her luxuriant hair was dark, with no trace of grey, the reading glasses propped on her narrow nose the only sign of the passage of years. She had brought her native French style to the house in Hammersmith, just north of the Thames, that she had entered as a young bride twenty-five years before.

The drawing room was her particular domain. Its decoration was chic, in shades of light blue and grey, with a few treasured antiques, silverware and family paintings, yet the sunlight pouring through the window picked out scratch marks on the woodwork from D'Artagnan's claws, several discreet patches on the curtains, the threadbare condition of the carpet. From another room came the melodic clinks of piano keys playing ascending scales and arpeggios.

'Always bills.' Leonie's frown deepened as she opened another envelope. 'Is that not annoying, Harriet?'

Harriet Maddox, the distant cousin who lived with them, made sounds of commiseration as she trimmed one of last year's hats with a new ribbon. There was a faded air to much of Harriet, from her mouse-coloured hair, pulled neatly back, to her carefully maintained but old-fashioned clothes. Only her grey eyes stood out, sharp and clear, in her thin face.

Catching sight of Evie, Leonie broke off her complaints. 'Where have you been?' she demanded fretfully.

'To a lecture on Egyptian artefacts at University College. Then the British Museum Library. I mentioned it over breakfast, Maman.'

'I didn't imagine you would be gone all day,' grumbled Leonie. 'And I'm not happy with you having gone to a lecture unchaperoned. There will have been any number of students present. *Young men*,' she added, rolling her eyes.

'None that interested me.' Evie flung herself into an armchair, unstrapping her shoes. 'Those boys are so awkward, so full of themselves. And boring.'

The piano in the next room took up the melody of 'Für Elise'.

Leonie sniffed. 'That's another thing. You should be taking more of an interest in young men,' she continued, blithely contradicting herself. 'When you're married you'll put all this studying nonsense behind you.'

Evie turned to Harriet in mute appeal. Leonie intercepted the look and wrinkled her nose. 'We know that Harriet likes to go to meetings where socialists talk about being vegetarian, and women not needing corsets. Harriet *peut s'amuser*, but she understands the realities of the world. *N'est-ce pas*, Harriet?'

'I think there's rather more to the Fabians than vegetarianism and no corsets,' Harriet protested faintly. 'Votes for women for one thing, and social justice and equality—'

Leonie sailed on, drowning out Harriet. 'It's different for the young, Evie. A woman needs to marry if she can. If she doesn't, who will look after her, support her?'

'I'll support myself,' said Evie.

Turning her back on her mother's scepticism, she spied a cucumber sandwich, left over from tea, only slightly curled. She pounced and returned to devour her prize, lazing sideways in her chair, legs dangled over the arm. Her hair had come loose, streaming down her back. Evie's face had been described as 'interesting' by people – mostly friends of her mother – struck by her mobile, expressive features. Hardly anyone called her 'beautiful', not even her mother, but she didn't care about that. In her – admittedly limited – experience, beauty did not equate to happiness, nor even contentment.

Her restless gaze passed through the bay window to the darkening street and brooded over the lamplit outlines of suburban villas, much like their own.

'You didn't have time for lunch?' said Leonie, reverting to solicitude. Evie shook her head mournfully and Leonie pressed the bell beside the mantelpiece. 'I'll ask Mary to bring some more hot water for the teapot.'

Evie had just started on her tea when the piano fell silent, and moments later a teenage girl entered the room, dark-haired, dark-eyed, tall and willowy, her features classically delicate. But for all her lessons in deportment, Grace bounced rather than glided, with a surfeit of bubbling energy that came with extreme youth.

Leonie greeted her younger child with some satisfaction. It was no secret in the family that Leonie pinned her chief hopes of at least one of her daughters making an advantageous marriage on Grace's shoulders. 'You have finished your piano practice?'

'Yes, Maman,' said Grace demurely. 'A whole hour.'

'*C'est excellent.*' Leonie turned back to Evie. 'Now that Grace is here, *chérie*, I want to speak to you about something important. This select party at Maltraver Towers to which Grace has been invited. Won't you reconsider and accompany her?'

Evie paused, the remains of another sandwich halfway to her mouth. 'That's impossible, Maman.'

'Oh, yes, do come!' pleaded Grace as she helped herself to tea.

'I can't. It's all arranged that Harriet will chaperone Grace. Harriet will enjoy it so much. I couldn't deprive her—'

'Don't mind about me,' said Harriet serenely. 'I'd be perfectly happy not—'

'Also,' cut in Evie, with a quelling shake of the head at Harriet, 'I've so much to prepare if I'm to attend university next year. My studies—'

'*Mais non*,' said Leonie, taking one of the demands for payment scattered before her and twisting it into a spiral. 'This is no time to burrow away in your books. The Crosbies move in the best circles. That is the real world, *ma chère*. It's important for Grace to make these connections; she has worked hard to meet the right people.'

Behind her mother, Grace assumed a pious expression, then winked at Evie, who snorted to suppress a laugh.

'It could be helpful for you, too,' Leonie continued, oblivious of the communication passing between her daughters. 'You could be *si jolie*, Evie, if you would only make a little effort with your clothes and your hair – if you flattered the men, gave them self-consequence, show attention when they want to tell you about themselves.'

'Encourage them to boast, you mean.' Evie's eyes danced with impish humour, but as she watched the bill being crushed between her mother's agitated fingers, she grew serious. Nothing had been easy since Evie's father had died. Feeling remorseful, she went to wrap her arms around Leonie.

'I'm sorry to disoblige you, Maman. I do understand – you want what you think is best for me. But I've no intention of spending a long weekend with a set of tedious people, trying to persuade a stranger of whom I know nothing to marry me, simply because he's rich and I'm not.'

Leonie tried half-heartedly to push Evie away, shaking her head in exasperation. 'You will find one day, *ma petite*, what the world is really like.'

~

The rest of the household had gone to bed, and Evie was alone. She brought the package to a table in the drawing room and examined the postcard. It lay docile and inanimate. She stroked it with her forefinger.

What had happened earlier? She recalled her conviction that an unseen stranger was watching her, how the card appeared to transform in her hands. She wasn't the kind of person to imagine things, yet she had no explanation to give. What would Papa have made of it? If only she could talk to him, ask him . . .

Evie propped the postcard before her and began to write up notes from the lecture she'd attended. Occasionally her eyes were drawn back to the photograph, to the fathomless water, the circling hills. She put it face down on the desk, so as not to be distracted. The only sounds were the scratching of her pen and the desultory crackle of the fire in the grate. This was her favourite time to work; at night there were no demands that she bury herself in domestic tasks, or squander precious hours in visits to hear small talk from the neighbours.

Evie chewed the end of her pen, reading over her notes while they remained fresh in her mind. She studied her pencil sketches of artefacts displayed at the lecture: a model boat, complete with a crew to sail a person safely to the afterlife; a figurine of a goddess with the body of a woman and the head of a lion; the mummified corpse of a small crocodile. She rubbed some lines out, lifting the paper to blow away rubber fragments, and sighed, dissatisfied; the drawings seemed crude, full of inaccuracies.

Twisting wayward strands of hair through her fingers, she tried to work out where she was going wrong. Doubt seeped through her. She'd never become an archaeology student with drawings like this, especially at University College under the revered Professor Flinders Petrie. It would have been different if Papa had still been alive. She would not have had to fight each step of the way to prove herself. He would have believed in her potential, in her right to a life of her own.

A faint thud sounded from somewhere inside the house. Evie laid down her pen and listened. The fire had died down; the only noise was her own breathing. She must have been mistaken – the sound had come from the street outside. Slowly, she relaxed and went back to her notes.

There it was again. Evie's head went up; the hand holding the pen froze. This time she made out footfalls, soft but distinct. Probably an inmate of the house had woken up and was moving about. And yet . . . there was something stealthy about the sounds that warned her the person making them didn't want to be over-heard. Her ears strained to locate the source. Somewhere near the back of the house, on the ground floor – the same floor where she sat working. She breathed deeply to shift the unease building in her throat, wondering why no warning bark had come from D'Artagnan. But he slept upstairs with her mother, and the door would be shut, muting sounds from the floor below.

More muffled steps. She pinpointed the direction; they came from her father's study, a place where no one ventured now. *A stranger in the house.* Her heart raced; her chest tightened. *You need to keep your head.* What to do? Wake someone? No question of calling her mother who was hopeless in a crisis. Or Grace, just seventeen, who would be equally panicked. The two servants – Mary Newby, the maid, and Mrs Hope, the cook – slept up in the attic rooms, remote from the rest of the house. Harriet perhaps? Harriet was calm and level-headed, yet she was no longer young, nor was she robust; unlikely to be much help against a desperate, probably much younger and stronger housebreaker.

Even as Evie hesitated, there came the distinctive creak of the door of her father's cabinet of curios, brimful of the treasures he'd amassed over the years. Evie pictured a burglar ransacking his things, mementoes of all that they had lost, and rage momentarily blanked out her fear. Her past. Her Papa. She would let no one steal it from her.

If she didn't act quickly, the thief would take what he wanted and be gone. There was no time to call anyone else.

With sudden resolve, Evie took the poker from the hearth and left the drawing room. The gaslight in the hall was turned down low. Conscious that the parquet could creak and give away her presence, she pulled off her slippers, moving along the passage in semi-darkness. At the far end, a light glimmered through the glass panels in the study door. Candlelight. She crept closer, her pulse pounding in her ears. Her face almost touching the glass, she made out a shadow moving near the desk. The poker in her unsteady grasp bumped against the door. Immediately the light went out.

If she waited any longer, she'd be too scared to act. Gritting her teeth, she flung open the door and marched in. Wielding the poker with both hands, she shouted to a hulking – unfortunately imaginary – male servant, 'Come on, Harrison! This way!'

A mistake, she realised at once. Her own silhouette must be visible against the gaslight from the hall – hers, alone. She paused to listen, but all was still. The only light came from the window, where moonbeams showed the lower sash thrown open, the curtains stirring in the night breeze. The intruder must have come in that way. Had he left that way too? Or was he still there, lurking in the dark?

As her eyes adjusted to the gloom, she began to turn, trying to control her trembling enough to keep the poker steady, searching the shadows. Nothing moved. No sound broke the stillness, not even breathing. *He must have made his escape.* Her teeth began to unclench, the rigidity to ease from her body. Her arms ached from holding the heavy poker aloft and she lowered them.

Unless . . . he was holding his breath.

Even as the thought came to her, muscular arms snaked through the dark and grabbed her from behind. Powerful hands tightened around her throat – and squeezed.

She struggled frantically as fingers pressed deep against her windpipe. Her knees gave way; her stockinged feet slid from under her as the attacker yanked her backwards across his body, knocking her off balance. She fought to take another breath, struggling to comprehend what was happening. A black curtain was coming down over her eyes and she knew she had only moments of consciousness left.

Evie scrabbled to find purchase for her feet, bracing them against the attacker's legs. With the last of her strength, she drove the poker wildly backwards, and was rewarded by a loud grunt and a recoil as his hands released her neck to clutch at his stomach.

She twisted to follow up her attack and struck him across the chest. Groaning, the intruder shoved her backwards. She fell against a bookcase, knocking her head, a sickening blow that sent lights exploding across her eyeballs. He ran for the desk, snatched something up from it and made for the window.

Evie staggered after him, swinging the poker at his back. A jolt vibrated up her arm as metal connected with muscle and bone. With a yell, the stranger let the object fall and dived through the half-open window.

She leant across the windowsill. Eyes streaming with pain, she made out an indistinct figure. Seconds later, it vanished over the garden wall.

Evie locked the window, her hands shaking. Racked by paroxysms of coughing, she slumped to the floor and lay prone, legs drawn up, wheezing as the room swam in and out of focus. It was a few minutes before she was able to explore, with tentative fingertips, the injuries at the base of her throat and the back of her head and several more before she was able to sit up and survey her surroundings.

Evie tottered to the desk and fumbled to light the oil lamp. The room was in disarray, books and papers lying scattered on the floor. She went first to the cabinet of curios; nothing seemed to have been disturbed. She turned to the bookshelves, the desk, trying to work out if anything else was missing. It wasn't an easy task; her father had been accustomed to leaving his possessions in an order understood by him alone. Most likely the intruder had been looking for jewellery or other small portable items of value. He would have been disappointed.

Her eyes went to a book lying open near the window. This must be what the stranger had dropped. She examined it: an ancient tome, bound in faded green leather, bearing a title in gilt script: *Perambulations Among the Relics of Ancient Britain: A History* by the Reverend C. R. J. Mickleford. She frowned, bemused. Hardly the kind of book to appeal to a thief. As she turned it over, puzzling, a piece of paper fluttered to the floor.

Evie picked up the scrap and unfolded it. It bore a drawing of a circle within a circle, the space between them filled by strange symbols. Within the inner circle was a complex pattern of whorls and spirals. She tried turning the paper sideways, then upside down, but couldn't make out what it signified. She fancied there was a picture in the pattern, but even as she gazed the lines mutated and dissolved. She felt an odd chill in the pit of her stomach. The longer she looked, the more disturbing the image became.

There was writing beneath the concentric circles, barely visible in the dim light. Evie held the paper over the lamp, making out faint words scrawled in pencil: a single word, 'Kuroskato', followed by a phrase, 'the circle of shadows'.

The coldness in her stomach became a chip of ice.

The writing was in her father's hand.

CHAPTER
Three

THERE WAS NO telephone in the Winstanley household, so Evie went out onto the street, where she managed to find a policeman on his beat, who summoned another constable with his whistle. Evie watched the two men examine the study window. As they turned away, she held out the paper she'd found.

'What's this, miss?' said the older man, holding the drawing at arm's length to bring it into focus. 'Is it a child's drawing? Vivid imaginations the young do have, don't they? Rather a nasty thing. You wouldn't want to find it under your bed.'

'It may be significant. The intruder dropped it. He could have been searching for it.'

'Hardly seems likely, does it now, miss?' said the man, while his junior smothered an embarrassed chuckle in the crook of his elbow.

She snatched back the paper, mortified.

Evie had hoped not to wake her mother, guessing what Leonie's reaction would be to the news that an intruder had got into the house and that her daughter had been rash enough to confront him single-handed, but her hopes were confounded. Disturbed by the noise of the front door opening and policemen entering, D'Artagnan began a belated, but lively, barking. Soon Leonie appeared, an excited D'Artagnan at her heels, her hair tumbling in loose curls over her shoulders, wearing a dressing-gown trimmed with such a quantity of billowing lace that the policemen's attention was more on her than on their search for evidence.

On hearing what had happened, Leonie raised an outcry. In times of crisis, she was apt to find English insufficiently expressive for her emotions and reverted to her native tongue. She did so now, using forthright terms about the inadequacy of the British police, who left a household of women undefended and failed to catch a single criminal. Evie fervently hoped the constables didn't have enough French to understand her.

Grace came trailing in their mother's wake, dark eyes wide with alarm. Evie was still trying to convince her mother that the danger was past when Harriet, too, joined them, wrapped in a serviceable tartan dressing gown, her mouse-brown hair plaited. Seeing – and correctly interpreting – the plea in Evie's eyes, Harriet sent Grace to find a tincture of lavender for the calming of nerves, and turned her efforts to coaxing Leonie back to bed, assuring her that Evie was more than capable of dealing with the police.

At last Leonie was persuaded to return to her bedroom, Grace and Harriet each taking an arm, with D'Artagnan bringing up the rear. The policemen left soon after.

Evie was thankful to be alone. Her head pounded, and her bruised throat ached with each breath, but she ignored the pain and went back to her father's books, increasingly convinced that, in some way she had still to fathom, the break-in was connected with his work.

A scholar, antiquarian book dealer and collector, over a long career Walter Winstanley had amassed a vast array of books dealing in the supernatural, a unique collection of arcane and occult lore, offering gateways into what he called *the realm of the invisible*. He had kept some of these volumes under lock and key, calling them his *forbidden books*, not because they were valuable and highly prized, but because he believed them to be dangerous. Everyone in the household had known not to touch them. As far as Evie knew, no one had taken them out since her father's death.

She scrabbled in a small drawer – yes, the silver key was still there, right at the back – then went to a cabinet of walnut wood, unlocked it, and inhaled the distinctive aroma of old books: decaying paper, antique leather and vanilla. Row upon row of volumes of all kinds and conditions lined the shelves. Many were rare, found in only a few libraries of the world; a few were unique, the sole surviving copies of studies of ancient lore. As far as she could tell, nothing had been disturbed since the day Walter Winstanley had come there for the last time.

She ran her fingers over the books until they rested on a large volume entitled *Ancient Cabalistic Symbols*, its black leather covers embossed with cabalistic spirals. She brought it out, relocked the cabinet and then, reluctant to put the key back in the desk where anyone might find it, dropped it into her skirt pocket.

She carried *Ancient Cabalistic Symbols* to the desk, trimmed the lamp and pored over the pages. More than once, she caught herself drifting into sleep and had to push herself upright.

On the verge of giving up and going to collapse on her bed, she came across a symbol that resembled the drawing she had found. Though the pattern differed in its details, the likeness was unmistakable – whorls and spirals, surrounded by a double circle. Beneath it was written:

This symbol is associated with the ancient Celts, but it has no known name. Its meaning and provenance are unknown, shrouded in the mists of the past. It appears to have been universally interpreted as a sign of dark magic and an object of dread.

She propped her aching head on her hands. *A sign of dark magic.* Papa would have known what it meant. But he wasn't here.

Walter Winstanley had had two great loves in his life: the first for his family, the second for his books. As a child, Evie had sometimes wondered what had brought her parents together – they were so different in many ways – but as she grew older she'd come to realise there was no mystery at all: it had been a love match.

Leonie had never taken much interest in the other great love of Walter's life, his passion for old books dealing in the supernatural; she was too wrapped up in the here and now to be curious about the past.

Of Walter's children, it was only Evie who shared his enthusiasm for literature. From early childhood, she escaped whenever she could from tedious domestic routine – sewing, darning, social calls to family and neighbours for endless chatter about nothing in particular – to her father's study, or to the bookshop he kept in Kensington. She would curl up in a secluded corner and read story after story, while her father worked nearby in companionable silence. For Evie – like her father – old stories and legends meant escape into another world, one of boundless possibilities and far horizons.

As Evie sat alone in the study now, her eyes ranged over Walter's book collection, stacked on shelves all around her, comprising everything from cheap pamphlets to rare first editions. Many were as familiar to her as old friends. There were studies of ancient legends and folklore from the British Isles and far beyond; witches and witchcraft; the gods of the Celts, Saxons and Norsemen; the lore of arcane magic and rituals; ancient monoliths, mounds and stone circles; the lost continents of Atlantis and Lemuria; hidden gateways to the Otherworld; documented apparitions of ghosts and spectres; and the growing science of psychical research. Among her favourites were the books about folklore and popular beliefs – stories that cast light on ordinary people's lives and how they viewed the supernatural as a matter of day-to-day reality, a world alongside their own.

The most prized works in Walter Winstanley's collection were his forbidden books. These were manuals on the occult, grimoires of learned magic and practical spell books, all giving instructions on how to wield power by means of magic. This written magic was far from the world of the humble, often illiterate village witch with her healing skills, her love potions, or even her ability to put a hex on a neighbour's crops or livestock. The grimoires dealt with magic as a shattering force to be controlled and channelled. The occult was about power, *real* power, which was dangerous in the wrong hands.

That, too, was a lesson Evie's father had taught her. There were certain men, he'd once told her, who should never have access to that power.

That had been on a trip to an auction in Harrogate. Walter had gotten hold of the pre-sale catalogue, circulated to antique book dealers, and his attention was caught by details of a collection of books on the supernatural that were to be sold as one lot.

The auction hall had been crammed full of objects, ranging from fine antiques and artwork to mundane household goods. It included a collection of china dolls, lined up in prams, that watched Evie in a way she found unnerving; she'd never liked dolls. A group of stuffed animals – hunting trophies from Africa and Asia, all beautiful and all dead – roused pity and sadness in Evie's heart. Harrogate was too far from the metropolis and the auction too small an affair to attract the big London buyers, yet the main hall was a hive of activity, with professional dealers rubbing shoulders with amateur enthusiasts, along with everyone and anyone from the locality in search of bargains.

The collection of supernatural literature had been set out for inspection by prospective buyers. Bales of old books, bound up with twine, left smears of dust on the deal table where they were displayed. Walter turned over the books, reading the titles, rumpling his greying salt-and-pepper hair with his fingers, as was his unconscious habit when he was preoccupied. Nearby stood a young, lanky, ginger-haired auctioneer's assistant, and old books were evidently not his thing for he stifled yawns, shuffled his feet, and fidgeted with his tie. He brightened when Evie – someone much nearer his age than the hard-nosed dealers – approached, and they soon got into chat.

The assistant told her that he himself had brought in the book collection. It had belonged to a retired schoolmaster in rural North Yorkshire. Despite losing his sight, the schoolmaster had refused to part with any of his precious books. He had lived on for years in his remote house with the help of two aged servants. Immediately after his death and funeral, his heirs, a niece and her husband, took possession of the house and lost no time in dispatching much of the dead man's furniture, personal effects and anything that might sell, including the books, to the auction house.

'They told me,' said the assistant, 'they had no use for books and old stuff, and meant to refurnish the house with everything new and up to date. They dismissed the uncle's servants, too. Seemed a bit harsh, for they were live-in servants, too frail and elderly to find other employment. Someone told me they went to the workhouse.'

'The workhouse!' Evie said with a shudder. 'It's all wrong. This is the twentieth century after all.' She was well informed by Harriet about the Fabians' campaign for the elderly to receive pensions, and she and the assistant enjoyed a talk about the need for social reform, until his superior found work for him to do and summoned him away.

Left to herself, Evie imagined how it must have been for the schoolmaster during his last years, alone except for his loyal servants. The assistant had told her that the niece had never visited, and Evie pictured him confined to the living darkness of his sightlessness, fingering the volumes he could no longer read, the words he could no longer lose himself in, stroking the grain of the leather bindings, the embossed titles. It all seemed to her achingly sad.

'Evie,' said her father. 'Come and take a look at these illustrations.'

She joined him, inhaling the characteristic mustiness of old books, old papers. Motes of dust floated through the air as Walter picked up the volumes, one by one, rubbing the leather bindings clean with his handkerchief. He drew out a series of woodcuts, collected and bound together in a single volume, depicting fantastical beasts: some scaly, some hairy, some winged, some crawling, some creeping out of the water.

'What are they?' To Evie, they looked the stuff of nightmares, all teeth and claws and scales. An odd pinch of unease clenched uncomfortably tight around her heart.

Walter, pushing his reading glasses higher on his nose, bent over the image before him. 'Elemental spirits, creatures of the invisible . . .' His voice trailed away into silence. He wouldn't be drawn further.

As they took their places for the sale, Walter drummed his fingers on the bench in front of him, casting glances over his shoulder. Evie guessed he feared the arrival of rival bibliophiles, many of whom he knew well by sight. Yet on this occasion, few bidders showed much interest in the books. Probably, serious enthusiasts hadn't heard about the sale or spotted the entry in the catalogue.

When the schoolmaster's books came up, Walter was able to buy the entire collection at what he called a modest price, though one which, Evie knew, would annoy her mother if she came to hear of him bringing still more books into the house. As he and Evie went to see to his purchases being bundled up for travel, he was gleeful as a schoolboy, selecting certain choice books to take with him on their train journey to London rather than trust them to a delivery service.

The next moment, Walter's head went up as a newcomer hurried into the hall, a burly, thickset man wearing a dark cape and a wide-brimmed felt hat. He came straight to where they stood.

'Afternoon, Winstanley.'

Walter gave a cool nod, eyes watchful.

The stranger tipped his hat towards Evie, revealing a bullet-shaped head surmounted by close-cropped receding grey hair. At first sight, he seemed unremarkable, until she caught the intensity in his face – the rigidity of the compressed lips, eyes that were colourless yet hard, like chips of frosted glass.

Walter didn't offer to introduce his daughter to the newcomer. The wariness in her father's manner transferred itself to her.

The man's attention cut to the woodcuts in Walter's hands. 'Pipped to the post, I see.' If he was annoyed, he didn't show it; his voice was liquid smooth. A smile lifted the corners of his thin mouth, though it came nowhere near his piercing eyes.

'Indeed,' Walter said shortly. 'But there's nothing here that would have interested you.' He hastened to bundle up the selected volumes in brown paper and string.

Stubby lashes flickered over the stranger's eyes. Doffing his hat again, he strolled off to appraise a stuffed tiger, poised in a position of rearing up, about to pounce.

Evie watched him go, filled with an odd sensation that with his departure the air around her was becoming easier to breathe. 'Who was that man?'

Walter said in a low voice, 'That's Robert Wenless. He's a specialist in the occult.'

'Like yourself?'

'No,' said Walter vehemently. 'Nothing like me.' His usually benevolent expression had sharpened, giving a pinched look to his nostrils. He spoke in her ear, as though worried they might be overheard, though Wenless was by now some distance away, inspecting a collection of rapiers and ceremonial daggers. 'Evie, my dearest girl, this is very important. Should Wenless ever come to the shop when I'm not there and ask questions about the occult books, you're to have nothing to do with him. Tell him he must return later and I'll deal with him myself. Then tell me. You understand?'

'Yes, of course, Papa. But why?'

Walter tugged at his lip. 'He's not the kind of man who should be . . . trusted,' was all he would say.

Yet Robert Wenless had never come to Walter's bookshop, or at least Evie had never seen him there. She'd almost forgotten about him.

Suddenly, she bolted upright, wide awake, as a thought struck her. The book the thief had dropped, the *Perambulations Among the Relics of Ancient Britain*. Hadn't it come from the Harrogate schoolmaster's collection?

The book still lay at her elbow. She opened it and began to read.

CHAPTER
Four

L EANING OVER THE desk in the circle of lamplight, chin
propped in her hands, Evie pored through the *Perambulations
Among the Relics of Ancient Britain.* Occasionally she shifted position and stretched, trying to ease the pain in her aching back, all
the while aware of the dull throbbing in her bruised throat. She
tried to keep her attention on the page, though it didn't help that
the Reverend Mickleford had a stilted, roundabout style of writing, and that she was exhausted. Even so, some part of her mind
kept active and busy, trying to remember when it was that a change
had come over her father. It was, she felt, important to work it out.

She had the impression that it had already been noticeable on
the train returning from Harrogate. He'd sat propped in a corner
seat, his new purchases clutched on his knees, his eyes closed in
thought, not sleeping, and hardly speaking.

The next step – just a few days later? – had been signalled by
him shutting her out from her customary position of working
alongside him in his study or the shop. It was time, he announced,
that she learnt to act like the young lady that her mother, and
indeed he himself, wanted her to be. His abrupt change of tone
had come as a shock; he'd always supported her desire for a more
fulfilling life. She'd tried to argue, but he was adamant, while her
mother sat by, nodding her approval. For the first time, Evie's
father wouldn't meet her eyes.

Then, a few weeks after Harrogate, Walter underwent a change
of heart regarding Evie's education. He fell in with Leonie's desire
that she be sent away to a finishing school in Paris to be given
'polish'. Evie was to go to a small *pensionnat* whose *directrice* was a

friend of Leonie's mother. They all agreed that Evie was beyond regular lessons and in some subjects could probably teach the teachers. Instead, she would be given the social skills considered appropriate for a girl whose goal in life was to marry well. Grace, too, was to be sent away from home to a school in Bath, though the prospect didn't appear as horrifying to her as it did to Evie. She had relished the opportunities for lessons in dancing, tennis and horse-riding, the piano and flute.

Evie was not so easily reconciled to exile. The last time she spoke to her father, she'd been full of bitter, angry words. She'd seen hurt in his eyes, but he wouldn't give way – she had to go. She couldn't help but suspect there was something else, something he was keeping back.

'Don't you see, Evie?' were his parting words to her. 'I'm doing this *for* you.'

~

Evie rebelled against the discipline of the little pensionnat, and was restless in its claustrophobic atmosphere, the *littleness* of everything. The teachers' attempts to give Evie *accomplishments* met with variable success. She enjoyed the dancing lessons, though the teacher was, to her mind, far too old to present the temptation some of the girls seemed to find in him. She worked at her French and at the piano, though she lacked Grace's patience in giving the instrument the practice it required. But the endless lessons in deportment and decorum and how to be *comme il faut* bored her. Most of her friendships with the other pupils were superficial. Over time, she forged a connection with two of them – a French girl, Marguerite Laurent, and an American, Rosalie Jassett – founded on a love of history and novels, curiosity about the world and a shared impatience at endless conversations in the pension- nat about fashions and the young men in their circle.

Still, Evie had worried about her father. She knew from letters she received from her older brother Pelham and from Harriet that Walter continued to be preoccupied by his investigations. Her mother wrote occasionally, her father hardly at all, adding brief postscripts to Leonie's letters.

Then Pelham had written, telling Evie that their father had given up the lease on his shop and let go the two assistants who had been with him for years. The rest of his family presumed that he was living entirely – and keeping his dependents – on the private income he'd inherited from an uncle, but this alone would hardly be enough to maintain the household. He seemed to have given up book-dealing altogether and spent most of his time, all day and late into the night, shut up in his study – 'researching', as he called it, though just what he was researching, no one knew.

Gradually, Evie grew accustomed to her life in Paris. She'd be stuck here for at least a year, she reasoned, so she might as well be learning something that interested her. The thought of the occult returned to her mind. Papa had wanted her to keep away from such studies, calling them perilous, but she was his daughter after all and inquisitiveness won out, as it so often did with Evie.

She went to the august halls of the Bibliothèque Nationale on the rue de Richelieu and attempted to talk her way in to consult its collection of grimoires. She was firmly rebuffed by the librarians, amidst looks of outrage that a young unaccompanied English woman had even heard of such scandalous books, let alone asked to read them.

Undaunted, she gave her energies a new direction. She had visited the holdings of the British Museum, but in Paris she had more time on her hands and began going daily to the Louvre, justifying this to the directrice as being in pursuit of improving her skill in drawing and knowledge of art history. In reality, she spent most of her time above the Egyptian chambers in the antiquities rooms, where so many treasures were housed, many of them plundered by Napoleon. She made observations about the artefacts, drawing them in meticulous detail, and began to teach herself to read the hieroglyphic writing. She spent her small allowance on books to help her understand the people who had made such objects, their beliefs and their gods.

The idea of studying to be a historian, perhaps even an archae-ologist, began to take shape in her mind. Papa had shut her out of his occult studies, but surely he would back her in this new ambition, if she showed him she was sufficiently determined and had already made strides in her learning. The path would present many challenges, especially for a woman of limited means, but such a life, after all, would be led within normal bounds. She would accept her father's desire to keep her safe and away from the occult.

Then, five months ago, she received a telegram from her mother saying that Papa had died suddenly of a heart attack.

Her father's death had meant the end of many things, including his daughters' education. There could be no question of continuing to pay exorbitant school fees. After the funeral, Evie remained at home and, along with Grace, began a new and harder life. Now it was Walter's family who were confronted with the task of turning out the detritus of a once precious collection. Leonie had not been able to bring herself to do it, nor to let Evie undertake it, so the books had stayed. Papa's study was closed up, and no one entered. Whatever Walter Winstanley had been working on during those final months was now lost, along with him.

~

Soon after, Harriet appeared, bearing damp cloths, a bowl and a mug.

'I saw the light was still on,' she said, handing the mug to Evie, who inspected the contents and grimaced. 'It's just lukewarm cocoa. The milk will soothe your throat. You've been through a terrible ordeal. How's your neck? And your head? Merciful heavens, what that brute did to you!' Furrows appeared between her brows as she gently searched the purple bruises flowering around Evie's throat. She held out the damp cloths into which she'd knotted ice cubes. 'I've brought these to bring down the swelling.' Ignoring Evie's protests that she was feeling much better and in no need of help, she used the cloths to bandage her throat.

'Have you seen this before?' Evie nodded towards the drawing while she sipped the cocoa, wincing as she swallowed.

Harriet looked at the picture – and gave a sharp intake of breath. Almost immediately, she covered up the sound, her face reverting to its usual unflappable expression.

'You recognise it,' Evie said.

'No.' Harriet avoided Evie's eyes as she fussed unnecessarily, readjusting the bandages. 'It's nothing.'

'You must tell me,' Evie persisted. 'Or I'll go right this minute to ask Maman.'

'She'll be asleep.'

'Then I'll wake her.' Evie sprang up, went to the door and set her hand on the knob. As she turned it, Harriet's voice followed her.

'Don't, Evie. It will only distress her.'

'I won't need to trouble her. If you'll tell me.'

'It will distress you, too.'

'Even so.' Evie returned to her chair.

Harriet's face had tightened; suddenly she looked much older. She sighed. 'You and Grace were away when it happened. Your mother – we all – wanted to spare you. There seemed no need . . .'

'This drawing, the double circle. It's connected to Papa's death?'

Harriet nodded. 'He'd been preoccupied. He wouldn't confide in anyone about what he was doing, not even your mother. That last night, he shut himself up in here. The next morning, Mary found him. There was nothing anyone could have done.'

This much Evie already knew. A heart attack, the doctors had said. He'd died alone, with no time to call out for help.

'What has this to do with the circle?' she asked.

'There were chalk markings on the floor, forming two circles and containing a symbol . . . like this one.' Harriet pointed to the paper. 'Your poor Papa lay in the middle of the circles.' She paused, biting at her lip. 'Something else was strange. I didn't think too much of it at the time – I was distressed. We all were, of course . . .'

'What was it?' Evie felt her heart skitter uncomfortably fast.

'There was water, everywhere.'

'*Water?*'

'All around him. The carpet was damp and his clothes soaked.'

Evie stared. 'Where had it come from?'

Harriet's narrow shoulders tensed. 'I . . . don't know.'

'You should have told me this before.'

'I wanted to.' Harriet's gaze fixed on her hands twisting in her lap. 'And I would have done. But your mother . . .' Her voice trailed off.

Evie guessed what Leonie would have said, pragmatic even in her grief. *People will talk, say Walter was mad, that he dabbled in black magic. It would be a scandal. We have to protect the girls.*

'I had a *right* to know.'

On the morning that the household discovered Walter Winstanley lying dead, Evie received a letter from him in Paris, the first in many months, penned days before. It spoke of his excitement at some new research he was undertaking. Though he gave no details, the letter finished, 'I hope, my dear child, I'll be able to explain more when next we meet.'

What had he meant to tell her?

Evie turned towards the bare expanse of carpet. Try as she might, she couldn't stop herself from imagining him sprawled there, eyes sightless, clothes drenched with water, limbs splayed out at impossible angles, mouth half open as though about to speak to his daughter – his last message that would remain forever unvoiced.

~

Towards the end of the night, Evie woke from a heavy sleep with a nagging awareness that there was something she needed to do, a connection she'd missed. She lit a stub of candle and picked up the *Perambulations Among the Relics of Ancient Britain* that lay beside her bed and skipped to a chapter titled 'Travels through the Northern Wilds of Yorkshire'.

Skimming the pages, her eyes landed on a name she knew. She read the passage, then let the book slide from her hands, pinched out the candle flame and stared, unseeing, into the darkness.

The passage detailed the reverend's journey to a place of dark legend, near the village of Wastdale. A lake called the Sithwater.

CHAPTER
Five

Two days later, Evie, attired in a pale lavender walking dress with matching jacket and her second-best hat, and overseeing several travelling bags, waited impatiently under the clock at King's Cross station.

It was mid-morning and the station was crowded, bustling with school children hauling trunks, men bound for their weekend leisure trailing bulky fishing tackle or golf clubs, harassed mothers with querulous youngsters in tow. People rushed hither and thither on important business, tripping over wheeled boxes and portmanteaux, grumbling at others to get out of their way. A melee of sounds reverberated through the cavernous space: the babble of voices, the roar of the trains, the shrill clamour of whistles, officials announcing platforms and departure times, porters offering to carry luggage. Overhead, colourful posters advertised travel to northern destinations: Edinburgh, York, Scarborough and the Highlands.

Evie brightened as a young man came hurrying through the press of people towards her.

'Pel!' she cried.

'I'm so sorry,' he said, giving her a swift brotherly kiss on her cheek. 'I didn't get your telegram till last night, too late to visit. Then this morning Mrs Lamb appeared just as I was going to close the surgery, and she wouldn't go away, though I'm certain there's nothing really wrong with her.'

'I hope you kept the nurse in with you. Don't let Mrs Lamb get you alone.'

'Evie, you shock me! I can't afford your suspicious mind; I need as many patients as I can get. Preferably those who don't possess the kinds of *beliefs* that some people don't trouble to hide from me.' He spoke lightly, but Evie knew that beneath her brother's calm exterior was a lifetime of armour constructed to protect himself from racial prejudice.

Pelham Salazar was Evie's half-brother, Walter's natural son by Pamina, a Jamaican actress. Pelham's youth had been spent touring with his mother; he had been ten years old when Pamina had brought her boy to meet Walter Winstanley. She was already gravely ill with the tuberculosis that would shortly kill her, and she appealed for his help raising Pelham. Walter had thus learnt for the first time that he had a son whose existence he had never suspected, and Pelham had found a father. Walter had taken on responsibility for Pelham, first out of duty but soon after out of growing love.

For Leonie, who had lost her only son in infancy, the sudden arrival of Pelham had provoked conflicting emotions, but for Evie it had been much simpler. She barely remembered Tom. Pelham was the only brother she knew.

Seeing the wrath on Evie's face, Pelham laughed. 'Mrs Lamb considers herself to be *exceptionally* broad-minded,' he assured her. 'She never tires of telling me so.'

Evie snorted derisively, eyes flashing.

'Never mind the Mrs Lambs of this world,' said Pelham. 'Tell me about the break-in.'

'Indeed yes, before Grace gets here. She needn't hear this; she's been distressed enough already.'

'Where is she?'

'Browsing at the bookstall. Let's find somewhere quieter to sit.' She put her arm in his and drew him through the crowds to a bench. They set the travelling bags beside them.

'So this intruder,' said Pelham, crossing one elegant leg over the other, and, with the sangfroid habitual to him, checking the crease in his well-cut trousers. 'You confronted him alone? That was courageous – but it was such a risk. You put yourself in danger.'

She poured out her tale while he listened in attentive silence. Their father, conscious of his son's rationalism, had never spoken much to Pelham about his occult experiments, fearful, perhaps, that Pelham would judge him, might even laugh. It was a reticence that Evie had previously respected. But now their father was gone, and she felt badly in need of an ally. As she ended her account, she brought out the scrap of paper.

'It's an occult sigil,' she told him.

'What on earth's a sigil?'

'It's more than a symbol; it's a thing of power in itself, imbued with magic. It can be used to summon a spirit. I found a passage about this particular sigil in one of Papa's books. Apparently, it signifies dark occult magic, though its precise name and meaning are unknown. But Papa knew what it was.' She pointed to the faint words on the paper.

Pelham read aloud: 'Kuroskato ... circle of shadows.' He grimaced. 'There's something deuced unpleasant about the pattern in the centre. It reminds me of something, though I can't think what.'

'When I suggested to the police it might be important, they all but laughed in my face,' she said bitterly. Then she caught the half-smile on Pelham's lips, and her heart fell. 'You don't believe me either. Look again and tell me what you see.'

He obliged, rubbed his sleeve across his eyes and stared, holding the symbol close, changing the angle. 'It looks ... different somehow.'

'It changes all the time.'

'An optical illusion,' he observed, tapping his fingers on the paper. 'I've seen such things before. The brain and optic nerves can be deceived by the most trumpery of tricks.'

'You have an answer for everything,' she replied with a sigh of exasperation, then took the paper, refolded it carefully and returned it to her purse.

'Why do you think it's important?'

'I believe it's connected with Papa's death.'

'What?' He saw her expression and the smile froze on his lips.

'Did they tell you that when they found Papa he was lying in the middle of a double circle and there were occult symbols, similar to this, drawn in chalk on the floor? Or that his clothes and the floor were drenched in water?'

His eyes narrowed. 'No,' he said slowly, 'they didn't tell me.' For a while he was silent, lost in thought. 'He may have been working on some kind of ritual from his books. That's what you think, isn't it? But our father died of natural causes. Even if he'd been dabbling in some crackpot occult experiment when his heart gave way, it was no more than a coincidence.'

'A coincidence? Perhaps.' She tugged at the fingers of her gloves. 'I believe there's some mystery around his death, and I mean to get to the bottom of it. The sigil is involved, somehow. Someone wanted it, wanted it badly.'

'Oh, come on, Evie. What possible connection could the burglary have with Papa's death? Why would an intruder have been after a scrap of paper?'

'That's just it. I couldn't work it out at first. The I examined the book he was trying to steal. The paper was hidden in it.' She drew *Perambulations Among the Relics of Ancient Britain* from her bag.

Pelham took it, pulling a wry face. 'Why would he bother to steal this? And more to the point, why on earth have you brought it with you? Light reading on the train? It looks excruciat—'

'The Reverend Mickleford,' Evie interrupted reprovingly, 'was a very distinguished scholar of pre-Roman Britain and an amateur archaeologist.'

'*Very* distinguished?' Pelham raised his eyebrows.

His smile was infectious, and in spite of herself Evie grinned back. 'Well, perhaps he's not so well known now,' she conceded.

Pelham flicked through the thick yellowing pages. 'And what does this distinguished scholar have to tell us that is worth ploughing through five hundred pages and more?'

Evie bit back the retort hovering on her lips. 'The Reverend Mickleford spent much of his leisure time walking the length and breadth of Britain. The book contains an account of a journey he made in 1867 to the North Riding of Yorkshire, in the course of which he visited a lake called the Sithwater, near Wastdale. It's a place of ancient legend.' She took the book from his loosened grip and turned to a page nearly halfway through. 'He found some symbols carved into rocks close by the lake. This is the drawing he made.' She indicated a complex pattern of whorls within a double circle.

Pelham touched an exploratory finger to the pattern and began reading the text beneath.

'Don't you see?' she said excitedly. 'It's the same symbol. The kuroskato. According to Mickleford, it signifies some kind of dark magic.'

'Dark magic?' He shook his head. 'You're letting yourself be led along by a fairy tale.'

'You might take this more seriously.' She snatched the book back, slamming it shut. 'Especially as a man of science. Why, Sir Arthur Conan Doyle, a doctor, creator of the most rational and scientifically minded of detectives, is also a member of the Society for Psychical Research. He visited Papa's shop several times in search of literature on ghosts and the supernatural.'

'Indeed. It only goes to show that even the cleverest of men may be deceived by his own emotions and his need to believe in something beyond the material world.' He furrowed his brow. 'You and I, Evie, we've never believed in the occult.'

'*You* didn't,' she acknowledged, 'but Papa did. And I—'

'Is *that* your motive?' asked Pelham. 'To vindicate Papa's work? But he's gone. It makes no difference to him now.'

'It makes a difference to me.' Her eyes were unfocused, her mind far from the busy station. 'I hated how people used to whisper about Papa behind his back, saying he was deluded, ridiculous even. He knew people were laughing at him. He acted as though he didn't mind, but I think he did.' Her breath hitched.

'I didn't know you felt like that.'

Hearing the sympathy in his voice, she glanced at him. 'Oh no. Not that.'

'Not what?'

'Pity. I can see it in your face. I thought I could count on you at least.' Pelham had been her comrade-in-arms in many stratagems to outwit Leonie's fiercely protective instincts and ideas about what was and was not seemly for a young woman.

'You *can* count on me, for anything sensible,' he said, exasperated. 'What is it you mean to do?'

'I looked up Wastdale, and it isn't far from Maltraver Towers, where we'll be staying this weekend.'

'Oh no, Evie.' He groaned, rubbing the back of his neck. 'Is *this* the reason you changed your mind about accompanying Grace?'

She considered telling him about the postcard, imagined herself trying to explain that she'd heard a disembodied voice and witnessed some kind of hallucination, but she could picture his reaction. Better not to tell him.

But she had seen it. She *had*.

'Of course.' She bestowed on him her sunniest smile. 'I mean to visit the Sithwater lake. You didn't think I'd voluntarily spend time at a country house party otherwise, did you? How unutterably tedious.'

'So tell me,' said Pelham. 'What are these tales about the Sithwater?'

'According to the legend, it's a place of death.'

'*What?*'

'You needn't look so rattled. You've already said you think it's all nonsense, so what is there to fear?'

'I still don't like the sound of it. You're not planning to do anything impulsive, are you?'

She folded her hands primly on her lap, like a vicar's daughter attending a sermon. 'If it's impulsive, it would be a contradiction in terms to say I was planning it.'

'Don't play games, Evie. Whatever the truth of these legends, the intruder who attacked you is real enough.'

She sat mulishly silent. When she spoke again, it was to change the subject. 'About the intruder. Just while I'm away, it would reassure Maman very much if you would come and sleep at the house.'

'Are you certain Leonie would welcome my presence?'

'Of course. You're the man of the family.'

He leant back, avoiding Evie's eyes. His hands fidgeted uneasily, straightening his cuffs. 'I'm not sure Leonie sees me that way.'

For a moment Evie saw again the lonely boy looking out of her brother's eyes. She bent her head against his shoulder before turning away, blinking rapidly, not wanting to stir up old ghosts, old griefs for him. 'Maman has to look beyond the past. Everything has changed . . . for all of us.'

She glanced up, sprang to her feet. 'Here's Grace. Not a word to her, please, Pel. It would scare her.'

'No, no, of course not.'

Grace came towards them carrying illustrated magazines and a slim volume under one arm. Half amused, half indignantly protective, Evie noted more than one head turn to watch her progress across the station concourse. Grace noticed none of them; she was absolutely without vanity and thought her own looks nothing out of the ordinary.

'Pel!' said Grace delightedly. As he stood to greet her, she reached to kiss his cheek. 'What brings you here to see us off?'

'The pleasure of your company, of course,' he said with a gallant sweep of his arm.

Evie went to summon a porter and the trio headed for the platform.

'You have your revolver still, Pel?' Evie asked quietly.

'Well, yes, but—'

'Bring it with you.' She tightened her hold on his arm. 'Please. If only to reassure Maman and Harriet. You won't need it.'

They reached the train and found their carriage, where their porter waited.

'A weekend at Maltraver Towers,' said Pelham. He grinned teasingly at Evie. 'You're moving in exalted circles now, girls.'

'Not I.' Evie tossed her head. 'I'm only coming to keep Grace company.'

'Who'll be there?' asked Pelham.

'Lady Maltraver's the dowager viscountess,' said Grace. 'The Honourable Phyllis Crosbie is her daughter. We became friends at school in Bath.'

'It was she who invited you?'

'Yes.' She paused, then added in a constrained voice, 'And there's Phyllis's older brother, Alexander. He's Viscount Maltraver.'

'I hear from Leonie,' said Pelham, 'that he's rich, well-connected, very young and very much unmarried. Another of your admirers, Grace?'

'I've no idea what he thinks, and I care even less,' snapped Grace, fire in her usually gentle eyes. 'I'm not going on his account.' She rearranged her hat and snatched up her bag.

Pelham's questioning gaze met Evie, who shrugged.

Grace climbed into the carriage. Evie searched her purse to tip the porter, but Pelham pre-empted her. She smiled gratefully and followed Grace up the step just as a shriek of the whistle and shouts of the guards announced the train's departure. Pelham swung away, soon hidden by swirls of steam as the train got up speed and hurtled from the station.

CHAPTER
Six

E VIE STOWED THEIR hats and outer clothes on the overhead rack along with their luggage. They had the compartment to themselves and settled in luxuriously. Grace brought out a volume of John Keats's poetry.

'Why Keats?' said Evie.

'How can you even ask? *A thing of beauty is a joy forever*, Evie.'

'Why, of course,' said Eve faintly.

With no spectators to cast censorious looks at her unladylike behaviour, Evie slipped off her shoes and huddled up in her seat. Soon she was deep in the *Perambulations* and a world of prehistoric landscapes, stone circles, barrows, monoliths and old straight tracks. Once they were beyond London, she took glances through the window, at passing fields, hedges, woodland and the steeples of churches surrounded by their attendant villages. In Evie's imagination, she saw beyond the mundane scenery to the ancient wild landscape described in the *Perambulations* and the people who had once lived in the old ways.

Towards the back of the book, she found a number of local legends that the Reverend Mickleford had gathered from the testimony of people he'd encountered on his travels. Mickleford had written them up in the dry, rather condescending style of a Victorian gentleman, but the tales had originally been handed down by word of mouth, and Evie guessed they must have sounded very different when spoken in the words and dialect of poor cottagers and farm labourers.

Turning over the pages, she came upon a tale from North Yorkshire, 'The Legend of the Sithwater'.

In the first days of the Roman invasion, elders of the tribe of the Brigantes went to Queen Cartimandua and asked her help to make a sacrifice to the old gods powerful enough to win their aid in defeating the invaders. A sacrifice of pure and highborn blood would be the most acceptable to the old gods. Cartimandua, already minded to come to terms with the Romans, declined, as did most of her children – all but the youngest daughter, who stepped forward to offer herself. Her parents wept and begged her to change her mind, her brothers and sisters sobbed and moaned, and lastly the young man who loved her, and whom she had promised to marry, fell to his knees and pleaded with her. To each of them she said no. The Druids came to lead her away, and she went with them willingly to the place of sacrifice by the Sithwater, there to suffer the triple death.

On the opposite page was a reproduction of a nineteenth-century oil painting by an artist whose name Evie didn't recognise. In the background, a line of distant figures looked on from a clifftop, their plaid cloaks bright in shades of red, yellow and green, and their plaited hair whipped by the wind. Shafts of sunlight picked out glints of sword hilts, circular brooches and golden torcs, the metallic gleam of diadems on the heads of the queen and her consort. One of the figures, a young warrior, had fallen to his knees and reached out imploring arms, chin sunken to his chest.

In the foreground, by the edge of the Sithwater, stood a very young woman, hardly more than a child, dressed in a sleeveless white robe, her waist-length hair loose, her bare feet and lower legs scratched and torn by brambles. A ring of druids in long dark robes surrounded her, men and women, stern-faced and wild-haired. One held a cudgel, another a length of cord and a third a silver knife. The girl didn't look at any of them. Her eyes were fixed on a point far out across the dark waters of the lake.

'Evie?'

Evie jumped and shut the book. 'Sorry?'

'I was calling you. You looked very far away.'

'Yes, yes, of course.' Evie smiled hastily. 'What is it?'

'I wanted to ask – do you think the ladies at Maltraver Towers will be wearing gowns like these?' Grace had the fashion pages of an illustrated magazine open on her lap, having set Keats aside to focus on more pressing matters.

Evie looked over Grace's shoulder at the elegant narrow silhouettes, surmounted by cartwheel hats. 'If they are, we'll look sadly out of place.' She hardly cared, but she caught Grace's wistful expression.

'Don't fret, Gracie.' Evie delved into a bag and presented her sister with the best of the apples. 'As you said, it's not as though you've any wish to enthral Lord Maltraver.' She hesitated. 'Why do you dislike him?'

Grace chewed on her apple slowly, giving herself time before she spoke. 'Nothing certain, just a feeling. He makes my flesh crawl.'

'Perhaps he's changed since you saw him last.'

'Perhaps . . .'

'I'm sure you have reason.'

'I feel . . . so embarrassed.' Grace's voice was little more than a whisper.

'Tell me,' Evie coaxed. 'I won't tell Maman.'

Grace's smile was tremulous. 'The first time I met him, nearly two years ago, I liked him very much. He'd just finished Eton and was about to go up to Oxford. He seemed so grown up.'

Evie held her tongue. Two years ago, Grace had been just fifteen.

'He was charming. He teased me. I thought that meant he liked me. I was ridiculously pleased. Flattered, I suppose. I was awkward and shy . . . and foolish.'

'We've all made that mistake.' Evie stroked her sister's arm. 'Grateful for anyone who approves of us, who notices us.'

'You're being kind,' said Grace. 'I don't think you've ever cared that much for other people's opinions. It wasn't until the day of the hunt that I saw another side to him. They put me on one of the smaller hunters. I was proud of being able to handle him. It was exhilarating, dangerous, but that seemed part of the fun. Then a fox broke cover. The hounds made after it, surrounded it, tore it to pieces. The sounds it made . . .' She clapped her hands to her ears, hearing again the cries of the dying animal. 'It was horrible.'

Evie turned rather white.

'Lord Maltraver went in among the hounds, took the mangled body and cut off its tail – its *brush* – and smeared the blood on my face. When I tried to get away, he gripped my arm to keep me still. I cried and begged him not to, but he wouldn't stop. They were all laughing, as though it was some huge joke. He tied the tail to my saddle and declared it was his gift to me, as the youngest person on the hunting field. That I'd been *blooded*. An old tradition, apparently.'

'Barbaric!' Evie protested. 'The brutes! Why didn't you tell me? Or Maman?'

'I felt ashamed,' Grace said in a low voice. 'And stupidly naive. It was I who'd begged Maman to let me go. I hadn't realised killing something would be . . . like that. And Alexander – Lord Maltraver – somehow made me feel complicit, as though I'd wanted it. There was a look in his face that . . . I can't shake off the feeling that there's something not quite right about him. But then, he's been through an awful experience. He lost his father when he was still a boy.'

'What happened?'

'A hunting accident. After all, we both know what it is to lose a father suddenly.'

There was some justice in Grace's remarks, but they made Evie look forward to the visit with nothing other than trepidation.

~

It was late afternoon when their third train, after wending its leisurely way along a small branch line, deposited them at a sleepy country station three miles from Maltraver Towers. A thick fog of steam billowed around the Winstanley girls as they descended with their luggage. Dense clouds crept along the platform, lingering at the far end.

Glancing that way, Evie saw a tall figure emerge out of the sea of grey mist, like a stage magician rising through clouds of dry ice via a hidden trapdoor to send shivers of excitement rippling through the audience. As the steam clouds dispersed, she made out the figure more clearly. A young man, tall with a slick of dark hair, in a well-fitting charcoal-grey suit and a high white collar. Handsome, too, no doubt about it, with high cheekbones and an easy grace in his movements as he turned to get his bearings, yet there was a watchfulness about him that reminded her of a wild animal, always on the alert. Their eyes met in the initial glance of strangers. Both looked scrupulously away, yet she had the impression that he was as aware of her as she was of him, coupled with a conviction that she'd seen him before, though she knew that to be impossible.

The guard's high-pitched whistle pierced her ears. Grace murmured something, but the clanking thunder of the train pulling away drowned her voice.

'I can't find my ticket,' Grace repeated, shaking out her handbag. Evie helped her search, and they eventually found the ticket in Grace's glove.

Evie shot a surreptitious glance under her lashes back down the platform. It was empty, and she felt a pinch of regret. *You didn't come here to look for young men,* she chided herself, *not even good-looking ones.*

The girls went through to the station forecourt, where tall chestnut trees, their candle-like flowers already emerging, shaded the open space. Beyond stretched open fields and woodland. The air was colder and fresher than in London, touched with the scent of the chestnut blossoms. The small crowd from the train thinned as people dispersed, on foot or into waiting carts and pony traps.

'Phyllis said they would send this,' said Grace, gesturing to a brash state-of-the-art motorcar, accompanied by a chauffeur in dark green livery to match his vehicle.

As they approached the motorcar, Evie's heart beat a little fast when she saw that the tall young man was there, stowing his bag in the space behind the seats. Seeing them arrive, he straightened and gazed at her with an unreadable expression. The next moment, the look had vanished, transformed into a smile that slowly widened, taking her with it.

'Are you ladies also bound for Maltraver Towers?' he asked. He spoke in the precise accent of an educated English gentleman, yet there was something about his voice – a warmth, like his engaging smile – that she liked. 'Can I take your bags?'

'That's my job, sir,' said the chauffeur.

'No matter,' said the young man, reaching for their bags and stowing them alongside his own. 'Shall we be off?' He offered his hand to help Evie mount the dashboard.

Evie found herself smiling as she stretched her gloved hand towards his.

'Hey there!'

Evie turned to see a man and a woman bearing down on them. A porter followed, laden with luggage.

'Are you going to Maltraver Towers?' the woman enquired of the chauffeur. 'This motorcar has been sent for us, I believe.' Her speech was deep and rich, like molten honey. The rest of her seemed commonplace in comparison, notwithstanding the opulent fur-trimmed coat that swathed her short, rounded form. Her curling strawberry-blonde hair (*not natural, surely*, thought Evie) was crowned with a modish hat adorned by a bunch of artificial cherries.

Her companion struck a drab figure in comparison: grey-haired, grey-suited and dusty-looking. His drooping moustache gave him a mournful expression, reminding Evie of the walrus who wept for the oysters even as he ate them. He followed in the woman's wake, bearing a closed wicker basket.

The chauffeur rubbed his moustache, clearly embarrassed. There was space only for four passengers.

The young man stood back. 'I'll walk. How far is it?' he asked the chauffeur.

'Upward of three mile, sir.'

Appearing unconcerned, the young man leant across to retrieve his bag. Evie noticed it was battered and worn, a contrast to his tailored suit.

It took the united efforts of the chauffeur and the porter to load the couple's various portmanteaux. Evie climbed into the backseat next to Grace, then turned to the young man. 'I'm Evelyn Winstanley, and this is my sister, Grace,' she said. 'We'll see you later then, Mr . . .?'

'Aubrey Penhallow.' He gave her a rueful look and stood back from the dashboard as the motorcar moved off in a haze of smoke.

It was the first time Evie had ridden in a motorcar. Jolted about on her perch at the back, obliged to hang on to her hat, she wasn't sure whether she cared much for the experience – too smelly, too loud, too uncomfortable.

The husband and wife sat in front while their capacious basket rested on the seat behind, next to Grace. Hearing something move inside, she peered into it – and started back as a whiskered face appeared out of the darkened interior and hissed at her.

'Osiris!' said the woman reprovingly. 'Where are your manners? I'm sorry,' she added, twisting round to Grace and raising her voice above the erratic spurts of the engine. 'Osiris is descended from the sacred cats of ancient Egypt. He senses things that humans cannot. He's especially sensitive to auras.'

'Is there something amiss with my aura?' Grace asked, bewildered.

'Of course not,' Evie assured her.

'Did I hear you say your name's Winstanley?' said the woman. Upon Evie's confirmation, she continued, 'I'm Madame Trent-L'Espoir.' She leant over the back of her seat and extended a plump hand loaded with intricately cut rings set with crimson, green and topaz stones. 'That's my professional name. L'Espoir was the name of my first husband, who's passed over. This is my second husband, Mr Trent.' Mr Trent nodded, acknowledging the introduction, before lowering his head to rest it on his walking stick. In contrast to his wife, he seemed to have little to say for himself.

The name Trent-L'Espoir struck a chord with Evie. 'Am I right in thinking you're a professional medium?'

The woman's smile was enigmatic. 'I think of myself as a communer with the souls that have passed over, a comforter to the living. I believe you girls have lost someone. I see a man, in late mid-life. Greying hair and beard, an embroidered waistcoat. Your father, perhaps? His passing was sudden? He had no chance to say goodbye.'

'Why, yes,' said Grace, open-mouthed. 'Our father died last November. My sister and I were away from home. You can truly sense his presence?'

Evie put a warning hand on Grace's arm. She remembered now where she'd seen the name Trent-L'Espoir. She subscribed to the *Ghost Hunter*, a periodical magazine that carried articles on supernatural phenomena of all kinds, such as apparitions, haunted houses, spectral ancestors and poltergeists. It had recently started running a series of investigative articles on spirit mediums, taking a sceptical stance and threatening to expose fraudulent psychics. The name Trent-L'Espoir had been one of those mentioned, though Evie couldn't remember the details. The name Walter Winstanley was widely known amongst people interested in the occult, and this woman might have heard of his death and could be playing on their sadness and loss. Evie resolved to be on her guard.

'I see him,' said Madame Trent-L'Espoir, leaning over to touch Grace's arm. 'He's sitting beside you, journeying through life with you.'

'Between Grace and the cat basket?' asked Evie. 'Is there sufficient space?'

'You are a sceptic?' said the medium, arching carefully plucked eyebrows.

'I'm yet to be convinced.' Evie lifted her chin and met the other woman's gaze.

'We'll convince you, my dear,' Madame Trent-L'Espoir said serenely. She bestowed a beatific smile on the sisters and turned back to resume a one-sided conversation with her monosyllabic husband.

Evie caught the sadness in Grace's eyes and clasped her waist. 'They're liars,' she whispered in Grace's ear beneath the roar of the engine. 'I'm sure of it.'

Nevertheless, a certain doubt remained in Evie's mind. There was so much about this mystery that only her father had known. Her longing to speak with him might make her an easy mark. Everything about Madame Trent-L'Espoir seemed contrived, from her dyed hair to her unctuous rolling vowels. Was it really possible that she could communicate with spirits beyond the grave? The idea seemed preposterous.

And yet . . .

CHAPTER
Seven

THE MOTORCAR FOLLOWED a high stone wall and turned into a drive crossed by iron gates set back from the road. A man hurried from the lodge alongside the gates to open them; they creaked shrilly as they moved apart and the car drove through.

They followed a long winding drive that curved downhill through dense woodland. The way was overhung with gloomy thickets of rhododendrons, bearing clusters of luminous white flowers that screened off much of the sunlight. Through the trees Evie caught occasional glimpses of the mauve-and-grey flanks of distant hills. Then, at the bottom of the valley, they came out into a wide gravelled space and Maltraver Towers stood before them.

Maltraver Towers was an imposing pile. At first sight, Evie took it for a miniature Norman castle, but as she drank in the details, she realised it was a Victorian reimagining of a medieval castle, built of grey stone slabs and complete with turrets and battlements. Behind the house, extensive parkland sloped upwards towards the top of the valley and the hills beyond. Evie was a little disappointed; she'd have preferred a genuinely old historic building, which would have been so much more atmospheric, even if this relatively recent construction would undoubtedly have better lighting, better heating and better bathrooms.

Servants admitted them up wide stone steps into the Gothic entrance hall, a vast echoing space, its walls decorated with stags' heads and antlers; a weapons collection of flintlock pistols, medieval swords, maces and axes; and some portraits of stern-looking Tudor and Stuart men and women whom Evie supposed to be ancestors of the present inhabitants. The stone walls made the interior feel cold and sombre, and though there was a massive stone fireplace, flanked by two suits of armour of complex Italian design, no fire burnt in the grate.

Evie went over to view the fireplace, drawn by the heraldic coats-of-arms emblazoned above it, studded with rampant scarlet lions, white stars and green salamanders with probing tongues. Beneath them was a Latin inscription: *Omnia possibilia sunt mihi.*

Evie translated it, murmuring the words aloud to herself, 'All things are possible to me.' As Grace came to join her, she remarked, 'They had no small opinion of themselves, these past Crosbies.'

'Evie, hush,' Grace said, tugging at her arm to bring her away.

Lady Maltraver arrived to meet them, a stiff-backed woman in a high-necked, peach-coloured day gown and a shawl of Spanish lace, her fair hair bleaching to grey, scraped up in a tight chignon. She clasped hands with the Trent-L'Espoirs, then turned to the Winstanleys, greeting them civilly but without great interest; they were Phyllis's friends, not hers. Her bulbous blue eyes narrowed as they took in Grace's unselfconscious beauty. Evie guessed well enough what was running through Lady Maltraver's mind – the same thoughts that struck many mothers of eligible and wealthy young men when they set eyes on Grace: *Such a pretty girl, but no money, no connections. I hope he doesn't make a fool of himself over her.*

'Grace! At last!' The Honourable Phyllis Crosbie darted down the broad stone stairs to meet her friend, encountered her mother's reproving frown and slowed to a decorous walk. She was a thin, sallow-complexioned girl, with her mother's sharp nose and baby-fine blonde hair. Excitement at seeing Grace had brought a glow to her skin, but immediately her face relapsed into sulky lines that Evie suspected must be habitual. Considerable expense would have been lavished on teaching Phyllis deportment, yet she moved awkwardly, even stiffly, as though unsure of herself and her place.

'I'm so glad you've come,' Phyllis said breathlessly. As she bore the sisters up the staircase, she was already reminiscing with Grace about their schooldays.

Evie followed in their wake, her gaze dropping down into the hall, where Lady Maltraver was conversing with Madame Trent-L'Espoir and her husband in eager tones. Despite her hauteur, Lady Maltraver seemed nervous, her hands plucking at her shawl. Curious, Evie strained to catch their words.

'We have the room all set up for this evening,' Lady Maltraver said. 'Can I take you to see it, and make sure that you have everything you require? Will you be joining us for dinner?'

'No food or drink for me,' cooed Madame Trent-L'Espoir mellifluously. 'I always fast before reaching out to the spirits. You might send some light refreshments up to our room for my husband. A fine herb omelette perhaps.'

'An omelette,' came Lady Maltraver's reply as Evie reached the gallery at the head of the stairs. 'Of course.' There were further words between the two women that Evie didn't catch, then Lady Maltraver spoke up: 'We'll all attend. My daughter – and my son.'

So, there was to be a seance that evening. Evie was amused by Lady Maltraver's eagerness to please the bourgeois Trent-L'Espoirs. In the hinterland between the realms of the living and the dead, it seemed that a dowager viscountess ranked lower than a professional medium. Ahead of her, Evie caught sight of Phyllis staring down from the gallery at her mother and was struck by the tight folds in the corners of her mouth, the resentment in her eyes.

'Where's your maid?' asked Phyllis, turning towards Evie. 'Did she go down to the servants' hall?'

'We don't have a lady's maid.' Evie felt the awkwardness of the admission.

Phyllis opened startled eyes. Recovering herself, she said, 'In that case, I'll send one of our maids to help you dress for dinner.'

Phyllis took the Winstanley girls along the main first-floor corridor to where a narrow door opened on a spiral stairway leading up into one of the high towers. She brought them to a circular room with two beds and a view overlooking the formal gardens and the sloping parkland beyond. The walls had been papered over with a bold, colourful pattern of violets on a shell-pink background, possibly in an attempt to hide patches of damp that had nevertheless seeped through in the far corner beside the exterior wall. On the other side of the staircase was a well-appointed, tiled bathroom, though some of the tiles had come adrift and there were stipples of brownish discolouration above the washbasin.

'Mama thought you'd like this room, so you can be together. The other guest rooms and the family rooms are down on the main corridor. You'll be quite secluded and peaceful here in the tower. And Janet's on the floor above.' Phyllis indicated the maid who was already there, unpacking their bags. 'If you should ring the bell, Janet will come. Janet, the Miss Winstanleys couldn't bring their lady's maid – she's ... indisposed – so you'll tend to them.'

'Very good, my lady.' Janet dropped a curtsey.

Evie felt a touch of anxiety. Having never been in so grand a house before, she hadn't realised that someone else would be unpacking their clothes, observing unmistakable signs in every-thing not on public show – the shabby brushes and cheap toiletries, the well-worn corsets and undergarments, the darned stockings. She ought to tip the maid, and wondered how much was custom-ary, whether she'd have to break into the banknote she kept for emergencies.

Janet was young, probably still in her teens. Wisps of curling red-gold hair escaped from under her prim cap, contrasting with the plain black dress and demure white pinafore that covered her supple figure. She kept her dark eyes lowered, as she had doubtless been instructed, yet they sparkled with an abundance of life. She would, decided Evie, not look out of place as a water nymph or a Shakespearean heroine in a Pre-Raphaelite painting.

Janet scooped up an armful of undergarments, dropping several on the floor, and as she bent to retrieve them her glance shot to Phyllis to see if her lapse had been noticed. But Phyllis stood by the door, chattering with Grace, catching up with the latest news about mutual friends.

Evie went to the window. Beyond the castle grounds, she made out distant moorland amidst iron-grey crags rearing against a lighter grey sky. The Sithwater must lie somewhere amongst those hills.

'I've heard the Yorkshire countryside's wonderfully dramatic,' said Evie. 'Is there a walk we could undertake tomorrow? The Sithwater is meant to be particularly interesting, historically. And picturesque, too, of course,' she added, seeing alarm in Grace's face. Her sister was no fan of long walks in search of places of historical interest.

'Sithwater?' said Phyllis doubtfully. 'I've never heard of it. It can't be anywhere near here.'

Somewhere far below them, a hall clock chimed.

'Seven o'clock already,' said Phyllis. 'We need to make haste. I'm afraid there won't be time for baths beforehand. Normally we dine at eight, but this evening we're dining at half past seven because of the seance.'

'Do you share your mother's interest in spiritualism?' Evie asked.

'The thought of seeing an actual ghost is quite terrifying,' said Phyllis, though she shivered in a way that suggested pleasurable anticipation rather than genuine fear. 'This house is haunted, you know. Alexander says all that's nonsense, of course. He wishes Mother wouldn't go ahead with the seance, but she's determined. Several of Mother's particular friends have had Madame Trent-L'Espoir.'

'What kind of ghost haunts this house?'

'A woman, dressed in grey, who says no word but wrings her hands, with a look of despair. She's been seen several times. Not by me, though,' Phyllis added regretfully.

'Is that all?'

'There's also a child that throws a ball for a little dog. You've seen that one, haven't you, Janet?'

'Not me, my lady,' said Janet. 'It was Sukey.'

'Oh, of course. Sukey.' Phyllis's face closed up like a book. When she spoke again, it was to reminisce with Grace over their visits to a teashop in Bath.

~

Phyllis soon departed to dress for dinner. Janet hovered uncertainly by the wardrobe where she'd stowed the Winstanley girls' clothes. Seeing her perplexed expression, Evie said, 'Please don't trouble. We're quite used to dressing ourselves.'

'Her ladyship expects me to attend to you,' Janet said. 'But I'm just a parlour maid, really. Sukey used to do all this for the ladies as didn't have a personal maid.'

'Sukey? The one who saw the ghostly child and the dog?'

'Yes, miss.'

'Perhaps she could help us then.'

'Sukey's gone.' Janet's voice sank to a whisper.

Something about Janet's agitation caught Evie's attention. 'Where did she go?'

'I don't rightly know, miss.' There was a shuttered look in Janet's face as she hastened about, taking Grace's discarded coat and skirt and brushing them vigorously. 'If Lady Maltraver should find I've been talking about Sukey, I'll be in that much trouble.'

'Evie,' said Grace, interceding in her gentle way. 'Leave the poor girl be. Come and help me instead.' She held a gown of pale blue chiffon against herself, assessing her reflection. 'This one, do you think?'

'Whatever dress you wear tonight, you'll have to wear the other one tomorrow. What does it matter?'

'It's all about first impressions. I think the rose silk is finer.'

Evie turned back to Janet, only to see her scurrying through the door.

'You're like a terrier sometimes,' observed Grace, lifting her hair aside and presenting her back for Evie to button up her gown. 'Digging and digging. Why should you want to know about an absent maid?'

'No particular reason,' said Evie slowly. She began to rummage for the clothes she intended to wear, tapping her forehead in frustration as she realised she'd forgotten to pack her evening gloves. 'Except that neither Janet nor Phyllis wanted to speak about her. I wondered why.'

Taking Grace's place at the dressing table mirror, Evie examined herself with a critical eye. The gown wasn't new and was pale biscuit in shade, which suited her colouring, trimmed with old lace but with no other decoration. Her dark slanted brows over wide amber eyes gave her face an air of innocent enquiry, though her hair – always unruly – was another matter. She unpinned it, shaking out the thick nut-brown waves, quickly brushed it, then put it up again, jamming in several pins and two dragonfly combs – made of bronze and studded with green semi-precious stones, a gift from her parents – in a haphazard attempt to keep it in place. To this arrangement, she added an old-fashioned necklace of large flat beads carved from jet that she'd borrowed from her mother to help hide the dark contusions round her neck. The rest of the bruises she concealed with an application of face powder.

Grace appeared behind her in the glass, wrapped in a soft-rose gown that moulded itself to her body, providing a warmth of colour that offset her dark loveliness. 'Here, let me help you,' she said, and took out the dragonfly combs, deftly brushed Evie's hair, put it up in a simple chignon, then pushed the combs back in at an angle.

'That's much better,' said Evie with real gratitude. 'If only it holds up till the end of the evening.'

As Grace moved away, Evie saw the room behind her reflected in the mirror. Shades of approaching twilight had begun to gather, muting colours and softening outlines. In the farthest corner, just below the ceiling, the damp patch she'd noticed earlier was bigger than before. Not only that but its shape had altered, too, having become rounded and . . .

She blinked, rubbed her eyes. The pattern was still there. It looked like . . .

'Grace!' Evie sounded a little panicky, even in her own ears. 'Do you see that stain?'

Grace came over, struggling to secure a string of pearls about her neck. 'What's wrong? Can you fasten this clasp for me? My fingers keep slipping over the catch.'

Evie pointed to the dark water mark. 'What does that look like to you?'

Grace stared in perplexity. 'A damp stain?'

'Do you see a pattern in it? Concentric circles, enclosing something that keeps shifting – almost as though it's alive?'

'I don't see what you're talking about,' Grace said plaintively. 'Are you trying to make me believe Maltraver Towers is like Count Dracula's castle? Don't tease me, Evie. You know I can't manage Gothic novels. I won't be able to sleep.' Grace, as was well known in the family, had been too terrified to get past the opening chapters of *Dracula*.

Evie sprang up. Lighting a candle that lay ready beside her bed, she took it to the wall above Grace's bed and held it up to the brownish stain. The circle of candlelight showed up an irregular discolouration of the wallpaper, a random distribution of stippled blotches. No pattern, no sinister meaning.

Bewildered, Evie pressed her hand to her mouth. 'It looks different now.' She turned back to where Grace stood watching, a little puzzled and uneasy, and blew out the candle.

'A trick of the light. I'm sorry I scared you,' Evie said with a smile, and Grace nodded, reassured. 'Here, let me help you with your pearls.'

∼

Evie and Grace made their way down the winding stair to the ground floor, following the distant hum of voices along an oak-panelled hall lined with heavy ornate mahogany furniture, tarnished paintings of hunting scenes, views of the house and surrounding parkland, and portraits of long-dead ancestors of the Crosbie family, who looked on disapprovingly.

'Do you think they all suffered from dyspepsia?' murmured Evie.

Grace smothered a giggle.

Evie noticed several rectangular areas of wall that stood out pale against the background. Had some paintings been removed from these spots? She was about to remark on it when a footman opened the door into the drawing room.

Several heads turned to observe them enter. At once, Evie became aware of several things: that it had been a mistake to wear the lace gown, which was sadly out of date; that her lack of suitable gloves was not going to pass unnoticed; and that it was going to be a very long evening.

CHAPTER
Eight

Viscount Maltraver came forward to greet them. Curly-haired and fresh-faced with soft, full lips and downy cheeks, he looked younger than his twenty years. He bowed to Evie as he took her hand, but his attention slid beyond her, lingering on her sister.

'Little Grace,' he said with a beam that twisted up the sides of his mouth. 'No longer so little, I see.' His voice, deep and assertive, contrasted with his still boyish frame.

A shiver passed through Grace that Evie knew she struggled to suppress. 'Lord Maltraver,' she said stiffly.

'No ceremony between us, I beg. I must and shall be Alexander to you.'

He swept them off to meet the other dinner guests. Two older couples, Dr and Mrs Marchmont, and Sir James and Lady Sankey, friends and neighbours of Lady Maltraver, were also attending the dinner and would remain for the seance. A young man was there too, and as he approached Evie she had an impression of a slight yet sturdy build, thick wavy hair that glinted chestnut in the candlelight, a smattering of freckles and a diffident expression.

'This is Mr Marcus Ellingham – a gentleman of the press, no less,' said Lord Maltraver, turning to him with a rollicking laugh. 'Come here to observe the decadent cavortings of the English aristocracy and reveal our intimate secrets to his readers, no doubt.'

'Alexander,' admonished his mother, bestowing a hard stare on Mr Ellingham. 'There's nothing decadent about us.'

'Then Mr Ellingham's readers are destined to be disappointed, Mama.'

'Are you enjoying your visit to Yorkshire, Miss Winstanley?' asked Marcus Ellingham.

She was murmuring some polite words in reply when she became aware of the tall, dark-haired young man who had just then entered the room to stand alone by the door: Aubrey Penhallow. Mr Ellingham fell silent, his eyes following the direction of hers. Could he tell what she was thinking? She felt suddenly self-conscious and fixed her attention back on their conversation.

They spent several minutes discussing the beauty of the landscape and the unseasonable warmth of the weather, yet all the while Evie thought restlessly, *Why did I even come here?* There was nothing here connected to the circle of shadows, just dull people having self-satisfied conversations about things that didn't matter. To think that Pelham had been concerned for her safety! He would laugh uproariously if he knew that the only danger she risked over the course of the weekend was of being bored senseless.

It was some consolation for Evie to find that Aubrey Penhallow was to be placed next to her at dinner. Seated close to him, she discovered with interest that he had striking green eyes – so few people had eyes that were truly green, rather than brown-green or hazel. It was another point in his favour, to put alongside his high cheekbones.

Lord Maltraver was seated on Evie's other side, at the head of the table, at right angles to herself and Aubrey Penhallow. He beckoned imperiously to a maid hovering nearby to bring the soup tureen she held. In her haste, she spilt soup on the tablecloth.

'Confound the girl,' he exclaimed. 'It takes these local people an eternity to learn the rules of service. I must apologise. It's not usually like this. We're short-staffed just at present. A temporary difficulty.'

'Is that because Sukey left?' Evie asked as she mopped up the soup with her napkin, smiling reassuringly at the girl, who was gulping back tears. She became aware of silence and looked round to see several sets of eyes on her.

A muscle twitched beside Maltraver's mouth. 'How on earth do you know about Sukey?'

'Your mother mentioned her,' lied Evie smoothly.

'I can't imagine why the mater would speak of Sukey,' Maltraver muttered, frowning at his soup spoon.

'Was Sukey afraid to stay here?' said Evie. 'I've heard this house is haunted.'

'Whatever gave you that idea?' Maltraver's eyebrows lifted haughtily. 'We're not in a Gothic melodrama, Miss Winstanley, even though we live alongside the Yorkshire moors. What happened to Sukey was simply the usual story. She took a fancy to one of the footmen and ran off with him, depriving me of two servants at one stroke. No doubt she's in London as we speak, living the high life – if the man hasn't abandoned her yet, having got what he wanted from her.'

'Did you take a shine to her yourself?' said Aubrey Penhallow, taking a lingering sip of wine.

Lord Maltraver winked broadly. 'In all honesty?'

'Indeed, yes,' agreed Penhallow with a glittering smile. 'We can speak freely here. She led you on, you'd say? There are many such girls among her class.' A sneer distorted the curve of his lips.

'Sukey was a regular little minx, and a man can't be blamed if—'

A loud clatter cut through his words as Evie dropped her bread knife onto her plate. All around the table, faces swung towards her. She glared back.

Marcus Ellingham intervened, nervously but determinedly. 'Gentlemen, this hardly seems a fit subject for a lady's ears.'

'Eh, yes, of course,' snorted Lord Maltraver. 'Pardon me, Miss Winstanley.' Though his tone was one of studied politeness, she caught the resentful gleam in his eye as he snapped his fingers at the butler to pour more wine.

Evie let her stare remain on him a moment longer, then lowered her attention to her soup. She felt mortified at having fancied herself drawn to Aubrey Penhallow. *Never judge a book by its cover – or a man by his face.*

As for Lord Maltraver, it was all too evident why Grace disliked him. Evie had already had enough of these arrogant men with their entitled airs, speaking scornfully of women and their social inferiors, and there were still several courses to get through.

'Mr Penhallow's an expert on the gees,' Maltraver burbled. 'He's going to advise me on my sporting ventures. No more nags that fall down or finish last.'

'Are you interested in horse racing, Miss Winstanley?' said Aubrey Penhallow.

'Not in the least,' she replied.

He seemed by no means daunted. Instead, he embarked on a steady monologue on horses – their care, exercise, nutrition and training. Maltraver, leaning over to listen, offered his own contributions, and the two men began conducting a conversation across Evie as though she wasn't there.

Long before dinner was over, Evie had come to loathe the precise, well-modulated tones of Mr Penhallow. She kept her head down, scowling, folding and refolding the napkin on her lap. When he began a lengthy account of the proper diet to feed up an under-par horse for the racing season, Evie thought she would explode. She looked across the table – and noticed Marcus Ellingham. He was staring fixedly at his plate, but she caught a twitch of his lip and realised he was trying to hide a grin. His reaction steadied her, making her feel they were accomplices. She waited till Ellingham caught her eye – then shook her head, frowning in mock reproof. Scarlet flooded his face. She smothered her urge to laugh behind her napkin, conscious of some sympathy for him; it couldn't be easy to have the kind of skin that made an open book of his emotions.

Lady Maltraver rose, the signal for the ladies to join her in the drawing room. As Evie stood, she leant towards Aubrey Penhallow. 'I must thank you for your conversation. It was so instructive. I feel that had I been so minded, and if only I had the money, resources and the least interest in the subject, I would now be well positioned to buy, nurture and train a prize-winning racehorse of my own.'

She smiled sweetly into his startled eyes and left the room in the ladies' wake.

CHAPTER
Nine

E VIE RAN UP a flight of low steps to a raised walkway at the
far end of the garden and stood, breathing in deeply, letting
the night air blow against her face. She'd slunk unnoticed from
the stifling drawing room, where Lady Maltraver was holding
forth about the chronic idleness of the estate's tenant farmers.
Beyond the garden, the open parkland was barely visible in the
darkness, and in the far distance the outline of the moors stood
out like a gigantic black-backed wolf against the starlit sky. Evie
wondered where amongst that dark mass the Sithwater lay.
Perhaps she could find a clue in the *Perambulations*. She was on
the point of going to her room to fetch it when a voice struck her
ears.

'Have you had enough of the evening's entertainment, Miss
Winstanley?' Marcus Ellingham stood at the bottom of the steps.
'Might I join you?'

His friendly manner was a welcome contrast to the chilly self-
absorption of the Crosbie clan. She smiled at him and he came
bounding up the steps to join her – like an oversized dog, she
thought, invited on a walk.

He offered her a cigarette. When she shook her head, he lit one
for himself. Batting the smoke away from her, he said, 'May I ask
why you're out here alone?'

She rested her forearms on the cold stone of the parapet. 'I've
no liking for what they call high society, Mr Ellingham. It all
seems to me like inconsequential chatter. Though perhaps,' she
added, trying to be fair, 'I'm being harsh because I feel conscious
of being an outsider.'

'Would you include Mr Penhallow under that indictment? When you sat beside him at dinner, I formed an impression, perhaps wrongly, that you would rather be elsewhere. Yet he's a smart-looking fellow. Some ladies would enjoy his company.' Behind the orange glow of his cigarette, his eyes sought her reaction.

'Looks aren't everything,' she said with a shrug. 'If you'd had to endure Mr Penhallow's company throughout dinner, you'd agree. He must be the most boring man in Yorkshire. Though Sir James may run him a close second. I don't think Sir James has had such an opportunity to tell a young woman so much about himself since the 1860s.'

From under Mr Ellingham's light lashes, she caught a shy gleam of delight. 'Mr Penhallow, by his name, must be from Cornwall.'

'Then Cornwall's welcome to him. No matter where they are from, all these men learn to speak in the same way.'

'The language of Shakespeare?'

'The language of power, Mr Ellingham.' Her gaze fixed on the point where the distant landscape merged with the dark sky, deep in her own thoughts.

'It's beautiful countryside, isn't it?' he continued, nodding towards the outlined sweep of the moors. 'Wild and remote. I occasionally came to this region as a boy. I had family nearby.'

'Indeed?' She regarded him with growing interest. 'Have you heard of a lake called the Sithwater?'

'Sithwater? I don't think so. Why do you ask?'

'Idle curiosity. I read in a guidebook that it's not to be missed.'

His eyes, shining in the moonlight, fixed on hers.

'You look sceptical,' she said.

'Simply curious.'

'About what?'

'About you, Miss Winstanley. I feel there's something—'

'You don't think I behave as a well-brought-up young lady should?' She tilted her head, regarding him.

He murmured, 'Not at all. You simply seem a little … *other-worldly* out here.'

'If you'll forgive me for saying so, I don't believe I'm the only outsider here.'

He drew in a shallow breath and blinked. 'What makes you think that?'

'I mean it as a compliment. I wonder what brings you, a journalist, to a high-society party in the depths of Yorkshire. Surely there's no story here to interest you, unless . . . What kind of newspaper employs you?'

Inwardly, she was assessing him. His newspaper probably didn't pay particularly well; his evening clothes had seen a lot of wear, and their cut wasn't entirely fashionable. He was evidently not a gentleman able to live idly on his private income; he'd had to make his way in the world. He wasn't a handsome man like Aubrey Penhallow, either; his blunt features, his freckles and the reddish tints to his hair were all too homely for classical good looks, but he had a pleasant, open face nonetheless.

'The *Ghost Hunter*,' he said, rubbing his nose self-consciously under her scrutiny. 'It's aimed at the popular market. Rather beneath you, Miss Winstanley. Not the kind of publication a lady would read.'

'On the contrary, I *do* know it. They've recently been running a series of investigative articles on spirit mediums. The writer takes a sceptical line, arguing that fraudulent mediums are cheating a gullible public.'

'That's it.' He bowed his head.

'Of course! *You* are the author. I'd thought your name seemed familiar. So, you investigate the supernatural. How intriguing. Are you yourself a believer?'

'Not at all.' He reddened and hurried on. 'I got into this kind of investigation by accident. To be honest, I don't know much at all about the occult. My previous work was writing reports on social events – society balls, garden parties, flower shows and cricket matches, things like that. Dull stuff, really. But my editor thinks I have a talent – if you can call it that – for blending in, not frightening the horses, don't you know? I'm not meant to let slip my real reason for being here. Yet it seems, Miss Winstanley, you've seen straight through me.' He regarded her nervously.

'You needn't worry,' she said, though her curiosity was piqued and she wondered how he had wangled an invitation to Maltraver Towers. 'I've no reason to give your secret away. I'm guessing you're here to write about Madame Trent-L'Espoir. What do you hope to—'

'Evie?' Grace approached the terrace, a pale, slender figure against the shadows of the garden. 'Lady Maltraver wants us all present for the seance.'

They returned to the house. As they entered it, Evie glanced down a darkened corridor and saw a man and a woman at the far end, standing close in conversation. The man had his back to her, and apart from making out that he was in evening clothes she couldn't be sure of his identity. As for the woman, there was no mistaking the red-gold hair escaping under her cap, glistening in the faint light from a single wall lamp. *Janet.*

As Evie watched, the man leant close to whisper in Janet's ear, took something from his pocket and gave it to her. The lamplight fell full on Janet's upturned face and Evie caught her expression – eyes wide, mouth ajar, seemingly mesmerised by her companion. The scene struck her as oddly disturbing. She craned over her shoulder to see more, but Grace was tugging at her hand to make haste.

The seance was to take place in the library, a long galleried room furnished with alcoves, heavy crimson curtains, more portraits of dyspeptic Crosbies and, to Evie's astonishment, remarkably few books. A collection of artefacts of Chinese origin – statues of striding warriors and wise-looking men with long moustaches, jade dragons, porcelain patterned with delicate blossoms, vases intricately decorated with flower buds, birds and butterflies – bore witness to the enthusiasms of a previous Crosbie. From a closed basket placed on a side table, stared the golden unblinking eyes of Osiris the cat. A circular mahogany table stood ready, draped with crimson chenille and set with chairs for each guest.

Lady Maltraver was already in place between Lady Sankey and Mrs Marchmont. Her eyes narrowed as her son strolled in, accompanied by his male guests, joking and laughing loudly.

Encountering his mother's frown, Lord Maltraver, who had been relating what was evidently a risque anecdote, abruptly fell silent.

All the men were there. Which one of them, Evie wondered, had been speaking with Janet?

Two servants glided around unobtrusively, putting out the gas lamps, leaving the room in semi-darkness. The only light came from a tall candle placed at the centre of the table and the fire that crackled in the grate. At a gesture from Lady Maltraver, the servants withdrew.

Madame Trent-L'Espoir came forward, casting off her enveloping black velvet cape to stand revealed in a white satin dress that caught the candlelight as she moved. She sat at the table, arms outstretched, breathing in deeply through her nose and out through her mouth.

Mr Trent bent over her, murmuring solicitously, 'Are you quite comfortable, dear? Is the light in your face?' He hovered, making adjustments to the supporting cushion at his wife's back, till she nodded her satisfaction.

Lifting his voice, he addressed the guests: 'Please take your seats. We must stay quiet while our spiritual intermediary searches out a path that will connect her to the astral plane.'

Evie wasn't sure what to expect. Her father had attended many seances and told her that most spiritualists were frauds. Grief and loss could make people all too willing to believe, even on the flimsiest evidence. He had described some of the mechanical devices used to deceive audiences by creating simulations of ectoplasm, moving tables and producing eerie sounds – disembodied voices, rapping and knocking. Yet occasionally, very occasionally, he had admitted to seeing and hearing things he couldn't easily explain.

Keep an open mind, she told herself. *Stay alert for signs of trickery.*

Mr Trent directed her to go between Lord Maltraver and Marcus Ellingham. As she took her place, Mr Ellingham grinned sidelong at her. Maltraver gazed around him with the insouciance of a toddler, his attention roaming over his guests as though seeking an ally. He gave several derisive snorts and yawned ostentatiously. His fingers drummed a restless beat on the table, like the pounding of hooves, louder and louder. His mother's eyes followed his moving hand and a frown sharpened between her brows.

'Please hold hands,' said Mr Trent as he seated himself between his wife and Lady Maltraver. 'Ladies, if you'd be so good as to remove your gloves, so you have direct contact with one another. By these means we form a unified circle to welcome our spirit visitors.'

The circle of candlelight threw wavering shadows on the walls and ceiling; beyond its reach the darkness pressed closer. They sat in near silence, the only sounds the ticking of the ormolu clock on the mantelpiece and a faint rustle as the cat stirred in his basket. Under half-closed lids, Evie scanned the circle of faces, strangely insubstantial in the low light – some excited, others sceptical, several frankly nervous.

Lady Maltraver licked dry lips, jaw compressed, eyes glazed. Evie recognised that look. *Anxious expectation.* Whom did Lady Maltraver hope to see? Her dead husband? Maybe others who had passed away? Evie felt unexpected sympathy for the straight-backed viscountess.

Mr Penhallow sat impassive, his gaze lowered – probably wishing he was playing billiards instead, Evie thought scornfully – while Grace and Phyllis looked apprehensive. To her right, Mr Ellingham's hand was cool and firm against hers. To her left, Maltraver's hand twitched in her grasp like a small, plump animal.

Madame Trent-L'Espoir, eyes closed, began to sway, then to contort and writhe.

'I say!' murmured Sir James Sankey.

'Hush!' admonished his wife.

Abruptly, Madame Trent-L'Espoir sat bolt upright and snapped into stillness. Her eyes opened. 'John is here. He passed over some years ago, after a long illness, bravely borne. His hair is white, his manner distinguished.'

John – the single most common man's name, thought Evie. *Just what I would have chosen.*

The faces round the table were blank. It seemed no one knew a John who matched the description.

'A young woman is speaking to me. I believe her name is Mary?' hazarded the spiritualist. 'She's trying to contact someone in the circle.'

Mary, thought Evie. *Another common, predictable name.*

'Could it be our maid Mary?' said Grace to Evie. 'Why would she visit us like this?' Her eyes widened. 'Maybe there's something wrong at home! Perhaps the intruder's returned! Surely, Mary can't have ... passed over?'

'Of course not,' said Evie. 'If something's happened at home, Maman would wire or make a call by telephone.'

'Sceptical thoughts hinder the channels of communication,' warned the medium, shooting Evie a frosty glare. 'I'll try a trance.'

Mr Trent readjusted his wife's cushions so she could lie further back, then went over to a phonograph on a side table and the lugubrious strains of 'Tit-Willow' from *The Mikado* filled the room.

Aubrey Penhallow suddenly shifted, scowling. Glancing around the table, his gaze encountered Evie's. He seemed to catch himself and lowered his head, hiding his face in shadow.

Madame Trent-L'Espoir lay slumped, her closed eyelids fluttering, her hands retaining their hold on her husband and Lady Maltraver. 'Ampheres,' she said with a radiant smile. 'Welcome, my lord.'

'This is excellent,' confided Mr Trent in a stage whisper to the rest of the company. He hurried to stop the phonograph before scampering back to rejoin his place in the circle. 'Ampheres was a high priest of Atlantis, the oldest and wisest of my wife's contacts in the spirit world. He's a powerful guide. We can trust in him.'

'Good evening, dear friends.' The medium's mouth shaped the words, but the voice was deep and manlike, the accent polished yet slightly foreign, though from which country, Evie would be hard put to say. 'I see some new friends have joined us tonight. Welcome all.'

'Well, really,' muttered Maltraver. 'Are we supposed to believe this rot?'

From across the table his mother gave him a quelling look.

'Lord Ampheres,' said Mr Trent, bowing his head. 'It's an honour to welcome you amongst us.'

Ampheres began a series of pronouncements. 'Your king needs to have a care to his health. Some women will be causing public disturbances in the name of rights for women; their actions are unwomanly. The women of ancient Atlantis were the guardians of hearth and home. It's they who made Atlantis a bastion of morality.'

'I thought,' whispered Mr Ellingham in Evie's ear, 'that the god Poseidon destroyed Atlantis because its people were immoral and transgressive. Do you think he knows?'

Evie erupted with sudden laughter, quickly suppressed.

'The coming winter will be worse than the last,' continued Ampheres.

'Ask him who'll win the Derby this year,' boomed Maltraver. 'That would be a useful prediction. You were sure it'll be St Amant, Penhallow. Not convinced myself. They say he's a vicious brute, undisciplined and unreliable. Needs the whip.'

Aubrey Penhallow didn't answer. He was still, his head resting against the back of his chair. He seemed asleep, but there was a faint gleam under his half-lowered eyelids.

Evie applied her logic to the question of the medium's authenticity. The voice that came from her lips sounded to Evie like that of a butler in a grand house; despite the slight accent, every syllable was carefully modulated, more ponderous and upper crust than the people he served. Who knew what a high priest of Atlantis would sound like? Surely nothing like this. What language would the people of Atlantis have spoken? Certainly not English. Perhaps specific languages had no meaning after death and the spirits spoke a universal language? Nothing the voice said struck Evie as having a supernatural origin; it just issued vague, lofty statements. She was convinced that Madame Trent-L'Espoir was a fraud.

Evie's hands, still in the grip of her neighbours, grew numb. There was a persistent itch beneath her upper arm where the lace sleeve of her evening dress rubbed against her skin. She considered taking back one of her hands to surreptitiously scratch it.

'What else do you see in the near future?' asked Mr Trent.

A long pause.

'Lord Ampheres?' said Mr Trent.

Again, there was no response.

'I fear we have lost contact.'

They sat on. Time passed. People grew restive. The numbness spread from Evie's hands up her arms.

The medium sat as if frozen, eyes open yet blank and unfocused. Then, with a hissing intake of breath, her lips moved and a new, lighter voice sounded.

'I see death.'

There were gasps around the room.

'Death?' Mr Trent sounded uncertain, confused.

Is this part of the act? Evie thought.

'Very close. It's here in the circle . . . the circle of shadows.'

Evie's throat tightened and she exhaled sharply. Had the words meant something to anyone else? But no, the faces around the table gave no sign of recognition. She narrowed her eyes, trying to make out the medium through the gloom. Her features seemed blurred, formless.

The high priest of Atlantis had gone, if he'd ever been there. The new voice sounded like that of a young woman, speaking with a northern cadence, soft and rolling. Evie, used to the range of southern voices, from cockney of the London streets to the clipped diction of the elite, struggled to pinpoint it.

'Some of you are going to die.'

Mr Trent's jaw dropped. 'W-hen?' he stammered.

Is this too part of the performance? she wondered. His fear looked genuine. How to tell?

'Soon.'

'Who?' whispered Mr Trent.

'Don't ask! I don't want to know.' Mrs Marchmont's voice cascaded into shrill panic. 'Take me home, George.' She lurched up, blundering against her husband.

'For your own safety,' said Mr Trent, 'I must warn you not to break the circle.'

Dr Marchmont wavered then reseated himself, pulling his wife down with him. She linked hands, whimpering quietly.

From Osiris's cage came a panicked yowling. The beast scrabbled against the door of its cage. The medium's body jerked backwards and forwards, as though yanked by an unseen force. Scream after scream came from her throat. One word was discernible:

'Why?' The medium slumped back, her quivering lips shaping a whisper. 'Why are you doing this?'

The terror in the voice sent a physical reaction through Evie, churning up her stomach, sending her heart pumping madly. She tried to keep herself steady. *Focus on the evidence. Is the voice genuine? What about the accent? A local girl?* It sounded different somehow.

'Let me go!' cried the voice. 'Please . . . I just want to go home.' The words faded away into sobs.

'This is h-horrible,' gasped Marcus Ellingham. His hand gripped Evie's as though he would shield her, though she felt his fingers tremble slightly.

On her other side, Lord Maltraver's hand was clammy with sweat. Repulsed by the sensation of wetness, Evie had to resist a visceral urge to pull her own hand away.

'Evie!' whimpered Grace. 'What's happening?'

People whispered their disquiet. Only the medium and Aubrey Penhallow appeared unaffected. Madame Trent-L'Espoir lolled in her chair, apparently unconscious, snorting and snoring. Aubrey Penhallow sat motionless, his green eyes shining like a cat's, fixed on a point behind Evie. Wondering what he was looking at, she twisted in her chair, but made out nothing in the thick shadows.

A dank stench of foetid water assaulted Evie's nostrils, then mingled with another smell, primitive and musky. She caught her breath, feeling a presence moving around them in the darkness, as though, just beyond her sight, some great lumbering thing was circling them.

'There's something down here!' screamed the girl's voice.

'That's it!' roared Lord Maltraver, scrambling to his feet, knocking over his chair. 'The show's over.' He went to the unconscious medium, shaking her by the shoulder. 'Stop these games, Madame!'

Mr Trent sprang up, pulling ineffectually at Maltraver's arm. 'Don't you know better than to wake a medium from her trance, my lord? The consequences could be very dangerous.'

Maltraver shook off Mr Trent's restraining grasp and yelled in the medium's ear. 'Mrs Trent-L'Espoir. Stop this!'

The medium moaned.

Evie felt something wet touch her face.

A drop. Another.

Then more and more drops.

'I say!' cried a man's voice. 'It's bloody raining in here. Maltraver—'

With a whoosh, a deluge of water came streaming down onto the round table, pouring over the watchers. In moments, everyone was drenched.

The downpour extinguished the candle, leaving the room shrouded in darkness save for the glow from the firelight.

Shouts, yells, screams, the scrape of chairs being pushed back as people scrambled out of the way.

'Lights! Turn on the lights!'

Amidst the turmoil came an inhuman cry. It took Evie several confused seconds to realise the sound came from the terror-maddened Osiris, who had burst out of his cage and was leaping over furniture, knocking over antique china and artefacts in his frantic attempts to escape from the room.

Swearing repeatedly as he stumbled over objects in the darkness, Lord Maltraver found the door, opened it and bawled for the servants. A stream of light chased back the shadows, revealing a scene of mayhem. Though it had slowed to a drip, water was still descending. Looking up, Evie made out a long, dark crack in the ceiling.

There was a babble of shaken voices. Over it rang out the wild howls of Osiris, now crouching with his back arched, fur on end, on top of a high bookshelf.

'Someone shut that animal up!' yelled Maltraver.

A footman climbed on a chair, reaching for the cat, and Osiris lashed out, scrambling out of reach. With a cry of pain, the man clamped his hand to his cheek.

'Fetch a ladder, you bloody idiot!' shouted Maltraver.

Osiris kept up his caterwauling, vibrations beginning deep in his throat, rising to a piercing crescendo.

'Sounds like a banshee,' gasped Evie.

'A b-banshee?' said Marcus Ellingham beside her. 'Isn't that an Irish spirit?'

She nodded. 'The ghost of a dead woman. Her cries are supposed to be a warning.'

'Of what?'

'That someone in the house will die.'

CHAPTER
Ten

THE NEXT MORNING, Evie rose early and made her way to the library, leaving Grace asleep. Shattered fragments of jade and porcelain had been cleared away, pools of water mopped up, and sheets draped across the circular table, but the carpet around the table was still saturated and the smell of damp pervaded the air.

Evie climbed on a chair, craning upwards. A network of cracks criss-crossed the ceiling, radiating in streaks of livid green and dull black from a central fissure above the table. Some kind of fungal growth bulged out of the jagged opening, sprouting a network of glistening threads. It gave off a putrid odour that caught in her throat and made her retch. Could *this* be dark magic – something so real, so organic, that you could see, smell, even touch it?

What to make of the seance? At first she'd been inclined to think the whole thing an elaborate charade. But the atmosphere had changed, as if winds of chaos had erupted into the room. An unknown woman's voice had predicted death – whose death? Followed by Evie's own conviction that some dark, unknowable presence had entered the library visible. Add to that the terror of the cat and, of course, the deluge of water – that had been real enough.

She paced up and down, twisting at her hair, then stopped, realising with disgust that her shoes were squelching on the sodden carpet. She shook her head. This wouldn't do. Her father might have had answers, but she had none – not yet, anyway. She would put the problem of the seance to one side, and return to her original reason for coming to Maltraver Towers: her search for the circle of shadows.

Conscious that she might at any moment be interrupted, she scoured the library till she found what she wanted: a map of the surrounding locality. She carried it to the light of a window set deep in an alcove.

Some minutes later, Mr Ellingham's head appeared round the door.

'Miss Winstanley. You're up early.'

'I couldn't sleep after what happened last night.'

'As to that, the mystery's solved.' He grinned at her, chin dimpling. 'At the time, I half believed we were witnesses to a supernatural visitation. It would have made a compelling story for my readers,' he continued regretfully. 'I already had the headline written in my head: *Supernatural presence haunts aristocratic mansion on the Yorkshire moors. Junior reporter present at sinister seance recounts the horrors he witnessed.* But at first light, Lord Maltraver and I checked the room above this. It's a guest bedroom suite, with an adjoining bathroom right above the spot where we sat last night. There's some kind of matter, disgusting-looking stuff, plugging the bath. The pipe beneath the bath had burst – that was the cause of the flood. Perhaps you can guess who was occupying that suite?'

'The Trent-L'Espoirs?'

He nodded. 'They deny engineering the leak, but we've no doubt they contrived it. They must have created the blockage and left a tap running, knowing that at some point the pipe would shatter.'

'How could they have timed the bursting pipe to coincide with the seance?'

'I'm not sure. But there's no other logical possibility.'

She was unconvinced. The timings, the mechanics, sounded so unpredictable and inherently unlikely. Nor did it explain the other things – the woman's disembodied voice, Osiris's frenzied panic, Evie's own sense of an unseen presence. She kept her opinions to herself, though. She barely knew Marcus Ellingham and didn't want him judging her as credulous, too eager to accept a super-natural explanation.

'There was a fearful row between Lord Maltraver and his mother,' he said. 'In the end, though, she conceded that the whole thing with the bathroom pipe looks decidedly fishy. The upshot is that the Trent-L'Espoirs are to leave on the morning train.'

'Why did Lord Maltraver ask you to investigate? Does he know about your work for the *Ghost Hunter*?'

'The thing is . . .' He hesitated, shot her an awkward glance. 'I'm afraid I wasn't entirely open with you last night. I didn't lie,' he added as her brows drew together, 'but I didn't tell you everything. I wasn't at liberty to do so.

'Lord Maltraver hired me. He's concerned about his mother's growing obsession with spirit mediums. There's reason to suppose that Madame Trent-L'Espoir is fraudulent. I've been gathering evidence for an exposé about her in the *Ghost Hunter*. It was arranged that I should come here ostensibly as a guest, so that no one should know my real purpose, especially Lady Maltraver.'

'So you knew Lord Maltraver before you came here?'

'Not at all. We move in very different circles, I assure you. My editor knows him and set the thing up. Do you mind?'

'Why should I?'

'That I wasn't altogether frank with you?'

'It doesn't matter what I think about it.'

'Oh, but it does,' he said in a rush, a rosy hue spreading from his neck as he reached out his hand as though to touch hers, then let it fall. 'I don't want you to believe me dishonest.'

'Of course,' she said briskly. 'But I must go and wake Grace.'

He trailed after her towards the door. 'Were you looking for something particular?'

'I was consulting maps.'

'Maps?' He looked baffled, then his face cleared. 'The lake you spoke of . . . the Sithwater. Did you find it marked?'

She debated whether to confide in him, but he'd mentioned that he knew the locality. 'I can't find anything by that name. But *sith*, or *sidhe*, is an old word for the fey folk. I discovered there's a lake some miles from here known as Fairymere, near a village called Wastdale.'

'Fairymere?' His brown eyes widened.

'You *have* heard of it?'

'Yes,' he said slowly. 'It has a bad reputation.'

'For what?'

'It's said . . . that people have gone missing. As for Wastdale, I know it a little – a dwindling community of the frail and the elderly. The rest left, long ago.'

'If I say I'd like to organise an expedition to visit Fairymere, will you back me?' She saw a question forming on his lips. 'I can't tell you why.'

'If you wish it.' He bowed his head.

~

Evie returned to her room to find Grace still sleeping, sprawled on her back, her cheeks flushed, strands of hair escaped from her plait clinging damply to her face. The room felt muggy.

Evie flung up the window. 'Come on, sleepyhead. The day will be gone.' She related to her sister her plan of visiting Fairymere.

Even when Grace sat up, yawning and stretching, it took her some time to take in what Evie was saying. 'Riding?' she said as she began to dress. 'But you dislike it so. And we haven't brought our gear.'

'Needs must,' said Evie. 'I would have preferred to walk, but it's too far. We'll find a way. Come on, or we'll miss breakfast.'

Grace trailed after her, stifling yawns.

At the breakfast table, Lord Maltraver was distinctly unenthusiastic when he heard Evie's scheme. 'Why would anyone want to go up on the moors when it's still three months till the first shoot?' he grumbled. However, when Marcus Ellingham added his voice to Evie's, declaring that Fairymere was a scenic spot, much renowned, Maltraver gave way. Eventually, all the house guests, along with Maltraver and Phyllis, agreed to go. It was decided that they should take a picnic luncheon to make the excursion, in Maltraver's words, 'more tolerable'.

At the stable, Evie considered her horse, a young chestnut mare, doubtfully. She and Grace had been obliged to borrow cast-off riding clothes from Phyllis. These were traditional habits – nothing so unconventional and daring as a divided skirt for Lady Maltraver's daughter. Evie fiddled with her borrowed riding gloves, trying to hide her anxiety, wondering again why convention dictated that women – supposedly the weaker sex – should be forced to adopt a much more difficult and precarious means of equestrianism than riding astride.

Grace was an accomplished horsewoman from her schooldays in Bath. Gathering up her skirts, she settled lightly into the saddle, arranging one bent leg over the pommel. On horseback, she looked decidedly more awake and animated. Even Phyllis's third best riding habit – a dark purple garment, too short in the arm and skirt for Grace – couldn't dim her beauty. If anything, she looked more ethereal than ever, at one with the skittish animal, hands light on the bridle, lustrous dark hair held back under her hat and a net.

'*La belle dame sans merci,*' called Lord Maltraver, as he waited for his own horse, a fine grey, to be led out. 'How well Keats writes of the torments of love. I believe he's your favourite poet? You see how well I know you, Grace.'

Grace quivered, a glow suffusing her pale cheeks.

A groom brought out a handsome bay, big and raw-boned, for Mr Penhallow. The horse jittered, rolling his eyes and whinnying. At that moment, Lord Maltraver, his back to the horse as he joked with Ellingham, let out a braying laugh. Startled, the bay horse pulled back sharply, hooves clattering on the cobbles, dragging the reins out of the groom's grip. The horse swung away towards the gateway, found Evie in his path, and reared up, the whites showing in his panicked eyes. Evie shrank back, but Aubrey Penhallow was suddenly there. Dodging the flailing hooves, he laid a hand on the horse's neck. The horse brought down his legs and circled, dancing and jerking. Penhallow followed, running caressing hands along the horse's back, all the while speaking reassuringly.

'Evie, are you all right?' cried Grace, bringing her own horse around. The others, too, watched with concern, though Maltraver wore an incredulous, almost childlike grin that made him, in Evie's annoyed eyes, look absurdly foolish.

'I think so,' said Evie. 'I'm sure of it. You go on. I'll catch you up in a moment. I just need to get my breath back.'

The others went back to busying themselves with their own mounts, tightening girths and scrambling into saddles.

Evie watched Penhallow murmur in the horse's twitching ears and stroke the muscular neck with circular movements. Under his touch, the horse grew calmer. Seeing them together, Evie realised Penhallow hadn't exaggerated his affinity with horses.

The groom turned to Evie. 'I'm so sorry, miss. Trafalgar's a great-hearted horse, but he's right nervous. His lordship wants him put down.'

'There's nothing wrong with him.' Though Penhallow spoke quietly, there was cold anger in his voice. 'He's been badly frightened, that's all.'

'*He's* been frightened?' said Evie indignantly. 'What about me?'

The two men disregarded her.

'Her ladyship,' said the groom, 'thinks as you do, sir. She won't hear of Trafalgar being put down. Says he was a good, faithful beast and we must keep him in his lordship's memory. We reckon it was the accident changed Trafalgar.'

'Accident?' Evie prompted, suddenly curious.

The groom checked who was in earshot and lowered his voice. 'Trafalgar was the previous Lord Maltraver's horse. When he died on the hunting field, people said the horse was to blame. That's why his new lordship – Master Alexander, that is – can't bear the sight of Trafalgar. He was very shaken up, poor lad.'

'He was there when his father died?'

'Right enough, miss. He saw it all.'

'What happened?'

'Trafalgar was a quiet horse in them days, for all he's so big. Something spooked him, mayhap a bird, and he bolted. Lord

Maltraver clung on till Trafalgar reared up, sudden like. The saddle slipped and his lordship fell under Trafalgar's hooves.'

'Did you hear that, Mr Penhallow?' said Evie. 'Aren't you afraid to ride him?'

'A man with intentions in his mind is far more dangerous than any animal that acts on instinct alone,' said Penhallow. Against the morning light, his eyes looked dark, their depths unguessable. He turned away, rubbing his cheek against Trafalgar's long nose. The horse whickered softly.

The groom went to load a pony with picnic hampers and blankets. Evie clambered onto the mounting block, promptly dropping her gloves. The mare swung round her head to nibble at Evie's skirts. Irked, Evie tugged back.

'You're not fond of horses?' said Aubrey Penhallow, retrieving her gloves and handing them back to her. 'Yet this expedition was your own idea.'

'Oh, I adore riding. It's so . . . bracing.' Evie grasped the pommel, scrabbling to mount. At the critical moment, the mare moved away, leaving Evie hopping, conscious of looking ridiculous.

'Can I help?' said Penhallow, a slight twitch to his lips.

'Not at all.' She felt at a disadvantage, half afraid he meant to pick her up and throw her onto the saddle. 'I could manage perfectly well,' she snapped, 'if I had a regular saddle instead of this ridiculous side saddle.'

'I'm sure you're right,' he agreed smoothly.

She regarded him suspiciously, uncertain whether he was mocking her, but he had turned away. He swung himself onto Trafalgar's back and rode through the stable yard to where the rest of the group waited.

The groom returned to give Evie a leg up. She landed in the saddle with a bump, conscious of how much farther away the ground appeared from this vantage point than she would have liked, and pulled nervously and entirely ineffectually at the reins. Luckily, the mare decided, of her own accord, to follow her stablemates along the path that led through the parkland and upwards, past monolithic stacks of gritstone rocks, towards the moors.

Eleven

E VIE SLITHERED OFF the mare thankfully, if not gracefully, and surreptitiously rubbed her aching legs and back as she took in her surroundings.

They'd emerged through a narrow cleft in an escarpment into an open space at the water's edge. The scene was much as she'd seen it in the postcard; the photograph must have been taken from about the same angle as the spot where she stood. It was a harsh and desolate landscape, and the strange sense of familiarity she felt, when she'd never been there before, cast an uneasy shadow over her mind. Such a lonely place, as though people didn't belong there. The silence of it crept round her heart.

The lake lay within the surrounding circle of hills, as though cradled in the hollow of a gigantic hand. Carpets of yellow gorse swept up the lower slopes towards crags of gritstone. On the farther shore, dense woodland of oak and birch reached to the water's edge. The mist of early morning had dispersed and the day was bright, the sky cloudless. The warbling call of curlews hung on the air and wading birds and ducks gathered to peck at the rocky fringes of the lake, hunting for anything that moved and could be eaten. Bulrushes clustered in the shallows, half submerged in black mud that gave off a stagnant smell, and beyond them patches of luminous green waterweed floated just beneath the surface. Further out, the water was clearer, though it was impossible to see what lay beneath the glistening surface. There was no breeze to stir up ripples, and the lake, like a dark mirror, reflected the open sky.

The Sithwater gave off the aura of a sentient being drowned in sleep. Evie could see why legends had become attached to it, why the druids had come here for their blood sacrifices, a place where they could be close to their gods. According to the Reverend Mickleford, the only inflow came from an underground spring, while the lack of a visible inlet or outflow gave rise to a persistent legend that the lake was bottomless, its source in another world. Most disturbing of all, to Evie's mind, was the story, repeated by Mickleford, that something otherworldly lived in its cold depths. She tried to shake off an unaccustomed feeling of oppression.

They tethered the horses to stunted trees where they could graze on the grassy slope and scrambled down with the rugs and picnic supplies to a pebbly beach.

Evie walked towards the water, seeking the location described by Mickleford. To her left rose low, crumbling cliffs, surmounted by rocks. A possibility . . .

'I can't imagine why you wanted to come here.'

Evie turned to find Phyllis at her elbow.

'Even on a day like this,' said Phyllis, 'Fairymere's such a gloomy place. The bottom slopes gradually down, then suddenly drops away. They say no one's ever measured the depth of the lake.'

'What about rumours of people going missing? Are the stories true?'

'Some are. Just a few years ago, a Sunday-school party came here for an outing. Not the sort of place I'd choose to bring children for a treat. When it came time to go home, two of the children had disappeared. The adults searched high and low. No trace of them was ever found. Not even their clothes left on the beach.' Phyllis shuddered, yet she spoke with a curious relish.

Evie and Phyllis went right up to the water's edge where Aubrey Penhallow stood motionless, as if carved man-sized from marble, wrapped in thought.

'Mr Penhallow?' said Phyllis.

He didn't answer, and indeed gave no sign he'd heard. He stooped, selected a rounded, flattened stone and skimmed it across the water. Once, twice, three times it bounced. As he tracked its progress, his lips curled back, disclosing white teeth and transforming his face into unsettling lines. For a moment, Evie thought he looked wolfish.

He swung to face Lord Maltraver, who was gingerly approaching across the stones. 'Fancy a dip?'

'Eh, no, not for me,' said Maltraver, backing away. 'I'm not one for deep water.'

'I thought the Sons of Dionysus were fearless,' Phyllis mocked, eyes dancing with mischief. '"All things are possible to me." Isn't that their new motto? One we both know.'

'Shut up!' said her brother, turning savagely on her, spittle flying from his mouth. 'You stupid little fool!'

Phyllis cowered back.

'Keep away from her!' said Evie, stepping quickly between Maltraver and Phyllis.

Maltraver scowled. 'My sister's a birdbrained idiot, but I'm not going to strike her, Miss Winstanley. You've no need to act like Joan of Arc.'

Even as Evie gathered herself up to retaliate, Maltraver, with a contemptuous toss of his jaw, swung away, blundering back up the beach.

'How dare he?' Evie glared at his departing back. She caught an unfathomable light in Penhallow's eye that she took for mockery and cast him, too, a scornful glance.

Penhallow turned towards Phyllis, who stood with her shoulders hunched and her scrawny arms braced tight across her chest. 'Are you all right, Miss Crosbie?'

'Yes,' said Phyllis, though her voice shook.

'Does he often lose his temper?'

'Only when he doesn't get his own way.'

Something flickered across Penhallow's face and he strode off, following Maltraver. Phyllis's gaze, lingering on Penhallow's back, struck Evie as despondent.

As Evie and Phyllis returned along the beach, Evie said, 'Who are the Sons of Dionysus?'

Sullenness had settled back in Phyllis's brows. 'It's supposed to be a secret. That's why Alexander got angry.' Seeing Evie's enquiring look, she shrugged. 'Why should I trouble to keep his secrets? It's a club he belongs to, at Oxford . . . where boys have their fun.'

A drinking club, Evie presumed. *How ridiculous, to have the chance of an excellent education and to fritter one's time away in that fashion.* 'Have you ever thought that you, too, might attend Oxford?'

Phyllis laughed mirthlessly. 'How can you ask? You've met my mother. No bluestocking would be tolerated in the Crosbie family. My role in life is to marry a suitably rich man whom my mother and brother will find for me.'

'But surely,' said Evie, pondering this, 'your family has enough money for you to be able to marry for love?'

'Love?' Phyllis stopped to face Evie, a jeer distorting her mouth. 'You're quite the romantic, aren't you? My family aren't as rich as they once were, partly thanks to death duties, though Alexander's gambling debts haven't helped.' She scowled in her brother's direction. 'The once great Crosbies are reduced to keeping up a charade and living beyond our means. Haven't you noticed that yet?'

'The missing paintings,' said Evie. 'They've been sold?'

'All the Canalettos have gone. And the Van Dyck. Mother's held out so far against selling the Titian. Alexander needs to somehow recoup his losses or marry money – a lot of it. An American heiress, perhaps. It might be a poor look-out for the heiress, though.'

Evie was inclined to agree. She wondered for a moment why Phyllis had confided the family's difficulties to her, but then she realised it was meant as a warning to pass on to Grace that Maltraver had no intention of marrying her. Ironic, Evie thought, that Phyllis clearly had no idea how much Grace loathed her brother. Phyllis assumed that Lord Maltraver was a catch any woman would want, even if he made his future wife's life miserable.

They crossed the small stony beach to where the others had spread out rugs and blankets and were unpacking the picnic hampers. Maltraver had himself under control again and was outwardly full of affable bonhomie as he brought out a basket of quails' eggs and heaped up toasts with spoonfuls of black caviar for the delectation of his guests. Yet sweat dribbled down his fore-head, and his hands fidgeted as he adjusted and readjusted his tie.

'Are you feeling well?' asked Marcus Ellingham.

'Never better,' said Maltraver with a sickly smile. 'Though frankly, I'd rather be anywhere than beside this blasted lake. It gives me the shivers.' He brought out several bottles of sparkling wine that had been packed in ice. 'This'll help the party atmos-phere. Jolly times. Who's for a little snifter?' He poured out glassfuls.

'Not for me or Grace,' said Evie.

To Evie's astonishment, Grace stretched out languorously, a glass in hand. 'Some for me, if you please, Alexander.'

'That's the ticket.' Holding her eyes with his, Maltraver filled her glass to the brim.

'What are you doing, Grace?' Evie protested.

Grace exchanged smiles with Maltraver, smiles that looked to Evie to be . . . *complicit*. Yes, that was the word.

'Don't be such a spoilsport, Evie,' said Grace over her shoulder.

Lord Maltraver's raucous laughter rang out, echoing across the water. To Evie's mind, that distinctive laugh was one of the most irritating of his mannerisms.

The others chattered as they ate and drank. Evie attempted to join in, but her eyes kept going to the lake. It seemed to have caught Grace's attention, too. She grew silent, drinking her wine, gazing dreamily at the water.

'Are you all right, Grace?' said Evie.

Grace dragged her eyes back. 'Oh, yes. I'm just so unaccount-ably sleepy.' Her voice had thickened and her eyes clouded. *She's not used to the wine*, thought Evie.

Grace cast aside her hat, stretched full-length on her blanket, and was immediately asleep. The others, too, seemed drowsy, no doubt from the food and the heat of the day, Evie surmised. Conversation became desultory. Flies buzzed heavily amongst the bulrushes clustered along the water's edge.

Lord Maltraver sprawled, head slumped, back against a tree. The others lounged on blankets, sipping their wine – all but Evie, and Aubrey Penhallow, who sat with long legs drawn up, arms resting on his knees, looking at neither the lake nor his companions, his gaze distant, his mind evidently far away again.

Sunlight danced on the water.

The curlews called to one another, like lost souls.

The flies buzzed louder.

A stealthy slap sounded at the water's edge.

Another.

Something was coming out of the lake . . .

Evie sat up, realising she'd been drowsing, dreaming that something was in the water. That wouldn't do at all; she'd come here with a task to do.

She cast a covert eye over her companions. No one was looking her way. Taking a leather shoulder bag she'd brought, she slunk off to the rock face at the far end of the beach and began to climb.

Several hot, uncomfortable minutes followed as she scrambled up the steep slope, made more awkward by the long flapping skirts of her borrowed riding habit. She'd forgotten her hat and her chignon came loose, exposing her head to the relentless sun.

When at last she reached the summit, she took stock, considering. The ground sloped gently till it reached a point overlooking the lake, where it fell precipitously away. Mickleford had provided no clear description of the location of the kuroskato carving, and no indications of its dimensions. Gritstone rocks were strewn everywhere across the summit; the carving could be on any of them.

Evie loathed heights and kept a wary distance from the cliff edge, averting her eyes from the drop. She went from boulder to boulder, crouching to inspect each in turn, using her handkerchief to rub away lichen and moss to reveal what lay beneath. When her handkerchief became too soiled for the task, she used handfuls of grass.

She turned her head as she heard a trickle of small stones. Someone was coming up the slope to join her on the clifftop. Lord Maltraver? Aubrey Penhallow? Unconsciously, she stiffened, but a moment later Marcus Ellingham appeared, slightly out of breath.

'Might I keep you company, Miss Winstanley?' He gave her a diffident smile from under his fair lashes.

She stood, a slight crease between her brows, wondering if she ought to send him off with a flea in his ear, not at all sure she wanted any witnesses to her investigation. And yet, after all, in contrast to the other men in their party, he'd been straightforward and friendly, and as a writer for the *Ghost Hunter*, he knew his stuff. Perhaps . . .

He must have seen uncertainty in her face, because he quickly added, 'No need to put up with me if you don't want. I'll take myself off.'

She relented and smiled. 'Not at all. I'd be glad of the company. You might be able to help me.'

Thus encouraged, he approached with enthusiasm.

'That's the pearl-bordered fritillary.' He pointed to small butter-flies, wings patterned in orange and black, darting through the grass. 'You don't usually see them this early. Can you make out the row of white pearl markings on the outer edges of the wings?'

Evie paused to watch the heedless dance of the butterflies before resuming her investigation of the rocks.

'You don't care for butterflies?'

'On the contrary, they're beautiful. But just now, I'm in search of something particular.'

'What exactly are you looking for? How might I help?'

She considered how much to reveal. 'A symbol,' she told him, 'carved into the rocks.'

'What kind of symbol?'

But she wasn't ready to take him further into her confidence. 'We'll know it if we find something.'

They searched for nearly an hour, while the sun passed through its zenith.

At last Evie halted, reluctantly accepting defeat. If the kuro-skato carving had been here, it must have long since vanished. She stood up, arching her back – cramped from long crouching – and thrust back the tousled hair that kept tangling across her face. She went as close as she dared to the edge of the precipice and gazed down at the glassy Sithwater, swallowing her disappointment.

What had she hoped for? Some clue to what had happened to her father – that was part of it, of course, just as she had told

Pelham. But if she was being honest, she'd also wanted something more, something to transport her beyond the drab everyday into another world. A dark fairy tale. Whatever it was she'd wanted, she'd failed to find it.

Far below, sunlight glistened on the water, turning it to a sheet of brilliant silver, blinding her.

'This is a strange place,' said Marcus Ellingham, coming up beside her. 'It chills me to the marrow somehow, even though the sun's warm.'

'It was a place of sacrifice,' said Evie.

'Do you mean human sacrifice?' He sounded unnerved. 'Did that really happen?'

'This was a sacred place for the druids – the priests and priestesses of the ancient Celts. The Roman authors said the Celts practised human sacrifice, though they may have said that because they thought the Celts were barbarians. What we do know is that for thousands of years people came here to make sacrifices of the best things they had – weapons, jewellery, drinking bowls. They hoped the spirit of the waters would grant them favours in return. The more precious an object, the more effective it was as a sacrifice. Sometimes people broke their treasures first, rendering them forever unusable, before casting them into the lake.'

'I see,' he said. 'Rather like King Arthur, on the point of death, who kept sending poor old Sir Bedivere to chuck Excalibur into the lake.'

'Exactly. Excalibur was too powerful and magical a sword to remain in the human realm. The things we love the most are only loaned to us. We never truly possess them.'

Sunlight beat on her face and she lowered her eyelids against the glare. She thought of the legend of Cartimandua's daughter, who had voluntarily sacrificed the dearest thing she had – her own life – in a desperate attempt to save her people from the Roman invaders. But according to the Roman historian, Tacitus, Cartimandua had struck a deal with the Romans, had betrayed the rebel chieftain, Caratacus to them, so if there was any truth in the tales, her daughter's sacrifice had been in vain. Just a story, perhaps, but still it seemed unutterably sad.

Evie was vaguely aware that Marcus Ellingham had left her side and was combing the strip of land at the very brink of the summit.

'Hallo, hallo!' came his shout. 'Could this be something?'

Evie turned to see him pointing to a flat rock near the precipice.

Cursing her debilitating vertigo, she clenched her hands, gritted her teeth together and steeled herself to walk to the edge. The ground was unstable; her boots slipped and scrabbled on the loose, sandy earth. All at once, Marcus was there holding her steady, his arms about her while her pulse raced, sweat trickled down the back of her neck and her breath came in faltering gasps. She half knelt, half collapsed by the rock, face turned away from the precipice, forehead pressed against the cold stone. Once she could no longer see the drop, her dizziness eased, though her heart still fluttered uncomfortably fast, like a trapped bird in her chest.

She pushed Marcus's arm away.

'Are you all right, Miss Winstanley?' he asked with concern.

'Yes,' she said between gritted teeth.

'Don't look down,' he advised unnecessarily.

Focusing only on what was in front of her, she traced with her fingers the place where a wide section of the rock face had been shattered. It looked like something there had been smashed out of existence, obliterated so that no one would ever find it again or uncover its dark secret.

The kuroskato?

How had Mickleford managed to find the sigil? Perhaps there had been a wider strip of land in his day between the boulder and the cliff edge, and since that time some of the earth had crumbled in landslides over the precipice. At all events, this had been a well-chosen location for the kuroskato – hidden in plain sight, overlooking the Sithwater.

She pulled at the moss below the defaced expanse of rock. Something else was there, concealed by long tough grass. She ripped away the turf, ignoring the cuts the grass blades dealt to her hands, seeking for what was hidden.

Words. Chiselled into the rock, then filled in with a substance that might have been red paint.

She ran her fingers over the letters, reading aloud:

'"The circle of shadows will be reborn. We shall rise."'

The cuts in the rock were fresh, not worn by prolonged exposure to wind, rain and snow. There was no moss or lichen in the indentations.

The circle of shadows will be reborn. We shall rise.

Her heart jolted under her ribs.

Whatever or whoever the circle of shadows was, it wasn't confined to the distant past. It existed right here. Right now.

She stood, wiping her hands against her skirt, keeping her back to the precipice.

Beside her, Marcus Ellingham read the inscription, his brow furrowed. 'What does it mean?'

She didn't answer. Indeed, she barely noticed him, caught up as she was in her exhilaration. This would be something to tell Pelham. Surely he would believe her now.

From the bag slung over her shoulder, she retrieved her notebook and a pencil, squatted down again and copied out the words, making a sketch map of the location. Absorbed in her work, she half forgot the sheer drop behind her.

At last, her task completed, she took a step away. Out of the corner of her eye, she caught a movement in the lake, far below. Something odd was happening. Clutching the rock for support, she braced herself to look. Rays of the lowering sun danced on the silver water, dazzling her. She shielded her eyes.

A shape like a letter V had formed across the surface of the lake. At its inverted apex a figure waded, waist deep, cutting a line through the water.

Long hair streamed out like a black banner. Lustrous dark hair.

'Grace!' screamed Evie. 'Stop!'

CHAPTER
Twelve

E VIE SCRAMBLED DOWNHILL, sliding on loose, treacherous scree, running recklessly fast. Hands cupping her mouth, she screamed Grace's name. Down at the beach, Phyllis pointed after Grace's distant figure, her thin shrieks amplified by the circling hills, while Maltraver flapped his arms beside her.

'What's the dratted girl doing?' he yelled. 'Has she gone raving mad?'

Evie ignored them.

Out across the water, Grace gave no sign she'd heard. She kept walking, immersed to her chest. Once or twice, she missed her footing; each time she righted herself and carried on towards the deeper water. The ends of her hair floated like a dark fan on the surface.

Evie flung aside her bag, tore off her boots and plunged in. The shock of the icy water made her tremble violently, but she waded deeper. The voluminous skirts of the riding habit became saturated with water. She yanked at the fastenings down her back, but they were out of reach. She tried to rip away the skirt, but the weave was too dense. She struggled on, forcing a passage through a forest of bulrushes, pulling her feet out of sucking mud, kicking free of whiplike tendrils entangling her legs.

Once beyond the weeds, she floundered on, chest deep in open water, calling to Grace, now nearly fifty yards ahead. Suddenly the bottom of the lake sloped downwards, pitching Evie out of her depth. She was no better a swimmer than she was a horsewoman, but no time to think about that. She struck out, paddling vigorously, fighting against the weight of her clothes. She went under, kicked out to find the surface again, murky water stinging her eyes and blurring her sight.

Where was Grace?

Frantically rubbing her eyes, Evie made out a dark head, swimming smoothly and purposefully ahead. With a jolt of disbelief, Evie realised that Grace wasn't alone. All around her, the water was churning. Something was moving just beneath the surface, circling her.

Treading water, Evie opened her mouth to scream a warning and found herself sinking inexorably downwards. The lake closed over her head. Icy water poured into her nose and mouth, went searing into her lungs. She tried to reach the surface but found only water. She was suffocating . . . drowning . . .

A sharp tug on her hair sent her spinning upwards into light and air. She gasped as hands held her up. She clung to Marcus Ellingham's wiry body through his sodden shirt, spluttering, panting, spitting out dank, mossy water.

As soon as she could breathe, she struggled against his hold, crying, 'Not me! Grace!'

She fought him, pulling them both under, but he kept his grip on her, swimming them both into shallower water, setting her down where her scrabbling feet found a bank of sand.

'Find Grace!' she yelled.

'I will. But you *must* stay here.'

She nodded, teeth chattering, as he struck back out into the deeper water. Seconds later, he dived below the surface.

Moments strung out as Evie stared, eyes burning, barely breathing.

Two figures broke the surface: Marcus with Grace unmoving in his arms.

Everything was silent. Evie's ears were full of water. Her heart seemed to stop beating.

Then she saw Grace's arm flap feebly and she gave an incoherent cry of relief.

Marcus carried Grace back into the shallows, Evie staggering behind them. At last he laid Grace on the beach. Evie ran to her sister and turned her on her side. Grace groaned, drawing up her knees, spasms shaking her ribcage, coughing as streams of brownish water gushed from her mouth and nose. She shivered convulsively, her clothes and hair drenched with water, her hands and face blue. Phyllis whimpered, looking on helplessly.

'Get blankets,' said Evie.

Within minutes, Evie and Phyllis had stripped off Grace's habit and wrapped her in a picnic rug. Marcus Ellingham returned bearing blankets and Evie wrapped Grace in them while he draped a cover around Evie's shoulders. Only then did she realise that she, too, was numb with cold, her heavy, wet clothes frozen to her body, her hair a sodden mass dripping down her back, her teeth chattering uncontrollably.

Sometime later, when Evie, Grace and Marcus, well wrapped and rubbing themselves vigorously, started to feel less deathly chilled, Evie turned on the Crosbies.

'Why didn't you stop her?' she demanded.

'I fell asleep,' moaned a wild-eyed Phyllis. 'Alexander, too. We woke to find Grace had gone into the water. I can't swim.'

'What about Mr Penhallow?' Evie looked round. For the first time, she noticed Aubrey Penhallow's absence.

'He left some time ago,' said Phyllis. 'He said he had business letters to write before the last post.'

'And you, Lord Maltraver? Can't you swim?'

'If your sister chooses to act like a silly little fool, it's no affair of mine.'

'Can't you swim?' she repeated.

'I have an . . . aversion to deep water.' He wouldn't meet her eyes.

'You coward!'

He made no reply. Scarlet blotches broke out across his cheeks.

'Evie,' gasped Grace, a blanket drawn around her chest, the rug over her legs. 'Alexander's not to blame. It was my own fault for swimming in the lake. You should apologise.'

'It's of no consequence,' said Maltraver, drawing himself up straighter. 'We know women struggle to control their rational faculties. Hardly surprising that Miss Winstanley should be overwhelmed by her emotions.'

It was at that moment that Evie's dislike of Lord Maltraver turned to active loathing. She bit her tongue on the words she wanted to say, conscious she might start screaming at him.

'You people all shivering and teeth chattering are making me feel cold,' said Lord Maltraver. He brought out a hip flask. 'Let's have a nip of brandy.'

'We don't take it,' snapped Evie.

'Your sister will. Won't you, little Grace?' He looked around for a glass, but they had been packed away. He poured brandy into his cupped hand and held it out to Grace.

Grace met his eyes, and something passed between them that Evie didn't understand. Grace stretched out to clasp his wrist and drew his hand down towards her. Then she reached out her pink tongue and licked the brandy from his palm, his thick fingers.

'Grace!' Evie felt shock, and something else – a kind of sickness in the pit of her stomach.

'Come on now,' interposed Marcus, taking in Evie's appalled face, 'before any of us gets pneumonia. We must return.'

Thirteen

THEY MADE THEIR way back to Maltraver Towers, Evie and her sister miserable with cold, shivering, their wet clothes clinging to their bodies. The journey back seemed interminable and Evie felt as though she'd never be warm again.

When at last the sisters reached their room at Maltraver Towers, Evie made Grace take off her wet things, doing the same for herself, finding them fresh clothes. She rang the bell and when a maid she didn't recognise came in answer, Evie sent her to fetch hot water bottles and warm drinks. Grace was strangely drowsy, her head lolling from side to side. Delayed shock, perhaps? When the maid returned, Evie took the hot water bottle and put it on Grace's feet, then sent the maid away. Perching on the edge of the bed, she held out a steaming mug, coaxing Grace to drink.

'Why did you do it, Gracie? You could have died.'

'I don't know what happened,' said Grace fretfully. 'All I remember is lying on the beach, vomiting water.' She pulled a face. 'Don't bother me, Evie. I don't feel well. I need to rest.'

'Lord Maltraver,' said Evie. 'You acted ... so strangely with him.'

'Go away, Evie!' Grace pummelled her pillow with her fists and turned her head away. 'Leave me alone.'

Evie bent over her, but Grace turned to face the wall, screwing her eyelids shut. She gave up and left Grace to rest.

As she closed the bedroom door, she heard rapid footsteps descending from the stairs above and drew back just as Mr Penhallow appeared round the spiral staircase. He didn't notice her in the shadow of the doorway, and almost cannoned into her, stopping himself just in time. Their startled eyes met. He seemed different somehow, with a strange, raw look on his face.

'That stair leads to one of the maids' bedrooms,' said Evie. 'Perhaps you were lost, Mr Penhallow?'

He'd mastered his surprise. The unguarded look was gone. 'I took the wrong staircase. A mistake.' He surveyed her, one eyebrow raised in amusement. 'You don't believe me, do you? So what do you suspect me of doing, Miss Winstanley?' He held her gaze a moment longer. To her embarrassment she felt herself reddening. 'What a *vivid* imagination you have,' he remarked.

She remembered the man she'd seen deep in furtive conversation with Janet in a darkened corridor. His back had been towards her and she hadn't recognised him, but suddenly she knew.

'I saw you with Janet last night,' she said. 'You were giving her money, weren't you? Making an assignation with her.'

He put his mouth so close to her ear that his lips almost touched her hair. 'What if I was?'

She recoiled. 'You're beneath contempt. I'll tell Lady Maltraver that you've been preying on a servant here, a vulnerable woman—'

'If you tell Lady Maltraver of your suspicions,' he said coolly, 'Janet will be immediately cast off, without a reference, into the outer darkness, into penury, misery, despair. And do you know what will happen to me, Miss Winstanley? *Nothing at all.* In our enlightened society, it's the women that pay, the poor ones most of all. That's just how it is – the way of the world.'

He smiled at her, a cold hard smile. As she stood back, he passed on down the stairs.

~

Dinner that evening was an ordeal for Evie. She suspected that most of the people around the table thought the same.

Mr Ellingham tried to introduce cheerful subjects, but his attempts were poorly received. Lady Maltraver frowned so forbiddingly at any mention of the disastrous seance that no one dared to speculate about it, or to raise the matter of the sudden departure of the Trent-L'Espoirs. Phyllis attempted to engage Mr Penhallow in conversation, but he seemed preoccupied, and had little to say on any subject, even horse racing. Eventually she gave up, fidgeted with her empty wine glass and poured herself more whenever her mother wasn't looking.

Evie, shaken by Grace's brush with death in the Sithwater, confined herself to pushing food half-heartedly around her plate. She watched Grace and Lord Maltraver, the only cheerful people at the table, conduct a flirtation in lowered voices, interspersed with giggles.

What was the matter with Grace? Just yesterday, she'd said she couldn't bear Maltraver. Women were entitled to change their opinions about men, of course, but Grace wasn't acting like herself. She looked flushed as though with fever, and tore bread with her fingers, leaving the segments scattered on her plate as she bubbled into laughter at one of Lord Maltraver's risque jokes, leaning in close towards him so that their shoulders almost touched.

Lady Maltraver missed nothing of the whispered interchanges between her son and Grace. 'You've not yet explained,' she said across the table to Grace in an arctic voice, 'what caused you to throw yourself into Fairymere. A thoroughly irresponsible action. You endangered other people's lives as well as your own.'

Grace went scarlet. 'I'm not sure,' she began, before turning to Evie in mute appeal.

'Grace sleepwalks,' Evie improvised. 'She has done since childhood. No doubt she was asleep by the water's edge and walked into the water without being aware of what she was doing.'

Grace smiled gratefully at her, as though Evie's transparent lie solved the problem. Evie cut up her potatoes without looking at them, keeping her attention fixed on Lady Maltraver, silently challenging her to repudiate the account.

'An inconvenient affliction,' said Lady Maltraver eventually, disbelief accentuating the lines between her nose and mouth.

'Yes, it is, isn't it?' agreed Evie affably, abandoning all pretence of eating her food. She turned to engage Mr Ellingham in talk and the subject was dropped.

After dinner, cards were set up in the drawing room. Aubrey Penhallow turned out to be an excellent player and won steadily.

'Lucky at cards, unlucky in love,' said Lord Maltraver. 'Good thing we're not playing for money. The mater won't ever allow that.'

'Perhaps you and I could play again at some future date, when you're not under the maternal eye,' suggested Mr Penhallow with a sardonic grin, as he shuffled the deck and dealt with practised hands. 'Your luck may turn.'

'High time it did.' Maltraver flushed, and ran agitated hands through his curls, disarranging them.

Penhallow finished dealing. Lord Maltraver groaned as he surveyed his new hand, turning for support to the decanter at his elbow.

Evie, playing in such a reckless way that she was soon eliminated, went to sit in an armchair with the *Illustrated News*, feigning an interest in the society pages. When the players' heads were bent over a new deal of cards, she flitted from the room.

Two minutes later, she was up in the quarters that had been occupied by the Trent-L'Espoirs. So much had happened in the course of that day that she'd had no time till then to investigate further the previous night's seance. The room lay in shadow, the heavy curtains closed, and the same dank, musky smell that had permeated the library was present here too, though much stronger. Evie lit a lamp and took it through to the tiled bathroom, resting it on a mantelpiece beside the deep claw-footed bath, the bottom of which was covered with an opaque greenish liquid. The pipe beneath had to have been completely blocked, Evie thought. She bent closer, holding up the lamp with one hand while with the other she covered her nose and mouth, trying to block out the stench.

Just above the malodorous liquid, a thick line of scum circled the bath, and Evie saw something glinting through the ooze. Several sharp and brittle-looking objects were stuck there, standing out like broken fingernails. She felt a deep reluctance to handle them, but they might be evidence – of something. Most were in fragments, but she spotted one that seemed to be whole. Using her handkerchief to cover her hand she tried to pull it free, but it had stuck fast in its bed of sludge. Grimacing with disgust, she grasped it between her thumb and forefinger and managed to prise it loose. It came away abruptly with a faint sucking sound.

She held the object up to the lamp, her brow furrowed. It was flattish and oval in shape, tapering at one end. The lamplight shone through it, picking out translucent colours: tawny brown and bottle green. The scale of an animal? Yet it was bigger than the scale of any creature, on land or sea, that she could imagine.

She wrapped the object in her handkerchief and tucked it in her pocket, then washed her hands at the basin. Tentatively she sniffed her fingers, where traces of the odour still clung, and spent several more minutes scrubbing under her nails, trying to get clean again.

Evie left the bathroom, carrying the lamp. Halfway along the corridor, a heavy velvet curtain was drawn across an alcove. She had an impression that the curtain had been open when she'd passed it a few minutes ago; a large Chinese vase had stood there. From behind the curtain came sounds – a woman's voice, moaning, a man's voice, earthy with desire.

Aubrey Penhallow, she thought, shaken. *It's not your business. Don't intervene.* She carried on past, shoulders hunched. Then, between one step and the next, she paused, tilted her chin and turned back. She wouldn't let him intimidate her a second time, nor stand by and let him prey on servant women. She yanked aside the curtain.

Grace leant back, quivering, in the arms of Lord Maltraver, eyes closed in languid delight, as he nuzzled greedily at her throat, his hands groping under her bodice.

Shock paralysed Evie. 'Grace!' she said at last.

Grace's black eyes opened, mirror-bright and alien, as though a dark light had been lit in a distant world. She stared at Evie as though she'd never seen her before.

Maltraver rolled his eyes. 'Your arrival is inopportune, Evelyn.'

'Take your hands off my sister!' Evie grabbed Grace's wrist, pulling her away.

Maltraver raised his hands, half laughing, like a schoolboy caught in a prank for which he knows there'll be no serious reprisals. He sighed ostentatiously and lit a cigarette.

'How dare you!' Evie raged. 'She's seventeen years old, a guest in your house. This is shameful! You are no gentleman.'

He pursed his lips, directing a stream of smoke at Evie. His tongue moistened his full, pink lips. 'Young and . . . unspoiled . . . is how I like 'em. And I can assure you, she was most willing.'

Evie slapped his face. The scarlet imprint of her fingers burnt on his cheek.

Swearing profusely, he fixed Evie with a venomous stare. 'I will not forget that, Miss Winstanley.'

'Good. I don't want you to forget it. Remember it every time you're tempted to assault a woman.'

'There was no assault. I tell you she was eager for it. It was *she* who followed me. Isn't that right, Grace?'

'Yes,' whispered Grace. 'I came to you.' Her chest heaved, her gaze never wavering from Maltraver.

'Grace!' Evie exclaimed. 'What are you saying?'

Maltraver smirked, smoking his cigarette and leaning back to watch the sisters; Grace limp and passive as a marionette in Evie's hold, Evie shaking with anger.

'You're disgusting,' Evie said to him. 'I'm minded to tell your mother.' Even as she said it, she knew her threat to be empty. Aubrey Penhallow was right about double standards. If Evie spoke out, it was Grace's reputation that would be wrecked, not Maltraver's.

He knew it too, for as he watched waves of impotent fury cross her face, he grinned, flipping the lit cigarette into the Chinese vase. 'Do as you will, Evelyn. But remember – all things are possible to me.'

Choking down her wrath, she stalked off, hauling the unresisting Grace along with her.

Grace dropped onto her bed, yawning as she pulled off her evening slippers. Evie slumped against a wall, still trembling.

Could Grace have been drunk? She hadn't drunk wine at dinner. Afterwards, perhaps?

'Are you going to tell Maman?' Grace's voice was sulky. 'If you do, she won't let me leave the house again. Not till I'm at least thirty.'

'I don't want to.' Evie shrank at the prospect of how much this would hurt their mother. 'But you have to explain what is happening ... because I don't understand.' She stood by Grace's bed. 'Just yesterday, you told me you couldn't abide Maltraver. What has changed?'

'*I've* changed,' said Grace, opening her black eyes very wide. 'I ... wanted him, so much. His hands to touch me ... everywhere.' She stretched out her arms, drew her fingers along her lips, as though feeling an invisible mouth on hers, her body writhed as though pressed against an absent form.

Evie rocked back on her heels, blurting out the first thought that came into her head.

'But he's nauseating!'

Grace's eyes blazed like black suns. She hissed at Evie. 'And you! All you care about is dry old stuff, and dead people in history books. Just because you care nothing about finding a man to love you and desire you and hold you in his arms, doesn't mean we're both doomed to end up as old maids.'

'Grace!' Evie recoiled, her hands to her mouth.

Suddenly Grace sobbed. 'I didn't mean it! I'd never want to hurt you. I don't know why ...' The rest of her words were drowned in incoherent tears.

Evie approached gingerly and hugged her. 'It's all right, dearest.' She didn't feel hurt – or at least, not very much hurt. What she felt most was fear for her sister, who was acting as if she had been replaced by a stranger. She was groping her way blindly along a tunnel, each step taking her further into the dark, leading she knew not where.

As Grace donned a dressing gown, Evie noticed strange marks on the back of Grace's left hand, a line of four angry-looking punctures, oozing blood.

'What's this?' said Evie.

Grace marvelled at her hand as though it didn't belong to her. 'I . . . don't know.'

'Did someone do that to you?' A fresh tide of anger swept over Evie. 'Maltraver?'

'No. Not him.'

'Did you . . . do it to yourself?' said Evie, hating the question, hating herself for asking.

Grace's brow cleared. 'Why, yes, that's what happened. My fork, at dinner.' She made a sudden vicious gesture of driving the fork into her own hand.

Seeing Evie's shock, Grace said, 'Don't worry, Evie, no one saw. I had my hand below the table and my glove covered it.'

'Why, Gracie?' Evie said unsteadily.

Grace's face clouded. 'I don't know. I must've had a reason, mustn't I?'

Evie determined not to let Grace out of her sight. When her sister went to the bathroom, Evie went with her, and after Grace got into bed, Evie locked the bedroom door and slipped the key under her pillow. She didn't look at Grace while she did it, but she could feel Grace watching her with resentful eyes.

Fourteen

Waist deep in water so cold it penetrates her flesh, sticks to her bones. Darkness all around. Mud climbs up her calves, her thighs, gripping her tight. She thrashes wildly, trying to tear herself free. Futile.

Then she hears it. Out in the darkness. A faint swish. Just below the surface, something's moving towards her. Coming fast . . .

She wakes. Darkness again, but this is the darkness of her bedroom in the tower. Somewhere, she hears water dripping.

The drips rise to a crescendo.

~

Evie woke with a start. Daylight shone around the edges of the curtains. Someone was knocking at the door, followed by rattling as a hand shook the handle.

She retrieved the key from under her pillow and turned it in the lock. Janet entered, bearing a tray of tea.

Grace lay in uneasy sleep, sweat plastered to her forehead, tossing her head from side to side, flinging out her limbs. Evie called to her. Grace's eyes opened and turned on her a look of blank darkness.

What's wrong with her? Something must have been here, in the room, while they'd slept, had got to Grace somehow.

Evie's gaze lifted to the discoloured stains above Grace's bed. A little bigger than before, perhaps, covering a wider area. No concentric circles, just irregular splotches. Had she imagined the pattern?

No. She had seen it. She *had*.

She hugged Grace. 'Do you know me?'

Long moments passed. Then, in a wavering voice: 'Evie?'

'It's me, dearest.'

Grace slumped back across the sheets, staring at the ceiling, her face empty.

Evie stood, biting her lip in thought. She said to Janet, 'Could you draw my sister a bath?'

Grace trailed after Janet to the bathroom, moving stiffly like an automaton.

As soon as Evie was alone, she searched the room. She burrowed through the cupboard by Grace's bed; explored the chest of drawers, throwing out underwear, corsets, petticoats, stockings; investigated the massive mahogany wardrobe, taking out each of Grace's garments, feeling for anything in the pockets or sewn into the hems. She shook out the hats, investigated the travel bags, then examined Grace's shoes, probing the soles, running her finger round the inner surfaces. Nothing.

Next she knelt on the hearth, peered up the chimney, then ran her hands up as far as she could reach, bringing them out black with soot.

Her eyes fell on Grace's bed. She darted to it, pulling off the blankets, the sheets, shaking everything out. She raised the mattress, and checked its underside, the wriggled into the space under the bed, and felt along each of the slats.

She clambered out. Wiping her hands on her handkerchief, she sat back on her heels, frowning.

She returned to Grace's mattress, lifted it and ran her hands along its whole surface, probing and pushing. This time, her searching fingers found a slit that ran just below the seam binding the mattress's edge – not a tear; a cut made with a razor or sharp knife. Through the slit came a smell of noxious water.

Evie drew in her breath with a hiss. She pulled out handfuls of woollen mattress stuffing through the slit, scattering it across the floor. It was heavy with liquid. More and more came out, and muddy water oozed through her fingers, forming puddles on the floor. She reached deeper in, only to draw back in disgust as she felt something slimy coiled tight around the metal mattress springs. Gritting her teeth, she forced herself to go on. Yanking hard, she felt something break, and drew out strands of livid green waterweed that tangled themselves tightly around her fingers. She untwisted them, screwing up her face in revulsion, and burrowed deeper. At last her groping fingertips touched something solid deep within the mattress.

She seized hold of the object and drew it out. It was small and cylindrical, fashioned out of some kind of organic shell-like substance. There was a crack along its length, into which she inserted her fingernail. It opened easily. Inside lay strands of dark hair, wrapped around a fragment of tightly folded parchment. She opened it tentatively. On it, depicted in blue-black ink, was the kuroskato sigil. As she gazed in horror, the central pattern wavered and reformed itself, like a living thing.

Evie pulled herself together and pushed back the wet stuffing into the mattress. She had no more handkerchiefs, so she took one of Grace's and laid the cylinder open upon it, the parchment and hair visible, just as Janet returned to collect the tea tray.

Janet stopped short, her eyes fixed on the cylinder, the tray wobbling in her hands. She set it down carefully, her face tight.

'Do you know what this is?' said Evie.

'N-no, miss. It looks right nasty.'

'The question is, how did it get into the mattress where my sister's been sleeping?'

'I couldn't say.' Janet twisted her hands.

'You had access to this room. This hair is from my sister's hairbrush.'

Janet's features reddened and crumpled. 'I know nothing about it.'

'If not you, then who?'

'I don't know. You'd best get rid of that *thing*, miss.'

'I intend to. Unless I keep it as evidence.'

Janet picked up a dish of tea. The china rattled as she set it down on the tea tray. Evie watched her for signs that she knew more than she was telling.

'I saw Mr Penhallow on the staircase that leads past this room. Do you know what he was doing?'

'I've no idea, miss.'

'That stair leads nowhere but to your bedroom.'

Janet flashed her a resentful look.

'What do you know about him?'

'I've never spoken to him.' Janet's flush had ebbed, replaced by pale wariness. 'One of the valets attends him.'

'You needn't be afraid I'll tell Lady Maltraver. I just want to warn you. I *know* he was in your room. Did he come to this bedroom too? Could he have put this *thing* in Grace's bed?'

'I'm sure he didn't.' Janet's expression was mutinous.

'For your sake, Janet, stay away from him. He'll bring you nothing but trouble. He's a bad man.'

'Begging your pardon, miss, what does someone like yourself know about a man such as him?' Something close to a sneer warped Janet's lips, quickly suppressed. She began to sort through Grace's bedding, picking things up from the floor where Evie had left them, and remaking the bed.

Evie tried another tack. 'Sukey – the maid who ran away. Did she go away with a man?'

Janet didn't turn around from her task; her back was rigid. 'I don't know nothing about that.'

A lie. 'What was her surname?'

'Huxley. Susanna Huxley.'

'Was she from somewhere in the north-west of England? Lancashire or Cheshire, perhaps?'

'Lancashire? Not she. Whatever makes you think so?' Janet came away from the bed, looking more self-possessed, though her mouth was drawn in a thin line. 'Her family were from the south. From Colchester way. Now, if you'll excuse me, miss, I've a lot of work to do here and can't stand chatting.' She scooped up an armful of discarded bedding and took it out with her, face averted.

Left alone, Evie paced up and down. At last she lifted her head, grabbed the cylinder – still wrapped in the handkerchief – and ran downstairs. A murmur of voices came from the breakfast room, but Evie strode off in the other direction, to the drawing room, which at this hour was empty. Logs had been laid in the grate but hadn't yet been lit. She put the bundle in the fireplace, lit a match and touched it to the kindling. Flames flickered, then flared green as poison, and Evie jumped back as they reached out to snatch at her. A rancid stench assailed her nostrils and a piercing wail rang out, like the suffering of a soul in torment, screaming as it died.

'What the devil's that?' said Marcus Ellingham from the doorway. He joined Evie as she stared at the green fire. The handkerchief had burnt away, exposing the parchment, scorched and blackened. It writhed and twisted as if in agony.

His eyes widened. 'What *is* that thing?'

'An abomination.'

'What's going on, Miss Winstanley? Won't you confide in me?'

She made no reply.

'Are you in some kind of trouble?'

'Why should you think that?'

'Because . . . forgive me. What happened at Fairymere . . .'

'I didn't thank you properly. We owe you a great deal. You saved my sister's life.'

He winced. 'I don't need thanks. I only did what anyone would have done. That's not what I meant. There was something already wrong, wasn't there? Your search among the rocks. The carved message we found – it meant something to you?'

'Perhaps. Is that all, Mr Ellingham?'

'No, not all.' He chewed at his lip. 'There are marks around your throat. As though someone had . . . laid violent hands on you.'

She clapped her hands to her neck, realising that in her hurry to dispose of the charm, she'd forgotten to put on the jet necklace or the concealing powder.

'Was that insolence the work of some man here? Tell me his name, and whoever he is, I will—'

'It happened at my home. An intruder broke into my father's study, but I gave him cause to regret it. Why should you think anyone here dared to touch me?'

'Forgive me, but your sister yesterday did not seem quite herself. And Lord Maltraver is not—'

'Not quite the thing?' Her voice was light, though her smile didn't reach her eyes.

Ellingham glanced round to make sure they were alone. 'I fear he's a bounder and can't be trusted with women. There's another thing, too, that gives me reason to doubt Lord Maltraver. Tell me, have you ever heard of the Sons of Dionysus?'

'Phyllis said something about it.' She was puzzled by the apparent change of subject. 'A student society at Oxford.'

'A very select society. Its origins go back hundreds of years. Maltraver is one of the current members.'

'What of it?'

'I've reason to think it may not be . . . a normal student society. Over the years, there have been whispers – I heard them myself when I was up at Oxford – that the Sons of Dionysus pursue an interest in the occult, that some members have gone further than the theory and actually practise the dark arts. All that may be just Oxford gossip, but there might be more to it. I intend to find out—'

A young footman entered the room. 'Lord Maltraver is looking for you, sir. He says it's urgent.' He stared inquisitively at the greenish flames, wrinkling up his nose at the odour.

Ellingham turned to Evie. 'I must go,' he said with a sigh. 'You'll wait for me? Please? I'll be back as soon as I can, and we can talk this over.'

Evie smiled noncommittally, waiting until Ellingham left. She felt a pang of guilt; he'd been her only ally throughout this nightmarish weekend, but she couldn't wait, not even for a minute. The only thing that mattered was getting Grace away from here.

She returned to the tower room to find Grace crouched on her bed, wrapped in a dressing gown, her hair damp, shivering, her teeth chattering. Seeing Evie, she held out her hands. 'I don't feel well. I don't know what's wrong with me.'

Evie sat beside her, put a hand to her forehead. 'You're feverish.' She held Grace's wrist. The skin was clammy, the pulse erratic. Her sister scratched repeatedly at her upper arm.

'May I see?' Evie pushed up the sleeve of Grace's dressing gown – and gasped.

Set into Grace's skin was a pattern, bluish in colour. With a clutch of terror, Evie recognised it.

The kuroskato.

Grace squinted, twisting her arm. 'What *is* that?' she cried, catching a glimpse.

Evie fought to seem calm, though her heart pounded and it was hard to breathe. *Don't scare her any more than she's scared already.* 'You must have cut yourself. There were lots of sharp rocks at the lakeside. The marks will fade.'

Grace looked uncertain.

'Gracie,' said Evie after a moment's frantic calculation, 'do you think you could manage the journey to London if we left at once?'

'We're meant to stay until Monday,' said Grace haltingly. 'Phyllis has plans. Won't they think it very rude if we leave now?'

'Not if I tell them you're ill. You could have caught a chill from the lake. The journey will be uncomfortable, but at the end of it Maman will be there to take care of you.'

'Oh, yes,' breathed Grace, tears in her eyes. 'I don't know what it is, but I feel weak and aching, as though I've been running for hours and somehow can't stop. Please, let's go home.'

'Then that's what we'll do.' Evie made her voice cheerful and encouraging. 'Get yourself dressed. I'll manage everything else.'

Within minutes, Evie had packed their belongings, found their hostess, given their apologies and asked for transport to be arranged to get them to the station for the morning train. Lady Maltraver put up no obstacle to their going, and readily agreed with Evie's suggestion that there should be no encounters to bid farewell.

'Don't let us detain you,' said Lady Maltraver. Evie fancied she saw barely concealed satisfaction in the viscountess's eyes at the prospect of getting rid of Grace.

Shortly after, Evie bundled Grace, wrapped in her coat, a rug and several scarves, into a dogcart. They'd encountered no one except a forlorn Phyllis, leaning over the banister to wave a distant farewell.

'All will be well now, dearest,' Evie whispered to Grace, so the driver of the cart wouldn't hear. 'I'm going to keep you safe. I promise.' She took Grace's cold hand and tried to warm it with her own.

Presently Grace retrieved her hand to scratch surreptitiously at the place where, beneath her sleeve, the kuroskato lay concealed. Evie said nothing, but she watched Grace's scrabbling fingers with dread in her heart.

PART 2

Oxford

Fifteen

'THIS IS ALL my fault,' said Evie, arms wrapped tight against her body, hugging herself in her guilt. In the window glass, she caught a faint reflection of her own face, looking oddly unlike herself – pale, brows knitted.

'How,' said Pelham emphatically, 'can it possibly be *your* fault? Or Grace's? The only person at fault here is that scoundrel Maltraver.' He clenched his fist and banged the window frame, a gesture so uncharacteristic it made Evie jump. 'That cad! If it hadn't been for you, Evie . . .'

They were in the attic room that had once served as their schoolroom. It was little used now, and their discussion wouldn't be overheard.

'Maltraver's an odious brute,' said Evie, 'and an opportunist. He took advantage of Grace not being herself. But that doesn't necessarily mean it was *he* who planted the kuroskato. I don't see how he would be involved with something like the circle of shadows. He's not clever enough, for one thing, and not much more than a boy. What would someone like that know about the occult?' She caught a slight smile on Pelham's face and snapped, 'Yes, I realise I'm also very young, but I was accustomed to helping Papa in his researches and I'm familiar with some of the basic principles of occult theory.'

She broke off and shook her head miserably. 'For that reason, because I knew enough to understand that magic might be real, and could be dangerous, I should have appreciated the risks. Papa said never meddle in things you don't understand, but I *did* meddle. And now this . . . *thing* has entered into Grace. What have I done, Pel?'

'We have to consider this logically. I still think you should tell Leonie everything.'

'You do believe me, then?'

'About Maltraver? Of course.'

'I meant the rest of it.'

Pelham gave her a searching look. 'Do you know how it sounds?'

'Of course. That's why I can't tell Maman. She wouldn't understand. She'd be so devastated that Grace ...'

They looked through the window towards where Grace had just emerged, dressed in white, a tennis racket under her arm, to meet a gaggle of girls about her own age, who fell upon her gleefully. They linked arms and set off along the street, chattering like a flock of starlings.

'Our neighbours, the Boswells,' Evie said, holding aside the curtain to follow Grace's progress. 'They're holding a tennis party. How normal Grace seems. Once we got away from Maltraver Towers, she seemed better. She won't speak a word about what happened in Yorkshire. She says she can't remember, that she must have been coming down with a fever.'

'Has it occurred to you,' said Pelham slowly, 'that Grace could have inflicted the marks on herself? We believe we make logical choices, yet our emotions, our desires, may overwhelm us.'

'You're talking like a doctor.'

'How else do you expect me to talk?' he said, looking stung. 'In my experience, people believe things because they *need* to believe them. They may convince themselves that they can commune with dead loved ones, or that they can make a charm that will procure someone's love. That doesn't make the things *true*.'

'You say that because you don't believe the power of occult magic is real. But what if it *is*, Pel?'

He didn't answer.

She tossed her head, flung herself onto a battered horsehair sofa and started to count off on her fingers. 'What about the physical occurrences? The cat that sensed something we couldn't? The water that came through the ceiling?'

'A hoax,' he said, coming to sit beside her. 'This journalist, Marcus Ellingham, said as much.'

'And what about what happened at the lake?'

'There's a possible explanation for Grace's action,' Pelham said, choosing his words with care. 'If her mind was under great stress ...'

'Are you saying you believe there's something not right ... in Grace's mind? That she'd actually attempt to take her own life?' Evie's fingers unconsciously tensed into claws, but she hid them, surreptitiously digging her nails into her stomach. 'How could you think so?' she said reproachfully.

He tugged at his collar as if it had grown too tight. 'I didn't say that. But it occurs to me ... what if that blackguard Maltraver tried to lay hands on Grace at some point over the weekend *before* you visited the lake? Such a shocking experience for a young girl could have sparked off emotions she couldn't acknowledge, even to herself – shame, self-disgust, a need for a ritual cleansing ...'

'You mean she felt she needed to atone for something *he* tried to do? Or did? That's horrible!'

'The mind is complex. We are only just beginning to understand *how* complex. Perhaps you have heard of Dr Freud, who practises in Vienna?'

'Freud?' she said distractedly, trying to straighten the tension in her fingers. 'I don't think so.'

'He says that things in ourselves that we can't face, emotions that frighten or shame us, are buried deep in the hidden places of our minds. Especially the secrets we can't admit to our conscious selves – our desires.'

She grew impatient. 'You think of Grace's situation as an *interesting case*?'

'That's unfair. I'm concerned about Grace ... and also about you.'

'Me?' She stiffened. 'You think that I, too, am being led by my unconscious mind to imagine things?'

With a nervous gesture, he pushed back his hair. 'Be honest with yourself, Evie. It's a possibility, isn't it? You say you want to follow the evidence, yet what real proof do you have that these occurrences were spun out of magic rather than the human mind?'

Evie frowned. 'Wait there.' She ran from the room, returning moments later with a handkerchief, which she unfolded to disclose the thing she had found in the blocked bath. 'This is physical evidence.'

Pelham took it between his forefinger and thumb and went to examine it under the window. 'It looks like a scale,' he said. 'Odd sort of colour – bronze-green. Too big for any fish I've ever seen,' he added, measuring it against his hand. 'Nearly the length of my thumb. A snake? Perhaps a constrictor or a python? Where did you find this?'

'In the bath, in the rooms occupied by the Trent-L'Espoirs.'

'So, it could be a clue to whatever hoax the spiritualists had plotted. Might they have smuggled a snake into the house, kept it in the bath?'

She recalled the copious amount of luggage the Trent-L'Espoirs had brought with them – over-generous for a visit intended to last a weekend. 'It's possible,' she admitted.

'May I take this?' He refolded the scale in the handkerchief. 'I'll be able to make it out more distinctly under a microscope. If I can't identify it myself, I'll ask Bertie Alcott. You remember him?'

'I do,' Evie said dubiously. 'He never has much to say for himself.' Bertie was a friend of Pelham's from their student days, an earnest young man who never encountered Pelham's sisters without becoming painfully tongue-tied.

Pelham grinned. 'It's true, he's not at his best when he's confronted by women, but he's a solid scientist. He's working for the Zoological Society. He'll be able to identify the animal this comes from.' He took out his pocket watch. 'I have to go, I'm sorry. I've evening appointments.' He shrugged on his jacket. 'Don't worry, Evie. We'll get to the bottom of your mystery. And we won't need to resort to occult theory to do it.'

He hurried off down the stairs. Evie wasted no time on fuming at his dismissal of her theories. Instead, she went to her father's study, lit the lamp and resumed her search for clues. She turned over stacks of papers, burrowed into pigeonholes, investigated the contents of tin strongboxes stacked one upon another.

Eventually she paused, rubbing her aching back, pushing back her tumbled hair. If there was any information about the kuro-skato in this room, it must be well hidden. It didn't help that she had no idea what she was looking for. Would she have to go through the pages of each individual book? Looking around at the sea of books, overflowing their shelves, her heart sank.

A rumbling in her stomach reminded her that the dinner hour was approaching. Emerging from the study, she met her mother in the hall.

'There's a letter for you,' said Leonie, indicating the half-moon table on which the evening post had been deposited. Evie picked up the letter, registering the unfamiliarity of the handwriting, executed in deep blue ink, that gave her name and address.

'A man's hand, *n'est-ce pas?*' Leonie squinted at the envelope with half-closed eyes.

'How can you tell?'

'These manly strokes – so firm, so decisive,' her mother said. 'So, *ma petite,* who is this man taking an interest in you? Is he suitable?'

Evie couldn't help but laugh. 'You should be a detective, Maman.'

'*Bah, non!*' Leonie's lip curled in distaste. 'A detective? Like those policemen who trampled mud over our carpets, asked stupid, inquisitive questions and entirely failed to find the intruder who tried to murder us in our beds? Such unsuitable work for a woman.' She lingered on in the hall, making some wholly unnecessary adjustments to a vase of dried flowers, evidently hoping to hear the contents of the letter.

Ignoring her mother's expectant air, Evie murmured something about dressing for dinner and bore the letter up to her room. Once alone, she tore open the envelope and read.

Dear Miss Winstanley,
Forgive me for taking the liberty of writing to you. Phyllis Crosbie furnished me with your address. Of course, you are under no obligation

to confide in me, yet I formed the impression that some hidden difficulty troubles you, and I want to assure you of my desire to be of help to you.

I am in Oxford, where I'm carrying out research into the activities of the Sons of Dionysus. I had intended simply to obtain material for an article, but I've discovered certain disturbing allegations relating to this secret society which I'd like to share with you. I hope to have more definite news soon.

If you should have need of me, please don't hesitate to write to my lodgings in Oxford.

Yours, most sincerely,

Marcus Ellingham

PS Just now I dined at a restaurant on the High, where I spotted Lord Maltraver having dinner with, of all people, Aubrey Penhallow. Thankfully, they didn't notice me. How strange that Penhallow should be here in Oxford! I suspect the fellow of being keen to ingratiate himself with the English aristocracy. Still, he should know better than to consort with Maltraver and his set.

Evie's hand curled around the letter, gripping it tight against her chest. The Sons of Dionysus. Lord Maltraver and Aubrey Penhallow. Were these things connected, and did any of them relate to her own investigations?

She felt mildly relieved that Ellingham hadn't taken offence at the abrupt way she'd left him at Maltraver Towers, yet she bitterly envied him his freedom of movement. He could travel wherever he would, in pursuit of a lead, of adventure. If there were clues in Oxford, they'd be his to uncover.

Whereas she . . . she was trapped in her respectable suburban life, slowly stifling. Just because she'd had the bad luck to be born a woman.

~

Evie woke the next morning to find the house in uproar.

Leonie had received a telegram from her mother, warning that her father, Grand-père, was seriously ill. Her parents lived in a crumbling chateau, which they couldn't afford to maintain or staff, and where the old man nurtured dreams of the golden summer of the nobility, before the Revolution came. Grand-mère was too frail herself to do much nursing, and their one servant was as ancient as Grand-mère.

'There's no alternative,' Leonie declared. 'I'll nurse him myself. Grand-mère says he may not last the week. She's sent for the curé.'

'Grand-mère does sometimes exaggerate,' said Evie, trying to strike an optimistic note.

'That's true,' reflected Leonie. 'The last time she invited the curé into the house, Grand-père recovered enough to throw him out and bade him never return. But no,' she continued, clutching the telegram. 'He's too weak to complain this time. It must be bad.'

Within an hour, Leonie was off in a cab to Victoria station to catch the boat-train, with hugs for her girls, interspersed with stern admonitions for them to mind what Harriet said.

A little later, Evie intercepted Harriet coming from the kitchen. 'I want to ask you something,' she said to her cousin. 'About Papa, before he died.'

Harriet eyed Evie uneasily. 'What more do you want to know?'

'Not about his death,' Evie said hastily. 'I wondered what he was doing during the last weeks of his life. How did he seem? Was he preoccupied?'

Harriet unbent a little. 'Your mother would know better than me.'

'It's *you* I want to ask. My parents shared many things, but not his work. It would distress Maman to speak of it.'

'I see,' said Harriet, considering. 'Still, I'm not sure how much I can help you. He didn't confide in me either. After he came back from Oxford, he shut himself away in his study. Undoubtedly something was preying on his mind, but I've no idea what.'

'He went to Oxford?' Evie asked, surprised. 'I didn't know.'

'He spent several days there, returned about a week before he died. He'd been to visit an old friend, Professor Lorimer.'

Her father had spoken occasionally of Fergus Lorimer, a friend from his time at Oxford, a brilliant student who'd stayed on to become a don. Evie had seen Lorimer at her father's funeral, sitting alone on a pew at the back of the church. After the burial, he'd approached to say words of formal condolence to Leonie and her daughters.

She fell silent, her mind deep in fresh speculation. So Papa had been in Oxford just before he'd carried out the ritual that had led to his death. Another reference to Oxford, coming in so short a time. Not a coincidence, surely.

'Evie,' said Harriet softly, 'it doesn't help to brood on the past.'

'I'm sure you're right.' Evie flashed her a bright smile, hoping it looked convincing.

Had Lorimer shared her father's interest in the supernatural? If so, Papa might have confided in him. Evie debated writing to Marcus Ellingham, to ask him to see Lorimer on her behalf, but if she enlisted Marcus's help then she'd have to explain everything to him. He might well disbelieve her – as a journalist for the *Ghost Hunter*, he took a sceptical line about the supernatural. Even if she could convince him and he saw Lorimer, it would then become his investigation, no longer hers. No, by hook or by crook, she would get to Oxford. If there were anything to find, she would discover it for herself.

~

'This scheme of yours,' said Pelham, 'to go hunting clues in Oxford. I doubt it will produce anything. And it could be dangerous.'

'It can't be both,' Evie snapped. They'd taken D'Artagnan for a walk by the Thames so that no one in the house would hear them arguing.

'Wait till Leonie comes back,' Pelham pleaded, 'and ask her.'

They went down the steps to the riverbed, exposed by the low tide. Evie bent to let D'Artagnan off his leash and watched him race merrily to the river, yapping at the water's edge as though challenging it to fight him. 'You know perfectly well Maman would never agree to my going alone.'

'I'm coming to the belief that it's my duty to tell her.'

At Pelham's words she turned to him, eyes blazing. 'You can't. You wouldn't. We've always been brothers-in-arms against the world.'

He poked at the rounded stones lining the riverbed with the toe of his shoe. 'Don't get on your high horse, Evie. It's not a matter of ideals, or even justice, but reality as we must live it. You can't go to Oxford alone. A young woman of your class and background, unchaperoned in a strange city, conducting an investigation or whatever it is you'd be doing – it won't do. This isn't just about social conventions.' He hesitated, rubbing at the side of his nose. 'It's also about the possible risks – for you. If I could go with you, I would, but I've several very sick patients whom I must attend to.'

'Of course,' she said, her chin raised. 'You must look after your patients. But I'm not one of them.'

'If you ignore my advice, I can't shoulder responsibility for your safety.'

'I am not asking you to,' she retorted.

'Then at least take Harriet with you.'

'I can't do that. She must stay here to take care of Grace.'

A hail of barking broke out. Evie ran after D'Artagnan, who was having an eyeball-to-eyeball encounter with a bulldog of uncertain temperament.

Pelham caught up with her. 'Grace won't be left alone. Mary will watch her in the day. I will join them in the evening and stay overnight. It's this way, or I tell Leonie the truth.'

'That's a low blow, Pel.' She squared up to him, arms folded. 'I confided in you, I trusted you, and now you're using my confidences to issue threats and ultimatums.'

'You're so stubborn, Evie!' Sparks of anger flew from him, shattering his usual self-possession. 'Can't you see I'm doing this to protect you?'

She began shaping a scathing reply, but at that instant a fight broke out between the two dogs. The next few minutes were spent trying to part the miscreants. Brother and sister united in telling the bulldog's owner, a man as belligerent as his pet, that his dog's manners needed attending to.

At length they got D'Artagnan back on his leash and began to retrace their steps towards the towpath. For a while neither spoke, and Evie chewed mulishly at her lower lip, but eventually she calmed down enough to realise she had no choice. Evidently Pelham was going to stick to what he saw as his duty. She consoled herself with the thought that once she got to Oxford, she would be free to outmanoeuvre Harriet and act as she wished.

'Very well,' she said through gritted teeth. 'I will ask Harriet. But what should I tell her? She wouldn't understand my mission, or sympathise.'

'You may be underestimating her,' he said, his voice lightening with relief. 'Harriet's no fool. But spin her any tale you like, so long as you have her company. Stay in a good hotel, a respectable place. Share a room so you're not alone. I'll supply the funds.'

His offer, made despite his reservations, touched her.

'That's good of you, Pel,' she said, 'but it's my investigation and I should bear the cost. I'll use part of my inheritance. It seems appropriate somehow.' Already, her nimble mind was running ahead to how she could keep the truth from Harriet. 'I could tell Harriet I mean to carry out research at the Bodleian.'

'The summer term started a few days ago,' Pelham observed. 'Maltraver will have gone back up to Oxford. You may run into him. Be careful.'

'I'm not afraid of him.' She drew herself up haughtily. 'He has no power over me.'

'There's something else,' he said. 'The student society you spoke of – the Sons of Dionysus. I asked Bertie Alcott about it. His younger brother, Toby, is up at Oxford, and according to him they're a loutish group of rich men's sons who think they can lord it over others and spend their time drinking, causing havoc and ... engaging in corruption.'

'Preying on women, you mean?'

'Yes.' His face was troubled.

'You needn't worry for me. I'm not Grace.'

'All the same.' He gave an anxious gulp, sending his Adam's apple bobbing. 'Please be careful, Evie. If anything happens — anything at all – send me a wire and I will come.'

'Of course I will,' she said to reassure him, though she'd already made up her mind not to contact him except in circumstances of direst need. 'What is it you fear? Is it just the bad behaviour of Maltraver and his cronies?'

'Isn't that enough? Maltraver won't have forgotten that you humiliated him. Don't underestimate him.'

'I don't,' she said, remembering the malevolence in Maltraver's eyes.

They were outside the house now, its white stuccoed front gleamed pale against the gathering dusk, the orange lamplight in the bay window cast an inviting glow. D'Artagnan pushed at the wrought-iron front gate with his nose, eager for his dinner and fireside.

'You didn't say what Bertie made of the scale,' she said.

'He . . . can't identify it,' he said slowly. 'It's from an unknown species.'

Each silent and preoccupied with their own thoughts, they entered the house.

CHAPTER
Sixteen

EVIE CONCOCTED AN elaborate story to justify her visit to Oxford, centred on Charlotte Babbington-Styles, an early Victorian amateur archaeologist who had taken part in excavations throughout North Africa and the Middle East. Evie told Harriet she wanted to examine Babbington-Styles's personal papers, including a diary of her excavations, held at the Bodleian Library.

Harriet knew about Evie's interest in Babbington-Styles and accepted the story unquestioningly. She was excited at the prospect of seeing Oxford. 'I'll write to my friend Ethel Maddeley for advice on places we might visit and how to navigate the libraries.'

Ethel Maddeley had once worked alongside Harriet for a firm of solicitors in Holborn. 'Didn't Miss Maddeley come into an inheritance?' Evie asked.

'Her aunt died, leaving her a house in North Oxford, and money besides. She's several times asked me to visit, but I haven't heard from her since we exchanged cards at Christmas. She was such great company when we worked together – interested in everything, always up for visits to the latest exhibitions.' Harriet looked rather wistful.

'Then our visit will give you an opportunity to renew the friendship.'

'I don't want to impose myself,' said Harriet. 'Now she's come into money, she probably moves in different circles to those we once shared.'

'If that's her attitude, then she's no true friend,' said Evie robustly. 'But probably she's simply scatterbrained and doesn't remember to write letters. I rarely remember to write them myself.'

'Not unless her character's entirely changed,' said Harriet doubtfully. 'She was always very punctilious about answering letters.'

~

The following day, Evie and Harriet arrived in Oxford by train and took a room at the newly opened Eastgate Hotel on the High Street. The hotel was constructed in the style of the seventeenth-century coaching inn that had formerly stood there, and so appeared in keeping with the general Oxford air of venerable age.

They left their bags unpacked and stepped out to view the city. Neither of them had visited Oxford before, and they were struck by how much the centre retained of its past, its buildings appearing like living ghosts, carved out of honeyed stone. Emerging onto Broad Street, they exclaimed at views of the Bodleian, the Sheldonian and the frontages of several ancient colleges. Through half-open gateways, they caught glimpses of velvet lawns, arched windows and fantastical gargoyles.

They visited Blackwell's bookshop, where Evie decided they should equip themselves with a Baedeker guidebook, and insisted she'd pay for it – a small gesture to assuage her guilt at having brought Harriet to Oxford under false pretences. Although she also judged that a busy Harriet, visiting the sights with Baedeker in hand, would leave Evie freer to pursue her own purposes.

As they queued at the counter, a voice said, 'Good afternoon, Miss Winstanley.'

Evie spun round. Aubrey Penhallow smiled, holding out his hand. She'd forgotten how tall he was. Taken aback, she shook hands with him awkwardly. 'What are you doing here, Mr Penhallow?'

'Much like yourself, I expect.' He nodded at the Baedeker she held. 'I've long wished to visit a place so full of history.'

'I thought perhaps you were here to see your good friend Lord Maltraver.' She watched for his reaction.

His eyes darkened. 'Why do you say that?' he said softly. 'Isn't he your friend, too, and your sister's?'

She felt he'd turned the tables and she herself was now under scrutiny. Uncertain about the possible meaning behind his words, she made no reply.

'You're interested in history, Mr . . .?' Harriet ventured, filling the awkward silence.

Belatedly remembering her manners, Evie introduced them.

'And poetry?' Harriet pursued. 'Shelley was here at Oxford, albeit briefly. He left under something of a cloud. We hope to walk in his footsteps.'

'*We* do?' echoed Evie.

Disregarding Evie, Harriet declaimed:
'Rise like lions after slumber
In unvanquishable number!
Shake your chains to earth like dew
Which in sleep had fallen on you—'

As Penhallow watched enthusiasm flower in Harriet's face, a smile touched his lips.

'Ye are many – they are few!' he finished.

'You know it,' said Harriet with evident surprise.

'*The Masque of Anarchy*? Of course, Miss Maddox.'

'It's a favourite of mine.' Harriet clasped her hands, pleased to have found a fellow literature lover.

Evie moved away to pay for the Baedeker, uneasily conscious that Penhallow and Harriet behind her had embarked on an animated discussion of the relative merits of Shelley and Wordsworth.

'How's your sister, Miss Winstanley?' said Penhallow as Evie returned. 'Fully recovered, I hope. Her illness came on so suddenly. I heard she caught a chill after her accident in the lake.'

'She's very well,' said Evie. 'Now.'

They stepped out onto the street, bustling with people, bicycles and ancient buildings – a contrast of old and new.

'Perhaps the air in the North didn't agree with her? Or the damp atmosphere? Or the company in which she found herself?'

'Perhaps.' Casting around for a way to escape the scrutiny of his green eyes, Evie became suddenly intrigued by a line of carved bearded heads visible over his shoulder.

Harriet looked from one to the other with a puzzled frown.

'You must have many places to visit, Mr Penhallow,' said Evie, now thoroughly preoccupied by the silent heads mounted on pillars, wearing expressions of classical gloom. She delved into the Baedeker, searching for an entry about them. 'Don't let us detain you.'

Taking the hint, he nodded. 'Of course. Good morning, ladies.' Doffing his hat, he left them.

'You don't like him, do you?' observed Harriet.

'Was I rude?'

'N-no,' said Harriet, 'but you weren't exactly warm.'

'Why should I be? Don't tell me *you* of all people are taken in by the superficial charms of Aubrey Penhallow? I thought you'd have better judgement.'

'Why shouldn't I like him? Do you know something against him?'

Evie deliberated how much to say. 'Only that he's rich and arrogant. As a socialist, you would consider him an exploiter of working people.'

'I'm not going to hold one young man responsible for all the evils of capitalism,' said Harriet drily. 'Perhaps Mr Penhallow isn't typical of his class. At least he appreciates *The Masque of Anarchy*. That should count for something.'

'Wasn't Shelley a seducer of women?' said Evie. All at once she shivered, recalling a dark corridor where Aubrey Penhallow, leaning so close to Janet that they almost touched, whispered into her red-gold hair.

'Shelley did treat both his wives shamefully,' Harriet admitted. 'But I believe you're thinking of Byron, dear. A much more disreputable character. Though now you come to mention it, Mr Penhallow does have rather a Byronic look.'

'It's not like you to judge by appearances.'

'You're right. The charms of young men are lost on me. It was merely an observation. It's such a coincidence that you encounter him in Oxford, so soon after meeting him in Yorkshire.'

'I don't believe it is a coincidence,' growled Evie under her breath. 'I don't think for one moment that he's here as a tourist.'

'Why else would he be here?' asked Harriet, who had caught the murmured words.

'I don't know . . . yet.'

~

Having missed lunch, they took an early tea at the hotel, after which Harriet declared her intention of making an impromptu visit on Ethel Maddeley. She looked anxious, uncertain of her reception as she put on her gloves. 'She still hasn't replied to me. Perhaps my letters went astray, or she's been unwell.'

'She'll welcome you, I'm sure of it,' said Evie encouragingly. 'And then you'll have a friend to accompany you in your sightseeing.'

Evie told Harriet she meant to rest before dinner, but as soon as Harriet had gone, Evie put on her favourite hat – a small, jaunty creation in brown velvet – and set out to explore the network of streets where most of the colleges stood, shut away behind their medieval walls and wooden doorways. She hoped she might spot Professor Lorimer, and scanned each bearded don that she passed, but spotted no one resembling him. In a short time, she found herself back on the High Street, surprised to realise how small an area the historic centre occupied. She loitered on some shallow steps, nose apparently buried in her notebook, discreetly observing passers-by.

The street thrummed with life: visitors like herself in smart town clothes and hurrying tradespeople in plain working garments, interspersed with the black gowns of students and dons. The latter were a breed apart from the townspeople: almost all were men, some sauntering in groups while others hurried along singly wearing a forbidding look that said, 'I'm on important academic business,' as they brushed past dawdling tourists. The gowns of the dons were longer and more elaborate than those of the students, some trimmed with fur or braiding. Many wore square black mortarboards that made them appear taller and more imposing. Taken en masse, they resembled a flock of flapping crows.

A flock? Evie fumbled through her memory and produced the phrase triumphantly. A murder of crows – that was it.

A young woman came hurrying along the pavement opposite, shoulders hunched, hands thrust in the pockets of her worn rust-pink coat. Most women wore hats in the street, but this one was bareheaded, her hair a golden-red blaze that clashed defiantly with the pink coat. At this distance, Evie couldn't make out her face, yet that eye-catching shade of hair seemed familiar. As the woman drew level, Evie caught her breath.

What on earth was Janet doing here, over a hundred miles from North Yorkshire?

'Janet!' she cried.

Startled, Janet looked round. Evie saw her eyes flash in recognition, then the maid was sprinting through the crowds, lifting her skirt to run faster.

Evie gave chase, racing across the road, eliciting a chorus of bells as a wave of students on bicycles swerved to avoid her. She ran in front of two horses pulling a milk cart, ducking as they reared and neighed in alarm. Abuse and yells followed Evie's progress as she reached the further pavement and spotted Janet pushing her way through protesting passers-by and veering off to the left.

Coming up seconds later, Evie followed Janet down a cobbled lane that led deep among the fastnesses of hidden colleges. Doors led from it – all shut – but no open roads. It turned several corners, and at each Evie strained to spot the red hair, but the path was empty. Had Janet gone through one of the closed doors?

Panting with exertion, clutching her hat and holding up her skirt, Evie sped round a further bend just in time to glimpse a pink coat surmounted by red hair disappear into the shadows under an enclosed stone bridge. Beyond the bridge, the lane divided and Evie hesitated. Which way?

The lane was bounded by tall stone walls. The path to the right ended in a medieval gateway to a college – firmly shut – so Evie turned left, her feet pounding over the hard cobbles, until she turned another corner – and there was Janet, doubled over, gasping for breath. When Janet glanced back to see if Evie was still in pursuit, the whites of her eyes showed like those of a hunted animal.

'Janet!' Evie's voice bounced off the high walls. She slowed down, trying not to alarm her quarry. 'Please, I don't mean you any harm. I only want to talk to you.'

Janet shook her head and ran on, vanishing round a corner. Coming up to the turning moments later, Evie emerged into a wide lane. Ahead, another enclosed bridge, this one set with windows, spanned the street. No sign of Janet. Evie ran to the head of the lane where the vista opened out into several alternatives, leading left, right and ahead. The space was crowded with people, but no one with a pink coat or red hair.

Frustrated at her failure, Evie retraced her steps. She tried a door set deep into a stone wall – locked. Just beyond the bridge she stopped, noticing for the first time a dark passageway, cramped between tall houses and so narrow she could touch both sides simultaneously. A discouraging smell of overcooked cabbage, grease and bad drains came from it – an unappealing place. She dived in, creeping cautiously along the passageway, calling out, 'Are you there, Janet?'

The passage took a right angle, past ramshackle tenements, and ended in a small courtyard before a public house. Evie hesitated, then pushed open the heavy door and stepped inside. The pub was an ancient building of low ceilings and dark alcoves, muggy with the reek of stale beer and tobacco. Several men leant against the bar in their working clothes, gawping at Evie's irruption into their world. Evie ignored them, stalking through a series of poorly lit interconnected rooms. As she peered through a smoke-filled fug, the landlord loomed up before her.

'Bain't no ladies allowed in here,' he pronounced, arms folded. 'If ye *be* a lady . . .' He smiled dubiously, revealing a missing tooth.

'Did a woman . . . another lady . . . come in here just a moment ago?' Evie said, trying to see round him. 'I need to speak with her. I've no wish to drink here, believe me.'

'No woman's come in here. This is a respectable house. You'd best be on your way.'

Afraid he might manhandle her, Evie capitulated. 'All right, I'm going.' She began to beat a retreat.

Somewhere overhead, a door opened and a burst of raucous laughter rang out. Evie froze at the sound, moved by a sudden conviction. She glanced furtively behind her – the landlord was paying her no further attention, deep in argument with a customer who objected to the quantity of froth on the head of his beer, and didn't see her as she began to climb the steep stairway, set into the ancient walls. At the top, she reached a dim, windowless landing where a door stood ajar. From behind it issued the buzz of strident talk and laughter, not the gravelly voices of working men but the refined tones of educated young men.

Evie peered through the crack in the door. She could make out a part of the room. The atmosphere was fuggy with smoke from cigars and cigarettes, heady with the fumes of beer, wine and brandy. A riot of young men sprawled over chairs and benches, perched on tables, most of them wearing mulberry tailcoats with engraved brass buttons, elaborate white cravats and salmon-pink velvet waistcoats. Several young women moved amongst them, all flimsily clad, their hair loose and streaming down their backs, pouring drinks, trading kisses and submitting to groping embraces. Evie saw no sign of Janet. A group of youths dressed in plain black gathered around a man who vigorously orchestrated proceedings. His back, kitted out in mulberry, was towards Evie, but she recognised the curling hair, the booming voice, the braying laugh.

Viscount Maltraver.

'What is the law, postulants?' he demanded, raising his glass.

'*Omnia possibilia sunt mihi*,' chorused the youths.

'All things are possible to me.' Maltraver smacked his ripe lips with relish. 'It is the only law. Drink up.'

Evie guessed from the youths' livid faces and general

unsteadiness that they'd already drunk a great deal, but obedient to Maltraver's order they tilted their pint glasses, attempting to down their drinks in one. Several gagged and retched, dribbling streams of beer. Others kept glugging amidst a chorus of encouragement, catcalls and yells from mulberry-coated students, thumping their own glasses on the tables. The youths hurled their emptied glasses against the wall, smashing them into fragments, joining the heap of shattered glass already there.

Maltraver gave the signal for another round to begin. Form was discussed among the mulberry coats and bets were laid. This time, more youths struggled to finish, skin blotchy, dripping sweat. One boy bent over, coughing and choking. Maltraver slapped him on the back, sending him staggering to his knees, brownish liquid spurting from his mouth and nostrils. Jeering laughter rang out. The boy collapsed, striking his head against the floor, and lay motionless in his own vomit. Maltraver straddled him, ripped off the boy's cravat and used it to force open his mouth. Yanking back his head by the hair, Maltraver poured the contents of a brandy bottle down his open throat, spilling more over his face and hair.

'You . . . will . . . take . . . your . . . drink!'

As Evie tensed, debating whether to intervene, the boy jerked, thrashed, violently expelled the liquid and lay gasping. Maltraver jumped out of the way with an oath of disgust and kicked the boy's abdomen, eliciting a groan.

'Get this human debris out of my way.'

Two youngsters hurried to scoop up the prone body, dragging him to a far corner.

Maltraver turned to the other youths. 'Learning to hold your liquor is the very least of the things that will be required if you want to show yourselves worthy of admission. Believe me, this is only the beginning. We want no mewling infants here. If you don't want what's coming, get out now!'

No one moved.

Maltraver snapped his fingers at a grey-faced youth, whose spindly knees wobbled alarmingly. 'Fresh glasses. Jump to it, gentlemen. Keep drinking.'

Evie noticed a shortish stocky student, leaning against the wall
not far from her hiding place behind the door. He too wore a
mulberry tailcoat but spoke to no one, giving his entire attention
to his own glass. Maltraver spotted him and waved cheerily. The
stocky student shrank back as Maltraver strolled towards him. At
Maltraver's approach, Evie drew back from the door to avoid
being seen. She could no longer see what was happening, but
Maltraver's strident voice carried to her ears.

'Evening, Zouch,' said Maltraver. 'Good to see you back among
us.'

The student said something in a low voice that Evie couldn't
catch.

'What a pity DD can't be here tonight. He has other business
– pressing business. Why the long face? Still missing Teddy
Windle? A great loss to our company. Still, no doubt one of the
new postulants will be happy to oblige you as part of the price of
admission. So young, so fresh.'

The student mumbled something in reply, set down his glass
and made for the door, followed by Maltraver's guffaw. 'Going so
soon, Zouch? Before we've found you a replacement for darling
Teddy?'

Evie had no time to get out of the way. The student barged past
her, tottering off along the corridor and down the steep stairway.

As Evie stood looking after him, she felt a thump between her
shoulder blades and spun round. A very tall, lanky youth sporting a
mulberry tailcoat and a wilted carnation in his buttonhole, teetered
over her, with one hand propping himself against the door. A strag-
gly moustache spanned his upper lip, his straight black hair was
sleeked down with pomade and his face and neck were liberally
daubed with adolescent spots. He gave off an aroma of strong spirits
and sweat, not altogether masked by a particularly pungent cologne.

He cast his bleary, clouded gaze over Evie's figure. 'Well, hallo,
sweetheart. Are you the evening's entertainment? Come and join
us.' He snatched at her with big unwieldy hands, but Evie shoved
him, hard, propelling him backwards on his unsteady feet. He
collided with the wall and grunted.

She pushed past him, and fled down the stairs, hoping he was in no fit state to run after. His voice followed her. 'Don't be shy, little minx. Come and join us. We've hardly begun yet.'

As she reached the bottom of the stairs, the landlord appeared: 'Hoy! You go ply your trade someplace else, my girl.'

Evie dodged round his bulk and was out of the door in moments, ribald comments pursuing her.

She kept running till she reached the main street, attracting disapproving glances. At last, she slowed, trying to get her breath back, outraged and disgusted at the scenes she'd just witnessed. Her close encounter with the tall youth had shocked her – and, yes, scared her too; in all her young life no one had ever spoken to her like that. A lesson learnt, she reflected shakily. Pel was right: she must be more cautious.

Walking more decorously now, she made her way back to the Eastgate. Harriet wasn't yet there; doubtless she was reminiscing with Ethel Maddeley. Looking at her wristwatch, Evie realised it was getting late. She'd have to dress for dinner. She started the business of pinning up her hair, her mind busy with new channels of thought – all of which made her uneasy.

Less than a fortnight ago, Janet had been in the North Riding. What was she doing in Oxford? Accompanying Lady Maltraver on a visit to see her son, perhaps? Yet in that case, there would be no reason for Janet to avoid Evie. Or had she – a disturbing thought – left her employment to join *Lord Maltraver*? Might Maltraver have enticed Janet away, offering to set her up as his mistress? Was she with Maltraver now? There'd been no sign of her in the debaucherous upstairs room.

The implications troubled Evie. Maltraver had been ready to seduce Grace, a girl with some social status, and a family to give her protection. A man like him would have no scruples about ruining a servant girl. She would vanish from the knowledge of her family and friends, just as Sukey Huxley had vanished.

Sukey Huxley. Evie snatched the name out of the air. Is *that* what had happened to Sukey? Had Lord Maltraver happened to her? Janet and Sukey had been friends. Might they both be here, in Oxford, in hiding together? There was a further possibility, that she might be with another man in Oxford whom Janet knew – Aubrey Penhallow. But Evie found it hard to think of Penhallow and Janet together. Her mind skirted away and went back to brooding on Maltraver.

Harriet arrived, breaking in on Evie's thoughts. 'I'm so sorry,' she said breathlessly. 'I got completely lost. All those streets in North Oxford, with their red-brick villas, look alike.' She sat to take off her outdoor shoes, hurried to the closet and laid out her gown with its accessories.

'How was your reunion with Ethel Maddeley?' asked Evie, as she struggled to drag a comb through the abundance of her hair.

'She wasn't there.'

'She'd gone out?'

'No,' said Harriet, a shadow crossing her face. 'The house was boarded up.'

'How very strange. Are you sure you had the right address?'

'Oh, yes. I knocked at a neighbour's door. The lady there told me Ethel departed suddenly, early in the new year. No one seems to know where she went.'

'I'm sorry, Harriet.'

As Evie turned back to the mirror, the room behind her fell away into shadow. The glass went dark.

She froze.

As if a veil had been whisked away, a double circle appeared in the mirror, shining like a moon seen underwater. The kuroskato. It almost touched the edges of the glass. Then, within the concentric circles, a living entity emerged, twitching and stirring, as if striving to escape its glass prison. The kuroskato began to revolve slowly, like a silver wheel. Mesmerised, Evie watched, unable to tear her eyes from it. Gradually, the double circle shrank as though retreating into a tunnel, and Evie felt herself drawn after it, sucked along in its wake. Somewhere in the tunnel ahead of her, a woman's voice cried out in terror and Evie glimpsed a figure following the kuroskato into unseen unguessable depths.

'Evie?'

The image fragmented.

'Are you feeling altogether the thing, Evie dear?' said Harriet.

Evie's heaving breaths filled the room. The mirror showed her own face, pale and drained, and Harriet's thin features frowning over her shoulder. Their eyes met in the glass, Harriet's showing blank incomprehension and a glint of anxiety.

'You don't see anything,' Evie whispered, 'in the mirror?'

Harriet shook her head.

Evie pulled herself together and made a business of putting in her amber earrings, avoiding Harriet's probing gaze. 'I think I almost fell asleep for a moment. How silly of me. It's been a long day.'

'We need an early night,' said Harriet. 'Are you sure you're well enough to come down for dinner? I could have something sent up.'

'Not at all,' said Evie, forcing her features into a smile. She saw that Harriet was already in her evening gown, a modest affair in green velvet with purple bands around the hem of the skirt. 'You look very fine, Harriet. We mustn't waste so smart an outfit.'

'You're always kind,' said Harriet with a wry twist of her mouth.

As Evie hurriedly finished dressing and followed Harriet down to the dining room, she couldn't shake off a chill of foreboding. She pondered the grim logic that if Janet had indeed come to Oxford in Maltraver's company, her reputation was in tatters and she'd never be able to go home. Surely, reflected Evie, there was some way she could help Janet. But to do that, she'd first have to find her. And it didn't seem as though Janet wanted to be found.

CHAPTER
Seventeen

THE NEXT MORNING, Harriet insisted on accompanying Evie as far as the Bodleian Library, marvelling at the high crenellated walls surrounding the main courtyard and the inscriptions over the entrances to the ancient schools. Evie climbed halfway up the stairs to the first floor, where she lurked for several minutes, giving Harriet time to depart, before slipping downstairs, back across the courtyard, through a further archway and onto Broad Street, where she pushed through the door of the first college she came to and approached the porter's lodge.

'I've an appointment with Professor Lorimer,' she announced.

'Professor Lorimer's not a member of this college, miss,' said the porter.

Evie straightened her wide-brimmed hat and tried hard to simper. 'Oh dear, I was mistaken. Do you happen to know where his college is?'

'He's at Talbot College, miss,' he replied obligingly. 'It's just a step.'

She followed his directions, taking a narrow road where college entrances opened on either side. A huddle of students spilled across the pavement. Amidst a clamour of male voices, one rose above the others, and Evie recognised its patrician tones before she spotted the owner, clad in a black gown edged with distinctive gold braiding, a gold tassel dangling from his mortar board. As though he felt Evie's eyes burning into his back, Lord Maltraver turned around, starting visibly at the sight of her. Collecting himself, he murmured something into the ear of a fair-haired youth, who inspected Evie, then replied. Both youths sniggered.

Maltraver made a formal bow towards her, an ironic smile curving his full lips. Evie stood her ground, refusing to acknowledge him, radiating disdain in every line of her body, then abruptly turned on her heel, pushing her way through the throng of students to the entry lodge.

Here, though, the head porter, dressed in black with a black bowler, a bristling moustache and a lugubrious manner, proved unhelpful. Upon her declaration that she had an appointment with Professor Lorimer, he checked a list and told Evie that she wasn't on it. Not to be put off, she handed him her card, accompanied by a note she'd written earlier that read:

Dear Professor Lorimer,
My father, Walter Winstanley, thought highly of you as his friend and a fellow expert on the occult, the subject to which he devoted much of his life. In the weeks before his death, my father was researching into some mystery. I believe he came to see you and may have confided in you. Would you afford me a few minutes of your time?
  Yours sincerely,
  Evelyn Winstanley.

The porter dispatched one of his minions with Evie's card and the note. The man crossed the quad, disappearing into the depths of Talbot College. In a few minutes, he returned alone and spoke to the porter.

'He can't see you, miss,' the porter relayed. 'The Professor's a busy man. He doesn't see many visitors.'

The two men turned their backs on Evie, expecting her to retreat.

Instead, she took another visiting card from her bag, wrote on the back in pencil: *It concerns the kuroskato – the circle of shadows. E. W.*

'Give that to him, if you please,' she said, holding it out to the young man. His questioning eyes went to the porter, who frowned, then nodded. The man went off again, and Evie noted the entranceway he disappeared into – in the far corner of the right-hand side of the grassy quad. This time he returned even more quickly.

'I'm sorry, miss,' he said, speaking this time directly to Evie. 'He says he can't see you.'

'I can wait.'

'He says we're to request you leave the premises, miss,' said the young man. He looked embarrassed; behind him the porter contrived to sneer without moving his lips.

Under the shade of her wide-brimmed hat, Evie felt herself redden. There being nothing else for it, she departed with as much dignity as she could muster. She feared Maltraver might still be outside, ready to jeer at her humiliation, but the crowd of students had dispersed.

She pondered her next move. In her bag was the letter from Marcus Ellingham detailing his determination to investigate the Sons of Dionysus. She took it out and read it through again, coming to the part where he offered her his assistance with her own investigations.

Do I need your help, Marcus Ellingham? Maybe I do, after all.

The address on the letterhead was for a lodging house in the streets beyond Carfax, and a few minutes' walk brought her to the door of a well-tended house, smarter than its neighbours. The landlady, dressed in a rigidly corseted style not seen since the early 1890s, made no attempt to hide her disapproval at seeing a young unaccompanied woman asking to speak with a young unmarried man. She wouldn't even confirm whether Marcus Ellingham was staying in her house, and Evie's request to leave a note was met with a rebuff, raised eyebrows and a sniff of contempt.

For the second time in the space of half an hour, Evie was forced to retire, humiliated, from an Oxford threshold. Uncertain of her next step, she returned to the Bodleian, this time climbing all the way up the stairs to the library, where she was confronted by a black-gowned attendant who informed her in an important whisper, 'No ladies are permitted unless accompanied by a fellow of the college or a letter of accreditation.' Evie had anticipated this problem, however, and produced a letter on headed paper from the Department of Egyptology at University College London (which she had previously purloined for this specific purpose), written in a passably good imitation of the writing and signature of Professor Flinders Petrie, testifying in glowing terms to the scholarship and moral character of Miss Winstanley. She was duly given admission and passed through.

She spent some time wandering through the Bodleian, familiarising herself with its sequence of reading rooms, so that she would be able to give Harriet an accurate account of having visited them. Even the sight of an unparalleled collection of books did little to soothe Evie's preoccupations. Belatedly, realising she was late to meet Harriet, she ran to the teashop where they had arranged a rendezvous for lunch. Harriet was already seated, and reported on a successful morning, describing the number of sights she had been able to tick off from her list.

'Though I had wanted, as you know,' she told Evie, 'to see the statue of Shelley at University College. I was told the college is closed to visitors.'

'Perhaps it was just as well,' said Evie, consulting the Baedeker, which she had propped open before her. 'According to this, he doesn't have so much as a stitch on.'

'Please don't be common, Evie,' said Harriet with some dignity. 'We're talking about *art*. It depicts his body after drowning.' She saw Evie smother a giggle. 'Not a subject for humour.'

'Of course, Harriet,' agreed Evie, abashed. *Drowning. Not funny, no.*

'What do you wish to do this afternoon?' said Harriet. 'Return to your studies?'

Though Harriet's tone was resolutely cheerful, Evie suspected her solitary morning of sightseeing had been a lonely business. Since she had nothing pressing to do until she'd worked out some means of getting into Talbot College, she offered to accompany Harriet on whatever expedition she had in mind.

'It would be pleasant to see something of nature,' said Harriet eagerly. 'Perhaps a walk along the Cherwell?'

The morning's sunshine had been dispersed by low-lying cloud as they went northwards through the water meadows. The air was full of the distant shouts of students on the playing fields. They passed a spot known as Parson's Pleasure, where, so the Baedeker informed them coyly, students were accustomed to bathe '*in puris naturalibus*'.

'I expect Shelley knew this spot well,' said Evie, half laughing.

Harriet tutted reprovingly and strode on ahead.

They crossed the Cherwell by a wooden bridge and found themselves in a landscape of wild grasses and flowers, twisting paths, dense undergrowth and scattered trees. They engaged in desultory conversation as they wandered, passing meadowland where sheep and cattle grazed.

'This is an excessively lovely place,' said Harriet. 'Have you ever thought you might become a student here?'

'It is beautiful,' Evie agreed, 'although some of the male students seem more interested in their sports than their books. It's extraordinary that the university is so behind the times that it won't permit women to take degrees and allows women's colleges to exist only on sufferance.'

Harriet nodded emphatic agreement. 'All the same, you could try, Evie. There must be scholarships for Oxford.'

'I'd need to be coached for the entrance examination,' Evie reflected. For a moment, she imagined walking in her father's scholarly footsteps, but she pushed the dream firmly away. 'Even if I succeeded in getting a scholarship, it would be so expensive – the boarding, the fees. How could we justify it? The University of London is more to my purpose. It's much more progressive. They welcome people without financial advantages and have been awarding women degrees for many years now.'

'You'll do well wherever you go. Marrying is well enough, but a woman should have a right to a life of her own, a career, a purpose, beyond any duties as a wife and mother – important though those are,' Harriet added punctiliously.

'What about you, Harriet? Do you think of the future?'

'Me? I think I'm a little old to take a degree.'

'You might marry, if you wished. If Maman was here, she'd find you a husband amongst these dons in the shake of a lamb's tail. I dare say you wouldn't want such a man, though. He'd be covered in chalk dust and badly dressed, obsessed with his researches and late for the dinners that you prepared. It's better to be free, after all.'

'Far better,' agreed Harriet. She seemed amused at something.

Evie regarded her curiously. 'You rarely speak so openly. Not in front of Maman.'

'Your mother sees a woman's life in more traditional terms. She has the right – and the duty – to do what she thinks best to ensure your future happiness. I wouldn't want to contradict her. That would be a poor way to repay her for her kindness to me when I could no longer find work. Once a woman grows older, she becomes more or less . . . invisible.' Harriet fell silent, her eyes on a flock of small, brown-feathered birds, chattering as they foraged through bushes newly come into leaf.

Evie was struck by the introspection in Harriet's face. 'Are you thinking of Ethel Maddeley?'

Harriet nodded. 'No one seems to know where she is, or even to care. I can't shake off a feeling that, in spite of her money, Ethel has become one of the invisible women.'

Evie thought of loss, loneliness and disappointed hopes, and realised guiltily that she knew little of what Harriet's past life had been like. Yet soon Harriet sighed and stirred herself, putting on her brisk workaday manner once more.

'The weather's changing. Foolish of me not to bring an umbrella. We'd better turn back.'

'Yes, let's,' said Evie. The clouds had indeed thickened, and drops of cold rain began to fall.

Wrapping their coats tight, they started to retrace their steps along twists and forks in the path. The rain increased. They were unsure of their direction, nor was there anyone in sight to ask their way.

Ahead, a dark line of willows traced the meandering course of the river. They directed their feet towards it and presently came to a narrow, blue-painted bridge.

'Surely this isn't the bridge we came by?' said Harriet.

'We can't have come far out of our way,' said Evie. 'If we follow the river downstream, it will lead us back.'

As they crossed the bridge, brown water churned below them, a layer of foaming scum floating across its surface. On the further side of the river, the main path passed through deserted playing fields bordered by hawthorn hedgerows. A path, no more than a dirt track, followed the riverbank leftwards. Somewhere off to their right, water tumbled noisily over a weir.

'This way, I think,' Evie said, pointing along the riverside path as the rain fell harder.

'It looks rather muddy,' said Harriet dubiously.

Evie pushed open a metal gate. They passed through and followed the river's edge, bordered by ash, alder and long-leaved willows, picking their way to avoid the worst of the mud and puddles.

All at once Evie stopped, rain pattering unnoticed on her face. The trunk of a willow tree, probably toppled in a storm, had fallen and now stretched halfway across the river, lying low above the surface of the water. Evie had noticed something in the deep shadows beneath the trunk. It seemed to be caught in the trailing branches, bobbing slightly with the movement of the swirling water. Evie went towards it.

'Where are you going?' called Harriet. 'We're getting wet here.'

'There's something in the river.' Evie was close to it now and was able to make out two long, narrow shapes gleaming in the dimness under the overhanging branches. Curiosity propelled her forward and she scrambled over the broken stump of the willow and inched along the fallen trunk, slippery with rain and moss, out across the river to mid-stream, ignoring Harriet's warning cries to be careful. She stooped there, clinging onto outspread branches, peering into the deep gloom beneath the trunk. The raindrops didn't reach under the shelter of the fallen willow where the surface was quite clear, like a mirror.

Beneath the mirrored surface, a woman lay face down in the cold embrace of the water, suspended in a tangle of ribbon weed, undulating gently in the eddying stream. Her hair fanned out across the surface, strands caught in trailing willow branches. The dark material of her dress was torn and rucked up in folds at the back, and from beneath it glistening limbs protruded, pallid arms and legs, tightly wrapped with weeds. She was barefoot, her toes two rows of small, bloated blobs.

Evie found it hard to believe what she was seeing. Even as she looked, something slithered out from under the woman's dress, wriggled between the bloated thighs and disappeared into the depths, and she gasped in uncontrollable horror. Instantly, she was back in the Sithwater, her sister drowning before her eyes as an unseen presence circled under the water. Her voice came out as a muffled whimper.

'Grace?'

CHAPTER
Eighteen

NOT GRACE, NO. How could she have even imagined it? Evie crouched on the willow trunk, averting her eyes from the horror in the water, shaking, heart racing. Shock blanked out thought, her surroundings melting away into unreality. The trees on the opposite bank seemed alive, circling, dancing. Was she going to be sick?

'Evie?' came Harriet's anxious voice. 'What's happening? What is it?'

'I'm coming.' Evie struggled to her feet, knees trembling under her. She swayed, grabbed at a branch to keep herself from falling. *No, no!* She fought to stabilise her legs, restore her balance. Only then could she stumble back along the trunk to where Harriet waited.

'There's a woman in the water. She's dead.'

Harriet's eyes widened and her lips twitched, yet her voice was steady. 'You're sure she is dead? Past saving?'

'Very sure.' Evie found it an effort to speak.

Harriet craned to see, one hand shielding her eyes from the rain. 'I can't make out anything. Could the two of us pull her out of the water, do you think?'

'No,' said Evie, shuddering at the prospect of approaching the body again.

'We must get help, and notify the authorities. One of us ought to stay here. We shouldn't leave her alone.'

Even in her dazed state, Evie was impressed at Harriet's calmness. 'Should I go?' she asked.

Harriet nodded. 'You'll be faster than me.'

'You're not afraid . . . to stay with her alone?'

'It's not the dead we have to fear. This poor woman is beyond all the suffering of this world. I'll stay here and pray for her.'

~

Evie ran along the path, reckless of mud and water, trying to outpace the horror in the river. Once she slipped and fell face down; she scrambled to her feet and kept moving. Rain blew in her face yet couldn't wash away the memory of the body floating face down in the brown water.

Ahead, the path curved, following the meandering river. Suddenly into sight strode a tall figure, head down against the wind, crowned by a flat cap to keep off the rain.

It was Aubrey Penhallow.

Evie ran full tilt towards him. 'We need help!' she cried. 'There's a body in the water!'

He stopped and looked at her in surprise, taking in her bedraggled appearance, the mud on her clothes and hands. 'If it's a body, there's not a lot I or anyone can do to help, Miss Winstanley.'

In her relief at finding another human being, she'd forgotten how supercilious he could be. Now she remembered, and the memory infuriated her. Immediately, she felt more robust.

'It's a poor woman who drowned. Harriet and I can't get her out of the water by ourselves. We can't leave her there. You must help us.'

For a moment he made no reply.

'Do you have an important appointment elsewhere, Mr Penhallow?' she asked ironically, annoyed at his apparent hesitation.

At her evident anger, his lips drew into a slight smile, and a searching look came into his eyes, almost as if he asked her an unspoken question. But all he said was, 'I'll come.'

As they turned back together, the rain slackened.

'Why are you here, Mr Penhallow?' Evie couldn't help asking.

'The same as yourself, Miss Winstanley – taking a walk.' He spoke smoothly, though moments later he added in a rather different voice, 'Sometimes I can't bear to be shut up inside the walls of a city.'

By the time they reached the place where Harriet waited, the rain had ceased.

'Mr Penhallow will help,' Evie told Harriet. She led Penhallow to the river's edge and pointed. 'She's down there, below the tree trunk.'

Aubrey Penhallow stripped off his coat, cap, jacket and shoes, scrambled along the trunk and knelt, staring down into the water. He reached out with a pocketknife to cut something free, then leapt down, chest-deep in the water, and began hacking at the ribbon weed.

Two youths appeared along the path, carrying fishing tackle. Quickly sizing up the situation, they laid down their lines to go to Penhallow's aid. Within a few minutes, the three men had hauled the body onto the bank and were laying it across the path. All three had cuts across their hands from the razor-sharp ribbon weed. Water streamed from the corpse's dark dress, soaking into the muddy clay of the path.

They turned the body over.

Evie uttered a small moan, which she stifled by stuffing her fist into her mouth. Harriet put an arm tight round her shoulders.

Black muddy water trickled from the corners of the slackened lips, clenched teeth just visible. Some river creature had burrowed into the soft parts of the bloated face. Cuts and abrasions covered the waxy flesh. She looked nothing like Millais's drowning Ophelia, nor any other Pre-Raphaelite dream of doomed beauty, yet under the daylight a hint of a red sheen was visible in the water-soaked hair.

'This is Janet,' said Evie. 'She was in service at Maltraver Towers.'

'How can that be?' exclaimed Harriet. 'Are you sure?'

Evie nodded, feeling sick.

'What was her surname?' Harriet asked. 'We must tell the police. They will trace her family and tell them the terrible news.'

'She's Janet Rae,' said Mr Penhallow, his voice rough, as though it rasped in his throat. He knelt on the other side of her body, his face pale even to the lips, his eyes darkened shadows. He looked like he'd received a terrible blow, Evie thought. Perhaps he really had cared for Janet.

Penhallow went to cover the body with his greatcoat, but Evie reached out to stop him. 'Wait a moment.'

He met her gaze with a frown, but stayed his hand.

Her attention had been caught by cuts on Janet's upper arms. Some of the lacerations had probably come from ribbon weed or sharp stones on the riverbed, but there were other marks too.

The men had pulled the black dress over her legs for decency's sake, but now Evie knelt and pulled the dress up higher, exposing marks on Janet's thighs that Evie had glimpsed when the body was underwater. There was a certain deliberation about some of the cuts, as though they'd been slashed with a knife.

'What are you doing?' said Harriet. 'Surely we should leave it to the police to examine her?'

'These cuts,' said Evie. 'Look, here—' she pointed '—and here.' She sat back on her heels. 'They look like . . .' Her eyes went to Aubrey Penhallow. Doubt filled her and she fell abruptly silent.

'Like what?' said Harriet.

'Nothing,' said Evie quietly. 'I was mistaken.'

Penhallow laid his coat over the dead woman, screening her from their sight.

Nineteen

THE LAST TRACES of rain had cleared, the sky had lightened, and a small crowd of passers-by had collected on the riverbank, seemingly with nothing else to do but speculate, appalled and fascinated, on the human form shrouded beneath Mr Penhallow's greatcoat. The remaining fisher-boy stayed with Evie and Harriet as they waited for the police to arrive and cart away Janet's body, and together they formed an impromptu cordon around the corpse, keeping spectators at bay. Evie watched him as he squatted next to the body to eat the meal he'd brought with him – his thin meagre face, wide mouth, his running nose that he kept wiping with his hand. Perhaps he'd caught a cold from his immersion in the river? He looked to be about sixteen.

'This must be a shock to you,' she said.

'Yes … and no, miss,' he said, taking a bite of his bread and dripping. 'She's the first one I've seen for meself, but there's been people drownded from time to time. Several of 'em recent.'

Were drownings in the vicinity of Oxford so commonplace? The boy was phlegmatic, already accustomed to the realities of life and death. Evie reflected that she herself needed to be more like that, less squeamish.

She looked around and realised that Aubrey Penhallow had disappeared. 'Where's Mr Penhallow?'

'He left just now,' said Harriet. 'He said something about having a pressing matter to attend to.'

'A matter more important than death?' Evie's lips twisted scornfully.

Her nostrils clogged with the ripe, queasy smell coming from beneath the dark grey coat. Large flies buzzed through the grass. One bluebottle hopped along a curl of hair, now drying to red-gold, and crawled under the coat to investigate. Evie looked away, nausea rising up into her stomach. With Penhallow out of the way, there was a task she needed to complete, but she shrank from it.

~

Back at the Eastgate, Evie had waited impatiently, expecting a summons by the police to give her statement, yet none came. Neither she nor Harriet had had an appetite for dinner, and eventually her cousin, looking drawn and pale, had admitted to having a crushing headache and went to bed, leaving Evie alone at a table in the public lounge, where an ebullient trio had played popular sentimental tunes: 'Tell Me, Pretty Maiden', 'Because', 'Violets'. A few couples had got up to dance.

The cheery inconsequential chatter and intermittent light applause that followed each piece had grated on Evie's already strained nerves. Didn't they know a young woman's life had been brutally cut short? She'd looked down to see her forefinger tracing a pattern of interlacing circles on the table.

This is no good. You have to do something.

Catching the eye of a waiter, she'd asked for directions to the police station. A few minutes later she was there, requesting to see the person in charge of Janet's case.

Now, at the Blue Boar Street police station, the two men seated in front of her were scarcely troubling to conceal their derision.

'You believe Janet Rae was the victim of black magic?' said Inspector Hammond, his heavy-lidded eyes fixed on Evie. Next to him, his junior, Sergeant Fiveash, hid a smirk behind his hand before looking grave again.

It had been rash of her to come. She was wary of giving anything away in her movements or her voice and was careful to sit upright in order to appear confident and self-possessed. Somewhere on the riverbank she'd lost her gloves, and her fingers now twisted together below the desk.

'I think it's something you should consider, Inspector. There are cuts on her body that are significant—'

'Miss Winstanley,' the inspector interrupted, making a steeple of his stubby hands and leaning towards her, 'a young lady such as yourself can have no idea of the havoc that the buffeting forces of running water can wreak on human remains.'

Evie kept her face impassive, though her fingers kneaded into her palms. It had been a mistake to come, to tell them what she knew, but she felt she owed it to Janet.

'The cuts to her upper arms and thighs weren't made by chance,' she said. 'They are occult sigils – symbols of magic power. Someone carved them into her body.'

Inspector Hammond's bushy eyebrows lifted into his hairline. Sergeant Fiveash gawped at her.

'What,' said the inspector, 'would a young lady like yourself know about these here *occult sigils?*'

Evie held his gaze. 'I've made a study of such things. These cuts must have been done before her death – by whoever murdered her.'

Inspector Hammond rolled his eyes and began sorting papers on his desk. 'There's no call to talk of killing and murdering, Miss Winstanley. Even if these cuts were made before death, Janet Rae could well have done them herself.'

'Why would she mutilate herself?'

'In my line of work,' explained the inspector, favouring Evie with a wide smile, 'we're never surprised at what women get up to when they grow hysterical. Especially when they're in the family way.'

'She was pregnant?' Evie twisted her fingers tighter, her nails digging half-moons into her palms.

'We won't know for sure till the police surgeon examines her. But she wouldn't be the first woman to choose the river as her way out.'

'You don't know that she was with child,' Evie argued, 'and you've no evidence that she chose to end her life. You're simply assuming it.'

'She was poor, unmarried, had left her home and her employment. Some man must have left her high and dry. It's very sad, of course, but it happens all the time.'

'She knew two men in this city: Lord Maltraver and Mr Aubrey Penhallow. Talk to both of them. Ask if they saw her here.'

'We don't need you to teach us our business,' growled the inspector, tapping the desk in a staccato beat. 'We've already spoken with Mr Penhallow. He came voluntarily to the police station and gave a statement about finding the body, and how he made the acquaintance of Janet Rae at Maltraver Towers.'

'He did more than make her acquaintance,' said Evie indignantly.

Sergeant Fiveash smothered a snigger in his sleeve.

The more she spoke, the more she seemed to tangle herself in knots for their entertainment. Her cheeks burnt and only pride kept her rooted in her seat, doggedly trying to establish her case.

'Girls of her sort are practised at arousing men's ... passions,' Hammond noted. 'Men can't help themselves. Not the sort of thing a young lady like yourself would know about, of course.'

She clenched her fists and half rose, ice cold with anger. 'It's the fault of the women? Is that what you're saying?'

Inspector Hammond's smile was complacent.

'And what about Lord Maltraver? He was Janet's employer, or at least his mother was. He *must* have known that Janet was here. Surely Janet came to Oxford with him—'

'Miss Winstanley,' said the inspector drily, 'sexual congress outside the bonds of matrimony is highly reprehensible, no doubt, but it's not against the law of the land. A matter for the clergy, not the police.' Looking meaningfully at his junior, he scooped up a sheaf of papers. 'Now, if you'll excuse me, it's getting late and I still have work to do.'

Sergeant Fiveash came to Evie's side. 'Can I show you out, miss?'

Evie leant forward, making one last effort. 'Will you at least conduct some enquiries into Lord Maltraver's movements?'

'Ask a peer of the realm whether he's been engaging in the

black arts and ritual murder? Not without any evidence, Miss Winstanley. In the meantime, I suggest you stop reading the penny dreadfuls and find something more wholesome to occupy your time.'

Hammond raised his hand in a gesture of dismissal. Seething, Evie had no option but to follow Sergeant Fiveash, who led her down steps and along a deserted corridor to a side door.

'Can I get you a cab, miss?' said Fiveash, twirling his moustache. 'It's late for a young lady like yourself to be out unescorted.' He smiled broadly, sending a smell of stale tobacco wafting into her face, and his eyes slid down her body. *Lingered*. She felt sickened. She'd had little experience of men staring at her so boldly, treating her with no respect, and crossed her arms protectively across her chest. She stepped backwards onto the street, careful not to turn her back on him.

'My hotel is just a few minutes' walk,' she said coldly.

As she walked along the narrow side road, she asked herself whether she'd mishandled the situation. Perhaps if she'd started with the disappearance of Sukey Huxley, explained that Janet Rae wasn't the first servant to disappear from Maltraver Towers, that this was part of a pattern, the police would have listened – or perhaps not. More likely they'd have viewed Sukey's case as that of another poor ignorant girl who'd brought her fate on herself, who'd deserved what she got. Evie shook with anger.

At the top of the road, she paused, uncertain of her way, and looked back. To her vexation, Fiveash still stood there, outlined in blue by the police lamp. Eager to escape his gaze, Evie plunged down a narrow high-walled lane. Almost at once, she realised she ought to have gone the other way, towards St Aldate's, but she didn't want to retrace her steps in case Fiveash was still there.

After taking several turnings, she passed under a streetlamp and paused. Beyond its circle of light, the night was dark, the end of the lane ahead lost in shadow.

Click-clacking footsteps echoed off the stone walls.

She looked back. A man's tall figure had passed the streetlamp and was visible as a blackened silhouette against its radiating light.

Just someone walking home.

He sped up, coming fast towards her, boot heels striking the cobbles.

Evie sprang away, her long, narrow skirt hindering her movements. Dread clenched tight in her chest. He was just yards away, his longer legs closing the distance between them quickly. Heart pounding, Evie ran, not looking back—

Another form appeared ahead, emerging from a public house. She sped towards it. 'Help!'

The second figure blocked her path and she caught the smell of spirits. She swerved, changing direction. Too late. Arms stretched out towards her.

'Evelyn? Miss Winstanley?'

'Mr Ellingham?' Astonished, she lowered her fist.

The hazy glow coming through the window of the public house illuminated the joy on his face. 'I can't believe it,' he said, chin dimpling in delight. 'You appear out of the darkness like an . . . otherworldly being.'

Evie scarcely heard. Breathing hard, she scanned the lane behind her. It was empty. A faint odour pervaded the air.

'It's so wonderful to see you.' Mr Ellingham seemed inclined to babble.

Evie cut him short. 'Are you wearing cologne?'

His face fell. Surreptitiously, he sniffed at his arms, his wrists. 'No. Should I be?'

She gathered herself together and smiled her relief. 'You're just the person I wanted to see, Mr Ellingham. I tried to leave a note at your lodgings, but your landlady was having none of it. I think she suspected me of writing you a *billet-doux*.' She'd meant it as a joke, but even in the darkness she could see that Mr Ellingham had turned scarlet and felt her own cheeks colouring in response. To cover her embarrassment, she said, 'Would you be so good as to walk me back to my hotel? I'm staying at the Eastgate.'

'Nothing would give me greater pleasure.' He held out his arm with a flourish and she put hers through it. 'The Eastgate's on the High,' he told her, oblivious to the fact that she must already know this. 'It's not far from here.' As they started to walk, he tripped, then righted himself with careful dignity.

'Have you been drinking, Mr Ellingham?'

He gave an ingenuous smile. 'Just a trifle foxed. I met with a couple of chaps from my student days. We talked of old times.' He followed her gaze. 'Why do you keep looking back?'

'I thought there was someone there. Did you see anybody?'

'Only you. Do you mean someone followed you?' He peered over her shoulder, fists clenched belligerently. 'What bally audacity!'

'Before you set off to fight any dragons, would you see me safely back to the Eastgate?'

'Why . . . yes, of course.' He turned back hastily, took her wrist as though it were made of porcelain, and tucked it under his arm again. 'I simply can't get over my surprise at seeing you. Why—?'

'I'll tell you,' she assured him, 'but not now. Meet me tomorrow.'

His arm shook slightly beneath hers. 'That would be delightful.' He fell silent, preoccupied with the careful placing of his feet.

Minutes later, back on the High Street, Evie's tension eased. Even if her knight errant was a trifle inebriated, no one was likely to accost her here, amidst the bustle of the evening crowds.

At the doorway of the Eastgate, she bade Mr Ellingham goodnight and ran up to her room. The curtains hadn't been closed, and light from the streetlamps poured into the room. Judging by the sound of regular breathing, Harriet was asleep. Not wanting to disturb her, Evie didn't switch on the electric light and crossed the room in darkness to look through the window. People crisscrossed the pavements outside, most hurrying home from work, the wealthy going out to dinner or the theatre. Several carriages passed, pulled by horses, then a motorcar, the roar of its engine rising above the buzz of the street.

Then, across the road she spotted a man standing motionless in the deep gloom of a shop frontage. His face was masked by a wide-brimmed hat and a muffler. She could make out little else, except that he was a big man, quite a bit taller than Marcus

Ellingham, and thickset. The light from a passing hansom cab picked out a gleam of eyes above the muffler: he was staring directly at her. She drew back.

A horse-drawn tram rattled on its rails down the centre of the road, bearing a gaudy blue-and-yellow advertisement extolling the benefits of a holiday in Bournemouth for those in search of rest, relaxation and a nerve cure. The tram blocked her view of the opposite pavement for a moment, and when she looked again, the figure had gone.

CHAPTER
Twenty

*C*hest-deep in the river. Something bumps her as it slowly rotates. She hears herself screaming: Grace! No! Grace! *She grasps the corpse by the collar and heaves it over. With a heavy splash, it topples onto its back. There's a stench of putrefaction. Muddy water spills from the slack mouth. Strands of grey in the sodden hair. Light eyes open on nothing.*

Not Grace, no. And not Janet.

Harriet.

Evie wrenched herself out of sleep, panting. She looked to the other bed, saw the sleeping figure there, caught the rhythm of gentle breathing. She pushed her knuckles into her mouth, stifling whimpers of relief.

∼

Early the next morning, Evie met a pasty-looking Marcus Ellingham at a tea room on Cornmarket. She'd lain awake long into the night, afraid of more dreams, flinching at sudden noises from the street, at random footsteps outside the door. No longer feeling guilty about deceiving Harriet, Evie had told her she meant to spend the day at the Bodleian. What mattered was to keep Harriet out of it, keep her safe.

Ellingham was a different proposition, young, physically active and with some knowledge of the supernatural, even though he was a sceptic. A potential ally? Violet smudges under his eyes and a pallor to his cheeks showed the effects of last night's carousing.

He'd made a concerted effort to dress himself smartly, however, and a fresh cut on his chin testified to his determination not to present himself with stubble on his face, though it also bore witness to the unsteadiness of his hands.

'Some tea, Mr Ellingham?' she asked, lifting the teapot.

He gulped, feeling at his collar, where a light sweat gathered. 'Thank you.'

'There's something I need to tell you. Many things, in fact. I hope you won't be tempted to dismiss what I say out of hand.'

He met her scrutiny with sturdy determination. 'Try me.' His eyes followed her movements as she passed him a teacup.

'The business I'm involved in,' she said, 'it's dangerous. You need to be clear about that. If you were to be drawn in, it could be dangerous for you too.'

'You are going to tell me and warn me off at the same time? I'm all ears.'

Between sips from her cup, she told him the story, from the moment the intruder broke into her father's study. The only thing she intentionally withheld from him was Grace's sudden amorous attraction towards Lord Maltraver.

When Evie had finished, she reached for a bun, sticky and loaded with currants, and bit into it, waiting for his reaction with an assumed air of assurance she was very far from feeling. The bun tasted like ashes as she chewed on it. What if he responded like her brother, with kindness but disbelief? Or worse, what if he laughed at her, as Inspector Hammond and Sergeant Fiveash had done? But Marcus Ellingham's reaction wasn't at all what she'd expected.

'You're incredible, Evelyn. You don't mind me calling you Evelyn, do you?' He swallowed hard. 'If I'm being too forward, just slap me down, don't you know?'

She dropped her bun. 'You're not going to say I'm a foolish girl, dabbling in things beyond my compass?'

His eyes widened. 'Who told you that?'

'Inspector Hammond more or less said so. It was ... dampening to my spirits.'

'The man's a fool. Yet you didn't let yourself be discouraged. That's what's so admirable about you. You let nothing put you off.'

'Grace says I'm like a terrier,' she said ruefully.

'That is *not* how I'd describe you.'

She smiled inwardly, busying herself in straightening her napkin and pouring more tea.

'Do you think the Sons of Dionysus could be involved?' he asked.

Was he too easily convinced? A doubt arose in her mind. 'Are you mocking me, Mr Ellingham?'

'Never.' He looked shocked.

'Well, my encounter with the Sons of Dionysus was rather horrible,' she admitted, 'yet they appeared to be no more than foolish, arrogant, very drunken young men. No whiff of the occult, no whiff of anything at all – except brandy.'

'The society's been in existence for centuries. Maltraver and the current batch of undergraduates merely inherited it. There's no hard evidence of current or previous undergraduates practising dark magic. And yet . . .'

'And yet?'

'I've a friend here from my student days, who edits *Jackson's Oxford Journal*. They've an office here on Cornmarket. He's been letting me go through back issues of the journal to find material for my articles, and I've looked for information about the Sons of Dionysus. There've been several disturbing allegations about them over the years. Complaints were made, some cursory investigations took place, but nothing ever stuck. No arrests, just rumours.

'I came across a case that could be significant. In 1892, a young woman went to the police with a tale of having been kidnapped by the Sons of Dionysus and forced to participate in a cabalistic rite involving arcane rituals, bloodletting and the sacrifice of a pig in an attempt to summon a demon. She claimed to have been made prisoner by the cult but escaped. The police dismissed her complaint as malicious slander against highborn young men. She went to the press.'

'Brave woman.'

'Yes, the story was published, giving her account. Then someone clamped down on it. Nothing more was said.'

'What happened to her?'

'I don't know. She dropped out of sight.'

'It could be significant.' Evie bit absent-mindedly into her bun. 'But it could equally have been play-acting on the students' part, a vicious game. Real dark magic requires deep knowledge and skill. As for poor Janet, I've no difficulty believing Maltraver would abuse a young woman, yet I struggle with the idea of him partici-pating in occult rituals. It doesn't fit somehow. He hated the whole idea of the seance at Maltraver Towers, mocked his mother for arranging it and commissioned you to expose the Trent-L'Espoirs as frauds.'

'Yes,' he acknowledged. 'It doesn't seem to fit with what we know. Nor do I understand why Janet Rae and Mr Penhallow should both be in Oxford. By what sort of bizarre coincidence—'

'Not a coincidence at all,' Evie interrupted. 'They were lovers, I'm certain of it.' Her voice sounded oddly small in her own ears, and she stopped, aware of Ellingham's eyes on her. She made herself continue in her normal tone.

'Penhallow's manner was so odd when he realised the dead woman was Janet. He showed grief, yes, but something else, too. A kind of wariness.' *Or fear?* she thought but didn't say. 'I think there was some other connection between the two of them,' she continued, frowning. 'I simply don't see what it was . . . I'm sure of one thing, though – somehow it's bound up with Maltraver. They were both here because *he* is here. There's some kind of link between Mr Penhallow and Maltraver. As for Janet – I don't know by what means Maltraver enticed her to leave her job, her home, and come with him or follow him to Oxford, but somehow he did. She vanished, just as Sukey Huxley vanished before her.'

'Sukey Huxley?'

'Oh, yes, I hadn't mentioned her. Sukey worked alongside Janet in service at Maltraver Towers, till she disappeared. I'm afraid the same fate may have befallen them both.' She paused, as nightmar-ish images loomed up suddenly in her head, realised her hands weren't quite steady and pressed her fingers into the snow-white tablecloth.

'You think,' said Marcus Ellingham, 'that Maltraver might have done this? He knew both women.'

'He might. Or he might have passed them on ... to someone else.'

Ellingham blinked in surprise. 'Who?'

'I don't know.'

She caught up her handbag, retrieved her notebook and opened it. Along with pages of notes, it included drawings of the unidentified scale from the bathtub, together with the sigil she'd found in Grace's mattress. She flicked through to the most recent drawings, made during her vigil on the riverbank, and propped the notebook open on the table.

'These drawings show the cuts on Janet Rae's body.'

The pictures – sketches of a woman's broken body, lying on her back – stood out incongruously amidst the dainty floral teacups, the willow-patterned plates, the paper doilies. Evie had drawn the face, limbs and torso with a few spare strokes, but the symbols scored into the arms and legs were delineated scrupulously in red ink.

Ellingham gaped at the images. '*You* drew these?'

'Someone had to bear witness to what was done to this poor woman.'

He nodded and gulped, looking a little green around the gills. 'You're right, I'm being ridiculous.' He made himself scan the drawings more closely. 'They don't look haphazard. There's some kind of design, a pattern. What do you think they are?'

'They're similar in design, but each has differences. There's a meaning here.'

'You recognise them?'

'I believe they're occult sigils.'

'Conduits for power?'

'That's it. It's said that an adept in the occult can use a sigil to summon a power from the realm of the invisible – though what these particular sigils might summon, I don't know. But look.' She tilted the notebook and pointed. 'If you superimpose the four sigils, one over the other, you can see they're composites. If you add the double circle, together they make this.' She turned over the page to show him her drawing of the kuroskato.

He bent closer, his chin on his hand. 'So this is the image on the paper in your father's study?'

'Yes, and on the parchment inside Grace's mattress, the thing you saw me burn.' *And now,* she thought, *it's marked into Grace.*

'What do they mean?'

'That's the thing. When I first found the kuroskato, I searched through my father's occult books, but I discovered almost nothing about it, not even in the pages of Paracelsus's *The Archidoxes of Magic*, which, as you may know, contains a learned discourse on the use of occult sigils and how they can be applied to amulets, either for apotropaic protection or to wield occult power.'

Marcus tried hard to look as though he did know, nodding sagely. Smiling a little, she pressed on.

'Reginald Scot's *The Discoverie of Witchcraft* lists seventy-two sigils for summoning spirits and demons, though I don't think these four are amongst them. I must check in a copy of Scot's book, or in Paracelsus – the Bodleian will have them. For now—' She stopped, hearing a light footstep, and glanced up to see their young waitress standing nearby, her eyes roaming with interest over the notebook's contents. Evie shut it and asked the girl to bring more milk and sugar. They waited till she'd gone before continuing.

'So you believe these sigils were used to perform dark ritual magic?' Marcus asked.

'Carved into Janet's body with that intention, yes. Though whether the ritual was successful in its magical purpose, or rather was carried out as a ghastly experiment by someone who doesn't grasp the reality of the occult, is quite another matter.'

'Might Janet have done this to herself?'

'I hardly think so. It would have taken great strength of purpose to inflict such deep, intricate wounds on her own body. If she'd lived, she would have carried the scars for the rest of her life.

Someone else did this to her. The cuts might have been done after her death, but I think ... I fear ...'

'That she was still alive when this was done?' He shivered and rubbed unconsciously at his own arms. 'This is a dreadful business.'

Evie sat, lost in thought, one finger tracing the pattern in the paper doily on her empty plate.

The waitress reappeared, bearing a fresh milk jug and a sugar bowl. She took her time and fussed over setting them down, her gaze flicking between Evie and Mr Ellingham.

They sat in silence till the waitress had reluctantly departed.

'You're very brave,' he said as Evie stirred her tea.

She shook her head. 'Not really. Lots of things scare me – horses; heights; angry policemen, as I discovered last night; angry voices of any kind; deep water ...' She sucked in her breath at the memory of Grace's dark head disappearing under the Sithwater. 'I just try not to let fear stop me doing things, if you see what I mean.'

'Indeed, I do,' he said gently.

She looked up to meet his gaze, and made the discovery that unremarkable brown eyes looking appreciatively at her were rather more gratifying to her ego than supercilious green ones, however well shaped, however remarkable the shade. Yet she wouldn't let herself be diverted from her purpose, certainly not by any charms that Mr Ellingham might possess. 'Do you believe there could be something genuinely supernatural in all this?' she asked.

For a while he didn't reply, making a business of adding sugar to his tea, stirring it with absent-minded force, the spoon clattering against the side of the cup. 'To be honest with you, a few months ago I would probably have said such things cannot be. But since I started investigating for the *Ghost Hunter*, along with all the preposterous frauds and cynical hoaxes – and I count the Trent-L'Espoir seance in that category – I've come across some strange occurrences that I can't explain by any orthodox means.' He peered into the teak-coloured swirl of his tea. 'I believe it not to be impossible that there is some malevolent presence at work here, that we should act on that assumption, arm ourselves to face it.' He ruffled his hair, forming it into russet-tipped peaks that should have made him look ridiculous but which she found oddly endearing.

'We?'

'Yes.' He set down his cup and stretched, his bleariness from the previous night had fallen away. 'Will you let me help you? I'd be honoured if you would put your trust in me.'

A sudden suspicion stirred in her mind. 'Is this offer made to provide you with copy for your newspaper articles? Because if so—'

'I give you my solemn word, I will write nothing for my newspaper till your investigations are finished. You would have an absolute veto over any disclosures I would subsequently make. Does that reassure you?'

Under her scrutiny, he took up a currant bun with a carefully insouciant air. He made a poor pretence at eating it, however, tearing out currants and scattering them across his plate.

She felt suddenly warm, less alone, at the prospect of having someone on her side. *Be honest, Evie, you're tempted.*

'On one condition,' she said at last. 'This is *my* enterprise. It remains *my* enterprise.'

He dropped the remains of the bun and broke into a dimpled grin. 'Understood, Captain.' He sketched a half-salute.

They raised their teacups to toast one another and the enterprise, only to find both cups contained only cold dregs. Evie waved to the waitress, hovering in the doorway. 'More tea, please,' she said. 'And do you have anything more substantial than buns?'

'Some sandwiches, miss? The bread's fresh baked this morning. And we've got some nice cress just arrived.'

Evie cocked an enquiring eyebrow at Ellingham.

He nodded enthusiastically. 'Top notch.'

As the waitress departed, Evie said, 'To answer your question . . .'

'My question?' He looked confused.

'Since we're to work together, you *may* call me Evelyn.'

A blush suffused his face, as though he'd been dipped in scalding water. The tide covered up his freckles like islands submerged in a scarlet sea.

'Did you aid your father a great deal in his work?' he asked, eyes riveted to the tablecloth.

She suspected him of speaking almost at random to cover his embarrassment. 'I helped with the bookselling side of things,' she said, 'and I learnt quite a bit about occult theory, though not the practice. But when he became more deeply involved, he kept me at a distance, literally so, and sent me to Paris.'

He shot her a shrewd glance from his still-pink face. 'Surely that was to keep you safely out of it. Don't you think we should respect his wishes? I will undertake to find out anything you need to know.'

'While I twiddle my thumbs and wait for you to report back? I don't think so.'

An awkward silence fell. The arrival of the cress sandwiches provided a welcome interruption. Once the waitress had departed to attend to a party of demanding elderly ladies, Evie continued, 'I believe Professor Lorimer may know something about my father's work, if only I can persuade him to meet with me.'

'About Lorimer . . .' Marcus pushed his chair back, clasping his hands behind his head with an air of being excessively pleased with himself.

Evie picked up the teapot. 'Professor Lorimer?' she prompted.

'I was at Oxford myself.'

'Why, yes.' She almost spilled the fresh tea she was pouring. 'At Talbot College?'

'No such luck,' he said with a grin. 'Talbotonians are mostly from the top drawer, with a smattering of scholarship boys – a token nod to the principles of democracy.'

'Then you were . . .?'

'One of the smaller colleges, a recent foundation, not one of the grand medieval affairs. But I came to Talbot College for some of my tutorials.'

'You knew Professor Lorimer?'

'I'm afraid not. I wasn't a bright enough chap to study myth-ology. Modern languages was my bag. But I'm sure I could bluff my way in to see him. He's got no reason to deny me, so long as I don't mention the circle of shadows till I'm actually through his door. I could pretend I want to return to Oxford, study mythology – as if I'd be such a muggins. Ask him for his expert opinion and all that. Then, once I'm in, I'll confront him, get him to spill the beans.'

'You could, I suppose,' said Evie, mulling this suggestion over but conscious that she very much wanted to be the one to speak to Lorimer. She drank her tea and devoured a sandwich, a plan forming in her mind. 'Do you know the porter at Talbot College?'

'Old Postlethwaite? Is he still there?'

'The man I met looked like he'd been there for about a century, so I suppose it's him.'

'He's not such a bad sort. He's got a forbidding exterior, but it's his business to keep strangers out. He was always quite friendly to me. We both like following the cricket, you see, and—'

'Excellent,' interrupted Evie. 'This is what we'll do. You'll go and talk to him and I'll . . .'

'What will you do?' He eyed her curiously.

'I thought I might disguise myself as a servant.'

'Servants in the colleges are called scouts, but male colleges don't have female scouts. There are no women in the men's colleges except for the occasional guest. You would stick out like a sore thumb.'

'Then I'll sneak in while you distract Postlethwaite.'

Marcus's face was sunk in gloom, his brow furrowed. A storm was evidently brewing, and soon enough it burst. 'But, Evelyn,' he protested, 'that would mean you take the risk—'

'I'm not asking your permission. I will do this with or without your help. As Walter Winstanley's daughter, I've a right to know what happened to him, and why.'

'I don't like it.'

'I understand that.'

'Are you always so stubborn?'

'Only when it's a matter of importance. And this is very important to me.' She scooped up her notebook, shook crumbs from her lap, rose to her feet and drew on her gloves.

'Where are you going?' he asked.

'To see Professor Lorimer, of course.'

'At this very moment?' He scrambled up.

'Why, yes.' She picked up her hat, securing it with the slapdash placing of a hatpin. 'We must waste no time.'

He hurried to the counter to pay, then ran after Evie, who was already sallying forth into Cornmarket.

'Evelyn, I don't like you doing this alone. Let me accompany you to tackle Lorimer.'

She shook her head. 'Lorimer's more likely to talk to me on my own than with someone else there to bear witness. My father was his friend, after all. I'll meet you later, if you like.'

'At the cafe again?'

Evie had no intention of subjecting herself to further inquisitive scrutiny from the waitresses. 'At the Martyrs' Memorial.'

As they crossed the road towards Ship Street, he said, 'Talbot College is reputed to be the headquarters of the Sons of Dionysus. And it's Lord Maltraver's own college. You will be careful?'

'Of course.'

CHAPTER
Twenty-One

E VIE LURKED IN the gateway of Talbot College, out of sight of the lodge, while Marcus leant at the open window, talking with an unseen figure. Cheery conversation wafted over to her, punctuated by outbursts of male laughter. Keeping his arm close to his body, Marcus twitched his fingers, beckoning to her. She dropped to the ground and crawled on hands and knees through the gateway, past the lodge, head lowered to keep the crown of her hat below the level of the window.

Once around the corner of the building, she scrambled to her feet, brushing the worst of the dust from her skirt and gloves, and followed the path skirting the quad. Two dons appeared, strolling diagonally across the grass, deep in talk, their gowns flapping around them, and as they approached her she caught their look of surprise at seeing an unaccompanied woman. She nodded graciously, acknowledging their presence, and continued on her way. It was a tactic she'd learnt long since from Pelham: when you were in a place where you'd no business to be, your best bet was to keep moving as though confident of your destination. To lack assurance or to hesitate would incur notice and possibly suspicion.

She felt their eyes on her back, but no call came to question her business in the college, so she walked steadily on, looking neither left nor right, till she came to a doorway in the far corner of the right-hand side of the quad. She stepped inside, into the sudden coolness of a white-painted corridor, and saw a flight of steep stairs ahead. Taking a swift scan round to make sure she was alone, she began to climb.

On each landing, doors led off to either side. On the third floor, Evie came to a heavy oak door with 'Professor Lorimer' inscribed upon it. She knocked. Receiving no answer, she pushed at the door. It opened to reveal, immediately behind it, another door.

Opening this second door, she found herself in a bright room, its two windows overlooking the quad. Bookcases, crammed with volumes, reached from floor to ceiling. She was reminded of her father's study, of a man whose whole intellectual existence was bound up in his precious books. The memory caught her unawares and she rested a hand on a chair back to steady herself.

Behind a carved oak desk stood an upright chair, and several mismatched armchairs were ranged around the room, bearing the imprint of the innumerable bodies that had rested on them. A strong odour of pipe smoke, mixed with the fustiness of old leather book-bindings, hung in the air.

Opposite the windows, a third door was closed. She knocked at it – no answer. She tried the handle – locked.

She waited, keeping on her hat and gloves, focusing on her breathing. She wanted the professor to find her cool and self-possessed, but inwardly her heart raced. What if he was furious with her for resorting to a ruse to invade his inner sanctum?

The minutes wore by, marked by the self-important ticking of a carriage clock. *What if he's not in college today*, she thought, *and I've done all this for nothing?*

Growing restive, she went to the bookcase behind the desk. The books here were bound in fine calf leather, adorned with gilt lettering – probably the professor's most prized tomes. She ran a gloved hand along the spines, recognising several titles from her father's collection. She lifted her finger – the tip was stained a reddish-brown from book dust. Another pair of gloves spoiled. Her favourite lace ones, too. *Ah, well . . .*

The top of a long low bookcase served to display a series of artefacts: reliefs and statues from India, ancient Greece and Rome; likenesses of Norse gods and Celtic spirits; the plaster head of a man, surmounted by horns; several masks with fearsome smiles and teeth and curtains of long, rough hair; a statuette of an ancient

Egyptian cat, gold hoops in its pointed ears; a collection of ankhs. One object in particular drew her attention – a small bronze statue of a young man with a wild, laughing face, his flowing locks bound by a wreath of laurel leaves and grapes, naked but for the skin of an animal draped over one shoulder. She drew closer, feeling an odd impulse to touch its smooth surface.

'Admiring my collection, Miss Winstanley?'

She swung round. A man stood in the doorway, his frame so large he blocked most of it. There was no mistaking the substantial form of Professor Lorimer, cloaked in his academic gown, and given added height – not that he needed it – by his mortarboard. He had been her father's contemporary, yet he looked older, his blotched and reddened face bearing witness to many years of copious dining. His thick thatch of black hair and lush beard were just as she remembered from her father's funeral. He was observing her from under bushy brows.

'So, despite my express wish, you've contrived to impose yourself upon me.'

Evie remembered her father saying that Lorimer came from a small community in the Highlands, and she could detect a trace of a Scottish burr in his accent. She could see herself through his eyes – just a girl, a slip of a thing, self-educated, and an imposter to boot; she didn't belong here. Discreetly, she groped for the desk behind her, clutching it for support, facing him with what she hoped came across as self-assurance.

'I wish to talk to you about my father's work.'

For a moment longer, he assessed her.

'Please, Professor, for my father's sake.'

He sighed. 'I can give you ten minutes. You'd better sit down.' He waved at the chairs. 'A glass of sherry?'

She started to decline, but without waiting for her reply he cast aside his mortarboard, went to a side table, moved a pile of books and busied himself with small glasses and a decanter.

Evie perched on a leather armchair and instantly regretted her choice: it creaked each time she moved. She folded her gloved hands on her lap, the fingers pressed together to hide the stains.

He brought her a brimful glass of amber liquid, then sank his weight into the armchair opposite her – his favoured chair, no doubt, for on a small round table beside it lay his pipe and tobacco. He seized them both, packed his pipe with big square hands, lit it with a match and sat back.

'Why do you have a statue of Dionysus?' she said.

'Miss Winstanley.' He spoke through reams of smoke, irritation in his voice. 'I'm a professor of ancient mythologies. Why would I not?'

She started to speak, but he held up his hand, palm outward, blocking her. 'Oh, I know what you're going to say. Clearly you've heard of the Sons of Dionysus, and your respectable female bourgeois soul is shocked. The rumours are much exaggerated. High jinks, drunken excesses, trashing property, rudeness and insolence, play-acting and make-believe. Sons of Dionysus!' he snorted. 'Sons of privilege, rather. Indulged their whole lives. The colleges have sanctions to keep them in check. The boys are well aware if they go too far they'll be sent down and shame their families. They'll grow up soon enough.' He regarded her shrewdly through rings of smoke. 'But surely you didn't come here to ask me about the Sons of Dionysus. Why *are* you here, Miss Winstanley?'

'As my note said, I'm investigating the circle of shadows.'

'It's a myth. No more.'

'How can you be sure? My father believed in its existence. I think he confided in you.'

Lorimer considered her broodingly, tapping the end of his pipe on the armrest of his chair.

There being no table to hand, Evie set down her glass of sherry on the arm of her own chair. Several drips rolled down the side of the glass. 'You seem disapproving, Professor. Is it because I'm a woman?'

Lorimer raised an eyebrow. 'I hadn't realised Walter's daughter was an advocate for women's rights. For your information, I'm *not* one of the dons still wilfully stuck in the nineteenth century, who objects unilaterally to the emancipation of women. I have even met some women of sound intellect, capable of reasoned argument – though not many, it's true. Nor, contrary to your evident expectations, am I myself a son of privilege. Not every don at Oxford was born with a silver spoon in his mouth. There's no call for you to gird yourself up to do battle with me.'

'Then why wouldn't you speak to me?'

'Young ladies have no call to go meddling in dark magic. Go home, Miss Winstanley. Play the piano, marry a nice young man and forget about the circle of shadows.' He flicked ash heedlessly onto the Turkish carpet, took up his sherry and quaffed it in several sips.

Ignoring his unsolicited advice, she said, 'You believe the circle of shadows is dangerous?'

'Dangerous?' He drew his lips back mockingly. 'A rather fanciful choice of words. We're at the dawn of the twentieth century, no longer in the Dark Ages. But the occult is *not* an appropriate subject for a girl of your upbringing. You need not deny it. I had the honour of meeting your mother. I can readily imagine the conventional life she envisages for you.'

'That's my mother's view. Not mine. I want to be a scholar, to ask questions and seek out answers, like my father.'

Lorimer flicked more ash onto the carpet. Evie wondered why he didn't have an ashtray, then realised he expected his scout to clear that up.

'Your father? Hmm. Walter didn't talk to you about the occult, did he? He wanted you kept out of it. I can only assume he didn't share your own opinion of your abilities as a scholar.'

She wavered: his words had cut her. It was true that Papa excluded her towards the end. She'd thought his intention had been to protect her, but what if Professor Lorimer was right and the real reason Papa hadn't wanted her involved was because he didn't think she was clever enough or strong enough to cope with the knowledge? *No, it can't be that. I won't believe it.* She pushed aside her self-doubt.

'I'm already involved. I don't intend to stop.'

Lorimer snorted, heaved himself out of his chair and went to pour more sherry.

'If I tell you what I already know about the circle of shadows,' she said, 'will you tell me the rest?'

Silence fell, broken only by the ticking of the carriage clock. Lorimer returned to his armchair, sipping his sherry, more slowly this time, eyeing her over the rim of his glass. Behind his over-bearing manner, she thought she detected curiosity in his gaze.

He sat back, crossing his legs with apparent indifference; ready to judge any mistake, any show of ignorance on her part. 'Well then?'

She mustered her resolve, striving to keep a confident exterior, and began: 'The circle of shadows was an ancient cult dedicated to wielding power through magic. They called themselves the *kuroskato*, meaning the web of power. This is their symbol.' She brought out her notebook, turned to the page with the kuroskato sketch, showed it to him. 'The concentric circles signify the power of the circle of shadows. The shifting pattern contained within is the elemental force they control. Am I right?' She watched him narrowly.

He took a cursory look at the drawing, puffing on his pipe till the embers glowed fiery red. 'How would mere humans control an elemental force?' he asked with an ironic smile, baring surprisingly white teeth.

'There are different ways, all of them based on spells of summoning. One such way would involve sacrifice.'

'What would be the purpose of such sacrifices?' His voice was dry as gravel, either from the pipe smoke or some other cause.

'Sacrifice gives power. If the sacrifice is accepted by the spirit or god to whom it is made, then in return the spirit will give magical power to the maker of the sacrifice.'

'Your father told you this?'

'No.'

'He must have done. How else would you have known about it?'

'I found it out for myself. I visited an old place of power, a remote lake in Yorkshire – the Sithwater. Something in the lake attached itself to my sister, and now she is marked by the kuroskato.'

Silence fell. Lorimer's attention went to the middle distance, his eyes unfocused, as though he saw something invisible to her.

'Professor?' she prompted. He swung his great shaggy head towards her. 'I'm right, am I not?'

Gradually the cloudiness in his gaze dispersed, as though he had returned from a far country. 'What exactly do you want to know?'

'Two things: the nature of my father's connection with the circle of shadows, and how I can free my sister from the kuroskato.'

He finished his glass, rose to pour another and returned with it. 'As regards your sister, I know nothing. I can't help you. All I can say is, you shouldn't have interfered.'

She clenched a fist against her mouth.

'As for your father ...' He paused, his fleshy face softening slightly. 'He and I met here. We were young and reckless, both fascinated by the history of magical belief.'

'When he was at Oxford?'

'*Here*,' he repeated impatiently. 'At Talbot College. He and I were both Talbotonians. Surely you knew?'

'No, I didn't.' The revelation stirred in her painfully. She could imagine her father as solemn, studious, with flashes of quirky humour, sharing a drink with a few trusted friends. Her eyes met Lorimer's. 'It seems strange he didn't speak of it to me.'

'Walter's time at Talbot was difficult. If you want to get on here, you need to learn the codes, how to keep on the right side of the people whose opinions matter. I could never make Walter understand. If he thought someone else was wrong, he came out and said so. He rubbed people up the wrong way. Other students began to cold-shoulder him. It wasn't just that he was a scholarship boy. He developed controversial theories, ideas that laid him open to mockery.'

'Ideas about the occult?'

His gaze darkened and he nodded curtly.

'Is there some direct connection between Talbot College and the occult?'

Lorimer stroked the wiry hair of his beard, his eyes like black marbles, unreadable.

'Professor?'

He tilted back his head, taking his time to drain his glass. 'There was an attempt in the sixteenth century to revive the circle of shadows, here at Talbot College. *It did not end well.* Members of the circle were arrested, tried by the church for heresy. Three were condemned to death by the fire. It was the darkest time in this college's long history. Walter and I heard whisperings about it. We were young, heedless, and the old tales piqued our interest. We were never – either of us – interested in practising the dark arts, you understand. We were simply intrigued. We did some research. There was a book, a grimoire ...'

'Did you find it?'

The opaque eyes narrowed. 'No. It was destroyed, along with most of the documents detailing the case, either by order of the Church or by the members of the circle themselves in an attempt to hide their traces. But enough information remained to absorb us, Walter in particular. After he left university, he collected books, documents.'

'And ... he found out some new information? That last time, when he came to see you—'

His beefy fists pounded his knees. 'He found nothing!'

Evie jumped at his suddenly energised display, bracing her hands against the armrests so he wouldn't see them twitch.

'Do you know how my father died, Professor?'

'A heart attack,' said Lorimer. 'Your mother said—'

'He was found lying dead in the middle of the kuroskato, drenched in water. What was he trying to do? You know, don't you?'

Lorimer's mouth opened, then closed again. He returned to the side table, this time searching for a bottle behind the decanter and pouring himself a generous measure of its contents. The bottle clinked loudly as he set it down. Keeping his back towards Evie, he said, 'The circle of shadows has long since perished.'

'You're wrong.'

He froze, then returned to his chair with his tumbler. Crossing one leg over the other, he relit his pipe, taking his time at the business, and began to puff once more. He was outwardly calm yet the pipe shook slightly in his hands. 'Would you care to share with me whatever evidence you have for such an extraordinary – and inherently unlikely – assertion?'

'I found a rock above the Sithwater. The symbol of the kuroskato had once been cut into that rock, but someone had destroyed it. The words "we shall rise" were there instead. And they'd been carved recently.'

'What?' He choked, coughing on his pipe; then lurched to his feet, striding about the room, his gown swirling about him. He stopped and faced her, lip curling. 'You're making this up.'

'Why would I?'

'You may be a young woman up for mischief. I'm told that hysterical imagining is characteristic of womankind.'

'Hysterical imagining!' Incensed, she seized the notebook, searching for where she'd drawn the mutilations on Janet Rae's body. 'Yesterday, a young woman who had worked for Lord Maltraver's family was found drowned in the Cherwell. These symbols were carved into her limbs. Look at them, Professor! Or are you too afraid?'

Lorimer glowered at her, the muscles along his jawline clenching. He fished in his pocket, brought out his glasses, fixing them over his nose and scrutinised the symbols.

'Do you recognise them? They're occult sigils, and together they make up the kuroskato. Tell me, what's their purpose and why were they cut into this woman's body? You know, don't you?' In that moment, she felt absolute conviction that he *did* know.

'That's enough!' He picked up his pipe, his hands so unsteady that he struggled to relight it. Some of the redness had leached from his skin, leaving it waxen. 'Stop importuning me with your ridiculous theories and get out!'

'Professor, you must listen—'

'Out!' he thundered. 'Or I'll summon the college servants to escort you from the premises.'

'My father thought highly of you. I would have credited you with more courage.'

He did not answer, simply glared, eyes glittering.

There was nothing else for it. She put away the notebook and marched out, struggling to appear composed as she descended the three flights of stairs, though her mind was seething in turmoil.

Just within the outer doorway, where no one could see her, she leant against the cold wall and fought back hot tears. She realised now how much she'd hoped Lorimer would give her credit for what she'd discovered. Bitter disappointment churned inside her. She felt diminished, invisible. *Are you going to give way to tears, like a child, because he wouldn't tell you how clever you are, as Papa would have done? You can't cry. Not now. Not here.*

She wiped her eyes on her sleeve, pushed her hair away from her damp face and tossed her head in a gesture of defiance, though there was no one to see.

Twenty-Two

As evie sheltered in the doorway, somewhere a bell rang, and soon students poured out into the quad, singly and in groups, chattering. She backed further into the entrance-way, keeping out of sight. She would wait till the crowd had cleared so that as few people as possible would witness her leaving humiliated. She glanced back up the stairs. So far no one had come down. If she heard footsteps descending, she'd have to leave at once; she'd no wish to come face to face with Lorimer again.

Astonishing that she hadn't known about her father's connection with Talbot College, that he'd never mentioned it to her, or what the college had meant to him. Even if he hadn't been popular with fellow students, as Lorimer had claimed, surely the place itself must have appealed to his delight in the past? According to Harriet's Baedeker, it was one of the oldest colleges, founded in the late Middle Ages.

Her eyes travelled round the age-worn buildings enclosing the four sides of the quad. On two wings, a Virginia creeper, just emerging into leaf, shrouded the honey-coloured walls. Across from where she stood, an archway set into the base of a massive square tower, four storeys high and surmounted by crenellated battlements, opened on a passageway leading deeper into the college. From the corners of the upper storeys, gargoyles fashioned as malevolent goblins jutted out against the sky.

Evie's eyes narrowed, her attention caught by the first-storey windows adjoining the tower. Through several of them she made out rows of bookcases beneath an elaborately carved wooden ceiling. *The college library.*

Lorimer had spoken of a grimoire. He'd said it was lost, but she wasn't sure she believed him. Might it be stored in the library? It seemed unlikely, yet surely there would be books on the history of the college that would tell her more. Could she possibly get into the library to investigate?

She shrank back into the shadows as two students passed close by. The taller of the two was fair-headed, blessed with angelic looks, while his companion was much shorter and stockier. The tall one laughed, and in that moment Evie recognised him as the youth she had seen with Lord Maltraver. When Maltraver had pointed out Evie, the boy had laughed in that distinctive way – light, rippling, positively delighted with himself. Evie retreated back along the corridor, out of sight of anyone chancing to look through the door.

Somewhere up above a door slammed and she heard heavy footsteps begin a descent. Within moments, whoever it was – Professor Lorimer? – would appear and find her cowering, caught between Scylla and Charybdis.

Several doors led off the ground-floor corridor going back past the stairwell, and she bolted along the corridor, trying one after another. The first two were locked but the third opened and with a fast-beating heart she stepped inside a large room, into a sea of battered desks and wooden chairs. The place was deserted. Suddenly, she realised she'd been holding her breath, and let it out with a gasp. She would wait here for the corridor to be quiet again. She positioned herself behind the door, out of sight in case someone tried it.

Beside her, on a row of pegs, hung two anonymous black gowns and a mortarboard. Her nose twitched at the odour that came off them, of mildewy, long-forgotten garments. A plan began to form in her head. Pelham, had he been there, would have told her not to act on impulse – *but he's not here, is he?* She inspected the gowns, choosing the longer and more voluminous of the two – made for a don rather than a student – and pulled it on, arranging its folds to conceal her clothes. The gown was meant to reach a tall man's knees, but on her smaller frame its lower edge came to just a few inches above the ground, though she reasoned the length was to her advantage, hiding much of her skirt.

The greater difficulty was her hair. She whipped off her felt hat and stowed it in her handbag. Then she undid her chignon, tightly plaited her hair and tried to bundle it under the felt skull cap, but the mortarboard rested precariously. In the end, she just stuffed the plait under the upturned collar of her blouse and hoped nobody would look closely at the back of her neck. No one who looked directly at her would be deceived, but from a distance they mightn't notice her odd appearance.

She returned to her post at the doorway onto the quad. No one was about. 'Carpe diem,' she muttered, then sucked in her breath and stepped out from her hiding place into the sunlight.

~

The desk where the librarian would usually sit was empty. The main aisle led in both directions. Alcoves opened at regular intervals, bearing shelves stacked with books. Shelves, flooring, the ceiling beams – all were fashioned from rich, dark wood. The air smelt strongly of musty books and faintly of floor polish. Which way? Male voices came from her left.

'As I have informed you, the book you require is not on the shelves. Another user of the library must be consulting it.' A querulous reply that Evie didn't catch. Then, with rising impatience: 'No, Mr McBride, I cannot demand that he return it forthwith. If you need to consult a book that is greatly in demand, you must arrive in good time.'

Evie turned the other way, passing several alcoves occupied by dons or students, reading, writing or, in one case, sleeping. Though the floorboards creaked at her tread, no one looked up. She kept her face averted, angling the mortarboard to shield her features, scanning the titles of volumes without finding what she sought.

Finally, she arrived at the two furthest bays, both of which were unoccupied. She investigated the left-hand alcove and her hopes rose – she'd found the history section. She ran her fingers along the leather tomes, hunting for what she needed. As she did so, a small, exceptionally youthful-looking student appeared. Ignoring her, he went to the right-hand alcove and selected several weighty history books. He dumped them with a thud on the table opposite, seated himself and, sighing heavily, took out paper and pens.

Cautiously, Evie returned to her search. There was no sign of the grimoire that Professor Lorimer had spoken about. *Of course not. You were a fool to hope it.* If the grimoire existed at all, it would be hidden away and inaccessible.

Then, on a high shelf devoted to the architecture of the college, she came upon *A History of Talbot College*, by 'A Gentleman Scholar', and reached up to grasp it. The volume was bound in tan-coloured leather. Its binding had come apart, and the pages were held together by faded ribbons. The date of publication was given as 1782. *There might be something here.* She looked sidelong at the boy. He was bent over his books, oblivious of her presence, humming under his breath, feet thumping out a restless rhythm.

Evie took a seat at the table in the left-hand alcove, her back to the aisle, propping up her legs so that her shoes weren't visible. The book smelt of damp and candle grease. As she turned the pages, motes of dust spiralled upwards.

She glanced over an account of the founder of the college, Sir Henry de Talbot, who'd been a court official under the last Plantagenets before switching sides to Henry Tudor. The author described him as a man notorious for being insatiably acquisitive and corrupt. She skimmed through details of various subsequent benefactors who had endowed the college with land and property. A chapter on the sixteenth century devoted many pages to the impact of the Reformation. Then, as she moved on to the following chapter, she realised she'd struck gold. She began to read:

The reign of Mary Tudor saw the darkest period in the history of the college. It began, in 1554, with the appointment of Dr Actaeon Fell as a fellow of the college. He was a magus, an astrologer, an alchemist and a secret practitioner of forbidden occult arts—

'Miss Winstanley?' The voice spoke in an amused drawl, its tone politely enquiring.

Evie shut the book, laid it down and slowly looked around.

Twenty-Three

MALTRAVER'S FRIEND STOOD at her shoulder, his blond hair gleaming like golden guineas against the dark wood backdrop of the library. Beneath his gown, thrown casually back, a figured-velvet waistcoat and a knotted muslin cravat proclaimed the tastes of a gentleman of fashion. His ethereal slenderness gave him an otherworldly appearance, and an incongruous thought flickered through Evie's mind that he would not look out of place with laurel leaves and grapes twined in his hair. As he observed her taking in his appearance, a quizzical gleam came to his eyes and a half-smile parted his lips, as though he were inviting Evie to join in some secret joke.

Behind him stood the shorter, stockier companion whom Evie had glimpsed earlier, a much less remarkable presence. He had an unhealthy pallor, making him look older than his actual age must be. His brown hair rose in a quiff and his eyes darted, avoiding Evie's, while his fingers rested on his stiff collar, rubbing it. She recognised him now as the solitary student whom Maltraver had mocked at the riotous meeting at the tavern. One of the Sons of Dionysus.

Her luck had run out.

She stood to face them, taking off the mortarboard and gown and laying them on the table. She realised then that several hair-pins had come adrift and she must look like a wild thing. Not wanting to appear at a disadvantage, she smoothed her hair with her fingers.

'How do you know my name?' She strove to keep her voice steady.

From his position across the aisle, the youngster had abandoned all pretence of working and sat open-mouthed, observing Evie's unexpected transformation. The fair-haired youth turned to him, flicked his fingers and said in an insouciant tone, though with a sense of a wire tightening: 'Go.'

The boy's eyes blinked repeatedly, swivelling to Evie with an expression like a frightened rabbit. He grabbed his things – leaving the history books – and stumped rapidly away, footsteps echoing on the wooden floor.

'Your fame – or should I say notoriety – has preceded you, Miss Winstanley,' the fair-haired youth drawled.

'Lord Maltraver?'

'Indeed. He's impatient to see you. Will you accompany us?'

'Why not?' she said coolly. *Don't let them see you look afraid. After all, you're in no real danger within the college. And you might find out more.* 'But you haven't yet told me who you are.'

'Have we not?' said the fair-haired young man, a flicker of amusement in his eyes. 'How very remiss of us. I'm Edgar Deverell-Drummond. And this little character is Zouch. Eh, remind me of your first name, Zouch – I'm persuaded you must have one.'

'Bernard,' said his companion quietly.

'Ah, yes, Bernard Zouch.' Deverell-Drummond sketched a half-bow to Evie. 'And now that we're all perfectly acquainted, it's time to depart.'

Evie collected her bag and started towards the main door, but Edgar Deverell-Drummond went in front of her. Though his manner was perfectly affable, he was blocking her path.

'Not that way,' he said. 'We don't want to run the risk of your presence in the college being discovered before you've had time for a cosy tête-à-tête with his lordship.' He nodded to Zouch. 'You've brought the key?'

'Yes, DD.' Zouch produced an iron key, several inches long, and headed for an oak door set into a Gothic arch in the farther wall.

'So you're interested in history?' said Deverell-Drummond to Evie, his tone conversational, with just a trace of light mockery. 'No doubt you'll appreciate what lies ahead. We're about to see one of the oldest parts of the college, built by our revered founder, Henry de Talbot, in . . . I forget the date. Sometime in the alarmingly distant past.'

Zouch unlocked the door and stepped through. Chin held high, Evie followed. Beyond the stone threshold, a spiral staircase reached both up and down, the only light filtered through narrow windows set deep into the stone walls. A few steps above, Zouch waited for her, half in shadow. The scrape of wood on stone signalled the closing of the library door behind her and prickles of unease lifted the hairs on the back of her neck. Glancing down, she saw Deverell-Drummond standing on the step below, pocketing the key, his head almost on a level with hers. He gave her a lazy grin and, with an extravagant gesture, pointed upwards.

Evie stiffened, lifted the hem of her skirt so it wouldn't trip her, and began to climb. It wasn't an easy ascent: the steps were mostly steep, being somewhat uneven in height, and dipped in the centre, worn away over centuries by the passage of countless feet. Through the narrow windows, she caught glimpses of the ground becoming ever more distant as they climbed and grew disorientated, nausea flowering in the pit of her stomach.

A childhood memory came into Evie's head – an illustration in a story of the Sleeping Beauty in a favourite book of fairy tales. In the picture, the princess was exploring the castle, her palm trailing against the curving wall to steady herself as she climbed a circling stair in the topmost tower. She was curious and without fear, for in her whole young life she had never encountered real malevolence. She didn't know it yet, but she was about to fall into the power of a wicked fairy, whose magic would make the princess fall into prolonged slumber – *a sleep like unto death.*

'Here we are,' said Zouch, his voice puncturing the bubble of Evie's memory. They stood near the head of the stairs, before a wooden door set into an ancient stone wall. Zouch wrestled briefly with the iron bolt, drawing it back with a clank. A burst of sunlight came through. Zouch ducked under the low lintel and disappeared.

Conscious of Deverell-Drummond right behind her, blocking her retreat, Evie followed to find herself in the very place she had most dreaded to be – on top of the tower. Sudden daylight, after the gloom of the library and the semi-darkness of the staircase, dazzled her, and she blinked rapidly. Wind whipped her hair, unravelling her braid, flattening flying strands against her face.

She was in a small space, bounded by ornate Gothic battlements. Beyond the boundary was nothingness. Vertigo coursed through her insides, raced around her head, making it spin. Her legs turned to water. She backed against the wall housing the staircase, seeking the solidity of stone against her shoulders, her flattened palms. She looked away from the distant ground and the landscape of Oxford, visible beyond the parapet and through the embrasures of the battlements, keeping her eyes locked on the confined space within the circumference of the tower. If she didn't see the drop, she might fool herself that she was safe on the ground.

Nine or ten young men were lounging nearby, all students. Most had cast off their gowns and several were in shirtsleeves. Some were half leaning, half lying against the pitched leads that covered much of the roof, except for the narrow path that skirted the parapet. They were talking, laughing, drinking from hip flasks, smoking cigarettes and cheroots. When they saw Evie, a rowdy cheer went up.

'Why, hallo, hallo, hallo,' said Lord Maltraver, coming towards her, hip flask in hand. 'Who do we have here? Miss Winstanley, as I live and breathe.'

Evie stared stonily at Maltraver, feeling thankful that her long, cumbersome skirt hid the shaking of her knees, just as her lace gloves absorbed the cold sweat dampening her palms.

'How's your luscious sister?' Maltraver's smile was ugly.

Cold fury swept over Evie. 'Don't you dare speak about her.' Her voice shook with a rage she fought to master. She chided herself. *You meant to keep control of your feelings and the first thing you do is let him bait you.*

'As you see, we'd planned for a suitably decadent afternoon at one of our favourite haunts,' Maltraver said genially. 'All that was lacking – at least for some of us – was female company. Women are so hard to smuggle into college, at least during daylight hours, yet *you* obligingly smuggled yourself in, Evelyn – I can call you Evelyn, can't I? I feel that since your sister and I have become so *close*, we are practically related.'

Don't let him see his words can hurt you. Evie squeezed her hands into balls.

Maltraver turned to Deverell-Drummond. 'Where did you find her, DD?'

'In the library,' said Deverell-Drummond languidly. He was sitting, legs stretched out, on the leads beside another youth whose long curling hair brushed his shirt collar. Between the two of them rested a small box, from which Deverell-Drummond had been inhaling something that was making his nose run. 'She'd disguised herself in someone's stolen cap and gown, but Zouch spotted her looking out from Staircase J.'

'Well done, little Zouch,' said Maltraver. Zouch glanced at him and looked quickly away. 'We'll have to find a reward for your loyal service.'

Maltraver turned back to Evie. 'So, tut-tut, Evelyn. Trespassing, pilfering – those aren't the actions of a nicely brought-up young female. We might ask ourselves, why were you so very keen to sneak into a male college? What were you so desperate to find?'

There was a snort of ribald laughter from a youth with slicked black hair who squatted on the pitched leads, his hands on his knees, watching Evie. She levelled a cool look at him. Under her icy contempt, he ducked his eyes.

'Staircase J,' repeated Maltraver musingly. 'Who's on that staircase? Who were you visiting, Evelyn?'

'Whatever I was doing is no business of yours.' But as she glared in his direction, she caught a sudden dizzying glimpse of the nothingness behind him and the nausea in her stomach redoubled. She felt herself sway and caught hold of a projecting stone to keep herself upright.

'Professor Lorimer's rooms are on that staircase,' said Deverell-Drummond.

'Ah, yes . . . Lorimer.' Maltraver's eyes probed Evie, as though he were trying to burrow beneath her skin.

His face began to fluctuate before Evie's eyes, backwards and forwards. Was she about to faint? She gripped the stone tighter, tried to brace her knees.

At that moment, Zouch caused a distraction as he brushed past her, sidling towards the door. Maltraver's voice called him back. 'Where are you slinking off to?'

'I've got a tutorial,' said Zouch over his shoulder. 'I can't keep cutting classes the way you fellows do. I'm not like you, Maltraver. I can't risk being sent down. I need my degree.'

'It's true,' said Deverell-Drummond with a titter. 'One day our Zouch will have to work for a living, side by side with the ranks of the great unwashed.'

'Work?' sneered Maltraver. 'What a misfortune. Even so, I rather believe you need to stay, Zouch. We must remain together, to entertain Miss Winstanley. We act as one. *Remember?* Besides, I was hoping you would be able to lend me the readies. Once again, I find myself in temporary difficulties. And none of the other chaps seem to have any cash about them. No need to look like a wet Sunday,' he added as Zouch jerked around, wearing an expression of sullen acquiescence. 'I have a transaction planned for this afternoon. If all goes well, I'll again be in funds. You'll be paid back.' Maltraver tucked his arm in friendly fashion into Zouch's and led him away to an angle of the tower, saying over his shoulder as he went, 'Watch her.'

Conscious that she was going to have to sit down before she fell down, Evie tottered the few steps to the pitched leads and dropped down beside Deverell-Drummond. She put her head down over her knees, fighting the dizziness.

'Are you quite well, Miss Winstanley?' said Deverell-Drummond.

'Yes.' Her throat had closed up, making it hard to speak.

'Would you like to try some snuff?'

She raised her head from her hands and saw what he was holding out to her: a small ornate snuffbox with the initials EDD spelt out in sparkling stones resembling sapphires. Above it, Deverell-Drummond's face appeared abstracted, his eyes unfocused.

'An old-fashioned habit,' he murmured, 'but it's enjoying something of a revival here at Talbot.'

The black-haired boy reached for the snuffbox but Deverell-Drummond waved him away. 'Not for you, Charlie. You can afford your own.' He turned to Evie. 'This is Charlie Pomeroy.'

'We've met,' said Evie.

'Indeed?' Deverell-Drummond looked curious.

'Upstairs at a public house, where the Sons of Dionysus were having one of your private meetings. Mr Pomeroy asked if I was there to provide entertainment, though he may have been too inebriated to recall the occasion.'

'How very ungentlemanly of him,' observed Deverell-Drummond. 'I must apologise for his uncouth manners.'

Charlie scowled down at his large feet, encased in hand-stitched brogues surmounted by spats.

Evie took deep, slow breaths. The light-headedness was lessening now that she was sitting down and facing away from the brink of the tower. She considered the powder in the snuffbox. 'I don't think I will,' she said. 'I don't think that's snuff, either. It's the wrong colour and consistency.'

'Oh,' said Deverell-Drummond, snapping the lid closed with a practised flick of the wrist. 'What do you think it is then?'

'I've read Sherlock Holmes, so I could hazard a guess. He injected himself—'

'While I,' said Deverell-Drummond, with a ghost of a smile, 'have a horror of needles.' He shuddered flamboyantly.

Beyond Deverell-Drummond sprawled a youth with long curling hair, a jaundiced-looking complexion, a meagre frame and bleary, bloodshot eyes. He grinned at Evie, as he took a swig from a brandy bottle. 'Are you falling for DD's charms, Miss Winstanley? I'd be careful, if I were you. More than one admirer has found him to be more than they bargained for. They say that Oscar Wilde knew DD when he was up at Oxford, and that DD was the original inspiration for Dorian Gray. That would make

DD around fifty ... or sixty? Something like that.' The youth leant conspiratorially towards Evie, across Deverell-Drummond's lap, treating her to a whiff of the alcohol on his breath as he confided in a stage whisper, 'Ask DD if he keeps a picture in his attic.'

Deverell-Drummond smiled sleepily, taking the bottle from the other's loosened hold. 'This is Cyril Roope, Miss Winstanley. He's always deliciously indiscreet.'

'That's not fair,' complained Roope. 'I can hold my tongue. Though I could tell Miss Winstanley tales that would make her toes curl.' He guffawed and groped for the snuffbox, spilling some of its contents.

'Cyril, you absolute idiot!' Deverell-Drummond exerted himself to snatch back the snuffbox. 'That stuff's expensive, and I've spent my entire allowance.'

'You could always get one of your adorers to fund your habit,' said Roope. 'What about that old gal, DD? She must be good for a few bob. She was so *eager*, wasn't she? You had to hold your nose for that one. We haven't seen her haunting your footsteps lately. Did you give her the old heave-ho?'

'Not really my thing, old boy,' said Deverell-Drummond. He leant back on one elbow. His smile had faded.

Roope, helping himself to more brandy, was oblivious. 'Oh, we all know about your tastes, DD.' He smacked his lips. 'We're all men of the world. At least ...' He broke off to bestow his befuddled gaze on Evie.

'Just look on me as a man of the world too,' she said quickly. 'You were telling us about Mr Deverell-Drummond's conquests?'

'Why, yes,' said Roope. 'Of course – the little mathematician.'

'Who's she?' said Evie.

'He,' Roope corrected. 'Women have no head for mathematics.'

'Cyril ...' came a murmur of warning from Deverell-Drummond, now lying stretched across the leads, his blue-eyed gaze fixed on the sky overhead.

Evie leant over Deverell-Drummond's prone form and shook Roope's sleeve. 'Who do you mean?'

'Theodore Windle,' said Roope. 'He's a student, here at Talbot – or rather, he was. He used to be very thick with Zouch. The scholarship boys stick together. Very bright is Windle. Predicted a double first and a grand career. But then Zouch introduced him to DD, and that was that.' He fumbled in his pocket, producing a slim gold case. He opened it upside down and several cheroots spilled out, rolling across the stone floor. He crawled to retrieve them, cursing.

Evie waited till he'd returned to his perch on the leads. 'Go on, Mr Roope. What happened to Theodore Windle?'

'He hung around DD like a lapdog, lent him money, neglected his own studies, eventually got notice from the dean that he was failing and needed to buck up his ideas.' Roope put a cheroot to his lips and patted his jacket in a search for matches.

'And then?' prompted Evie.

'He ran away,' said Roope, taking a long draw on his cheroot and sighing with pleasure. When he spoke again, he slurred his words and Evie had to lean towards him to make out what he said. 'Last term. Disappeared one night. Left the dean a letter saying he couldn't hack it.'

'Did he go back to his home?' said Evie.

There was a silence. Roope's pupils glazed, his attention wandering. Beside Evie, Deverell-Drummond seemed to be asleep – at least, his eyelids were closed.

Maltraver's voice broke in softly. 'I heard that his parents received a letter from him saying he was too ashamed to face them and meant to go off and sink himself in some miserable post in the colonies, hobnobbing with the feckless and rancid natives. Their *darling Teddy* wasn't coming home.'

'Poor little Teddy,' murmured Deverell-Drummond dreamily. His golden head lay pillowed in the crook of his arm, his eyelids fluttered, his lips just parted. Somehow, he reminded Evie of Girodet's 'The Sleep of Endymion'. It was a painting she'd often seen at the Louvre; voluptuous, full of hidden meanings. She tried to remember the story. The moon goddess, Selene, stricken by passionate jealousy, had begged Zeus to cast the beautiful shepherd boy, Endymion, into an eternal sleep so that no one else should ever have his love. Evie frowned in bemusement. In her present dire situation, it seemed nonsensical to be conjuring up classical allusions. Why had her mind gone there? Her attention went beyond Deverell-Drummond – and was caught by Zouch who stood a little way off. Like her, he seemed to have been struck by a sudden thought: all the blood had left his face, save for a scarlet blotch on each cheek, and his mouth hung heedlessly open. It seemed to Evie that he was struggling to understand something that hovered just out of reach.

Twenty-Four

'WOULD YOU CARE to see the view, Evelyn?' Maltraver asked. 'It's quite something from up here.' His smirk had the tautness of a rubber band as he held out his hand as if to haul her up from the leads.

Fear and anger wrestled inside Evie. Anger won. She'd be damned if she'd let Maltraver intimidate her.

She stripped off her gloves, slippery with sweat, and stuffed them into her skirt pocket. Ignoring Maltraver's proffered hand, she jerked like a marionette towards the parapet and braced her hands on the stone, forcing herself to look over the drop. As her eyes went downwards, all the breath ripped out of her body.

Far below her was a paved courtyard. From it, a cobbled pathway led to a perimeter wall, into which was set a closed wooden side gate. Away to the right was the college chapel with its narrow spire. Over the outer wall of the college, Evie caught glimpses of a busy street and, beyond it, a sea of spires, towers and high walls. As she stared, everything – the paved square, the buildings – began to shift and dance. The ground pulsated, seeming to rush towards her. She swayed and closed her eyes, battling the tide of panic rising up from her stomach into her throat.

'This is the north side,' came Maltraver's voice. 'Over there is Broad Street.'

Evie forced her eyes open, keeping them fixed on the intense blue of the sky. *Don't look down. Don't look down.* She clutched the parapet, the only solid thing in the spinning world.

Maltraver's eyes lingered on her whitening knuckles as she gripped the stone. She heard his voice dimly.

'A fine sight, isn't it? The dreaming spires, the dutiful tourists with their guides, and all the gullible little plebs. Oxford is our playground, and from this vantage point we can see our toys in play. One day, the world itself will be our playground. Charlie's father intends for him to go into politics. DD is destined for high finance. As for myself, I have plans – big plans.' His self-satisfied, arrogant voice provided a buzzing accompaniment to her jangling nerves. Evie's entire body was nerveless, as though it no longer belonged to her, as though at any moment she would topple over the parapet and plummet to the ground below.

Maltraver murmured in her ear. 'You're not as . . . generous as your sister. A little prudish, are you not?'

Grace. He had hit on the one thing that could lash Evie into sufficient anger to combat her terror. She turned towards him, her back to the drop.

'Grace loathes you. All your money and titles and privileges don't make you appealing to a woman. That's why you put a spell on her, didn't you?' She spat out the last few words.

Maltraver kept his eyelids lowered, as if contemplating how to respond. Then he flicked his gaze sidelong like a guileless toddler, an incredulous smile breaking across his face.

'A spell? You think I dabble in black magic? You really are raving, Evelyn. Oh, I know you've been spreading ludicrous stories about me. A police sergeant warned me that you've been dreaming up malicious fantasies that I was somehow involved in Janet Rae's suicide. And now you turn up here at Talbot, nosing around. Curiosity killed the cat, you know.'

'What are you afraid I'll find? The circle of shadows?'

'The circle of shadows?' He blinked and guffawed. 'What's that? A game for children?'

'A cult of dark power. But I think you already know about them. Perhaps you're even involved yourself.'

'Meddling little fool!' His face suddenly darkened and his hand shot out and grabbed her arm as it lay on the parapet. He shook her like a rag doll until her teeth banged together, cutting her lip.

'Let go of me!' she cried. 'I'll report you to the college authorities, to the police!'

He threw back his head and roared with mirth. 'Be my guest. Tell me, who do you think they'll believe? A hysterical girl creeping unchaperoned around a men's college, or us gentlemen?' He gestured to his fellow students, who had stopped talking, all eyes now focused on the confrontation.

Evie appealed to the onlookers. 'If you call yourselves gentlemen, you'll help me.'

Deverell-Drummond unravelled himself and approached, propping himself against the parapet close to Evie. For a moment she hoped he'd come to her aid, but he simply took out a cigarette, sheltering a match in his cupped hand to light it, and looked on with interest. Zouch shuddered and turned away. No one else moved.

'No one's going to intervene, Evelyn,' said Maltraver, his voice thick. 'You're alone, and you're the star of the show. You might as well enjoy it.' His words terrified her in a way that had nothing to do with vertigo.

She twisted round, facing the drop into the square below. Along the cobbled path from the side gate, two figures were approaching, one wearing the short gown of a student, the other – taller than his companion – in a dark suit. She thought she recognised the latter, but at this height she couldn't be sure. She filled her lungs, readying herself to yell out for help, but a hand wrapped tight round her mouth and she couldn't make a sound, could barely even breathe.

'It would be such a pity to slip and fall,' came Maltraver's voice, his breath against her neck. 'This warm little body, this clever little brain, all splattered. A nasty mess.' She struggled and fought, but he pulled her painfully tight against him, his flaccid mouth seeking hers. She tried to turn her face away, the smell of his sweat making her retch, then felt his erection and recoiled in shock. She drove her shoe heel viciously into his ankle, making him grunt in pain, yet still he kept his hold on her. She raised her right hand to slap him but he grabbed it with his left, twisting her arm brutally behind her back.

'Not this time, Evelyn.'

She tried to wrestle her right arm free, but he pinned it to her side, shoving her back against the parapet till she was half lying across it, wedged into an embrasure, her head and shoulders suspended over the vortex of empty air. As she writhed, she caught a glimpse of the world beneath her turned upside down, the ground rushing up to meet her. With her left hand, she felt in her pocket for her crumpled gloves, pulled one out, groped the rough stone of the parapet at her back, found a notch and pushed it through.

'She's dropped her glove,' said Deverell-Drummond a moment later, looking over the drop. 'Naughty girl.'

'What does that matter?' said Maltraver, lifting his mouth from Evie's throat.

'I think it might,' Deverell-Drummond drawled. 'Someone's picked it up. He's looking up here.'

'Who is it?' snarled Maltraver between clenched teeth, his spittle splattering Evie's face.

'I'm not sure,' Deverell-Drummond reflected, his eyes narrowed against the light, 'but he's seen us. He's rather dashing.'

'You idiot, DD!' Maltraver wheeled to face the parapet, letting Evie go so abruptly she fell against the stonework, banging the side of her head.

'Ah, mea culpa,' said Deverell-Drummond, producing a monocle from his breast pocket with a flourish and peering through it. 'I think we both know him.'

Following his gaze, Maltraver exploded into expletives.

Evie pulled herself upright, wiping her face and straightening her clothes. She felt her arm gingerly as she too stared over the edge.

Down in the square the man in the charcoal suit was staring up at them, one arm lifted to screen his eyes from the sun as he tried to make out what was happening on top of the tower. The student beside him tried to urge him away, grasping his sleeve. The man shook the student off, shouted something indistinct and dashed forwards, disappearing from view beneath the shadow of the tower.

'It's Mr Penhallow,' Evie wheezed, trying to catch her breath. 'He seems annoyed.' Her whole body trembled with shock, but she saw the dread in Maltraver's face and permitted herself a grim smile of triumph.

'You bitch!' said Maltraver.

She laughed in his face. 'Time to let me go.'

He gave her a look of sour loathing. 'It was just a game, Miss Winstanley. High spirits and all that.'

'A game?' She put a world of contempt into that word, glaring savagely at him till he dropped his eyes and backed away. She wouldn't give him the satisfaction of seeing how much he'd succeeded in terrifying her. 'At all events, the game is over, *Lord* Maltraver.' She snatched up her handbag from where it lay on the leads. Her hands and knees still shook, but the rush of adrenalin carried her through. She turned to Zouch. 'Will you open the door and show me the way out of here?' He nodded, followed her to the door, unbolted it and stood aside to let her pass.

'Penhallow's here to see me,' said Maltraver to Zouch. 'Bellamy's brought him. Bring him up here with you. Don't let Postlethwaite or his flunkeys see.'

Evie plunged down the tower stairs, her legs as wobbly as a newborn lamb's. The downward spiral seemed to pitch her forwards, and at one point she missed her footing and almost fell headlong. Zouch tried to hold her steady, putting his hand under her elbow, but she shoved him away.

The pounding of fists against wood echoed up through the stairwell.

One floor from the ground, she stopped and leant against the wall, breathless and panting. 'Mr Penhallow seems rather agitated,' she gasped, seized with a mad desire to laugh. 'I believe he's trying to break the door down.'

'He'll attract attention,' muttered Zouch. 'We need to hurry.'

But Evie didn't move. Instead, she considered Zouch. His eyes slid away, avoiding hers.

'So it was you,' she said, 'who told Maltraver I was here.'

Zouch seemed to fold in on himself. 'You don't know what they're like. What they'll do if you make them angry.'

'What will they do?'

Zouch shook his head wordlessly. His face shone with sweat.

'Tell me about Theodore Windle – Teddy. He was your friend, wasn't he? What happened to him?'

'None of your bloody business,' said Zouch in a low voice.

'I heard Maltraver taunting you, at the tavern.'

Zouch's eyes shut tight.

'You can't trust Maltraver.'

'And you're saying I can trust you? It's no affair of yours.'

Evie could see he would say no more. She turned and went down the last few steps. From the other side of an oak door set deep into the wall came a flurry of yells and hammering from Aubrey Penhallow.

The door shuddered violently as Penhallow threw himself against it.

'He's a madman,' said Zouch in alarm. 'The lock will give way.'

Evie fumbled with the iron bolt. It was stiff, and rust came off on her fingers, but at last she raised it. The door flew inwards and Aubrey Penhallow bounded in. Evie was almost struck by the door and had to jump backwards as he grabbed Zouch by the lapels, shouting, 'What have they done with her?'

He started as he caught sight of Evie in the shadows behind the doorway and released his hold on the spluttering Zouch. She saw the shock in his eyes as he took in her appearance. She began to straighten her clothes and pushed back her dishevelled hair, trying to regain her composure.

'What happened up there?' demanded Penhallow. He looked almost devilish – pale, muscles taut, fists clenched.

Behind him, the student who'd brought him to the tower gave a hapless shrug and slunk discreetly away.

'Did Maltraver threaten you? Did he *hurt* you?'

'He . . . I'm all right. Now.'

His eyebrows met in disbelief. He searched her face.

'Maltraver wants me to invite you up,' said Zouch.

'He can wait,' snapped Penhallow.

Zouch backed away from the menace in Penhallow's face, pleading, 'It wasn't me.'

Penhallow turned back to Evie. 'Come away from them.'

She stood frozen. He put out his hand, but she shrank back, shaking her head. He raised his other hand; it held her glove.

'Please,' he said in a gentler tone.

Pulling herself together, Evie brushed past him, heading for the arched opening that led back into the front quad. Mr Penhallow, careful not to touch her, fell into step beside her.

'Are you sure you're all right?'

'Yes,' she said impatiently, feeling a trickle of warm blood on her chin and wiping it away with her hand.

'What did Maltraver do to you?'

'He called it a game. The Sons of Dionysus at play.'

She caught the flash of raw fury in his eyes.

'My glove, if you please.' She held out her hand imperiously and he laid her lace glove – now crumpled, stained and torn – in her palm.

'Have you ever heard of the circle of shadows, Mr Penhallow?' she asked suddenly, trying to catch him unawares.

His expression was one of blank incomprehension. 'What is it?'

'It's ... a mystery. But I'm fairly certain of one thing – that there's a connection between the circle of shadows and two women who were in service at Maltraver Towers: Sukey Huxley and Janet Rae.'

Behind the impassive features, she thought she saw his jaw tighten, his pupils narrow, but the reaction – if it was one – was fleeting. When he spoke, his voice was cool and self-possessed, and the enigmatic look was back on his face.

'You're brave, Miss Winstanley,' he said. 'That much is obvious. But allow me to warn you: don't go near Lord Maltraver again, or any of his friends. They ... have no scruples.'

'No scruples? *You* tell me that? *You* who pursued a poor vulnerable servant woman for your own base gratification?' The tide of her own emotions took her aback.

He tried to speak, but Evie reacted like an outraged Amazon queen, her words spilling out in a torrent. 'You tell me that I should avoid Maltraver, that he's an immoral man – so why then are you seeking him out?'

He drew himself up stiffly. 'I offered to bring Lord Maltraver and his friends some financial advice – racing tips – in return for a consideration. It's a matter of business.'

'Oh, business!' she jeered. 'And that justifies everything.' They were nearly at the lodge. Postlethwaite had spotted Evie and his expression became scandalised.

Evie turned back to Penhallow, who stood grim-faced and silent. 'I can't make you out, Mr Penhallow,' she said, 'or understand why you would shake the hand of a man like Maltraver, having warned me against him. But one thing I see clearly: either you are as base as he is or you are weak, and a coward to boot.'

All the colour blanched out of Penhallow's face. He opened his mouth as though to say something more, closed it again, then turned on his heel towards the shadow of the tower where Zouch was waiting.

CHAPTER
Twenty-Five

E VIE SPED ALONG Broad Street, dodging passing pedestrians, feet pounding the pavement, hair flying. She arrived at her rendezvous with Marcus Ellingham nearly an hour after the appointed time, expecting him to have given up and left, but he was sitting patiently on the steps of the Martyrs' Memorial on St Giles'.

He sprang to his feet. 'Evelyn, your face! How did that—? I was worried something had happened to you.'

'Something did,' she said grimly.

Marcus spread out a handkerchief on the step beside him.

'What's that for?'

'For you to sit on, so your clothes don't get dusty.'

A sudden laugh escaped her at the ridiculousness of the gesture. 'Marcus, have you *seen* the state of my clothes?'

He blinked. 'You do look a little . . . rumpled,' he admitted.

She put a hand to her hair, assessing its tangled disorder, then took a mirror from her handbag and discovered smears of dirt and dust on her face, bruising to her cheek, and blood from her torn lip staining her chin. The hem of her skirt was also torn.

'I look a ruffian.' She felt deflated. In her mind, she'd been a flashing-eyed warrior queen confronting Aubrey Penhallow, but on appraising her chaotic, battered and wan-faced reflection, she realised she looked nothing of the sort. And Harriet was hardly likely to believe she'd got into such a condition while reading in the Bodleian. She wiped at the blood and dirt with her handkerchief.

'I brought you some refreshments.' Marcus indicated a paper bag at his side. 'In case you didn't get time for lunch.'

She realised she'd eaten nothing since leaving the cafe that morning and investigated the contents of the bag with interest. 'Chocolate! Oh, excellent. Pastries and ices.'

'They're from Boul's on Cornmarket. They should be good. Though the ices are a little melted.'

She took a pastry filled with crème pâtissière and bit into it tentatively. A delighted expression came over her face. 'It's really good. I haven't had one like this since Paris.'

He beamed at her pleasure. 'The chef at Boul's is French.'

'So much better than currant buns and cress sandwiches.' She found herself, to her surprise, gurgling with laughter – *a reaction to stress*, she reasoned. She was back on solid ground. She'd escaped from Maltraver and his crew, and faced down Penhallow.

'Will you tell me what happened?' he asked as Evie finished her cake and licked the last of the creamy mixture from her fingers.

She recounted her adventures, starting with her hostile reception from Professor Lorimer and ending with her escape from the Sons of Dionysus.

Marcus listened, aghast. When she came to her struggle with Maltraver, he sprang up, face dark with rage. 'I'll make that rat pay for daring to lay a finger on you!'

'It's all right, Marcus,' she said, seeing him look round wildly, as though he intended to march on Talbot College and wring Maltraver's neck. 'I managed to extricate myself. Sit down, please. People are looking.'

He slumped down. 'It's my fault,' he gasped, his head in his hands. 'I didn't take the danger seriously enough.' He continued with a touch of bitterness: 'It was a lucky chance that Penhallow arrived. I shouldn't have let you go without me.'

'I didn't need Aubrey Penhallow to rescue me,' she said tartly. 'I'd seen him there – that's why I dropped the glove. And it was my choice to see Lorimer alone.'

'Of course.' He bit his lip. 'Forgive me. I shouldn't presume.'

She turned her attention back to her untamed curtain of hair. Most of her hairpins had gone, so she twisted the strands up into a long plait, tying it as best she could.

'You seem so calm,' he said, watching her wrestle with her hair.

'Not really. It's my way of coping, I suppose.' She considered her own response for a moment. 'If I thought about it . . . well, I'd rather not think about it, that's all. Maybe later, when all this is over and there's time.'

'You won't stop, will you?'

She didn't reply. The truth was that she couldn't stop, not with the kuroskato still etched into Grace's arm. Not with the questions she had about her father – bigger questions now, since her meeting with Lorimer – remaining unanswered. But she didn't want to explain all this to Marcus; it was too personal, too painful.

He must have seen her resolve, because he didn't waste time in trying to change her mind, instead saying quietly, 'Will you let me come with you next time? So you don't face danger alone?'

'Why, yes, it will be good to have a friend at my side.'

'Your friend.' His mouth twisted. 'I hope I'm that to you, at least.'

'Of course,' she said, a little uncertain where the conversation might be leading.

A moment later, he spoke in his usual straightforward way. 'What are your plans now? How can I help?'

'My first problem is what to say to Harriet to explain the bruises.' She took out her hat, surveyed its crumpled and misshapen state with dissatisfaction, and endeavoured to pull it back into some sort of respectable order. 'I'll tell her I slipped on a staircase. All that polished wood in the Bodleian.'

Marcus started to say something more, but Evie glanced at her wristwatch.

'Oh, my! I have to go. If Harriet doesn't see me walking sedately out of the front door of the Bodleian at the appointed time, she'll smell a rat.'

'Can I walk you there?'

Evie pulled on her hat, examining her reflection in her hand mirror. 'Walking with young men is exactly the kind of unsuitable pastime Harriet is supposed to be guarding me against.' She saw his face fall. 'She might make an exception if she came to know you.'

'Can I see you tomorrow?' Marcus asked, as she gathered up her belongings.

'For what?' She frowned as she surveyed her ruined gloves.

'We could have lunch, compare notes. Or take a picnic on a punt.'

She scrabbled in her bag for another hairpin to secure her hat, reflecting on her best course of action. 'A trip on the river? An excellent idea. Don't bother about a picnic, though. We'll have work to do.'

Twenty-Six

S he opens the door and steps out onto the top of the tower.
Above her, a sliver of new moon, the only light in the velvet night sky.

Below her, all the land is under water. Oval objects drift with the tide. One floats near her and she makes it out — a livid face, suffused with blood. It turns towards her. Dead eyes open. The dead mouth speaks.

'Save us. Save yourself.'

She runs to the door. It's locked.

Somewhere close by, a woman screams.

Then a man's voice, full of warmth and darkness. 'This is why we're here.'

Slowly, she turns. Penhallow is there, silver and black in the moonlight. He holds out his hand and in his palm is the kuroskato.

'There's nothing to fear.'

~

'Evie?'

A fumbling sound in the darkness. A thud as something fell to the floor. Harriet lit the lamp and its glow chased Evie's dream back into the shadowy corners of the room.

'What's the matter?' said Harriet. 'I heard you scream.'

'A . . . dream.'

'I'll leave the lamp on, shall I?'

'Thank you.' Evie pressed trembling palms to her cheeks, stifling her whimpers with the blankets.

~

Over breakfast in the hotel, Evie unfolded the letter from Grace that had arrived that morning, propping it against the coffeepot.

'What does she say?' asked Harriet as she poured herself tea.

Evie leant her chin on her cupped hands, scanning the lines written in Grace's even, rounded hand. 'All is well,' she announced. 'Maman has written from France. She's still with Grand-père, but he's convalescing and she hopes to return home in a few days.'

'Oh, thank God!' breathed Harriet.

'Yes, it's excellent news. Grace says D'Artagnan's missing me and Maman. He sulks a lot, insists on sleeping on Grace's bed and won't play with his toys, or even eat unless Grace feeds him his favourite meals by hand—'

'Never mind the dog,' interrupted Harriet. 'What about Grace?'

Between sips of coffee, Evie read on. 'She seems absolutely recovered, writes that she's smothered in attention. She's never alone; by day Mary is constantly with her, and in the evenings Pel is there. They play cards and board games, and walk D'Artagnan together. She's sleeping really well. She means to go to a poetry recital of the Romantics in Kensington tonight.' Evie frowned a little till she came to the next line, 'Ah, but Pel will go with her.'

'He's a good brother to you both,' observed Harriet, unfolding her napkin and drawing a plate of scrambled eggs towards her. 'Will they perform Shelley?'

'I don't think so. Grace says it's an evening of Coleridge, Wordsworth and Keats.'

With the daylight and Grace's letter, the horrors of the previous day and her broken sleep had retreated. She selected some toast from the rack and began to butter it liberally, her mind on her next move.

Harriet, too, had received a letter, which she perused while nibbling a corner of toast. She gave an exclamation of delight. 'It's from Maude Washington. She's come to visit a friend of hers in Oxford . . .' She screwed up her eyes, trying to make out the name.

'Diana Gordon-Stukes,' she said at last. 'They're inviting me to dinner.'

'How lovely,' said Evie absently. She considered the selection of pots of jam laid out, choosing the raspberry.

'I don't think I should leave you on your own.' Harriet frowned as she folded away the letter.

'Nonsense.' Evie waved her toast. 'I'll be perfectly all right.'

'Your mother would disapprove.' Harriet looked uncomfortable.

'Only if we tell her.' Evie smiled coaxingly.

'You'll come back here when you've finished your studies?'

'Straight back here,' Evie assured her. 'I'll dine at the hotel in solitary splendour. They know us now and will give me a quiet table. So, you see, you really don't need to hurry back.'

~

The weather was warm for early May, with puffy clouds under a blue sky. A small crowd gathered at Magdalen Bridge, waiting to embark on the flotilla of punts, rowing boats and canoes that bobbed on the water. Evie couldn't help but notice that everyone but herself was kitted out for a day of pleasure on the river. Most of the women wore white linen or muslin, some carried flimsy cotton or lace parasols and all had wide sun hats, trimmed with artificial flowers and bunches of ribbons, to shield their tender complexions. Evie, by contrast, wore clothes selected to convince Harriet she was bound for a day in the library: a demure skirt, blouse, woollen cardigan and her brown velvet hat, all serviceable rather than decorative.

She leant over the parapet of the bridge and spotted Marcus Ellingham in a flat-bottomed punt, waving to catch her attention. He at least was looking the part, in white flannel trousers, navy jacket and a straw boater. She went down the cobbled slope to the water's edge, dodged past the youths who were giving a hand to the less agile and jumped lightly from one boat to the next till she reached Marcus. He guided her into the punt, arranging green- and white-striped cushions for her comfort. She gathered he meant to carry out the traditional manly role, leaving her to recline in picturesque indolence.

'Which way?' he said. 'Up or d-down?'

Most of the punts were heading downstream, passing under the shadow of the bridge. 'Up, if you please.'

She settled herself among the cushions, tilting her hat-brim to keep the sun's glare from her eyes. As they drew away, she glanced back at the stone arches of Magdalen Bridge and saw a well-built, thickset man in a brown suit in the place she had occupied moments before, standing a little apart from the knot of spectators, arms propped against the parapet. She couldn't make out his features, which were shaded by a wide-brimmed hat, but she saw his head tilt to follow the movement of their punt. Then he pushed back his hat and she glimpsed his eyes – strangely colourless, yet opaque, like frosted glass pebbles. They were fixed on her.

Evie caught her breath.

Marcus, his back to the bridge as he pulled into his stroke, looked questioningly at her. 'What's up?'

'There's someone on the bridge. I think I know him. Turn around, carefully so he doesn't see you looking.'

Making a show of struggling with the pole, as if it had stuck in the riverbed, Marcus shot a glance back over his shoulder.

'Who?'

Evie looked again. The man had vanished.

'Never mind. I may have been mistaken.' Though she didn't think she had.

Dappled sunlight filtered through the trees and danced over the surface. It was cooler down here on the water, where a chill pervaded the air, and Evie huddled herself in her cardigan. Marcus proved to be dexterous – he must have punted many times as a student – and the boat slid smoothly through the water.

Once out of sight of the watchers, Evie scrambled round and knelt on her seat, facing forwards to scan the tree-lined banks ahead on either side of the winding river.

'Are there no buildings near the Cherwell?' she asked.

'Not once you're past Magdalen Bridge. It's all parkland, trees and playing fields. What are you looking for?'

'A building where Janet Rae's body might have been stored. She was murdered sometime during the night after the Sons of Dionysus met. Agreed?'

'Agreed.'

'So, whoever killed her needed a place to carry out the ritual. You can't just lug a body – unconscious or dead – through the street. Her killers needed a place where they wouldn't be disturbed, where no one would hear if she ... cried out.' Evie stumbled on the last words, shivering in spite of the warmth. She forced herself to be dispassionate. 'Then, how did she actually die? Her body looked as though she'd drowned. The police seem to agree. But even if that's what happened, she may not have drowned in the Cherwell.'

'You mean she could have been killed somewhere else, then brought to the river?'

'Exactly.'

'But where?'

She said, unhesitating: 'Talbot College.'

Marcus's eyes widened. For the first time, he seemed to doubt her logic. 'But the college is full of people.'

'They would need access to a secluded place.' Evie recalled the iron key in Zouch's hand.

'And Talbot's nowhere near the Cherwell. Nor the Isis.'

'The Isis?'

'It's what people in Oxford call the Thames.'

'Oh. At all events, it makes no odds, because even if Talbot College stood right beside the Cherwell or the Isis, if someone threw Janet into the water hard by the college, alive or dead, she would have floated downstream, not up. Yet upstream is where we found her.'

'You've thought it all through,' he said, frank admiration in his eyes. He stopped punting, letting the boat float slowly through trailing willows.

'Not really.' She shrugged her shoulders. 'Because what I think makes no sense.'

She stood up. 'Let me take a turn. I've never tried before.'

As they swapped places, the punt wobbled. Marcus caught her sleeve to keep her from falling in, bringing them close for a moment, before she drew away.

Despite rapid instruction from Marcus in the essentials of punting, it was harder than it looked. The pole was cumbersome and heavy. Damp from the wood penetrated the thin material of her gloves. The unaccustomed movements made the muscles in her arms and hands ache. She was, alas, no better on a punt than she was on a horse. Curiosity satisfied, she was relieved to relinquish the pole again to Marcus.

Thereafter, they made much better time. Eventually they came to where a fallen willow trunk stretched part-way across the river.

'This is where I found her,' said Evie.

Marcus lifted the pole upright and drove it deep into the river mud. Evie examined the site. The grass had been trodden down and streaks of mud showed where Penhallow and the fisher boys had heaved the weight of Janet's corpse. A scrap of dark cloth caught on a twig came from the dress Janet had worn. Nothing else seemed to have been disturbed.

They were alone on this stretch of the river. Insects hovered on the water, going about their business. Dragonflies circled Evie's head, now skimming low over the surface, now dancing out of sight through the undergrowth. A flash of blue and orange darted across the river, disappearing into the trees on the opposite bank – a kingfisher.

Evie twisted round, intending to tell Marcus they'd better go back, but she paused, frowning, lifting a hand to her eyes. Something was smeared over a patch of overhanging willow leaves, glistening as it caught the light. Rolling up her sleeves, she sent the punt rocking perilously as she reached out for the trailing willows.

She brought her hands back and found that her palms were coated in a sticky substance, viscous and slimy. Turning them over, she saw something small and flat stuck to the back of her hand, semi-opaque and shot through with a shimmer of bronze-green. She tried to pick it up using her thumb and forefinger, but it slid from her grip, tumbled into the river, and sank slowly beneath the surface. With a cry of annoyance, she plunged her arms up to the elbows in the water.

'What is it?' demanded Marcus.

She ignored him, groping around for the object in the murk and waterweeds. Suddenly she gasped, snatching back her arms. 'There's something down there! A shadow. It's moving.'

Marcus dropped down beside her, keeping one hand on the pole. The boat began to drift. 'I don't see anything,' he said after a moment. He turned to Evie. 'A fish?'

Her bare wet arms gripped the side of the boat. She was shuddering. 'I don't think so. Something much bigger than a river fish. I just caught a glimpse underneath the weeds.'

She could make out only shimmering reflections of the willows, the sky overhead, the wavering outline of the flat-bottomed boat and their own two forms – an inversion of the world above, rippling in ephemeral lines. The shadow under the water must have been a trick of the light and the water. 'I must have been mistaken,' she mumbled, mortified at her own excess of imagination.

'Hardly surprising that you'd be nervous, here in this spot. We could carry on upriver? We'd have to drag the punt over the rollers when we get to the Upper Cherwell.'

'I don't believe her body came from further upriver. Let's explore the lower reaches.'

Marcus tried to tug the pole. 'It's stuck here,' he muttered, and as he twisted it a stream of dark liquid rose to the surface, along with a trail of bubbles. A rank, musky smell accompanied the effervescence. They coughed and retched.

Marcus wrenched the pole free, sending the punt swinging away, out into the middle of the river. 'That was disgusting,' he observed when he'd brought the punt some distance downstream. 'Some blighters throw their rubbish into the river—'

'Didn't you recognise the smell?' Evie sat hunched up in the prow of the boat, her hand across her nose and mouth.

'Eh, something horrible, but—'

'After the seance, the whole library reeked of it, where the water had come through the ceiling. The same smell was in the bathroom above.'

'I believe you're right. Do you want us to go back and search?'

'No.' She shook her head. 'It may be cowardly, but there's no way of finding what might be down there, short of swimming.'

'Do you want me to—'

'No,' she said quickly. 'Let's get away from here.'

'Whatever you say, Captain.' Marcus spoke lightly, but he looked relieved.

For a time, neither spoke. Marcus seemed content simply to watch Evie from beneath his lashes as he punted, while Evie's mind worked busily at possible links between the seance at Maltraver Towers and the Cherwell in Oxford. One obvious link was the thing she'd seen so briefly on the willow leaves, which she was almost certain was a scale like the one they'd found in the bathtub . . . from an unknown species. The other connection was even more obvious, for it was all around her: water – life-giving and lethal, pouring, dripping, swirling and ever-changing, like the fluctuating heart of the kuroskato. She exhaled slowly, resting her forearms along the gunnels, letting the sun warm them and dry the drops of river water on her skin. Was she getting any closer to a possible answer? Her mind couldn't make sense of it – too disturbing, too unreal. Her dream swam back into her mind: Penhallow, the kuroskato in his hand. *This is why we're here.*

She started to speak, then stopped herself. What if she was wrong – wildly, madly wrong? Even Marcus would think she'd lost her mind.

They passed Magdalen Bridge and the Botanic Gardens, finally reaching the water meadows of Christ Church, and Evie's mind came back to her original purpose – to discover how Janet's body might have been brought down to the river unseen. The trees and tangled undergrowth bordering the water meadows would offer possibilities, at least under cover of darkness.

As they approached the spot where the Cherwell met the Isis, the current grew stronger. They passed a small island, several buildings, including warehouses, and a wharf that came to the water's edge, close to where the stone arches of Folly Bridge spanned the Isis.

'I wonder,' said Evie, scanning the cluster of buildings. 'Could Janet have been hidden somewhere nearby? But that leaves the problem of how her body travelled *up* the Cherwell from this spot, against the current, without being caught in the weeds. Unless someone rowed her in a boat – surely not a punt? Yet why go to the trouble of taking her far up the river before throwing her in? It makes no sense. If I was in this place at night, with a murdered woman on my hands and in a hurry to dispose of her, I would weigh her body down and cast her off the bridge so that she went to the bottom of the river and wouldn't be found.'

'If you ever turn to crime yourself, Evelyn, you would surely have a steady head for it.'

Evie raised a sardonic eyebrow.

'An underground river called the Trill Mill Stream emerges somewhere about here,' said Marcus, bending into his stroke to give a wide birth to a boatful of raucous tourists. 'It's said that students sometimes row along it as a dare, though the pastime is strictly forbidden.'

'Does it pass near Talbot College?' she asked as she studied the bank, elbows propped on the gunnel.

He grinned. 'Not very near, though the centre of Oxford is quite small. Talbot College is less than ten minutes' walk from this spot. The Trill Mill goes through the western part of Oxford, an area that once went by the name of Paradise, though in truth it's a poor area of narrow streets. Cholera was once rife there. That's why the tunnel was built, to close off the river, which was full of filth, and send it underground.'

They came to the foot of Folly Bridge.

'This is far enough, I think,' said Evie.

'We could head a little way back up the Cherwell,' suggested Marcus, pushing the pole away from the boat, propelling them into a slow graceful arc, 'and take some refreshment as an incentive to thought?'

'We'd have to leave the boat,' she reminded him. 'And besides, we don't have a picnic.'

'Um ... as a matter of fact, we do.' He pointed out a hamper stowed under her seat. 'It's from Boul's. I got them to include the chocolates you liked.'

In spite of her distraction, she laughed. 'What could be more idyllic?'

They went a little way back up the Cherwell, tied the punt to overhanging branches and retrieved the hamper. Evie brought out sandwiches, slices of savoury pie and a flask of lemonade and shared them out. She cooed in delight as a mother duck swam past, followed in close formation by her line of ducklings, and leant over the side, throwing crumbs to lure them closer.

'So you do like some girlish things?' said Marcus. 'It's not all murders and dark secrets.'

'Is it *girlish* to love ducklings? Look how their little heads wobble as they try to keep up. There's no need to come over all *manly*, Marcus. Surely you love them, too?'

'The ducklings?' He lowered his eyes. 'Yes.'

But already Evie's train of thought had moved on. 'The man on Magdalen Bridge.'

'You thought you knew him?'

'I do. His name's Robert Wenless.'

'Wenless!' Marcus sat bolt upright, making the boat rock wildly. The ripples scattered the ducklings and their mother led them away, quacking in protest.

'I see you do know him.'

'Only by reputation.'

'And that reputation . . .?' Her eyes searched his troubled face.

'People in occult circles say Wenless has gone beyond the theory, that he experiments with the dark arts. I don't know exactly what he's done; it's hard to find anyone who'll agree to be interviewed about him. People who've encountered him seem . . . frightened. I've tried to interview him for the *Ghost Hunter*, but he ignores my requests. I don't know what he's doing here in Oxford, but I don't like it.'

'He's not a former student?'

'An Oxford man? I don't believe so.'

'So no connection with the Sons of Dionysus, or Talbot College?'

'Not that I've heard. How do you know of him?'

'The day my father bought the collection of occult books in Harrogate, Robert Wenless appeared, too late to bid for the books. He knew my father had them. I wonder . . .'

'You think he might have been the dastard who attacked you in your father's study?'

Evie nodded, but her mind had gone further back, to that day at Harrogate – her father's glee, the way his face had changed when he saw Wenless, how his hands had tightened on the book he held. 'Papa wouldn't tell me much, but I could see he distrusted Wenless. Could he be mixed up in this circle of shadows business?'

'If he is, Evie, if there's even the remotest possibility of such a thing, I urge you, in all sincerity, to give this up. He's a dangerous man. I couldn't bear it if anything happened to you.' Shivering, he drew close and took her hands. His own were shaking and his breathing came ragged and fast. Anguish swam in his eyes.

At last she understood the thing she'd been trying not to understand. *He really does care for me. And he's afraid . . .*

'I can't do that, Marcus,' she said, gently withdrawing her hands. 'It's Grace. She's marked by the kuroskato. I have to follow this through.'

'Grace, yes.' He hung his head. 'But you will let me help you?'

'You already have. You saved Grace's life in the Sithwater. I'll never forget.'

'Anyone would have done the same,' he murmured, evidently embarrassed. Then, with a visible effort, he pulled himself together and brightened. 'But there's something else I can do for you. A surprise.'

'A surprise? Something even better than the chocolates?'

Marcus brought out a canvas bag that had been stowed behind the basket and reached inside. 'Much better,' he said, and laid a book upon her lap.

Evie looked at it in astonishment. 'The book on the history of Talbot College!' she exclaimed. 'How did you get it?'

'I bluffed my way into Talbot this morning. Spun the junior porter a yarn, and once I was in I sidled off to the library.'

'I made such a mull of it,' she said, slightly crestfallen, 'when I attempted the same thing.'

'No fault of yours,' he assured her. 'It's so much easier for a man to creep in unnoticed. I had brought my gown to Oxford, in case I attended any college social events.'

'But why did they let you borrow this? It's a reference book.'

'An unofficial loan,' Marcus admitted. 'I thought you'd want to read it for yourself.'

'You stole it. Very resourceful. I fear this investigation is leading you into a life of crime.'

'Yes.' The dimples in his chin deepened mischievously. 'And I'm thoroughly enjoying it.'

She laughed, an infectious sound, and he joined in as she untied the ribbons binding the cover and their heads bent together over the book.

She looked up to find Marcus's gaze fixed on her with an intensity that startled her, as though she was the centre of the world. No one had ever looked at her like that before. He stretched out a hand, as though to touch her cheek, then froze. Something shifted between them, a disturbance in the air. Her heart began to beat fast. She had a conviction that he wanted to kiss her. She'd never been kissed – not like that. Did she want this? She heard Grace's voice saying, 'Just because you care nothing about finding a man to love you and desire you and hold you in his arms . . .'

Slowly Evie leant forward and their lips met. She acted impulsively, out of curiosity and to blot out the memory of Maltraver's brutal assault, rather than from desire, yet she was surprised at her own reaction to the sensation of Marcus's mouth on hers

– warm, sweet, tender. She felt him quiver with delight. 'Evelyn,' he murmured unsteadily, reaching up to stroke her hair, 'you are—'

At that moment, Evie heard the splash of oars and voices ringing across the water, heralding the approach of a boatload of tourists, and she drew awkwardly away. She lowered her gaze to the book and kept it there. *What on earth am I doing? No complications! This isn't the moment. Not now. Not yet.* With one hand she turned over the pages while crumbling cubes of bread with the other, tossing them into the water for the delectation of a throng of quacking and diving mallards that had gathered around the boat. When she raised her eyes again, minutes later, Marcus was giving all his attention to the waterfowl, trying to tempt over several coots that were circling a respectful distance from the ducks. From where she sat, only the back of his neck and part of one ear were visible, all bathed in scarlet.

The next moment, the romantic aspirations of Mr Ellingham slipped completely from Evie's mind as she sat bolt upright, letting a salmon-and-cucumber sandwich fall to the bottom of the boat.

'Listen to this,' she said, pointed to a passage in the book, and read aloud:

'In forbidden tomes, Dr Actaeon Fell discovered the existence of a secret occult sect called the Circle of Shadows.'

'Could this be what we're looking for?' he asked, embarrassment fading in the pull of the investigation.

'I truly think so,' she said, and read on:

'It became Actaeon Fell's ambition to revive the sect. He gathered around him eight like-minded fellows of the college, each of them so steeped in evil, so abandoned to every Christian or moral principle as to be prepared to embrace the old ways of those ungodly pagan priests, the Druids. One of these men was the warden of the college, Thomas Alderbury, a man utterly mired in every conceivable form of

*corruption. With the connivance of Alderbury, Fell fashioned a cham-
ber beneath Talbot College wherein occult dark arts could be practised
in secret. Fell became a master adept, Magister of the new Circle of
Shadows. For thirteen years, these nine men carried out their evil rituals under the aegis and protection of the college. It was whispered that
they even made sacrifices to an ancient water demon in a blasphemous
attempt to harness its powers.*

*At last, some of the college servants plucked up the courage to report
the doings of the Circle of Shadows to the Church and State authorities.
Warned of his impending arrest, Actaeon Fell disappeared, along with
one other. No trace of them was ever found. Alderbury and six others
were arrested, imprisoned and put on trial in circumstances of the great-
est secrecy to avoid the contagion of Fell's heresy spreading throughout
Oxford. Alderbury and two of his deputies were declared heretics,
banned for eternity from the Kingdom of Heaven and burnt alive for
their heinous crimes. The remaining four, whose family connections and
elevated social positions made it impolitic to execute them, were imprisoned in solitary confinement for the remainder of their lives.'*

Evie fell silent, the book resting on her knees, a brooding look on
her face.

Marcus gave a low whistle. 'So, the circle of shadows did exist,
and flourished at the heart of Talbot College.'

Evie's brow furrowed in thought.

'But surely,' said Marcus, 'that can't have happened now. I mean,
for one thing, and I know it's in poor taste to talk about it, but
Janet Rae wasn't eaten by a monster. Dash it, you yourself found
her body.'

'An elemental is a metaphysical being. According to Paracelsus
and other authorities on the occult, it sucks the life force of its
victims, leaving the physical body intact.' She spoke absently, her
mind running on ahead.

'Oh,' said Marcus slowly. 'That sounds . . . appalling.'

Suddenly, Evie leapt up, snatched her hat and gloves and jumped
from the punt, sending it lurching. She scrambled up the riverbank, tugging impatiently at her skirt as it caught on brambles.

'Where are you going?' cried Marcus. 'Wait for me!'

'You need to take the boat back. I can't wait, I'm sorry. There's something I need to check.'

She took off in the direction of the Botanic Gardens.

Marcus shouted, 'What about the book?'

'You can return it,' she called back. 'I don't need it anymore.'

Twenty-Seven

E VIE SAT IN Duke Humfrey's Library, the oldest reading room of the Bodleian. At any other time, she would have revelled in her surroundings – the painted ceiling; ornate, carved beams; the stacks of shelving reaching high overhead, crammed with the knowledge of centuries – but today she'd no leisure to admire it all. For nearly three hours, she'd been investigating beliefs, myths and legends of the ancient Britons. On the table before her was a book entitled *A Mythology of Elemental Spirits of Fire and Water, Earth and Air*. Bound in black leather, it contained delicately coloured full-page illustrative plates. The frontispiece gave the publication date as 1873 but stated it was a copy of an older volume, long since lost. The book lay open at an entry that read:

Of all the legends of the water elementals associated with the British Isles, the most terrifying is that of the afanc, one of the immortals known and worshipped in ancient times. It is not certain whether there was one afanc or many. It was said to roam the waters, making its lairs in ancient wells, remote lakes, underground seas and rivers. The afanc preys on the unwary, dragging them down to the watery depths, drowning and devouring them. While the physical form of the afanc is the stuff of nightmares, it is more than a monster, for like all the immortals it has an invisible, metaphysical dimension as well as a visible, physical one. The afanc forms a living link to the realm of the invisible.

One might suppose that all rational people would give the afanc a wide berth, but over the centuries there have been a few hardy souls, adepts of ancient magic, who have attempted to compel the afanc by means of feeding its devilish appetite and, when it is sated, speaking spells of terrible power to bind it. By such unhal-lowed means, the most skilled adepts may strive to take the afanc's powers for their own and thereby make themselves masters of magic.

Beside the text were two illustrations, the first of which was labelled, 'The metaphysical dimension of the water elemental or afanc.' It depicted a spiralling, whirling pattern, as shimmering and constantly shifting as the water it represented. The second illustration was called, 'The physical dimension of the water elemental or afanc.' Someone had tried to obliterate this picture with diagonal pen lines, scored deep into the paper. Evie angled the page towards the glow from the desk lamp and peered closely. Then she caught her breath, for beneath the defacing pen marks, she made out something that resembled the outline of a great gaping mouth.

She laid down the book and sat still, chewing on her thumb, half closing her eyes. Eventually she stirred, drawing towards her a sheet of paper and a pencil, and began to write.

Dear Professor Lorimer,

I believe I'm drawing closer to the secret of Talbot College. If I'm right, it concerns the legend of the afanc. If you will not speak with me, I will have to take my discoveries elsewhere, and possibly reveal your own part in all this. I think you will agree that such revelations, should they come to light, would damage the reputation of the college – and your own.

Yours sincerely,

Evelyn Winstanley

It is blackmail, she admitted to herself as she folded the sheet, slipped it in an envelope and sealed it. *But if it works . . .*

~

Evie emerged from the Bodleian just as twilight fell. The multiple openings off the main courtyard – doors, windows and archways – seemed aware of her presence, like watchful eyes. As she crossed the space, she cast uneasy glances behind her.

A short walk brought her to the lodge of Talbot College. Bracing her shoulders, she approached the window. Once more, Postlethwaite was presiding. The look he gave her was far from friendly. She disregarded it.

'Will you give this note to Professor Lorimer?'

His mouth pursed in disapproval. For a moment, she thought he might refuse, but he wordlessly extended his hand and almost snatched the note. She watched him put it into Lorimer's pigeon-hole, then turned on her heel and left.

The great wooden double gates of the college had been closed for the evening, leaving a wicket gate open. As Evie stepped over the threshold, she almost cannoned into Cyril Roope, about to enter. He reached out to grasp her, but she sidestepped, evading him, while just behind him Edgar Deverell-Drummond sniggered softly. Several other students from the founder's tower were there too, but of Lord Maltraver and Charlie Pomeroy there was no sign.

'Good evening, Miss Winstanley,' said Deverell-Drummond. 'How delightful to see you here . . . again.'

The others fell back, making no attempt to incommode her, then filed through the entrance one after another. She felt a twinge of concern about her note to Professor Lorimer, waiting in his pigeonhole. Surely Postlethwaite wouldn't let a student touch correspondence meant for a don? At all events, there was nothing she could do about it now.

She set off into the gathering dusk.

~

Ahead of her, Evie made out a rotund figure stomping along Turl Street – Bernard Zouch. On impulse, she followed him towards the High Street, where he turned right and vanished into the covered market. Close on his heels, she saw him stop at a bakery stall and buy pink meringues, then sit on a bench to consume them, swiftly, joylessly, cramming them into his mouth. Evie went to sit next to him.

'Good evening, Mr Zouch.'

He looked up startled. Pink sugar sprinkled his chin while misery haunted his red-rimmed eyes. For a moment she thought he would rebuff her, but then he seemed to collapse in on himself. He scrunched up the paper bag containing the last of the meringues and held it, staring at his feet. She thought she had never seen anyone so defeated.

'What do you want?' His voice was flat, uninterested in anything Evie might have to say.

'Information,' she told him. 'Have you heard of the circle of shadows? Or a man called Robert Wenless?'

He shook his head.

'Then tell me about the Sons of Dionysus. Why did you join them?'

At the name, he clenched the bag in his fists, crushing the remaining meringues into powder.

'They aren't your friends, are they? Maltraver and Deverell-Drummond and Pomeroy and the others,' Evie prompted. 'Not true friends.'

He kept a listless watch on the burly holder of a grocery stall and his assistant lads, who were packing up vegetables and tins into boxes and wheeling them away, bantering light-heartedly with one another.

'Anything you tell me about the Sons of Dionysus will be in confidence,' Evie said. 'I won't tell them. Or the college author-ities, or . . . the police. I swear it.'

He turned towards Evie, as though he saw her for the first time. 'You were brave, up there on the tower. I'm sorry about that. I didn't know they'd go so far, not with a woman. I'm not brave, you see. And Maltraver is . . .' The whites of his eyes rolled and Evie was reminded of Trafalgar the horse – his wild eyes, flattened ears and flailing hooves. It occurred to her that man and beast shared a common terror of Viscount Maltraver.

'Tell me about Teddy Windle,' she said gently.

Zouch flinched, as though the name hurt him.

'Maltraver taunted you for caring. You *did* care for him, didn't you?'

Slowly, he wiped his mouth, then put his head in his hands. For a while he said nothing, and Evie thought he would refuse to answer.

'I loved him,' he said eventually, the words seemingly drawn up from a deep well of misery. 'And Teddy loved me. He really did.'

'I see.'

'No, you don't,' he said bitterly. 'What would a girl like you know about it?'

'Tell me, then. What don't I know?'

Now he had made the admission, the floodgates opened and his secret poured out.

'Teddy's parents – his father's a vicar – brought him up with very strict morals. Teddy was full of guilt. He thought we ought to restrict ourselves to a platonic love, not contaminated by sins of the flesh. He said that was the only way we could be together. I don't really believe in all that higher-love stuff – love is love, isn't it? – but I was willing to go along with whatever Teddy wanted. Then I made an unforgivable error.'

Without warning, he smashed his fist against the bench so hard that Evie winced. Blood oozed from his knuckles.

'I introduced Teddy to Edgar Deverell-Drummond. I'm not sure what possessed me. Hubris, I think. I was trying to show off that I had important friends, Maltraver and his set. It's not easy for fellows like Teddy and me. We didn't go to their schools. We don't have their money, or their connections. And they treat us with utter disdain; mocking our accents, our clothes, our backgrounds, our families. And if we try and hide who we are, pretend we're like them, it's worse – they laugh even more, because that means they've won the game. I didn't understand all that then. I had this idea it would help Teddy and me if we got into their set. We'd form better connections. Dear God! I've been well punished. I lost him and everything else that mattered.'

'Can't you write to Teddy? Be reconciled?'

'I've tried. He doesn't answer.'

'Where did you send the letters?'

'To his parents' house, the only address I had for him. When I got no reply, I believed he no longer wanted anything to do with me, or perhaps his parents had destroyed my letters. But you heard what Maltraver said on the tower – Teddy never went home; he's gone off abroad somewhere and won't come back. I won't ever see him again. And I never knew the world could be so empty.'

His face crumpled and he wiped his eyes with his sleeve, making sounds she initially took for laughter but realised were racking sobs.

Did love make you so vulnerable? Did it hurt so much? Evie wanted to say something that would comfort his despair, but the idea in her head would devastate him still more if she voiced it. Even as she searched for words, he lurched to his feet and staggered away, leaving her alone in the emptying market as all around her the sellers packed up their stalls.

Betrayal, loss, guilt, pain. If that was what it meant to open your heart to love, it must be a terrifying thing.

~

Evie and Harriet sat at a corner table in the public lounge at the Eastgate, where a pianist in evening dress played Strauss waltzes. Evie nursed a cup of coffee, pretending to listen to the music. Harriet, too, seemed pensive. She hadn't returned until sometime after Evie had finished dinner, making a sudden appearance in the public lounge, weary from having walked back from Diana Gordon-Stukes' home in Jericho. Evie was planning her next move should Lorimer refuse to see her when she became aware that Harriet was speaking.

'. . . No one has seen her since that day,' said Harriet.

'I'm so sorry.' Evie leant towards her. 'What did you say?'

'Ethel Maddeley,' repeated Harriet. 'I've learnt more about her disappearance from Maude's friend, Diana Gordon-Stukes. It turns out that Diana and Ethel were part of the same set in North Oxford. They used to go to afternoon concerts together and public lectures, that sort of thing. According to Diana, Ethel didn't simply leave Oxford, she vanished altogether. Ethel started acting strangely, avoiding Diana and their circle of friends, making excuses to decline invitations. About four months ago, Ethel went out late one afternoon, telling her maid she'd be back late that evening and not to wait up for her. She never returned.'

'Does Diana have any idea what happened?'

'There's been no trace of Ethel, not in the hospitals or the . . . the mortuary. As for the police, they've drawn a blank.'

Evie, who by now had formed her own views on the efficiency of the Oxford police, rolled her eyes.

'Diana and her friends,' continued Harriet, 'are deeply troubled. They did wonder if there might have been some unhappy love affair, whether poor Ethel might have done away with herself. But if she did, she left no note. And why hasn't her body been found?'

'And there's more. Diana told me that three days before Ethel went missing, Diana was on top of a tram, passing along the High, when she saw Ethel walking with a young man. Ethel's about my age; Diana says the young man was perhaps thirty years younger. There was a radiance in Ethel's face, and a lightness in her step. Diana had never seen her like that before.'

The strains of a new waltz began, spritely and joyful.

'I don't want to distress you,' said Evie slowly, 'but you said she was well off and had an inheritance. Is it possible that someone – this young man, perhaps – might have murdered her for her money?'

'We considered that,' said Harriet. From the way she spoke, Evie realised that her cousin was well aware of the darker side of human nature and wondered again how much she might have underestimated her. 'Diana has a theory that the young man was some kind of confidence trickster who encouraged Ethel to make false investments, persuaded her to invest in some dubious scheme and did away with her to cover his traces. But the police say there were no unusual withdrawals from Ethel's bank. Her money's still there. She simply . . . disappeared.'

A sickening sinking feeling pinned Evie to her chair. 'Did Diana describe him?'

'He looked like a student,' said Harriet, 'though he wasn't wearing a gown. Very young, debonair, well tailored. Diana doesn't care very much for young men – well, doesn't care much for men at all, really – but she said even she could tell he was exceptionally handsome. He was bareheaded and had a fine head of fair hair. *Like an angel*, she said. *Beautiful as Lucifer.*'

~

As Evie and Harriet passed the reception desk on the way to their room, the clerk behind the desk called Evie over to give her a note that had been delivered by hand for her a few minutes earlier. She waited until she was alone to open it. It was short and to the point:

Miss Winstanley,
Come to my college rooms at two o'clock tomorrow. There is something I should show you. If, after that, you still have questions, I will tell you what you want to know, though you may wish I had not.
Fergus Lorimer.

CHAPTER
Twenty-Eight

T HE NEXT MORNING, Evie, uneasy and unwilling after the Ethel Maddeley revelation to leave Harriet alone, suggested they spend the morning together. She had told Harriet about her appointment with Professor Lorimer, explaining it by yet another falsehood – that Lorimer had agreed to help her organise coaching to prepare for her entry examinations to the university.

They visited the Ashmolean where Evie discovered the Egyptian galleries and promptly whipped out her notebook. She was stationed before the red-glazed ceramic sculpture of a seated lion, frowning in concentration as she tried to capture its benign majesty with her pencil, when Marcus Ellingham materialised from behind a pillar.

'Are you following me, Marcus?' said Evie.

'Not at all.' He fiddled with his tie. 'Well, perhaps. I haven't seen you since you ran off yesterday.'

'So, you were loitering outside the Eastgate?' she said, amused.

He nodded eagerly. 'That was it. But you came out with your companion and I wasn't sure whether I should approach you.'

'I'm glad you didn't. Harriet mustn't get wind of anything. She's anxious already this morning.'

'Of course.'

'I meant to seek you out and tell you what I've discovered, but there's been no time. I'm glad you're here.' She moved her coat to make space on the bench.

'Don't let me disturb you,' said Marcus as he joined her. 'Artist at work and all that.' His eyes went to the drawing in her notebook.

'There are no lions left now in Egypt,' Evie said, as she continued working on her lion's indented whiskers. 'They were hunted to extinction sometime in the eighteenth century. It makes me sad, somehow. The person who created this sculpture was capable of appreciating the beauty of a world that has such beings in it. So why are people also capable of destroying their fellow creatures?'

She thought of Ethel Maddeley and Teddy Windle. Both had sought love from another human being and found something very different.

'I have been wondering about love,' she said.

'About love?' he repeated.

'Yes. Did Oscar Wilde have the right of it?'

'What do you mean?'

'That each man kills the thing he loves.'

'Love needn't be like that.' He tugged at his ear, looking self-conscious as a teenager. 'It can be real. I—' He broke off, springing up awkwardly as Harriet came into view, raising her eyebrows at the sight of Evie deep in conversation with an unknown young man.

'Harriet,' said Evie, 'this is Mr Ellingham. I met him at the weekend party in Yorkshire.'

Harriet and Marcus shook hands. Harriet said, smiling faintly, 'Another person from the North Riding who has found his way to Oxford?'

'Yes, it is a coincidence, isn't it?' Evie scooped up her pencils, returning them to their box, and packed everything into her handbag, eager to hurry Harriet off before Marcus inadvertently revealed something that would cause her carefully constructed fabric of lies to unravel.

'I'm afraid we must go, Mr Ellingham,' she said. 'We're taking an early luncheon.'

'Evelyn has a rendezvous with Professor Lorimer of Talbot College,' said Harriet to Marcus, a note of pride in her voice. 'He wants to offer her advice on coaching with a view to her taking the Oxford entry examination. Evelyn is very clever, very studious.'

'I know she is. I mean, I'm sure she is,' he said nervously, catching Evie's warning look. 'She, uh, looks as though she would be a clever sort of person, don't you know?'

As Harriet said goodbye and headed for the stairs, Marcus shook hands with Evie, retaining hers for a moment. 'Lorimer?'

'Yes, he's agreed to talk. I've been thinking, Marcus. Might it be possible that Lorimer himself is the Magister of the circle of shadows?'

His eyes widened in horror. 'How could that be? Surely not!'

'After all,' she reflected, 'who knows more about the occult arts than he? The more I think about what he told me, the more certain I am he was lying, about my father, about his own involvement . . .'

'Then don't go to him,' Marcus pleaded. 'Or at least don't go alone.'

She shook her head. 'I have to. Don't you see? He'll only speak about my father if I'm alone. And I *have* to know.'

Marcus gripped her fingers tightly. 'Please, be careful. He—'

But on seeing Harriet look back enquiringly, Evie retrieved her hand from Marcus's grasp and hurried after her.

∿

At precisely two o'clock, Evie called at Professor Lorimer's rooms. This time, the outer oak door was open. When there was no response to her knock on the inner door, she twisted the handle, found it unlocked, and entered Lorimer's study. No one was there. Was this to be a re-enactment of her first visit? But Lorimer himself had fixed the time . . .

She waited, more or less patiently, with no company but the regular ticking of the carriage clock. At length, she knocked at the door to his private quarters. Getting no answer, she opened the door cautiously, but found the bedroom unoccupied. A sense of unease crept up her spine like a small animal and wrapped itself around her throat.

The strident chime of the clock rang the quarter hour. Evie went to the window, gazing down on the quad, wondering if she might see Lorimer's bulky form making its way towards Staircase J. Someone was indeed striding along the perimeter, but it was a much younger man, gown flying, mortarboard hiding his face and hair. The figure stopped outside Staircase J and looked towards the window where she stood. She jumped out of sight, catching her breath, after a moment peeking around the edge of the curtain. No one was there.

She heard steps coming fast up the stairs, too fast for the ponderous tread of Professor Lorimer. She ran for the bedroom, shutting herself in. The newcomer could be going to any of the rooms on that staircase. No reason to think they were heading for Lorimer's rooms. Even so . . .

She heard the landing door open.

Heart racing, she dropped to the floor, wriggled backwards under the bed and lay there amidst a thick layer of dust and the smell of old shoes, keeping the door in view. Surely, the visitor wouldn't come into this room?

With a soft click, the bedroom door swung wide.

From her vantage point, she could only make out a pair of dark-trousered legs and a pair of shoes – handmade, well polished, exceptionally large, equipped with spats – then realised she'd seen them before, on Charlie Pomeroy. She lay, trembling, sure at any moment he'd peer beneath the bed. And there she'd be, caught like a rabbit in a trap.

A moment later, she became aware that the carpet beneath her was warm and damp. What *was* that? She inched about – and discovered she wasn't alone under the bed.

She stuffed her fist into her mouth to stop herself from screaming.

Twenty-Nine

Fergus Lorimer's black eyes stared into Evie's, the dark pits of the pupils enlarged and fixed. A trickle of scarlet seeped from the corner of his slack mouth, losing itself in the wiry black thicket of his beard.

For what seemed an endless time, she lay absolutely still. Then, at last, came the sound of the bedroom door closing, of footsteps crossing the study, followed by the closing of the door to the landing.

She counted to ten slowly, her eyes fixed on Lorimer, just as his were on her, as though he found her endlessly absorbing, a moment of communion between living and dead. With a sobbing breath, she scrambled out from beneath the bed, ran to the landing door and locked it, then returned to the bedroom. She couldn't bear the thought of touching Lorimer, so she put her weight to the bed and rolled it over on its casters.

Lorimer's corpse lay contorted in death, head twisted towards his right shoulder. He had been stabbed in the heart. There was no sign of the weapon used to do it. Just a terrible, gaping wound. His upper chest, waistcoat and shirt were saturated in blood. More blood had pooled onto the carpet around him in a spreading stain.

She knelt beside him, taking care to avoid the blood. Something lay upon his barrel-like chest – a piece of ancient parchment, bearing a design executed in black ink. It was heavily stained with blood, but she recognised it immediately: a spiralling pattern within a double circle. The kuroskato.

She lurched to her feet, grabbing the wall as the room revolved around her.

What next? Get help.

She started for the door, then stopped as she remembered Lorimer's note. What had he meant to show her? She returned to his study and made a hasty search of the things on his desk and in the drawers beneath, then rifled through his books, papers, totems, amulets and statues. Nothing.

With a crushing sense of the inevitable – hadn't she known all along where it must be? – she went back to Lorimer's body, knelt beside him, took off her gloves – no point in ruining another pair – and gingerly explored the outer pockets of his jacket, but she found only his pipe, handkerchief and tobacco pouch. The corpse was still warm, his blood quite liquid, which meant his murderer must have left just minutes before she'd arrived.

She took a ragged breath, drew back the lapel of his jacket and stuck her hand into his inner breast pocket, recoiling as her fingers encountered sticky wetness. Gritting her teeth, she probed further and retrieved an envelope, splashed with Lorimer's blood, bearing his name and the address of his college. The handwriting, with its graceful old-world calligraphy, was achingly familiar.

It was from her father, Walter Winstanley.

~

The shadows lengthened across Inspector Hammond's desk and Evie's temples ached. The inspector's heavy-lidded eyes watched her every movement while beside him Sergeant Fiveash smiled and nodded, but Evie trusted Fiveash's affability even less than she did Hammond's scrutiny and she knew she had to keep her head, be careful of her answers. The contrast between their attitude to the violent death of Janet Rae, a poor servant girl, and that of Fergus Lorimer, don of an Oxford college, couldn't have been more marked.

Hammond's questions kept coming.

'And your appointment was for what time?'

'Two o'clock.'

'Yet it wasn't until ten minutes to three, according to the

statement of Mr Postlethwaite, that you came to the lodge to raise the alarm. Why did you delay so long?'

'I waited for some time in the study. I didn't think it proper to venture into what must be a private room.'

'But at length you did look into the inner room.'

'Yes.'

'And not immediately seeing Professor Lorimer, you looked under the bed?'

'Yes.'

Hammond's bushy eyebrows climbed and Fiveash smirked into his moustache. Licking his lips, the sergeant took up his pen to make notes of Evie's answers.

'And still it took you many minutes to raise the alarm,' said Hammond, making a steeple of his fingers. 'What were you doing in that time?'

'I fainted.'

'You *fainted*?'

'It was the shock of finding his body . . . all that blood.'

Swooned – that was the word. Like a heroine from a Victorian novel. If that was their expectation, she was happy to play along with it. She repressed a wild, inappropriate urge to laugh.

'You can confirm that there was no trace of the weapon used?'

'None.' They had asked her this question already. 'But there was a piece of parchment lying on his body, with a symbol upon it. You saw that, I suppose?'

Hammond sat back, visibly exasperated, running his hands through his hair. 'Lorimer wasn't killed by a piece of parchment, Miss Winstanley. Perhaps you don't realise the importance of this question of a weapon?'

'Enlighten me, Inspector.'

'If there's no weapon present, that rules out the possibility of Professor Lorimer's death being self-inflicted.'

'Ah, yes, I see. How foolish of me not to realise.'

'So,' said Hammond, rolling his eyes and drumming his fingers on the desk. 'Either someone took away the weapon after Lorimer stabbed himself, which hardly seems likely, or he was murdered by someone who took away the weapon.'

'What sort of weapon was used, Inspector?'

'A long knife. Or a dagger, perhaps.'

'I noticed one or two weapons fitting such a description amongst the artefacts in the study. Beastly looking things.'

'We have examined them and found no trace of blood,' said Hammond, grinding his teeth. He seemed to find Evie in her new persona as a naive Victorian schoolgirl every bit as irritating as Evie the occult detective. 'Someone removed the knife.'

Both men's eyes went to Evie's clothes. No possible place there where she could have hidden one. It had been lucky, she reflected, that she had put on a formal, form-fitting dress for her interview with Lorimer, or she might have been subjected to the humiliation of a search of her clothing. They had gone through her handbag, of course, and opened up her pencil case, though to her relief they hadn't bothered to examine her note-book. As for her father's letter, it was safely tucked inside the corset she had put on to give the dress its proper outline – the first time she'd ever been glad of wearing one. The sticky sensation of Lorimer's blood against her skin made her squirm with disgust, and she chided herself – she couldn't afford to be squeamish.

'So, you suspect murder?' said Evie. 'Have you spoken with Lord Maltraver?'

'We have made all proper enquiries,' said Hammond. 'Viscount Maltraver has nothing to do with the matter. He was on a train returning from a visit to London at the very time you made your dramatic discovery.'

Evie opened her mouth to speak, but Hammond cut across her.

'Yes, we did check with the train company. And independent witnesses verify that his lordship spoke the truth. So, you see, you must stop these malicious allegations against his lordship.'

'And the man who came into Professor Lorimer's study?' she

asked. 'I told you about him. I believe it was Charlie Pomeroy.' Her head was hurting worse than ever.

'We have talked to Mr Charles Pomeroy. He readily admits he had a tutorial with Professor Lorimer, for which he arrived at a quarter past two. Not seeing any sign of the professor – and not having your foresight to search under the professor's bed for him – Mr Pomeroy went away again.' Hammond took a cigarette from a box on his desk, lit it, sat back and surveyed Evie through narrowed eyes. 'Do you know what the really curious thing is about his testimony?'

Fiveash threaded his moustache through his fingers as he too leant forward to study Evie's face.

'I can't imagine,' said Evie.

'That he saw no sign of *you*, Miss Winstanley. Though on your own account you were there.'

She had an answer ready. 'I was hiding under the bed. That's why he didn't see me. Though I saw his shoes.'

'You recognised him by his *shoes?*' Hammond was incredulous.

'Yes. Expensive, hand sewn, with a distinctive pattern stitched into them.'

'You hid under the bed, next to the body of a murdered man, rather than reveal your presence to Charles Pomeroy and ask for his assistance. Why did you do that, Miss Winstanley?'

'I heard a knock at the door. I feared it was the murderer return-ing, so I hid.'

'That wasn't very rational, was it?'

'You have established, have you not, Inspector, that women are *not* very rational.'

Hammond grew brick red.

'Was it before or after you fainted that you hid under the bed with a corpse?' Sergeant Fiveash asked, his cheery smile revealing his canines.

Evie turned to him. 'I fainted twice, Sergeant. Once when I was under the bed. Then, as I got up, the room swam about me and I fainted again.'

'This second time, you fainted for over half an hour?'

'I must have done. I was prostrated by the shock of my discovery.'

Evie knew they didn't believe her, but neither could they prove she was a murderer – not without finding a murder weapon. In the end, they let her go.

~

She left the interrogation room – back stiff with pride, though her temples still throbbed – to find Harriet waiting for her at the front desk of the station, a lonely-looking figure sitting upright, hands folded, on a bench. Seeing her face brimming with concern, Evie's heart sank.

'Dearest,' said Harriet, hurrying to embrace her. 'What's been happening? I've been so worried.'

'I'm very sorry.'

'Sorry? What for?' Harriet released her, searched her face. 'Such a terrible experience. I blame myself. I should never have let you go alone.'

Evie bit her lip. In her heart, she felt sure it was very much her fault. If she hadn't made it her business to seek out Lorimer and make him talk to her about the circle of shadows, he would still be alive. The pain in her head intensified. Of one thing she was certain: she would have to tell Harriet the truth. She dreaded the prospect.

'Have these policemen been bullying you?' Harriet glared at the constable behind the desk, who wisely kept his head down, focusing on his paperwork. 'You're a witness, not a suspect.'

'I'll tell you,' said Evie miserably. 'But not here.'

'Of course,' said Harriet.

They left the building and set off along St Aldate's and turned up the High Street. Evie stumbled at the corner, confessing to having a headache, and Harriet said they should stop at a chemist for a remedy.

'No laudanum,' said Evie, pulling away. 'I need to keep a clear head.'

Back at their room at the Eastgate, she sat Harriet down and relayed the whole business, starting with the night the intruder came and her discovery of the kuroskato. She held nothing back. Harriet didn't speak or interrupt. The only time she showed emotion was when Evie voiced her suspicion that the disappearance of Ethel Maddeley was connected to the mystery, when she gave an involuntary moan of anguish and her hands tightened as she kneaded them together.

When Evie finished, she forced herself to meet Harriet's eyes. The look in them made her burn with shame.

'Does anyone else know this?' Harriet asked.

'Pelham. At least, he knows the first part, not about what's happened since we came to Oxford. He wanted me to keep him informed, but I was worried he would come tearing up to Oxford and leave Grace alone. You mustn't blame him. He wanted me to confide in you, but I wouldn't, at first because I feared you too wouldn't believe me, but then, after we found Janet's body, I thought you'd be safer if I could keep you out of it. But now that Professor Lorimer has been murdered, I realise I have to warn you.' Her voice dwindled almost to a whisper. 'Though you may rightly hate me for what I have done.'

Harriet's face was ashen. 'All the lies you told me about coming here for your studies, to pursue a career.' Her voice rose. 'Every time you said you were researching Charlotte Babbington-Styles ... all utter balderdash!' She shook her head incredulously. 'I would never have believed you capable of such deceit.'

'I wanted to keep you safe.'

'And that is supposed to make me feel better?' Harriet spoke with a cold anger that Evie had never seen in her before. 'I trusted you, Evelyn.'

Evie winced.

'How can I ever face Leonie again,' continued Harriet, 'knowing what I let you do? The police could have kept you in prison, charged you.'

'No, they couldn't. They had no evidence against me, and they knew it.'

'As for these appalling young men, the Sons of Dionysus ...'
Harriet's hands twisted spasmodically.

'They are not the worst of it,' said Evie. 'The circle of shadows
– it's real, I'm convinced of it. Whatever you think of what I've
done, Harriet, do you believe me?'

'About the supernatural?'

Evie nodded.

'I believe ... that *you* believe it.'

'That's not the same thing.'

'No, it is not.'

They sat in silence till the room was almost dark. Harriet got up
and turned on the electric light switch. 'Well,' she said, turning to
Evie. 'Are you going to open it?'

Evie looked at her, bewildered.

'Your father's letter.'

Evie had forgotten all about it. She gave a long, drawn-out sigh
and said, 'Of course.' She crossed to the window and scanned the
street below, but could see no one watching them. She closed the
curtains, returned to the bed and, reaching into her bodice, drew
out the letter in its bloodstained envelope. She read the contents
aloud.

My dear Fergus,

*I believe the quest for which we have sought an answer for so long,
and of which we spoke the last time I was with you at Talbot, may be
close to a resolution. We may even be able to make good our old dream
to revive the circle of shadows. One for the twentieth century, that
would benefit mankind, with all the dross of fear and superstition
swept away. We shall have it in our grasp to prove the reality of occult
magic. Those who laughed at us all these years will be humbled and
forced to eat their words.*

*You will remember that I told you of Harold Catterick, a school-
master with scholarly interests like our own, living in retirement in an
isolated house on the Yorkshire moors. I visited him last year and
endeavoured to persuade him to speak of his findings, but his sight had
been failing and I fear his mind was also, as he no longer knew the*

contents of his own collection. He seemed afraid of something, but he could not or would not tell me what it was.

Several months ago, I saw an auction notice of the sale of his books and realised he must have died, for he would never have agreed to the sale while he lived. I went to the auction in Harrogate. Robert Wenless, of all people, turned up there. Thankfully, he was too late to outbid me for the books, though his presence convinced me I was on the right track. It's essential to keep all this quiet so that Wenless doesn't get wind of what I'm doing and how much I've accomplished.

Now that I have Catterick's books in my possession, I've been going through them, and I came across something extraordinary hidden away inside a study of ancient Britain by the Reverend Mickleford. I believe it to be a copy of an ancient spell, to summon and bind the being of which we have spoken, even without due sacrifice. I cannot yet read the spell, for it is in an Old Tongue which defies my scholarship, but with the help of Catterick's collection I am working on a translation into Latin, a more appropriate language for wielding occult mysteries than uncouth English. I believe that I am on the brink of success. If so, I shall be able to speak the words of power that have not been heard for years uncounted.

Actaeon Fell believed the old way of sacrifice was necessary for a summoning. I disagree, yet I will proceed with due caution, for this ritual must be done correctly; the spell must be spoken at the proper time, taking the right precautions. To do otherwise would be dangerous and could rebound on the speaker. If anything should happen to me, you will know that I have failed. Oh, but if I should succeed, Fergus . . . if I should succeed . . .

Ever your devoted friend,
Walter

PS If I have time, I'll visit you again in Oxford, for there is a matter in Fell's grimoire that I wish to consult for my final preparations.

Evie clutched the letter. So Lorimer and her father had acted in collusion, and Lorimer had had the grimoire in his possession. Had her father translated the spell and performed the ritual? What had come in response to his summoning?

'What do you think, Harriet?'

'What do I *think?*' echoed Harriet, grey eyes sharp and clear, arms folded tightly. 'I think that he does not mention his family and what will become of them if he fails in his rash attempt. I think that men in their pride put their desire to fulfil their own ambitions first, without a thought for the effect on those who love them. Even the best of them. Even your father.'

'Don't say anything against Papa!' Evie's voice came out half choked.

Harriet pursed her lips, went to a drawer and started pulling out clothes and other belongings.

'What are you doing?'

'Packing. Get me your portmanteau, if you please.'

'You want us to leave?'

'Yes, by the evening train. We'll just have time if we hurry.'

'But why, when I'm getting so close?'

'Evie, it's my duty to keep you safe, and I intend to carry out that duty.'

'So you *do* think there's something in it? That Papa was right about the reality of the occult?'

'No, I do not. But don't you see? Either *I* am right, in which case you are wasting your time pursuing this elusive circle of shadows, or—'

'Or?'

'Or *you* are right, in which case this secret has killed several people already, including your own father. Either way, we must be gone from here and forget all of this ever happened.'

'I can't do that, Harriet. I'm sorry, but I'm not leaving Oxford or stopping this investigation. Running away and wilfully closing our eyes to the truth won't help matters. What about Grace and the mark of the kuroskato that she bears? There's no hiding from the circle of shadows.'

Harriet's face set in lines of grim determination. 'If you will not come home of your own volition, I'll have to tell your mother. It's my duty.'

'You *can't*! That would distress her horribly—'

A knock at the door interrupted them.

Evie opened the door to find one of the hotel staff holding out a telegram in a basket.

'It's from Pelham,' she said. 'What can he have to say that's so urgent?' Then a sudden gust of fear yanked at her heart as she read aloud:

I much regret the grief this will cause you. There is something very wrong with Grace. I am afraid for her sanity and her safety. We need you to come home.

PART 3

The Circle of Shadows

~

CHAPTER

Thirty

'WHERE DID YOU find her?' said Evie.

'At the river's edge,' said Pelham.

Evie's eyes searched his stricken face.

'Yes,' he answered the question she couldn't bring herself to ask. 'She was in the water.'

'Oh, Gracie!' Evie sobbed.

Harriet clasped an arm about Evie, her other hand reaching to grasp Pelham's.

They stood at her bedside, where Grace lay sleeping. Her black hair spilled in waves over the white lace of her pillow and curls stuck damply to the sweat on her forehead. She was murmuring indistinctly.

'Why doesn't she wake up?' said Evie. 'Her breathing's so heavy.'

'I gave her laudanum,' said Pelham. 'I had no choice,' he added defensively, catching Evie's expression. 'She hadn't slept in two days. That in itself could have made her delusional.'

Harriet listened, frowning. 'What's she saying?'

'Lines of poetry, I think,' said Pelham. 'Whatever it is, she keeps repeating it, as though there were safety in the words. A refuge from whatever disturbs her mind.'

Harriet stooped, her ear to Grace's mouth.

Grace murmured, 'Sister, I would have command, if it were heaven's will, on our sad fate.'

'It's from Keats,' Harriet said, straightening up.

'Why, yes.' Evie sniffed, drawing her sleeve across her damp face. 'She went to a poetry recital of the Romantics.'

'That's when her illness began,' said Pelham. 'Two days ago. The event was at a hall in Kensington. I'd meant to escort her there, but one of my patients suffered a sudden collapse, so I met Grace afterwards to escort her home.'

'She was alone?' said Evie.

'Yes. At least, she was alone when I met her at the exit. It was a fine evening and we walked back to Hammersmith. She was strangely excited, though, almost fey. In the night, I heard someone moving downstairs in Papa's study. I thought it might be the intruder returning. I took my revolver – and came upon Grace herself.'

'What was she doing?' said Harriet.

'Drawing pictures.' He indicated some sketches on the dressing table.

Evie went to look. The drawings depicted angelic ladies with rippling hair, in medieval clothes, riding palfreys, and knights in full armour, only their hands and faces visible. 'They look like illustrations from the *Morte d'Arthur*. What happened then?'

'She wouldn't go to bed,' said Pelham. 'She was ... agitated. I stayed up to keep her company. The next morning, she seemed worse. I don't believe she'd slept at all. I cancelled my appointments and stayed with her. Mary helped; we watched her between us. But in the afternoon, she fell asleep – or I thought she did. I meant to keep watch, but like a damned fool I dozed off in an armchair. When I woke, she was gone.' He ran his tongue round his dry mouth. 'D'Artagnan was scratching at the door. She hadn't taken him with her. That worried me even more, for whenever she goes walking, he's her constant companion. I brought him with me, and a good thing I did, for if he hadn't been there ...'

'He followed her scent?' prompted Evie when Pelham trailed off into silence.

'Yes,' he said at last. 'Across Hammersmith Bridge, to the other side of the river.'

Evie knew the landscape well – woodland and orchards, few houses. 'It's quiet there.'

'As you say,' he agreed, his voice harsh with anguish and self-blame. 'D'Artagnan raced down the steps to the towpath. I followed. The tide was coming in fast. There was a mist over the water and the twilight was settling in, so it was hard to make out anything clearly. I ran by the river, calling her name, but there was no answer. Then I heard D'Artagnan barking, his paws rattling over the stones. I ran after him, and that's when I saw her, up to her knees in the Thames. A moment later, she would have been out of my sight and lost, but D'Artagnan was there, holding on to her skirt. She was trying to push him away, but he wouldn't let go. He wouldn't let go . . .' Pelham's voice cracked and he wiped impatiently at his eyes.

Evie went to him and hugged him, a weight of pain like lead in her stomach. 'This is my fault, not yours.'

She broke away and turned back the blanket, exposing Grace's arm. 'I went looking for the circle of shadows – and I found it.' The sigil had darkened into a deep shade of violet and seemed to float just beneath Grace's skin.

'Evie, all this about the supernatural – it's just not . . .' Pelham made a helpless gesture.

Evie turned away to hide a sudden humiliating quiver of her lip. She found herself missing Marcus. He would have listened to her, trusted her judgement, whereas her own family . . .

She pushed the thought away. *Don't think about it, not yet. Deal with it later.*

~

In the early afternoon, Evie curled up in the armchair in Grace's room, reading a letter from Marcus that had just arrived, while D'Artagnan slept on the bed next to her. Just before leaving Oxford, she had scrawled a few lines to tell Marcus that Lorimer had been murdered, and that she was returning to London to look after Grace. Judging by the swiftness of his reply, it must have been sent by return of post. The letter was full of his anxiety for her – how awful it must have been to discover Lorimer's body and concern about her possible narrow escape. He ended by saying:

For your sake I'm glad you're home. I've no right to insist, but I beg you, please, Evelyn, to stay there, at least for now. After what has happened to Lorimer, no one is safe, least of all you. If you will trust me, I have a plan for how I may trap Maltraver and expose the activities of the Sons of Dionysus. It's worth trying, I think. I'll let you know, as soon as I can, whether or not I succeed.

The words 'no one is safe, least of all you' had been underlined.

She chewed at her thumb, pondering Marcus's words. What could his plan be? Most importantly, would he really be able to take on Maltraver and the Sons of Dionysus, let alone the circle of shadows? She thought of replying to warn him against attempting anything without her, or at least to ask him to explain what he meant to do. But would he listen? Any more than she herself would listen to attempts to dissuade her? She worried, too, that he would act rashly so as to keep her out of it and shield her from danger, in which case no words of caution from her would stop him.

A sound came from the bed and she looked up from the letter to see Grace stirring. Marcus temporarily forgotten, she called Mary and asked her to heat some soup, then watched Grace eat, the spoon dipping slowly and listlessly into the bowl.

'How are you feeling, Gracie?'

'Much better.' Grace finished the soup, returning the bowl to Evie with hands that shook.

Evie sat on the bed, watching her sister's face, the hectic flushed patches, the sheen of cold sweat on forehead and upper lip. She took Grace's hand. It felt chilled. She took the other too, tried to warm them both between her own.

'Why did you go into the river, dearest?' said Evie, kissing Grace's hands; tears blotted her cheeks, trickled onto the coverlet. 'Is your life such a burden to you that you wished to make an end of it?'

'Not at all,' said Grace, through lips that were cracked and dry. 'I don't want to die. I was trying to escape.'

'Escape from what?'

'From *him*.'

Evie stopped crying, lifted her head. A space seemed to open up inside her mind, and through it some understanding filtered.

'He keeps calling to me,' said Grace. 'He says I must come to him. But I don't want to, Evie. I don't want to! He's loathsome. I *hate* him. I hear his voice in my head all the time. It's all I hear. I try to drown it out.'

'With Keats?'

'Mmm.'

'Don't worry, dearest.' Evie hugged her tight. 'We'll keep you safe.'

Her mind went back to Maltraver Towers and the sigil hidden in Grace's mattress. Could something like that have been contrived again?

She pulled away and tilted Grace's chin so she could see her face. 'Have you seen him again recently? Lord Maltraver?'

Her sister's eyes narrowed into black slits and she turned away, stuffing the corner of her pillow into her mouth to stifle her wail.

'Please, Gracie. This is important. Was he at the poetry recital?'

Grace hunched up into a ball, whimpering.

'Did he approach you? Speak to you?'

Grace nodded, not looking at Evie.

'Did he give you anything?'

Grace didn't answer, just rocked backwards and forwards, forearms cradling her head, blocking out the unbearable.

Evie ran to the door and called for Mary, who came swiftly.

'Has Miss Grace finished the soup?' Mary asked.

'Never mind that,' Evie said, pulling out clothes from her sister's wardrobe and dropping them on the armchair. 'What was she wearing for the poetry recital?'

Mary pointed out a coat, a blouse and skirt. Evie ran her hands over them, investigating the pockets. 'Which handbag?'

Mary wasn't sure, so Evie went through all of them, finally finding a small, embroidered evening bag containing a programme for the recital and a purse containing only a few coins and a bus ticket. She turned the bag inside out and ripped apart the silken lining, disregarding Mary's tongue-clicking disapproval.

Nothing.

As Evie slumped discouraged onto the bed, the torn bag on her lap, she heard giggles.

'You won't find it here.' Grace was sitting up in bed, scratching briskly at the kuroskato symbol on her arm. Mockery danced in her eyes, crinkling the corners of her mouth. 'He bade me tell you – he has it safe.' As Evie turned to her, appalled, Grace threw back her head, sending her long hair flying down her back, and broke into peals of laughter.

A cold tide of dread coursed through Evie, chilling her blood. She had thought the Magister could be Lorimer – until he had been murdered – or perhaps the elusive Robert Wenless, against whom her father had warned her. But all along it had been Maltraver, the man she had despised, yet fatally underestimated, hiding in plain sight.

~

'She's under a spell,' said Evie. 'It's Maltraver's doing.'

Pelham had been drowsing, exhausted, on the drawing-room sofa, a barely touched glass of brandy beside him, but when Evie entered he dragged himself awake, suppressing his yawns. He looked far from his usual dapper self, his jaw blue and unshaven, his unkempt hair standing on end, shadows of sleeplessness blurring his eyes. 'Tell me,' he said.

'He met her at the poetry recital. I believe he used a symbol of the kuroskato, probably on a sheet of parchment, as he did before, to waken the kuroskato in her arm into life.'

'On a parchment? Where is it?'

'I've looked everywhere.' She shook her head, her features a mask of misery. 'Grace says *he* has it, and that this time we can't break his hold on her.'

Pelham groaned and put his head in his hands.

Evie huddled up alongside him on the sofa, arms wrapped tight round her knees. 'There's something else.'

Alerted by her tone, Pelham turned to face her.

'Grace told me that when she walked into the Thames, she wasn't trying to kill herself but to escape from a voice calling her to come to him.'

'Him?'

'Maltraver.'

Pelham swore, then apologised, then swore again, his hand clenching round his brandy glass so tightly the knuckles showed white. 'He deserves to be dead in a ditch.'

'Yes,' said Evie. She hesitated, then asked, 'Do you believe me now, Pel?'

He didn't answer her directly but stared unseeingly at his fingers clasping the glass. 'I'd rather, first, that you told me all of it. So far I've only heard from you and Harriet the bare outline of what happened in Oxford.'

As she told Pelham how she and Harriet had discovered Janet Rae's mutilated body, his weariness dropped away and he sat upright, gazing fixedly at her. When she related how she'd found Professor Lorimer stabbed in the heart, his mouth dropped open. Finally, she produced their father's letter to Lorimer. Pelham read it and groaned. 'Poor Papa.'

'Don't you think that this is real evidence?' she ventured.

'It's evidence of something,' he said slowly.

'You believe Papa was self-deluded?'

'I didn't say that. But this is hard to take in. It goes against everything my reason tells me. You really think Papa was involved in the practice of occult magic?'

'Yes.'

'Lorimer too?'

'I'm not sure how far Lorimer was actively involved. He had Actaeon Fell's grimoire and he knew much more than he told me. He was really afraid.'

'With good reason, it seems.' He tugged distractedly at his hair. 'You say Papa was trying to summon this creature? This . . . afanc?'

'The night he died, he carried out a summoning ritual. He was within the double circle of the kuroskato, for protection. But the ritual went wrong somehow and the afanc crossed the circles.'

Pelham clenched his jaw. 'You're saying our father called up a monster out of a fairy tale and it killed him.'

'The afanc is a water elemental. Elementals aren't only physical beings, they also have a metaphysical form, invisible to us.'

'Visible or invisible, I can't believe a monster killed our father, or that he would engage in human sacrifice to try and control it. He was the gentlest man.'

'He spoke of sacrifice as the old way,' said Evie. 'He would never have resorted to it. He tried another way – and failed.'

'I saw his body, when he was laid out. No creature had touched him.'

'An elemental doesn't consume a body physically. It feeds on its life force, and the person dies.'

'No. The whole idea's unthinkable.' He reached for the decanter and poured more brandy with hands that shook slightly.

'Does the brandy help, Pel?'

'Not so much.'

'Can I try some?'

He poured her a little. Evie took a sip, spluttered and pulled a face. 'That is truly disgusting,' she observed, putting the glass down. She turned back to Pelham. 'Then you must think that I, too, am deluding myself. Or that I'm deranged.'

'Not at all, but . . . the things you say are objectively impossible.'

The door opened and Harriet entered to catch the tail end of the conversation.

'It may go against your scientific reasoning, Pelham,' said Harriet, 'but until and unless you develop a hypothesis that fits all the evidence better than Evie's supernatural theory, we need to assume she's right. She's been right about the danger to Grace, after all, and that's the important thing now.'

Evie stared at Harriet. 'But . . . you didn't believe me before.'

Harriet's clear, cool gaze met hers.

'Ah, I see.' Evie nodded. 'You thought we could run away, put it behind us.'

'Something's got inside Grace,' said Harriet. 'The girl's possessed. We have to help her, even if that means jettisoning everything we thought we knew about the world. There's no point sitting here, twiddling our thumbs and saying such things can't happen, because they evidently have.' She picked up a bundle of knitting from the sofa. 'Grace is still asleep. I'm going to take over from Mary.'

'I'll come up later,' said Evie. 'We can share the watching through the night.'

'Mind, this doesn't mean I've forgiven you,' Harriet said to her. 'And don't drink too much of the brandy,' she added severely. 'Leonie marks the levels.' With this parting shot, she left them to it.

Pelham had gone to stand by the window, looking out over the rain-slicked street, stretching his cramped, weary body. Evie stared at his back, not venturing to speak, letting Harriet's words do their work.

Abruptly, he turned and strode towards Evie, a new resolve in his face. 'Harriet's right – harsh, but right. There's no point sitting here, dithering, waiting for doom to fall. I don't know about this water monster – I can't say I'm convinced – but as far as the danger to Grace is concerned, we must assume that it's real and act on that assumption. So, does this *malign influence* have a limited range? What if we take Grace to France? Would she be out of its reach there?'

'That could work, I think. When the kuroskato possessed her before, she started to recover almost as soon as we left Yorkshire. When can you go?'

'Tomorrow morning. We'll take the early boat train.' Already, with the prospect of action, Pelham seemed surer of himself. 'We'll keep her safe. Surely he can't reach her across the sea.'

Across the sea. In her mind's eye, Evie pictured all the vast expanse of ocean between England and France. She saw Grace in the water, her clothes floating around her, sinking, and then *something* coming out of the darkness towards her. 'The thing is, it's a long way to France. Across water. If Grace is desperate to escape his voice in her head . . .'

Pelham's eyes widened as he grasped her meaning. 'We'll watch over her,' he said, 'and not let her up on deck, commandeer a cabin for her and make sure she stays in it. As for Maltraver, if he dares to come after Grace . . . I'll pack my revolver. What does he look like?'

She gave him a description.

'And you, Evie.' The look he gave her was uneasy. 'You should come, too.'

'Harriet will go with you. The two of you will watch over Grace perfectly well without me. I need to stay here and go through Papa's books again. There may be something that will tell us how to defeat the circle of shadows. It's the only way to put an end to this.'

'I shouldn't leave you alone,' said Pelham doubtfully. 'You may be in danger too.'

She shook her head. 'It's Grace who's at risk. It's she who carries the kuroskato. Not me.'

'Then promise me you won't go to Oxford or confront Maltraver while I'm away.'

'I promise,' she said solemnly. 'I'll wait quietly here till you return from France. Then we can think together of what to do next.'

'Evie, if you're bluffing me again . . .'

'I've no intention of confronting Maltraver,' she assured him. 'Certainly not on my own. Truly, Pel. I'm so very sorry about deceiving you. And Harriet. Indeed, I'm not sure Harriet will ever speak to me again.'

He gave her a swift smile. 'Harriet will forgive you eventually. And don't worry about Grace. We'll take every care of her. I'll return soon, and then you and I will face the circle of shadows together.'

CHAPTER
Thirty-One

S HORTLY AFTER TEN the next morning, Evie stood on the steps of a tall, narrow house in Camden Town and rang the doorbell. When the maid answered, Evie told her, 'I'd like to see Madame Trent L'Espoir.'

'She's not an early riser, miss. She keeps late nights.'

'Tell her I'm Walter Winstanley's daughter.'

Evie waited on the topmost step, her back to the slanting rain, and consulted her wristwatch. Harriet and Pelham had left at dawn, bundling Grace between them in blankets and shawls, having cabled ahead to book Grace a cabin for the crossing. By this time, they should be on the boat.

The previous night, she'd searched her father's books again, revisiting the lore of occult spells and sigils, turning up nothing that suggested a fresh lead. Discouraged and feeling she'd let Grace down, she'd gone to bed exhausted, only to waken in the early hours out of some half-remembered dream. Feelings of intense emotion had come into it, emerging from some hidden recess of her memory: the seance at Maltraver Towers; Lady Maltraver's face in an unguarded moment, full of loss, sorrow and fearful anticipation; the way she'd looked at her son as his fingers drummed a restless rhythmic beat on the table, like the pounding of hooves. Then there had been the terror of the horse, Trafalgar, when he heard Maltraver's voice.

Lady Maltraver's face; the sound of fingers drumming; the wild neighing of a frightened horse. In Evie's sleep-fuddled state, these seemingly unrelated incidents had assumed a new significance. *What connects them? Something . . . something. If you can just grasp it . . .*

Could there be another way to protect Grace? Evie would keep her word to Pelham: she'd neither confront Maltraver, nor return to Oxford. But she hadn't promised to stay cooped up at home, waiting for news.

The maid returned, breaking Evie's train of thought. 'Madame Trent-L'Espoir will see you, miss.'

'Thank you.'

There was little light in the hallway, a narrow space decorated with Anaglypta wallpaper in arsenic green. Evie followed the maid up a flight of stairs, passing paintings of scantily clothed goddesses from various mythologies in various states of ecstasy, until she arrived at a drawing room on the first floor. 'Madame will be here in a moment,' murmured the maid and left her alone.

Evie was struck by how closely the room resembled a theatrical set and imagined herself walking on stage: *Scene three, the spiritualist medium's boudoir.* The walls were azure blue, probably to mimic the heavens, but to Evie's heightened senses the colour felt oppressive, making the walls loom forward over her. The space was crowded with furniture: sofas and armchairs, a chaise longue and cushions, all upholstered in heavy fabrics, velvet and brocade. There was a plethora of knick-knacks, small painted tables, gilt-framed mirrors, a vase of peacock feathers and another of irises. The colours were deep but vibrant – purple, crimson and viridian – and the overall effect was like being inside a jewel box. A rich scent filled Evie's nose, patchouli mixed with something else, making her head spin. Seeking relief, she went to the windows overlooking the street and pressed her palms against the glass, cold and damp with condensation. Rain beat hard, trickling in rivulets down the windowpanes.

As she watched, the individual raindrops moved and regrouped themselves into the shape of the kuroskato, glittering like diamonds through the glass. She reeled back and covered her eyes to blot out the sight – though she couldn't keep out the sounds that accompanied the manifestation, the screams of a woman overwhelmed by terror.

This is why we're here.

A line of raindrops snaked up her arm, spiralled along her skin, seeking out her life force.

No! NO! I won't give way to fear.

She forced herself to look again and saw only raindrops.

'A pleasure to see you, my dear.'

Evie started and fought to compose her features before she turned.

'Unexpected,' continued Madame Trent-L'Espoir in honeyed tones, 'but still a pleasure.'

Settling herself with unhurried motions, the medium eased into a sofa, indicating for Evie to do likewise. Evie sank into the deep softness of an armchair, taking off her gloves but keeping on her hat. Madame Trent-L'Espoir blended with her surroundings, as though prepared for a command performance. Her hair was concealed under a silk turban, with an onyx shaped like an eye nestling in the centre, while her curvaceous body was draped in a voluminous robe, something between a kimono and a dressing gown, patterned in leaves and flowers picked out in gold thread. In contrast to the opulence of her attire, her face looked rather drawn.

'You must forgive my informal way of receiving you.' The medium reclined further back, her body limp as though boneless, massaging her temples with her fingertips. She surveyed her visitor closely from under her lashes. 'We had a meeting last night that continued very late. The spirits were so eager to present themselves, to make contact with their loved ones on this side of the veil.'

Osiris appeared and leapt lightly onto his mistress's lap, and she caressed his silver-grey fur with bejewelled fingers. He settled himself, front paws tucked under his chest, regarding Evie through almond-shaped golden eyes as though she were prey hiding under a dresser.

'Would you care for tea?' The medium summoned her maid and gave her instructions.

'Madame Trent-L'Espoir,' began Evie, when the maid had departed, 'I'm sorry to call on you without warning, and so early in the day, but it's a matter of urgency.'

The medium shuddered slightly, holding up an admonitory finger. 'Not, I beg, before the tea arrives.'

Evie fidgeted with the golden tassels on the cushion beneath her arm, searching but failing to find some bland subject of conversation. What did small talk matter, anyway?

Eventually, the maid returned bearing a silver teapot, its spout arched like the neck of a swan, and a plate of lemon biscuits.

'Mint tea,' said Madame Trent-L'Espoir, 'is all I can stomach in the mornings. It purifies the body and makes the mind receptive to the spirits.'

Evie took a sip. The mint tasted pungent on her tongue. As she tried to work out her line of engagement, the medium said:

'You have come to consult me?'

'What makes you think so?'

'My dear, I can see him.' The medium gave a serene smile. 'Your father, Walter Winstanley. He's standing behind you.'

Evie glanced over her shoulder. 'There's no one there.' *Of course not. Did you really expect there to be?*

'You're wrong, my dear,' said the medium, unabashed. 'You lack the sixth sense that would enable you to see the spirits. That doesn't mean they're not there.'

Evie put down her teacup. 'Madame Trent-L'Espoir, I haven't come to consult you about the spirits. Will you tell me why Lady Maltraver asked you to conduct a seance at Maltraver Towers? Did she confide her real reason to you?'

Under her loose robe, the medium stiffened. 'Lady Maltraver hoped to see her lost loved ones. Many come to me for comfort.'

Evie shook her head. 'Lady Maltraver had a very particular reason. Did she tell you the secret she believed her husband's spirit might reveal to her? A secret her son was determined would never come to light? That's the real reason he was so opposed to the seance, isn't it?'

Madame Trent-L'Espoir's expression was one of blank bemusement, but her hands had tightened unconsciously on Osiris, who yowled in protest and lashed out at her fingers. 'I can't imagine what—'

'She fears that her son murdered his father.'

A wail erupted from the cat's mouth and he sprang from the medium's lap, tail lashing. Beneath the turban, the medium's face had turned bone white. 'That, Miss Winstanley, is a terrible allegation. Terrible.'

'Yes.' There was no mistaking the dread in the other woman's face. *You're right,* Evie told herself. *And she knows it.*

'I can't imagine, I'm sure,' said the medium unsteadily, 'what would possess you to say such things.'

'I have my reasons.' Evie held up her hands, ticked off on her fingers. 'The previous Viscount Maltraver died in what was, to all appearances, a tragic hunting accident. The son was close by when something spooked the father's horse, Trafalgar. But the son was always a risk taker, a gambler. At a stroke, he became his own man, and a viscount, with an independent allowance and no father to stand up to him. As yet, he hasn't come into the full inheritance; it will be held in trust till he comes of age in a few months. In the meantime, he's an inveterate gambler and has got into debt. His mother's seen all this. She knows her own son. Perhaps she examined Trafalgar and found blood, or signs the horse had been drugged, or indications that the saddle girth had been tampered with. Not hard proof, but enough for her to suspect.

'Her suspicions would have eaten away at her as she watched her son grow to become the man he is now. Whatever he'd done, I doubt she would ever consider going to the police – she dreads a scandal that would indelibly tarnish the family name – but for her own sake she needed to know the truth, so she called you in. I believe you both intended for Alexander's father to manifest at the seance, perhaps with some additional ... help from yourself. Lady Maltraver hoped to test Alexander's reaction, to see if, confronted by his father's ghost, his guilt would become apparent. His bluster that night was to disguise how nervous he was, though it has taken me until now to understand why. He was afraid that the spirit of his dead father might actually appear, like Banquo's ghost.'

'All this is nothing but supposition,' said Madame Trent-L'Espoir quietly. 'Why are you asking me these questions?'

'Viscount Maltraver is a danger to my family – to my sister, Grace.' Evie's fingers dug into the arms of her chair. 'If you're any kind of true medium, you'll know what I mean and what kind of danger he presents. He has power – occult power.'

The medium's breath escaped with an audible gasp from between clenched teeth.

'If I had evidence that Viscount Maltraver murdered his father,' said Evie, 'I could use that information to confront him or go to the police. I could protect my sister.'

Silence filled the room, broken at last by the noise of Madame Trent-L'Espoir clearing her throat. 'I can't help you.'

'Madame, you could prevent a terrible evil from happening.'

'You don't understand. I *can't* help you. I have no evidence, no proof to give you. It would be my word against the Crosbies'.'

'Please—'

'You must ask Viscountess Maltraver.'

'There's no use in that. Whatever she feels about her son, she'll never admit to his crime, never risk the shame of seeing him hanged for murder. She would much rather sacrifice my sister than her son.'

'I cannot help you,' the medium repeated firmly. 'For your own sake, Miss Winstanley, you need to leave this be. Take your sister far away. Don't let him near her.'

Evie closed her eyes till she was sure she had mastered herself, then stood up, feeling around for her bag and gloves. 'I've taken up enough of your time.'

'Wait.'

Evie stared.

'There's something you need to know, about the seance at Maltraver Towers. There was a presence there.'

Evie lifted her brows. 'Ampheres from Atlantis? John and Mary?'

The medium looked affronted. 'There's no need to mock the spirits in that way, Miss Winstanley. But it's not my own spirit connections I'm thinking of. There was something else. I felt it. A power. A door opening.'

The water pouring through the ceiling. The blocked bath in the room above. The scale of an unidentified creature.

'The afanc?'

The word seemed to shiver in the air between them.

Madame Trent-L'Espoir dropped her teacup into its saucer with a clatter. 'An afanc – an elemental? Is *that* what came?' She chewed on her lip, her eyes round. 'You think you know about the powers invisible, but you know nothing. You understand *nothing*. You have no idea what it is you're meddling with.'

'I'm not afraid,' said Evie stoutly. *Not for myself, at least.*

'You should be,' said the medium. 'You really should be. Your father—'

The maid entered, consulting the card in her hand. 'Viscountess Maltraver is here.'

As the maid departed, Lady Maltraver entered, moving quickly, her furled umbrella dripping onto the carpet. Her gaze fell on Evie and her back stiffened, her protruding eyes, normally so forceful, now full of doubt.

'Miss Winstanley,' she said, inclining her head, noticeably biting back whatever she'd intended to say. Evie read the un-spoken words in the hand clenched on the handle of the umbrella, the strained corners of the turned-down mouth.

Evie crossed to the door, opened it, then paused and swung round. 'Your suspicions are right, Lady Maltraver. Your son is a murderer. A monster. He's ready to sacrifice anyone and anything for his own desires. His own father isn't his only victim. He's caused the deaths of others, too: two women who worked for you, Janet Rae and Sukey Huxley. He betrayed them. You've been wilfully blind to what he's been doing under your own roof.'

The viscountess-dowager recoiled as though Evie had struck her in the face. She shot an accusing look at the medium. 'What have you told her?'

'Nothing,' muttered Madame Trent L'Espoir. 'She worked it out for herself.'

Evie reached towards Lady Maltraver in supplication. 'He means harm to my sister. Please, help me.'

Lady Maltraver held herself with stiff composure, her expression frigid. 'Your sister,' she said in clipped tones, 'is a tart. Whatever becomes of her she will have thoroughly deserved.'

Evie dropped her arms and looked at Madame Trent L'Espoir, who turned away, though not before Evie saw the fear mixed with shame on her face. The older women had closed ranks in self-preservation. There was no point in wasting any more time here, or making appeals to the pity of a woman who had none. Feeling Lady Maltraver's hate-filled eyes drilling into the back of her neck, Evie walked out of the room, down the stairs and out of the house.

Her funds were rapidly dwindling, so rather than look for a hansom she meant to return as she'd arrived, in an omnibus. In her preoccupation, she hadn't brought an umbrella and her hat soon became waterlogged under the downpour. As she made her way along the street, avoiding puddles, her boots slipping on the wet paving stones, her head down against the driving rain, the medium's words echoed in her head: *You think you know about the powers invisible, but you know nothing. You understand* nothing. *You have no idea what it is you're meddling with.*

Pedestrians hurrying along the pavements pushed past her, intent on their own business. She was in a crowd, yet entirely alone. All she could feel was water, drenching her clothes, pounding her skin, getting in her eyes and blinding her.

Thirty-Two

E VIE SAT SLUMPED at her father's desk, her head on her arms. Outside the window, the early-afternoon rain showed no sign of slackening, dripping through the shrubbery leaves and churning the lawn to mud.

'Evie, my dearest.'
She raised her head. He sat in his armchair by the empty hearth.
'I'm so terribly sorry. I've left you alone.'
'Papa.' Tears rolled down her cheeks. 'You have to help me. What was it you found?'
'My dear child. You don't know what you're asking . . .'

Her head shot up. Had she heard something? Something hollow, echoing? A knock at the front door, perhaps? She rubbed her face, dispelling the dregs of sleep, as Mary entered bearing an envelope.

'A telegram, Miss Evie.'

Evie took it eagerly. 'Pelham said he'd send a wire when they reached France.'

Mary folded her hands in front of her and showed no signs of leaving. She'd been in service in the Winstanley household for more than ten years and she, too, was eager to hear news of Grace.

Evie tore open the envelope. 'It *is* from Pelham.' For Mary's benefit she read the message aloud, her voice sinking lower with each terrible word.

G has vanished. We watched cabin where we thought she slept but it was empty on reaching Calais. At first, we assumed worst. Now find she bribed a steward. Convinced she never left England. She may return home. H and I taking next boat to England.

Eight more words followed, which Evie did not read out to Mary:

Do not leave the house. Await our return.

'Oh, the poor girl!' Mary stifled sobs. 'Where could she be?'

'I don't know.' A lie, of course. Evie sat very still but her hands twisted the telegram. She had a very good idea of where Grace would be: she'd gone to the Magister, into the dark. She turned to Mary, trying to project reassurance. 'I'm sure all will be well. I have to go away. I'll take an overnight bag.'

But Mary folded her arms, a flush blazing in her cheeks. 'I'm sorry, Miss Evie, but Miss Harriet and Mr Pelham left instructions that on no account were you to leave London until they returned.'

'And how did they say you were to stop me?'

Mary's colour deepened. 'I'm not sure. But if you insist on going, I'm coming with you. You're not going anywhere alone.'

Evie hesitated. She didn't want to place Mary in an impossible position, but she also had no intention of putting her in danger. 'Very well,' she said. 'I'll stay here and wait for news.'

Mary's relief was palpable. 'I could make you something to eat. You haven't had anything since breakfast. It's Mrs Hope's afternoon off, but I can make a sandwich or soup. You must be so worried about Miss Grace. You need to keep up your strength.'

'Thank you.'

Mary smiled through her tears and scurried off.

The moment she'd gone, Evie went to a litter of papers on a table near the fireplace and burrowed amongst them. It had been Papa's habit to keep all kinds of papers, on the vaguely hopeful grounds they might someday prove useful: old bills he had previously settled, letters, theatre programmes, sales catalogues, articles and pamphlets of all kinds. Somewhere amongst the papers on the table, she'd noticed a timetable for trains to Oxford.

She found it at last, but as she opened it something fell out and dropped to the floor – a sheet of paper, folded into quarters. She picked it up. It felt stiff, as though it had once been immersed in water. She unwrapped it and stared at the object inside – a small square of what looked like tree bark, beaten thin. Its colour was similar to that of parchment, stained here and there with darker patches, and it appeared to be of great antiquity, brittle to the touch, as though it might snap at any moment. Carefully, she turned it over and saw lines written in an angular black script – words in what Papa had called the Old Tongue.

Was it possible that she'd found it? Could *this* be the summoning spell? She didn't know, unable either to read the words or to understand them.

Rubbing her aching forehead in frustration, she set down the tree bark with its indecipherable message and her gaze fell on the folded sheet of paper that had enclosed it. Written on the paper were more lines, these in Latin script and in her father's hand. Papa's translation of the spell? The ink had run a little, but the words were still legible. She read them – and her heart beat erratically. She got to her feet clumsily, knocking into the desk, and lurched about the room, her mind in turmoil.

Mary came in with a loaded tray, which she set on the desk. 'Here's your food, Miss Evie.'

'Thank you.' Evie indicated the sheet of paper and the piece of tree bark. 'Do you recognise these?' She struggled to keep her voice steady. 'Were they . . . out on this desk the night my father died?'

Mary screwed up her eyes. 'I think . . . yes. At least this funny old bit of parchment or whatever it is looks familiar. I can't really say about the sheet of paper. Your father had so many papers lying about, didn't he?'

'Yes,' said Evie faintly. 'He did.'

'I remember now,' said Mary more confidently. 'After they took away your dear father's body and I was setting the room to rights,

I saw this scrap of parchment on the desk, all sodden with water like, and worried it might be something important. So I wrapped it up in a piece of paper that was on the desk beside it, for safe keeping. I put it with some of his other papers.' Her eyes went to Evie's face. 'Are you all right, Miss Evie? You look ever so pale. Why don't you sit down a minute?'

Evie let Mary push her gently into the chair.

'You've had such a shock, miss, what with Miss Grace going missing,' said Mary, pouring her a cup of tea. 'Don't you worry yourself. Mr Pelham and Miss Harriet will find her, you'll see. We'll get good news soon.'

Evie didn't answer. She couldn't.

You've been blind.

She sat like a statue, the paper and the piece of bark clasped between her palms. All along, she'd assumed the intruder in the study had found what he'd been looking for, but she'd been wrong.

'I don't wonder you're upset,' said Mary into the silence. 'I expect Mr Winstanley was working on these things right before he died. Maybe it was the last thing he ever did.'

'Yes.' Evie whispered, her eyes fixed on the summoning spell. 'The last thing he ever did.'

Thirty-Three

THE TIDE OF rush-hour crowds at Paddington station parted to stream around Evie. She scanned the passing faces for Grace, though without much hope: her sister was almost certainly already in Oxford with Maltraver.

Evie had left a letter for Pelham and Harriet, explaining what she meant to do. Then, telling Mary she was going to lie down on her bed, she'd waited till the maid was busy in the kitchen and slipped down the stairs. Within moments she was shutting the front door quietly behind her.

A guard announced that the Oxford train was arriving. Evie hurried to the platform and found herself a corner seat in a third-class carriage. She hadn't brought so much as a handbag, carrying everything she anticipated she'd need in her coat pockets. The compartment filled up with a squash of clerks, typists and office workers, and two youths in working men's clothes who launched into a lively discussion about football fixtures. Others travelled in silence, reading books and newspapers or dozing. The air was cramped, claustrophobic and heavy with smoke from the engine.

Evie took up as little space as possible, keeping her elbows in to avoid touching the much larger man occupying the seat beside her, and was suddenly struck by a wave of fatigue, having barely slept in the last twenty-four hours. She knew she would need all her strength for whatever lay ahead, so she laid her head against the window and tried to rest, but the roar of the engine, combined with the clash of wheels and intermittent shrieks of the whistle, made sleep elusive. Once or twice her head drooped, but each change of pace or direction jolted her awake. The Latin words of the translated spell ran through her mind in time to the rhythmic pounding of the train.

In the centre of the double circle. In a whirling, spiralling vortex. Falling into it, down . . . unable to breathe . . . drowning . . .

The whistle wailed like a lost soul and Evie's eyes flickered open. For a moment she couldn't think where she was, but then saw that everyone in the compartment was staring at her. She must have screamed aloud. Her hands went to her face, and then a woman leant forwards and touched Evie's knee. 'Are you all right, dearie?'

'I was . . . dreaming. Thank you. I'm all right now.'

The woman nodded, her attention still on Evie.

Evie hunched up in her corner seat, tucking her trembling hands away from the woman's curious gaze. There was something familiar about the stranger's accent; Evie had heard it recently, though she couldn't remember where or when. She thought of asking the woman where she was from, but decided it wasn't that important and it would mean getting into more conversation and fielding more questions.

Evie couldn't shake off a suspicion that the afanc was hiding somewhere in the compartment, in some shadowy corner just out of sight, and looked for it surreptitiously under half-closed lids. Her legs twitched spasmodically, as though the afanc was about to shoot out from the darkness under her seat and seize her by the ankle. Had she called it up just by *thinking* the words of the summoning spell? She tried to blank the spell from her mind, but the words danced mockingly behind her eyes.

With a hiss of steam, the train pulled into Reading station. Most of Evie's fellow passengers rose to leave, one or two eyeing her as they departed. *They all think I'm raving*, she thought, not sorry to see the back of them.

One man remained. Middle-aged, bearded and unremarkable, he sat in the corner opposite her, immersed in the evening paper. Evie kept her eyes averted, gazing through the window. It had

finally stopped raining, though puddles dotted the station platform. A wind was rising, starting to disperse the clouds, and a few
stars were visible.

The man had let his paper fall and his attention now crept
towards Evie. He coughed. Did he mean to strike up a conversation? If so, she wanted none of it, so she picked up a discarded
newspaper from the seat where the woman had sat. It was yesterday's *Manchester Guardian*. Ah, *that* had been the woman's accent.
She thumbed the pages, pretending to be interested.

She tried to form a plan of action for once she reached Oxford.
She imagined herself telling Inspector Hammond, *My sister has
been abducted by means of dark magic and Viscount Maltraver is
behind it*, and pictured Hammond's reaction. No, there was no
point at all in going to the police.

Instead, she would look for Marcus, whom she hadn't heard
from since receiving his letter. She had sent him a telegram from
Paddington saying, 'Coming to Oxford tonight. Wait for me. We
will tackle Sons of D together.' With every hour that passed, her
anxiety for him grew, along with her terror for Grace.

All this was her fault. She'd drawn Marcus into her reckless
investigations, then left him alone in Oxford while she'd run off
to London to save Grace. What if something had happened to
him? She clung to the hope that she'd underestimated his
resourcefulness. As the memory of his warm brown eyes and
eager homely face came into her mind, she felt a little comforted
and less alone.

Her eyes fell on the open page of the newspaper, and a very
different visage appeared – a face she recognised but which had no
apparent place in the article it accompanied. She gripped the
newspaper, reading and rereading the words, trying to make sense
of them.

The article was headlined 'Rising Stars of the North' and was
about young actors and actresses from the north of England who
were making their mark on the stage despite hailing from places
distant from the metropolis and from backgrounds that were far
from privileged. One of the actors was Mr Kit Hollins from

Manchester, who had enjoyed a singular success the previous year in a production of *A Tale of Two Cities*.

Evie looked again at the picture, which was captioned 'Mr Kit Hollins as Sydney Carton'. It showed a young man, hands bound behind his back, in front of a guillotine. His long, dark hair – probably a wig, unless he'd grown it for the part – reached almost to his shoulders, but there was no mistaking his face.

It was Aubrey Penhallow.

Penhallow was a professional actor.

Like the turning of a kaleidoscope, the landscape of Evie's mind shifted. Impressions, ideas and assumptions tumbled over one another as she saw moments from the recent past with new eyes. From the outset, she'd been conscious of something enigmatic and unpredictable about Aubrey Penhallow. He could call up charm seemingly at will, then the next moment his whole personality would transform. She had labelled him a shallow money-grubber, a cynical seducer of women, but what if he was something much worse than that? Of course, Aubrey Penhallow, or Kit Hollins or whatever his true name was, had no direct link to the Sons of Dionysus – he was no student – but that hardly mattered. He could still be a member of the circle of shadows. He might even be – her fists clenched at the thought – the Magister himself.

Her dream came back to her – Penhallow on top of the tower, waiting for her, the kuroskato in his hand. She'd dismissed it as a nightmare brought on by the events of the previous day, but now . . .

Of course! *That* was why Maltraver had been so eager to ingratiate himself with Penhallow. It wasn't just about money, but about something much more important: access to power. It would explain, too, why Maltraver had always seemed to her, for all his iniquity, to fall short of her idea of a mastermind of the occult.

Yes. Someone else stood behind Maltraver, someone far more intelligent, someone who could act a part: Aubrey Penhallow.

And Grace was in his hands.

She leant forward, clutching her stomach, and a moan escaped her.

'Are you ill, miss?' The bearded man half rose towards her.

'That's no business of yours,' she retorted fiercely.

He sat back down sulkily. His newspaper went up again.

Evie stared wide-eyed through the window at the darkness. Reflected in the glass, she saw a woman's body floating face down in the water. Janet's ... or Grace's? How much longer did Grace have? Surely the most secretive rituals of the circle of shadows would not take place till a late hour? Torment like a physical pain tightened around her throat.

A faint glow shone over the darkened countryside. Through a gap in the ragged, hurrying clouds emerged a curved sliver of light: the new moon rising.

CHAPTER
Thirty-Four

E VIE RACED THROUGH the streets of Oxford, clutching her hat to her head, ignoring the frowning disapproval of a few passers-by at the spectacle of a young, respectably dressed woman, alone at night, running, purposefully and without decorum. Eventually, she came to a main junction and stopped, bracing her hand against a wall, doubled over, chest heaving. Away to her right snaked a double line of streetlamps leading to the most populous parts of the city. She followed them, plunging into a network of narrow streets, searching for the road where Marcus's lodgings stood. Had he received her wire? *Please be there, Marcus, I need you.*

Lorimer's corpse swam into her mind, and she brushed aside tears. For the first time, she was conscious of just how much she'd begun to rely on Marcus. She needed to find him safe and well, but the maze of streets conspired to confound her. She emerged by Carfax Tower and realised she'd missed the turning to his lodgings. Fuming at herself and the delay, she searched for the right road.

Some way ahead, a tall form in a dark suit appeared, coming from the High Street. She caught only a glimpse before he turned northwards, along Cornmarket, but she had no doubt it had been Aubrey Penhallow. If she followed him, he might lead her to Grace, but if she was wrong about him being the Magister, she would be going further away from Marcus and any possibility of obtaining his help. Yet if she hesitated any longer, she would lose sight of Penhallow altogether. She had to decide.

Dismissing doubt from her mind, she raced after Penhallow along the wide expanse of Cornmarket. There was no sign now of the dark-suited figure. He could have taken a turning, of course, or entered a house or restaurant or public house. She ran full tilt, pushing past startled pedestrians out for an evening stroll. At last, she glimpsed him, far ahead and walking swiftly, heading up St Giles', and she slowed her headlong pace, trying to blend into the background. The road opened out, forking to either side of a church, and he took the left-hand turn. When she came to the junction, she looked along the Woodstock Road, stretching into quieter, more suburban districts. Where *was* he? She hurried down the road, raising her skirt and lengthening her stride – and suddenly there he was, not far ahead. She slowed, fearful he might hear her pounding footsteps and look behind him, and focused on getting her laboured breathing under control.

Up ahead, her quarry suddenly stepped out of sight. Coming up to the spot a minute later, she saw a door with a sign overhead that read *The Woodstock*. She pushed at the brass door panel, and found herself in the entrance hallway of a small, shabby hotel that smelt of wood polish, its brown walls decorated with engravings of old Oxford. A party of new arrivals were gathered at the reception desk, where the proprietress, a tall woman wearing widow's black, her hair a sleek brass helmet, was wreathed in smiles as she greeted them. At the sound of the entrance bell, she glanced up, and on seeing Evie her eyes hardened. It took Evie a moment to realise that a young woman with no luggage entering a hotel alone after dark might raise certain questions. But the proprietress's attention was distracted by a man asking the way to a recommended restaurant; he produced a map and she was obliged to examine it to give directions.

Penhallow stood alone, his back to Evie, reading a sheet of paper. She was confident he hadn't yet seen her and was trying to work out how best to accost him when he put the paper in his pocket and headed up the stairs at the back of the entrance hall. She began to follow, but then paused. It would be foolish to confront him without a weapon. Evie waited till the proprietress turned her back and darted forwards to seize a walking stick from a stand by the entrance, then flitted up the stairs like a shadow to the first floor.

Penhallow was nowhere in sight. Evie considered knocking on each door in turn, to see if he answered, but changed her mind at the faint sound of a door swinging to on the floor above. She took the stairs up to the second floor, emerging onto another corridor, under the roof. It was quiet up here. The gaslights were turned down low, their glow doing little to relieve the gloom, but she could see a door standing ajar. She walked soft-footed towards it, past several closed doors, her sweating hands slipping on the walking stick. When she reached the door, she stood outside it, listening. A faint creak issued, as of someone within moving across bare floorboards. Was he in there? With Grace his prisoner? She would need to take him by surprise to have any chance of defeating him. She grasped the walking stick and braced herself to attack.

'Miss Winstanley,' came a voice behind her. 'What on earth are you doing?'

She swung round, bringing the stick up in a sweeping arc.

With an agility that caught her by surprise, Penhallow leapt back out of range. Gritting her teeth, she swung the stick again, but it was unwieldy, slowing her attack. He ducked under her weapon, sprang at her, grabbing her wrist, applying pressure until, with a choking cry, she dropped the stick and it fell with a clatter. By no means subdued, she kicked at his shins, but he evaded her and seized her other hand, gripping both and holding her off.

'What *is* the matter with you?' he gasped.

'I know who you are.' She tried to prise herself free.

An odd light came into his eyes. 'Do you indeed?'

'I know what you've been searching for. I know where it is. I'll give it to you. *If* you let my sister go first.'

An expression of blank incomprehension came into his face. It would have been convincing if she hadn't known he was an actor.

'Your sister? Grace?'

'Of course, Grace! I only have one sister.'

'I know nothing of her whereabouts.'

She snarled her disbelief and tried to rip her hands free to punch him.

The door before them flew open and a grizzled man in shirt-sleeves appeared, his face wet from shaving and his tie undone.

'What the blazes is going on here?' He glowered at Aubrey Penhallow, who was holding Evie at arm's length as she twisted furiously. Both of them were breathing hard with the struggle.

Penhallow scowled and retorted, 'Nothing that's any business of yours.' Nonetheless, he released Evie, who stood mutinously, rubbing her wrists.

'I'll be the judge of that, you young whippersnapper,' retorted the man. 'No gentleman would lay violent hands on a woman. I'm not too old to teach you some manners, sir!' He looked to be at least twenty years older than Penhallow, who rolled his eyes in exasperation.

'What if the lady lays violent hands on the gentleman?'

'Let the lady speak for herself,' fumed the stranger. He turned to Evie. 'Is this ... gentleman ... troubling you, madam?'

Penhallow took Evie's arm, pulling her close. He whispered in her ear. 'If you want to find Grace, we should talk this over, you and I, without an audience. Do you agree?'

Her heart racing, Evie considered his words dispassionately. Whatever he was, Penhallow represented Evie's best, possibly her only, chance of finding Grace. The stranger *couldn't* help her. The police *wouldn't* help her. Evie nodded her acquiescence.

'Just a misunderstanding,' said Penhallow to the hotel guest. 'Isn't that right?' he added, with a meaningful look at Evie.

'Thank you, but all is well here,' she said.

The man still looked dubious, but Evie kept nodding and smiling at him and eventually he pulled his door closed.

Alone in the corridor, Evie and Penhallow confronted one another.

'Why on earth do you think I have Grace prisoner?' he asked.

'Either you, or Maltraver, or both of you.'

His expression tightened. 'Maltraver's connected with this?'

'You know he is.'

His eyes rested on her searchingly, as though he would read what was passing in her mind. 'We could go to my room and talk there without interruption.'

She didn't move, only fixed a hostile glare on him.

He stooped and picked up the stick. Evie backed away, arms raised defensively, but he held the stick out to her by its handle. 'I'll show you how to use it, if you like.'

She snatched it from him, feeling foolish.

Penhallow turned his back, as though to demonstrate trust – or a low opinion of her aim – and set off along the corridor. She contemplated the back of his head, the thought running through her mind that if she were quick she might strike him there, perhaps succeed in killing him. But if she did so, her last chance of finding Grace in time could be gone. So she kept pace behind him as he led her along the corridor, unlocked a door and held it open.

'After you, Miss Winstanley.'

Evie marched through, and came to a halt in the middle of a simply furnished room with a bed – not slept in – two chairs and a dressing table, and a mirror over the mantelpiece. Signs of Penhallow's occupation were minimal. She and Penhallow crossed glances like flashing blades, and a memory came into her head of the first time she'd seen him, coming through a cloud of steam at the train station in Yorkshire. She'd been reminded then of a magician, a master of stage illusion. She should have known, then, what he was.

A fresh suspicion shot through her. Did he have Grace prisoner in this room, and had she too walked into his trap?

She lifted the walking stick higher, grasping it in a business-like manner. 'Move away, Mr Penhallow.'

With a curl of his lip, he stepped backwards to the wall and stood, arms folded, watching her. There were few places where someone might be hidden. She opened the door to a cupboard built into an alcove by the fireplace, but apart from a few coat hangers and spare blankets, it was empty.

'What are you looking for?' He sounded amused.

She ignored him and knelt to investigate under the bed, mindful of what she'd found the last time she'd looked under one. She had to lay down the stick and stretch herself out on the floor, and though it took only a matter of seconds to ascertain there was nothing there, during that moment she felt acutely vulnerable.

Penhallow, though, was still leaning nonchalantly against the wall. 'Are you satisfied that we're alone?'

She was back on her feet. 'Where's Grace? Have you taken her to Talbot College?'

'I told you, I know nothing of your sister's whereabouts.' The humour had gone from his face. 'But if you're searching for Maltraver, I can tell you where he is – or, rather, where he will be at eleven o'clock tonight. He believes I'm to bring him his winnings.' His mouth tightened with contempt. 'Consequently, he's eager to afford me his time. Here.' He took a note from his jacket pocket and held it out to her.

Evie thought it must have been the message he'd received at the reception desk. She took it and read:

I can spare you a few minutes tonight. Come to the side gate of the college, on Brasenose Lane, at half past eleven. M.

Was this a trick? She'd never seen Maltraver's handwriting. The only thing she knew for certain about Aubrey Penhallow was that he wasn't Aubrey Penhallow.

'We have some time,' he said, consulting his pocket watch. 'It's not yet ten. We might as well make ourselves comfortable. Can I take your coat?'

'It's rather cold in here,' she said, keeping the coat wrapped around her. She took off her hat and gloves and laid them on the dressing table before taking a chair near the door.

A glimmer of ironic humour flashed across Penhallow's face as she propped the walking stick against her armrest. He took the other chair. 'So. You say you know who I am?'

'You're a professional actor. Your name is Kit Hollins.'

His expression barely changed, except that his vivid green eyes regarded her with interest. 'Where did you get that idea?'

'The *Manchester Guardian* had an article on promising new-comers to the theatrical profession. There was a picture.'

His smile was humourless.

'What of Aubrey Penhallow?' she demanded. 'Does he exist? Are you impersonating a living man?'

'That toff?' he said mockingly. 'Who thinks only of making money and seducing parlour maids?' He snapped his fingers. 'A puff of smoke. Though I've met enough men like him to make him an easy creation.'

The man in front of her looked the same, but the way he held himself was different. A certain rigidity had gone out of him and his voice was warmer, softer. The clipped accent of the wealthy, well-educated southern gentleman had vanished, and his intonation had taken on an unmistakably northern burr.

'Does anyone else know the truth about me?'

'No one.' Too late she realised such an admission was dangerous. 'Except Marcus Ellingham. I've told him everything. He'll meet me here later.'

His eyes gleamed at her feeble ruse. 'You've no call to be afraid of me, Miss Winstanley. I'm thinking we have a common enemy, you and I.'

'Lord Maltraver?'

'Aye.'

'What is your grievance against him?'

'I too have a sister – or had one. You already know of her. Her name's Sukey. She worked for Lady Maltraver.' His face twisted into lines of pain. He stared unseeingly at his hands.

It seemed like a veil had been lifted and at last she saw the man behind it. His aloof manner and poised unconcern were gone. What remained was grief – unless that, too, was an act. Might she trust him? He probably could have overpowered her if he'd wanted, yet he'd done nothing to harm her, had shown no sign of intending to do so. Still . . .

'I am very sorry to hear that, Mr Hollins.' Evie paused. 'Forgive me, but I don't understand. I was told the name of the missing maid was Sukey *Huxley*?'

'Who told you so?'

'Janet Rae.'

His face darkened. 'Probably Janet was trying to protect my identity, by keeping the name Hollins out of people's minds.'

'Janet knew who you really are?'

'Knew me and helped me. And for that, she died.'

Evie's horror must have shown in her eyes, for he added, 'I didn't kill Janet. I've never killed anyone. But I should have done more to keep her safe, and for that I feel responsible.'

'Will you explain?'

He sprang up and paced restlessly for a moment, then leant against the mantelpiece with his back to her. 'Three months ago, Lady Maltraver wrote to my parents, telling them that Sukey had run away. It was a brutal, cold-hearted letter. She held Sukey herself responsible. She said our Sukey was a—'

He broke off. She saw his expression, reflected in the mirror over the mantelpiece, become suddenly tigerlike, teeth bared in a silent snarl. Below the cuffs of his tailored suit, his fists clenched tight. She watched him, not venturing to interrupt.

For a while there was silence between them. When he spoke again his voice was steadier. 'Lady Maltraver said our Sukey must have gone off with some man. My parents were frantic. They didn't believe Sukey would have run away without a word to them. My father went to Maltraver Towers, but Lady Maltraver wouldn't receive him. She sent her flunkeys to turn him away. He went to the police to report Sukey missing. They just laughed at him.'

He lifted his head, staring unseeingly into the mirror, and when he spoke again, his voice was hoarse. 'Sukey's a bright lass, but she's always been naive, wanting to think the best of people, wanting to be loved. We thought, if she'd run away with someone, or taken a place elsewhere, she'd have let us know, but we heard nothing. Sukey and I, we'd been close, but then I went away, with the acting. She got this job in Yorkshire. I was touring with a company when she disappeared. As soon as I could get free, I made a push to find out the truth. I had no clue to her whereabouts, only that she had been at Maltraver Towers, so I decided to go there.'

Evie thought of what it must have meant for him to enter the socially elite world of the Crosbies under a disguised identity, knowing that the least slip could spell disaster. Many things now made sense to her – how his whole personality had appeared to shift, how he'd made her like him one moment and loathe him the next.

'That must have taken a lot of courage,' she said.

He shrugged and ran a hand through his dark hair. 'It was for my sister.'

'How did you think up the role you would play?'

'In one of her letters, Sukey had mentioned that Lord Maltraver was forever gambling and seemed always in want of money. I told a mutual acquaintance – a theatre-goer, a man of Maltraver's class – that I wanted to meet Maltraver, telling him I wanted to see if I could pass myself off as a gentleman in order to prepare for a role I was to undertake. The man was happy to introduce me – I daresay he was glad to think of Maltraver being humiliated by an imposter. So Aubrey Penhallow was born, gentleman of the turf, with his insider knowledge of the track, dead certs and easy money.'

'Did you make all that stuff up – about racehorses?'

His eyes met hers in the mirror and he gave a wry grin. 'As a lad, I worked for a time as a groom in a racing stable, though I grew too tall to ever think of being a jockey.'

'Are you a gambler?'

'Never on horses. A mug's game.'

'So what do you gamble on?'

'Myself.'

'You thought Maltraver was involved in Sukey's disappearance?'

'From the moment I met him, I thought it possible. I may be just a jobbing actor, Miss Winstanley, but I could see he was a wrong 'un. The difficulty's been finding out anything for certain, so I've tried to get close to him.'

He sat down again, opened a plain cigarette case and offered one to Evie. She shook her head. He struck a match on the sole of his shoe, lit his cigarette, then sat back, holding it between long fingers, blowing out thin columns of smoke.

'Sukey was friends with Janet. I got Janet alone, told her who I was and gave her money to let me see the room they had shared. Most of Sukey's possessions had been destroyed on Lady Maltraver's orders – she didn't even send them on to our parents – but Janet showed me a few things she'd kept back, pretending they were her own; she told me it seemed a waste to burn it all. There were a few novels – daft stuff really, but Sukey liked that kind of thing. Romances.' His jaw worked. 'Inside one of them I found part of a letter, addressed to me. Sukey never finished it. She must have put it in the book for safe keeping.'

'Do you have it?'

He nodded.

'Might I see?'

He stubbed out his cigarette, went to the dressing table and retrieved a small leather case, battered and worn. From it he drew a letter and offered it to Evie.

She read:

My dear Kit,

His lordship has declared his love for me and offered to marry me. I rely on you to break the news to Mam and Dad.

Alexander says it must be a secret marriage. His mother would never allow it, for she is a proud woman and neither of us is of age. He has a special licence. I'm to join him in Oxford, where he knows a clergyman who will unite us.

Can you imagine it, Kit? Your little Sukey, a lady? You need have no fear for me. Alexander swears he will respect my honour and there'll be nothing between us till we are wed. I will write as soon as I reach Oxford.

Evie pictured Sukey as she wrote the words, her hand gliding over the page, imagining a bright future, her lover at her side. And all the time, Maltraver . . .

'This is . . . awful. Cruel beyond anything.' She stumbled over the words. 'Mr Hollins, I'm so very sorry. I fear . . .'

Kit nodded. 'I think so too,' he said, his voice harsh. 'Sukey's dead.'

Evie held out the letter and Kit returned it to the leather case. He seemed lost in some dark place. She stayed awkwardly in her chair, wondering whether she dared try to comfort him or whether it would be considered a liberty. But before she could make up her mind, he had turned away, found another cigarette and sat opposite her again. The tip of the cigarette glowed between his fingers, his feelings, once more, under control.

'You could return to the police with this letter,' she suggested without much conviction. 'It's evidence of Maltraver's complicity in whatever happened to Sukey.'

A sardonic smile crossed his face. 'Do you really think the police would help a man like *me* make a case against a lord?'

'No,' she admitted. 'I don't suppose they would.' For a while she was lost in thought. 'So, you and Janet . . .?'

He shook his head. 'Janet was helping me, that was all.'

She had thought this story was hers, but it was just as much Kit's. She recalled her encounter with Kit on the stairs at Maltraver Towers, how she had assumed he had gone to seduce Janet. He had let her think it, to keep his real secret hidden. *What a fool you've been, making assumptions about people, so confident in your own judgement.*

'I see,' said Evie slowly. 'You acted the part of a cad to put me and everyone else off the scent. Yet what did you mean by saying it's because of you that Janet was killed?'

He sighed, took another draw on his cigarette and flicked ash into the grate. 'I told Janet what was in Sukey's letter, because I feared Maltraver would try to seduce her too. Janet told me he was always chasing the female servants. Our poor Sukey was the only one who took him seriously.' Rough grief was back in his voice.

'So Janet knew what Maltraver is.'

'I warned Janet never to be alone with him, and I told her why.'

'And yet, even after you told her, she came to Oxford in his company.'

'In one of her letters, Sukey had said that she saw Janet as a true friend, with too much nous to waste her life as a skivvy.

When I met Janet, I thought her sharp, all right – sharp as a knife – but she liked money and was glad enough to take mine. I should've suspected then what she might do with the knowledge I gave her.'

'You mean . . . she tried to blackmail Maltraver?' She drew an incredulous breath. 'That was so reckless.'

'I think so. Not so sharp after all.' Bitter anger passed across his face, though Evie couldn't tell whether it was directed at Maltraver or Janet or himself. 'Maltraver's not the kind to pay out money and trust his liberty to a girl of her class. I reckon he thought he'd be safer if Janet was dead.'

'But he didn't dare harm her in his own house,' she said, piecing together what must have happened next. 'Too big a risk of him being caught.'

He nodded. 'I'm thinking he did the same thing he did with Sukey – lured Janet away with promises of money and a better life, telling her to speak to no one and he'd see her right. Well, we both know where Janet fetched up . . .'

Evie shivered and tried to thrust away the memory of a drifting body with pallid, bloated limbs and matted hair, drifting slowly back and forth in the current. She had to concentrate on what needed to be done. 'How do you mean to—'

'My plan, you mean? I've been angling to get Maltraver to meet me alone, where none of his servants or cronies can intervene and it's just the two of us. Tonight, he's agreed.'

'And then?' she prompted, for he had fallen silent.

'I'll make him tell me the truth of what he did to Sukey, and where he's hidden your Grace.' Kit held himself with almost unnatural calm, his expression unfathomable. The only clue to what he was feeling was the whiteness of his knuckles as his fists closed on the armrests of his chair, the bones standing out sharply beneath the thin layer of skin.

'You're confident you can do that?'

He raised an eyebrow, gentle mockery twisting his mouth. 'You doubt me? He's barely grown and never done a day's work. I wasn't always an actor, Miss Winstanley.'

'I'm sure you can handle yourself in a fair fight, Mr Hollins, but physical force alone may not be enough – probably *won't* be enough. There's more to this than a group of ruthless, predatory men. I've been investigating Maltraver and his cronies for some time, and there's much you don't yet know. I've made certain discoveries. These men are involved in occult magic. Professor Lorimer at Talbot was going to speak to me about it – but I found him murdered.'

Kit's eyes widened.

She continued in a rush, 'You may find all this hard to believe.'

Beneath his stillness, his gaze was steady on her face.

Her chin lifted. 'Marcus Ellingham believes me.' She winced, realising how defensive that sounded.

'Does he now? And where is Mr Ellingham? If he thinks you could be in danger, shouldn't he be at your side?'

'He wrote me that he had a plan to trap Maltraver.' She broke off, took a shaky breath and continued uncertainly, 'He may have succeeded.'

Kit didn't answer, but she saw doubt in the way his brows drew together.

'You don't think he's capable of defeating Maltraver, of outwitting him?' Her voice sounded oddly hollow in her own ears, as if she was trying to convince herself.

'I can't say. I hardly know Ellingham.' His tone was carefully neutral. 'But Maltraver was well enough and at liberty when he sent me that note earlier this evening.'

She nodded and whispered, 'Yes, of course.'

Had something terrible happened to Marcus? If so, it would be because he'd been trying to help her, because he cared for her. It would be her fault. While she, for her part, hadn't even been thinking of him, or not enough. Guilt flooded her. Was she so full of fear for Grace that she had no space for anyone else?

Kit must have seen something of her anguish written on her face, for he said quietly, 'He ... matters to you?'

'It's not that,' she said quickly. *Too quickly?*

'You blame yourself, then?'

She gulped and nodded.

'But you told him what happened to Lorimer?'

'Oh, yes.'

'So he knew the risks. He's a grown man and it was his choice.'

'I suppose so.' But it wrung her heart, after all, to think that a man might have gone to his death while trying to help her.

Kit waited, watching her expression change as she struggled through her conflicting thoughts, her emotions. Then, his long body shifted and he spoke briskly, 'So what are these discoveries you've made, Miss Winstanley?'

'It's complicated,' she told him. How long might it take to convince him? A glance at her wristwatch showed it was already half past ten.

Kit followed the direction of her gaze. 'We have a while before I go to meet Maltraver. If he's holding Grace prisoner, I'll find her and bring her back to you. Will you tell me what you know?' A faint smile touched his mouth. 'I may not be Marcus Ellingham, but I think I can manage *complicated*.'

She embarked on her story, keeping nothing back, trying to focus on the telling, yet a part of her tried to gauge how he was taking it. His face gave little away, and she remembered his skill as a card player.

Only when she'd finished did he speak. 'So you think these friends of Maltraver's, the swaggering schoolboys I met on top of the tower, played a part in what happened to Sukey, to Janet, to the professor?'

'Yes. But don't you see? They're not just students playing at being bad. The circle of shadows stands behind them.'

'This cult you speak of?'

'Yes.' In spite of herself, her voice wavered. 'Don't you believe me?'

'Since you ask me outright, I have to say that I don't, Miss Winstanley.'

She cried out in exasperation, leapt up and began pacing the room, arms crossed against her body.

'The things people do to one another,' he said, observing her restless movements, 'are far worse than any tales of spirits or ghosts or . . . monsters in the water. It's people that are the real monsters.'

'But don't you see?' she said again, drawing closer to him in her desire to convince him. 'It's both. These men resort to terrible methods to get what they want. They use supernatural means for evil ends. You've seen the power of the supernatural yourself – at the seance.'

Kit shrugged. 'That was all trickery.'

'Not all of it. A girl spoke, cried out for help. Her accent resembled yours – a Manchester accent I think. Forgive me for asking – was it your sister?'

'I heard no girl's voice. If it was Sukey, I didn't know it. I wish to God I could hear her voice again.' He pressed his hands to his head as if it ached unbearably. 'I don't remember much. A lot of nonsense about a high priest of Atlantis, and then . . . I'm not sure. Perhaps I slept. It was dull enough. The next thing I recall was a deluge of cold water, people shouting and everything in darkness.'

Evie's mind went back to the seance. Surely Kit had been awake? She remembered how his eyes had shone like a cat's in the darkness.

What was it that Madame Trent-L'Espoir had said about an unseen presence at the seance? *A power. A door opening.*

An idea began to form in her mind. She barely heard Kit saying apologetically, 'I don't want to offend you, Miss Winstanley. I don't doubt you've had a great deal more education than I, but I can't say what I don't believe.'

'I understand,' she said absently, her mind still on her idea. Her dream flashed back to her then – Kit on the tower, the kuroskato in his hand, telling her there was nothing to fear, that that was why they were here.

Kit took out his pocket watch. 'Ten past eleven. Time I was going.'

She snapped back to the present moment. 'Time *we* were going, Mr Hollins.'

His green eyes opened wide. 'You want to come with me to meet Maltraver?'

'Of course. He has my sister. Do you expect me to wait here quietly while you go off to tackle him alone?'

'If he sees you with me, he won't trust me.'

'I'll keep out of sight. You can call me once you have him ... secured. Between us, we'll make him reveal where Grace is. Is that a plan, Mr Hollins?'

'Right enough,' he said doubtfully. 'Has anyone ever told you you're uncommonly rash?'

'My brother, Pelham, says so all the time.'

'I'm thinking he has the right of it. You're an independent spirit. And you have courage, I don't doubt.'

'Not really,' she said. 'But this is too important. You're willing to take the risk. Why shouldn't I?'

He regarded her sombrely for a moment but then unbent a little, a smile warming his eyes. 'We'll go together. It's time we were off.'

He went to the door and opened it with Evie on his heels. 'Your hat and gloves,' he said, gesturing towards the dressing table.

'Oh, yes.' She took a step towards them and spun round just as the door closed.

'Mr Hollins!' She rushed forward, hearing the key turn in the lock. 'No!'

His voice came from the other side. 'I'm sorry. It was a shabby trick, but this business is too dangerous for a girl, no matter how brave she may be.'

'Let me out!' She hammered her fists against the door. 'You chivalrous idiot!'

'I'll confront Maltraver. And find your sister.'

'Not this way! You can't do it like this. Don't you understand? You need me. You don't know what you're up against. It's not enough to play the hero. The circle of shadows is real, Mr Hollins!'

She continued to yell, demanding and imploring that he return, pounding against the unyielding oak. Eventually, she stopped to listen, but from the other side of the door there was only silence.

Thirty-Five

'Is something wrong?' came an unknown male voice from outside in the corridor.

Evie rattled the doorknob. 'I'm locked in! Let me out!'

There was a brief pause, and then the voice came again. 'There's no key in the lock.'

Evie squealed with exasperation. 'Then get one of the hotel staff!'

'Oh, yes. Right you are.'

'Please, hurry!'

'Wait there,' the voice added unnecessarily. Slow footsteps departed.

It had been more than twenty minutes since Kit Hollins had left and Evie's fists were a mass of bruises, her knuckles raw and bleeding, her throat hoarse from shouting. She slumped down against the door as more precious minutes ticked past. She checked her wristwatch, imagining what must be happening. Kit must have met Maltraver by now. Had he got through the gate of Talbot College?

Then a woman's voice sounded. 'What's going on here?'

'Please, let me out!'

There was a rattle of a key turning in the lock, then the door swung open. The hotel proprietress stood there, blocking Evie's way, her hard eyes raking her up and down, taking in her wild, unruly hair and the abrasions on the backs of her hands.

'Mr Penhallow locked you in and took away the key? We don't want no perverted goings-on here, I'll have you know. This is a respectable house.'

Evie sidled past.

'We don't have none of your sort,' the woman bawled after her. 'Out you go, my girl, or I'm calling the police.'

By that time Evie was racing down the stairs, the words 'Brazen hussy!' assailing her ears.

~

The streets around Talbot College formed a labyrinth in which it was all too easy to become confused. A jumble of interconnected colleges, libraries, accommodation and offices fitted together like the pieces of a jigsaw, their dimensions hidden behind high walls. At the heart of the maze was Brasenose Lane, a narrow, cobbled road bounded by stone walls soaring up more than thirty feet on either side and studded with several doors facing the lane, one of which, at least, must lead into the precincts of Talbot College. All were locked.

Evie retraced her steps towards Turl Street, trying to formulate a plan to get past the locked front gate and the night porters in the lodge. Then she stopped. Someone was coming towards her wearing an academic gown, their footsteps echoing off the high walls. Evie tensed to turn and run, but something about the stocky figure and the way it moved, stomping along the cobbles, seemed familiar. She called out: 'Mr Zouch?'

Bernard Zouch lurched to a stop beside her under a streetlamp, swaying slightly, considering her doubtfully. His eyes grew owl-like as he recognised her. 'Not a good idea for you to be here on your own at night. If Maltraver and his friends found you . . . Not good, Miss Winstanley.'

By the streetlamp's yellow light, she saw that Zouch's face was waxen, his eyes unfocused.

'Mr Zouch, are you drunk?'

'Not drunk enough.'

'Have you been with the Sons of Dionysus tonight?'

For a moment, it seemed he wouldn't answer. He rocked backwards, contemplating the wall before him. 'One of their dinners,' he mumbled. 'Drink was consumed. Everything to excess. Part of the fun of the thing. Jolly good show.' He turned still paler, his forehead covered with sweat, then clutched his hand to his mouth and tottered off to the gutter. Sounds of retching and vomiting followed.

As Evie waited, a plan formed in her mind, born of desperation, and she fought to control her impatience. Zouch eventually wandered back, looking more alert.

'Are you alone?' she said.

He looked blank. 'Always.'

'What about the others? Maltraver, Pomeroy, DD, Roope? Where are they?'

He frowned. 'They were at the Bear earlier, but they went back to college. I think they've special business tonight. I'm not invited when they have their *special business*. Not one of the inner circle, you see. I stayed on at the Bear for another drink.'

He sounded so lost that part of her shrank from what she intended doing. She didn't want to cause him more unhappiness, but she saw no other way.

'What happened when Teddy Windle disappeared?'

'One day,' Zouch whispered, 'he just wasn't there. He didn't come into hall for breakfast. I went to his room – his bed hadn't been slept in. His clothes were gone, and his valise, but he'd left behind some of the things he cared for most, as though he'd packed in a hurry – a book I'd given him, an illustrated guide to birds of the world. Even though he and I weren't so close anymore ...' His face clenched with suffering. 'He loved that book.'

'Did he disappear after a night when the inner circle had their *special business*? Did Teddy go with them?'

He stared blankly, looking at nothing, and she realised then that he already had an idea, or at least suspected – had known it for a while.

He gulped, as though choking down a lump of grief, and pulled at his tie. 'The night before, Teddy and I were having a quiet drink with a few of the others. DD came over and invited Teddy to go with them. DD said they didn't want me to tag along, that I was surplus to requirements. Teddy just . . . got up and left, as though DD was the Pied Piper.'

She drew in her breath. 'This will be hard for you to hear, and I'm very sorry . . . but I believe they murdered Teddy.'

'I didn't know, not for sure,' he murmured. 'But he would never have gone off to the colonies, not without letting me know. That wasn't like him at all. So when Maltraver said Teddy had gone abroad, that day on the tower, I knew, really . . .' He blinked rapidly, head jerking.

She was afraid he was about to burst into tears. There was no time for sorrow – not yet. She jumped in hastily: 'Can you get me into the college? Show me the place they meet when they have their *special business*?'

'I can't do that. I can't go against them. Don't ask me.'

'I'm not asking you to. I'll face them alone.'

He stared at her, amazed. 'You're mad.'

'Not mad. Desperate. They have my sister, you see.'

He gaped, open-mouthed. 'Then I'm very sorry. But you don't know what you're asking. If they find out I've blabbed . . .'

'Don't waste time being sorry. Help me. For my sister's sake. For Teddy's sake. For the others.'

'There've been others?' He groaned and rubbed tears from his cheeks with the sleeve of his gown while she waited, trying to curb her impatience, combating an urge to shake him. 'All right,' he said eventually. 'I'll show you the way in. But I won't face them. If we meet them, you're on your own. You've got to be quiet as the grave.' He tittered a little hysterically at his joke. 'For both our sakes.'

He led her further along the lane to a wooden door, studded with ironwork, set deep into the wall. 'Here's the Talbot postern.' He took out a key, put it in the lock and turned it. 'Students aren't meant to be out this late. One of the perks of being a Son of Dionysus – we've got copies of most of the keys to the college.'

She was afraid the hinges would creak as the door opened, but they must have been kept well oiled for it turned inwards silently.

A door opening. Her gaze fixed on the postern as Madame Trent-L'Espoir's warning ran through her mind.

'Miss Winstanley?' came Zouch's whisper. His face showed dimly in the faint light of the new moon and a few scattered stars. They were at the edge of a lawn, surrounded by tall trees. Branches waving in the night breeze showed dark against the midnight sky. 'We're in the warden's garden,' said Zouch. Ahead, Evie made out the great mass of the college. One or two lights showed, but most of the buildings were in darkness.

A faint clanking came from somewhere ahead. They both froze.

'You have to go back,' Zouch hissed, suddenly galvanised into action, trying to push her back to the postern. 'I can't bear it!'

'I'm not turning back!' she whispered fiercely. 'It was just a random sound. We've got to go on. If you won't help me, I'll go alone, and if they catch me, I'll tell them *you* opened the door for me.'

Zouch gave her a look of terror and loathing.

She felt a wrench of pity for him. 'If you help me, I won't tell them anything, even if they catch me. Please, Bernard.'

He shook visibly and she thought he might vomit again, but he pulled himself together and led her down a path, through an iron gate that thrummed alarmingly as it swung back, along several passageways and out into the open again. 'This is the Old Quad,' said Zouch in her ear. 'We're in the original part of the college.'

'How is it that you know where the inner circle meets?'

'I used to spy on them to try and find out their secrets. I don't anymore. I don't want to know.'

They crept along a cloister, alongside marble busts of past dignitaries of the college embedded into the walls like a row of white ghosts. The elongated shape of a sundial stood in the centre of the grass.

'The members of the inner circle – are they all students?'

'Not all. I've seen others being let into the college late at night. I don't know who they are. They keep their faces hidden.'

At the farther end of the cloister, they came to a closed door.

'This is the way down to the cellars,' he said. 'It's as far as I come. You'll find an electric light switch on the wall as you go down the stairs.'

'Won't the light give me away?'

'Yes, but you can't manage without it. It's pitch dark down there. You'll find cellars, leading into one another. Against the left-hand wall of the third cellar, hidden behind racks of the warden's finest port, there's a secret door. I don't know how to open it. There's no key. But if the members of the inner circle are already there, the door will be open.'

Zouch took out another key and inserted it into the door's lock. 'It's unlocked,' he said after a moment. 'Someone must be down there. Don't think too badly of me.' His face worked as though he wanted to say something more. 'I wasn't cut out for a hero.' He trudged away and was soon lost in the darkness.

Evie turned the iron handle; it felt bitter-cold in her hand. The door swung open. Over her head, the electric light was already on, illuminating a long flight of stairs descending into shadow. She had to be close now. She fought down a wild urge to career down the stairs screaming Grace's name.

You'll be no help to Grace if you give way to panic.

It took all her force of will to move deliberately, carefully, as she went down the steep staircase until she reached the bottom and found herself in a vast cellar. Tall wine racks divided the space into bays while a central aisle ran down the middle. Most of the racks were full, and she could see little past them. Electric lights were suspended at intervals from the ceiling, splashing pools of light over the central aisle, leaving the further reaches of the bays in deep shadow. Her nostrils filled with the earthy odour of vintage wines, overlaid with the heady aromas of brandy, sherry and port. She passed under an arched doorway into a further cellar, then into the third cellar, where a rack against the left-hand wall had been pushed back. In the space behind, she made out the outline of a door, the same dingy colour as the wall; it had to be all but invisible when the wine rack lay against it. There was no handle, nor any other means of opening it that Evie could see, so she set her shoulder against it and pushed. It stayed stubbornly closed. She put her ear to the door but heard only the frantic pounding of her own heart.

She cast around for something to use to pry the door open, and then noticed, amidst the thick layer of dust covering the floor, several glistening wet patches. The electric light bleached out all colour, but she caught a distinctive smell, of something animal yet metallic. Fresh blood.

Her heart lurched as though it would jump out of her body. *Not Grace, please, not Grace . . .*

Evie followed the trail as the smears widened and thickened, becoming a slick, and entered the farthest cellar. Here, the imprints of running feet had scored tracks in the dust, making a trail that angled between two tall racks. Beyond them, against the back wall, dense with shadows, was a huddled form lying in a pool of darkish liquid.

'Grace? Kit? Oh no!'

As Evie hauled the limp body over, more blood pumped in a sticky tide from the wound in the chest where the handle of an intricately carved dagger protruded.

Lord Maltraver wore a brownish-red robe, soaking in his blood. His eyes were protruding and unseeing, his teeth clenched in the agony of his final moments.

Evie's mouth opened in soundless shock, swiftly suppressed. Her hands were covered in Maltraver's blood and she tried to wipe them clean on the edge of his robe. It was a strange thing, made of rough brocade with velvet facings, wide sleeves and a silk lining. The colour looked like carnelian red, the lining perhaps violet, though in the washed-out light it was hard to be sure. It resembled the kind of garment one might wear for a theatrical performance.

She remembered Grace's message. *He bade me tell you – he has it safe.*

Ignoring the turmoil in her stomach, Evie explored the blood-soaked folds of Maltraver's robe, searching for a pocket but finding none. Then she slid her hands into the pockets of the evening suit beneath the robe, and felt along the length of his still-warm body. Nothing.

She sat back on her heels. She'd been so certain he would have the sigil.

She lurched to her feet and ventured further into the cellar, knowing she had to make sure whether Grace was there. In a far corner, stuffed out of sight, she came upon a small heap of discarded clothes that looked like they'd been used for rags. On top of the pile were the remains of a pink coat. She lifted it, saw it had been ripped and cut almost to shreds, and let it fall, horror tightening around her heart.

She scoured the surrounding darkness. No one else was here. It was just her and Viscount Maltraver's dead body.

Grace must be on the other side of the door. And Kit too . . . if the circle of shadows hadn't already killed him. The time for hiding was past. She returned to the door, lifted her hands and pounded.

'Grace! Kit!' No answer. Again she banged on the door. 'This is Evelyn Winstanley! I've come for my sister!'

The door stayed closed, immovable. Its thickness muffled all sound. She kept hammering. Again, nothing.

She felt the edges of the door, probing the thick black dust. Her grasping fingers found a hidden latch, set into the frame. She pushed it, yanked it, twisted it. At last, with a soft click, it snapped back and the door swung slowly open.

Evie crossed the threshold into a large, circular, windowless chamber, illuminated by several braziers whose flames cast flickering shadows against the walls. By their light, she made out a design scorched into the floor, covering much of its surface: two circles with occult symbols filling the space between them. In the centre of the circles moved a shape, constantly shifting and turning as it contorted within the confines of the prison forged by the sigil, seeking a means of escape. Evie thought she glimpsed eyes and a gaping mouth.

Around the edge of the chamber ran a narrow raised platform surmounted by eight high-backed chairs, elaborately carved in age-darkened wood. On a dais set against the far wall was a ninth chair, of similar design and antiquity, yet raised higher and with more intricate carvings on the back and the armrests. Evie had braced herself to confront her enemies, but she was alone. She spun around, expecting at any moment someone to swing out of the shadows and attack.

Then she looked down, and saw that she was standing at the centre of the double circle, at the heart of the ever-changing, ever-twisting kuroskato. Caught in a tangled web of lies. So many lies. As if from out of nowhere, words her father had once said surfaced in her memory: 'These ancient forces are utterly alien to the little world of humans, they don't have our emotions; love, pity, loyalty and trust mean nothing to them. To master the unseen powers, you must become like them.'

Love, pity, loyalty and trust mean nothing.

In that moment, many things fell into place. She understood what lay at the heart of the circle of shadows. Yet even as she worked out the pieces of the puzzle, she realised that her knowledge had come too late.

'Evelyn? Save yourself! Run!'

The voice echoed, weak and quavering, as though rising up from a great distance. She realised it came through an open trapdoor set in the floor, close to the outer edge of the chamber. Light filtered dimly from the space below.

Slowly, Evie approached the trapdoor. The top of a ladder emerged from the gap, along with a dank smell like drains and dirty water. She gripped the top of the ladder and, with shaking hands, stepped onto it. After taking one dizzying glimpse down past her feet to the depths below, she shut her eyes, her fingers so numb they threatened to release their hold, sending her plummeting downwards. *Don't think. Just do it.* She didn't need to see where she was going. She thought she already knew.

She started her descent.

Thirty-Six

A S SHE FELT her foot touch the ground, Evie swung round, peering through the gloom as she caught her breath and got her bearings. She was far beneath the wine cellars, in an underground chamber. The air was damp and foetid, the stone walls green with slime and running with water. What light there was came from oil lamps set in niches part-way up the walls, several lanterns and a faint glow from the braziers that filtered down through the trapdoor in the ceiling high overhead. Set into the centre of the stone floor was a square opening that gave onto a flooded shaft resembling a giant's well. The surface of the water gleamed in the lamplight like a black mirror. Evie couldn't guess its depth.

Eight figures stood at some distance from her. They wore brownish-red robes, like Maltraver's, and several carried lanterns. Each was masked in a hood in the same carnelian red, covering the head and neck, leaving only slits for eyeholes. On the chest of each figure the emblem of the kuroskato was embroidered in gold. Near the far wall, Kit Hollins was bound upright to a wooden post, his arms pinioned behind his back. He wasn't moving and his head was slumped on his shoulder. Unconscious . . . or dead?

There was no sign of Grace.

And except via the ladder, there was no way out.

For a moment, no one moved. Then a slight muscular figure stepped forward and stripped off its hood.

'I knew you'd do it,' Marcus Ellingham said. 'I knew I couldn't be mistaken in you.'

There was joy in his face, and something else – a tension, visible in the taut muscles of his neck, the way his tongue shot out to moisten his lips, the way his voice quivered, the way his chest heaved visibly as though he'd been running. The hood had ruffled his chestnut hair, which rose up in peaks. The blood-red robes were too big for him, the sleeves too long, and he had to push them up above the elbow. If she could only concentrate on how absurd he looked, maybe that would help her feel less afraid. Instead, rage and fear almost choked her, but she forced them down and tried to slow her panicked breathing, to curb the frantic pounding of her heart. *Keep your head. Think. If you give way now, you're lost.*

He held out his arms to her.

'Don't touch me!' she shrieked. 'Keep away!' She rubbed at her lips, wiping away the memory of his Judas's kiss.

Marcus flinched.

She'd been played for a fool. Betrayed. Bitterness coated the roof of her mouth, her tongue; her heart contracted into a hard knot. *No time for that now.* She shook it off. The essential thing was to use the cards she'd been dealt – a meagre hand, true, yet it was all she had.

'What's your price, Mr Ellingham, to let my sister go free? And Mr Penhallow too. If he isn't dead already . . .' She was fleetingly surprised at how strong her voice sounded.

'That fool? Oh yes, he's alive, just unconscious.' Marcus's admiration shone in his eyes, even as he nervously stroked down his hair. 'Won't you ask for yourself, too? I always said you were brave.'

Evie gave him a look of derision. 'The spell to summon the afanc and bind it to your will. That's what you want, isn't it? You were searching for it in my father's study the night you tried to strangle me.'

'Not that.' His mouth contorted as though in pain. 'That wasn't me. I never wanted to hurt you.'

'Liar.'

A hungry light came into his eyes. 'Do you know where it is?' He must have seen the answer in her face. 'You have it, don't you? Clever girl! I knew you wouldn't let me down.'

Somehow the ordinariness of him made it even worse. He looked like a normal, humane man – he even smiled like one and met her eyes – but he was nothing of the kind. *Love, pity, loyalty and trust* meant nothing to him. He'd passed beyond all such emotions.

A cold dread flowed through Evie's veins.

'I don't have it here,' she said. 'I didn't want to risk bringing it with me, but I know where it is. In a hotel room, here in Oxford. I won't tell you which. But if you let Grace and Mr Penhallow go, I'll take you there.' She met Marcus's watchful gaze and held it, putting as much conviction as she could into her stance. 'I give you my word.' No tremor in her voice. 'But if you harm them, you'll never have it.'

Marcus stroked his chin as he contemplated Evie. Silence fell. It was broken by a loud splash as if, down in the shaft, something stirred beneath the water.

Marcus's attention shot to the water, then back to Evie. 'You're lying. You have it here. Give it to me.'

She took a step back. 'Not till you let Grace go. Let me see her.'

'Grace isn't here.'

Evie's heart seemed to stop. Her eyes locked onto his. 'But she's . . . alive?'

'I swear it,' said Marcus, white-lipped, hands outstretched. 'I'll swear by any gods or powers you care to mention, by your life, or mine. I mean no harm to Grace. She's alive and you have it in your power to save her.'

Did she trust him? Not at all. But she was caught in a choice that was no choice. Give the circle of shadows the spell, or they'd take it by force.

He moved towards her.

Outrage and visceral horror nearly choked her. She almost begged – *Please, Marcus, don't do this* – but she could see in his eyes that Marcus Ellingham had turned his back on pity, and she couldn't bear to have his hands on her, searching her body.

'I have it.' The three words fell from her sullen mouth, echoed round the dark space, bounced off the clammy walls.

Marcus gave a wordless cry of triumph. Around him, the figures in red coverings shifted, murmuring to one another.

'I'll give it to you,' she said, 'if you let Grace go.'

'You have my solemn word.'

For whatever that's worth, Evie thought bitterly. Feeling in the pocket of her coat, she brought out a folded sheet of paper and held it out. 'My father made a translation of the spell. This is it. So, you have what you want. Much good may it do you. Now let Grace go. Mr Penhallow, too.' She swallowed hard. 'And me.'

Marcus took the paper and Evie stepped backwards, out of his reach.

'This is it.' He held the paper against his heart. 'The summoning spell. The key to the realm of the invisible.' His eyes closed in ecstasy and he appeared transfigured, a light blooming in his face. Evie barely recognised him. Was that how her father had looked when he'd completed the translation, before reading it aloud to summon . . . whatever it was that came? Marcus seemed to have forgotten she was there.

'Mr Ellingham,' she prompted. 'We made a bargain, you and I. Let the three of us go.'

Slowly Marcus opened his eyes, regarding her as though from a long way off – from the lofty heights of his dreams. He sighed. 'I deeply regret that it's not that easy.'

She read the truth in the fixed hardness of the brown eyes she had once thought so warm, honest and true.

I never knew you.

She flew at him, trying to tear out those lying eyes.

He held up his forearms to fend her off while two of the other red-clad figures seized her and bore her, kicking and struggling, to a second wooden post. Within moments she was bound there with ropes, still snarling her defiance.

Marcus ignored her cries and curses. His attention was all on the summoning spell.

Evie lapsed into watchful silence. Better not to expend her energy in vain efforts. There might be a chance later.

Marcus stowed the summoning spell reverently in his pocket and approached Evie. 'I'm sorry about the ropes. Are they hurting you? I could loosen them.' He began to investigate.

'Don't you dare touch me!' Though her arms already ached from being yanked behind her back and pinioned, she writhed away from him.

He let his hands drop. 'It won't be for long,' he said quickly, excitedly, as though his own conviction might convince her too. 'I want to explain, so that you understand.'

Evie stared at him incredulously. *He thinks if he explains himself, I'll admire his greatness*, while another part of her mind – the coolly strategic part – said, *Play for time. There may be a way to escape, even now.*

'I've been waiting for this moment for so long,' said Marcus. 'Mr Penhallow nearly spoiled matters, blundering into the ritual chamber. I admit, I didn't expect that. Maybe we underestimated him, you and I, Evelyn. I rather wondered, at one time, if you liked him. Some women might think him a handsome chap, but not you, Evelyn. You saw through him. He's not very bright. He knows nothing of the power of the occult. He was no match for me.'

'We should kill him, Magister,' said one of the red figures. Evie recognised the voice of Edgar Deverell-Drummond, his normally silky tone tinged with anxiety.

'I've told you,' Marcus said sharply, waving him away. 'There must be no pollution of this place by unhallowed blood.' His gaze dwelt fondly on Evie.

She felt sick.

'When Pomeroy appeared,' said Marcus, 'with the news that you had found a way into the college, I knew I'd succeeded.'

'You said we wouldn't use names.' The surly voice, coming from under the drapes of a tall, lanky figure, was that of Charlie Pomeroy.

'You're a coward, Pomeroy,' said Marcus, 'but you've nothing to fear. Miss Winstanley won't disclose your identity. She'll keep the secrets of the kuroskato.' He drew closer to Evie and murmured in a confidential tone, 'These fools from the Sons of Dionysus thought the circle of shadows was just another game; they relished the theatricals. They didn't understand real power. They've learnt better since.'

'Where's Grace?' Evie interrupted.

'Don't worry,' said Marcus soothingly. 'She's safe. My word as a gentleman. It's not of Grace we should be talking but of *you*, Evelyn. I've been following you, step by step, while you danced ahead of me, like a fritillary butterfly.'

Evie felt again the sun beating on her face, saw the butterflies flutter through the grass. Realised how he had deceived her.

'You led me to the hidden rock face,' she said. 'You let slip that you had family in the North Riding. That was careless of you. I should have realised what it meant. You knew all about the Sithwater, its past as a place of sacrifice and power. You went there as a youngster. *The circle of shadows will be reborn. We shall rise*. You knew those words were there because *you* had carved them. And when Grace went into the water, you *knew* there was something else there.' She stopped, almost choking on her rage.

Marcus swept away Evie's protests with an emphatic gesture. 'Of course I knew. But I didn't send her into the Sithwater. Her own weakness did that. Still, it gave me an opportunity—' He paused, tongue circling dry lips. '—to win your trust.'

Trust meant nothing to him but as a means of betrayal. Into her head, as though at random, came a piece of advice her mother was fond of giving her, though Leonie could have had no idea in what circumstances Evie would use it: *Men love to speak of their achievements. If you want to keep a man's attention fixed on you, say to him, 'Tell me more about yourself.'*

She had to keep him talking, while she worked out a way to fight back.

'You told me you knew nothing about mythology and folklore, that you didn't know Professor Lorimer,' Evie said. 'You lied.' She frowned, trying to think through the problem logically. 'Ah, I see – it was Lorimer who told you my father had discovered the summoning spell. Only Lorimer knew.'

'I was his most brilliant student,' said Marcus with a fond smile.

'But people at Oxford didn't like Lorimer; they dismissed his research as hocus pocus. Nor did they like me, his protege. After my finals, Lorimer put me forward for a research fellowship at Talbot, but a cabal was against me, a group of closed-minded, dried-up old men who believed the Oxford system was the apex of the life of the mind and must be protected from infiltration by such a man as myself.'

'So you became a journalist,' prompted Evie.

'Can you credit it? Me, with all my abilities, reduced to following the doings of so-called high society, pretending the trivial lives of the rich and well-connected, with their endless parties and social conventions, were of importance.'

'You took a job with the *Ghost Hunter*,' said Evie. Marcus's account of his life looked so different now, seen from this angle. 'And you wrote article after article denying the existence of magic and the supernatural. You must have found that amusing.'

He nodded appreciatively.

'And you were safe,' said Evie, 'for no one would suspect sceptical Marcus Ellingham of being a master magus. And the *Ghost Hunter* was useful too. It gave you the opportunity to make contacts.'

'You're so astute, Evelyn.'

'Don't call me that.'

'I wanted more. Much more.'

'To revive the circle of shadows.'

That gentle smile that she'd thought so ingenuous and appealing spread across his face like a bloodstain. 'I'd found the ritual chamber when I was a student here. The revelation that Actaeon Fell's secret chamber still existed in the very bowels of Talbot College would have frightened Lorimer half to death. He was sound enough on the theory of the occult, but he shrank from the practice.'

'So you used Lorimer to meet the Sons of Dionysus,' said Evie, piecing it together.

'I knew I'd need assistance to revive the circle of shadows, so I persuaded Lorimer to let me give his students a talk on my occult researches. I watched my audience carefully. Some were members of the Sons of Dionysus, but back then it was no more than a student society, all pantomime, till they met me. Most were no more than privileged buffoons. Yet I spotted a few with potential – ambition, resourcefulness, a willingness to disregard conventions of morality.'

'Men like you.' Evie put a world of scorn into those three words.

He started and blinked, then recovered himself. 'I met with my chosen candidates, persuaded them to reveal their true selves, what they really wanted in this life and what they were prepared to do to get it. I told them I knew the means if they were prepared to pay the price. I chose carefully, taking only a few. I required total loyalty, complete commitment. This little band of students formed the nucleus of our cult and helped me restore the ritual chamber. But I also admitted several others, men I had closely observed and found to be, as you say, men like me.'

'But Lorimer wasn't a man like you, was he?' She shaped it as an accusation. 'He was my father's friend. And like my father, he had a conscience. He drew the line at murder. So you betrayed him too. You used his trust in you to get close to him, to kill him.'

'You gave me no choice.' Marcus spoke with soft reproach. 'You told him that a woman found dead in the Cherwell was marked with the kuroskato. You put pressure on him. He might have revealed to you that I was his former student, a devotee of the occult, and that would have ruined everything.'

She thought of Lorimer, who'd tried to warn her, sprawled on his carpet, convulsed in death. If she hadn't gone to him . . .

'Don't blame yourself, Evelyn. You are blaming yourself, aren't you?'

'It wasn't my fault.' Her voice shook. 'You murdered him, not I.'

'Even so, you believe yourself responsible. You see, I *know* you, Evelyn, I understand how you think. That foolish, loveable, soft weakness of pity within you. Lorimer was a coward, unable to face the truth about the great mysteries to which he devoted his life. And so he died. He's not worth your regret.'

His callousness about a man who had been his mentor, his friend, chilled her.

'Would you like to hear something amusing?' he said. 'About the Sons of Dionysus?'

Behind him, several of the red figures shifted apprehensively.

'They were just a pack of entitled rich boys holding ridiculous pretend rituals where they dressed themselves up as druids and sacrificed a chicken or two. The circle of shadows was just a make-believe game for them until I showed them what it really meant. And here's another joke,' he continued. 'When I was an under-graduate, Lorimer proposed that I be adopted into the Sons of Dionysus, but the president of the society rejected me on the grounds that I came from inferior stock. And now look at them.' He swept a hand towards the acolytes, several of whom shrank back. None stood their ground. 'You see how they grovel? Because only I can give them what they want – the powers of an ancient immortal spirit.'

'So you're doing all this for earthly power. Have you succeeded?'

'Succeeded?' he said warily.

She pushed on. 'Has the afanc given you what you want? You've summoned it before. Why's this spell different?'

His gaze wavered. 'It's not easy to master an elemental. We can summon it to feast, but it's another thing entirely to bind it to our will. The spell your father discovered is the most powerful, most ancient magic ever devised for such a purpose. If this spell is cast correctly, with the proper rituals, the afanc will serve me, and my loyal followers.'

'So the afanc still won't do your bidding, after all the sacrifices you've made to it, all the deaths. You've failed. That's why you needed this summoning spell. Is all this worth the cost?'

Marcus drew himself up. 'I'm prepared for the undertaking, ready to pay the price.' His glance darted back and forth, and Evie had the impression he was listening out for something. *He's terri-fied*, she thought. *He says the others are frightened, but he's more scared than any of them, because he understands the risks.*

'You ask why I do this.' He gestured towards his heart. 'The delights of power, even the pleasure of revenge over fools who underestimated me, are not enough to justify the things I have done – or the things I must do. I'm an adept, a seeker after know-ledge. Much like your father, who was a braver man by far than Lorimer. You recognised that quality in me, were drawn to it. That's why you care for me, even now, in spite of yourself.'

She laughed in his face. 'You're not remotely like my father. He would never have used power to harm or dominate other people. You're no adept. You're a travesty.'

A flush more purple than crimson suffused his face. 'Perhaps I overestimated you, after all – your strength of mind. You mustn't think I take pleasure in sacrifice. But there's no alternative. Your father thought the ritual could be carried out without resorting to the old way. He was wrong, and his death proves it. For the summoning spell to be strong enough to bind the afanc, we need another sacrifice.'

Evie suddenly felt as if she stood above a yawning chasm; Marcus, the red figures, her surroundings – everything fell away. She groped to understand what he meant by *another sacrifice*. He'd lied to her, that much was clear, just as she'd feared he would.

'Where's Grace?' she demanded. 'What have you done with her?'

'Grace is safe enough.' He sounded regretful, melancholy. An eternity of slow moments passed. He sighed. 'It's *you* that's not safe, my darling.'

Marcus brought out an object from a pocket beneath his robe: the kuroskato sigil on a piece of parchment, a twin of the one Evie had found in Grace's mattress.

'The sigil binds her. It only works on those who are weak-willed, like Grace. Her emotions overwhelm her; the power of the occult works easily in her. I had no hand in her walking into the Sithwater. Why would I? She heard the ancient spirits of the Sithwater call to her and she obeyed. She's so much less than you. Yet you came here, for her.'

'I love my sister. If you knew anything about love, you'd understand.'

'That's your failing, Evelyn.' He gave a gentle shake of the head. 'Love is a weakness. You have let it overrule your judgement. That's why you've come here in her place. Grace has served her purpose, for she has brought you here, and in trying to save her, you came willingly.'

At last, she understood. Maybe in some unconscious part of her mind, she'd long since guessed. She was to be like Cartimandua's daughter. The willing sacrifice.

'You see, Evelyn, *you* are a much better sacrifice than your sister. You're courageous and clever, and you don't give up. A strong sacrifice is pleasing to the immortal spirits. A willing sacrifice is more pleasing still. Yet the most important reason why it must be you, my darling, is the bond between us. *He who walks the path of the adept must be prepared to give up the thing his heart most desires to get what his will most wants.* That is the sacrifice that most delights the immortal spirits. You said as much yourself, when we stood above the Sithwater and you spoke of how the druid priests sacrificed their most treasured possessions. That was the moment I understood what I needed to do, what would be required of me. For the potency of the sacrifice to be optimal, I could not bring you here by force or by spell. You had to come by your own will and workout a means to do it for yourself. I could not smooth your path. Yet you did it. You are utterly resourceful and determined, a fit mate for the highest adept.

'You say I don't know what love is, but I do. In giving you up, I will be cutting out a part of my own heart. The price of being able to summon and bind an immortal . . . is everything I have to give.'

He gulped back sobs. Tears crawled down his freckled cheeks.

A slim figure approached, peeling off a hood to disclose the gleaming blond head and boyish beauty of Deverell-Drummond, eyes bright with anticipation. 'Magister,' he murmured, 'if you're unable to do what must be done, because this woman means something to you, then I—'

'Keep back!' Marcus screamed at him. 'Or I'll give you too to the afanc.'

Deverell-Drummond gaped and fell back, scrambling out of reach.

Marcus turned to Evie. 'Don't you see, my own Evelyn? I have to do this.'

Useless to beg. Pointless and humiliating. Evie bit her lip to stop herself from sobbing, blood trickling down her chin. She gathered the remnants of her courage around her. 'I'm not *your* Evelyn,' she hissed, though her throat felt so tight it was hard to get out the words. 'I'll die cursing you. I'll take *that* curse to the afanc.' Terror numbed her body. If the ropes hadn't been holding her upright, her legs would have given way. 'My life for hers,' she said. 'You swear it.'

'I swear.' He held out the parchment between finger and thumb, spoke words in Latin and released it. The parchment burst into green flames, the sigil writhing and contorting. An inhuman scream came from it, and then it was gone. 'It is done. Grace is free.'

Across the cellar, Evie heard Kit stir. He groaned, then swore.

'Mr Penhallow, too,' she said. 'You must let him go.'

Marcus shook his head. 'He's seen too much already, even if he's too ignorant to comprehend the great mysteries.'

'It was you!' yelled Kit. '*You* killed Sukey!' He strained at the ropes binding him; his eyes, full of hate, bored into Marcus. 'But you won't murder another woman. Let Evie go. Take me instead.'

'Playing the hero, Mr Penhallow?' sneered Marcus. 'It won't do, you know. *You* won't do.'

'Why not?'

'The sacrifice should come willingly. You did *not* come down here willingly.'

'But I'll die willingly. If you let her go.'

'Would you now?' Marcus regarded Kit thoughtfully. 'How touching. Even so, I doubt you will fulfil other criteria. The adept should, if possible, sacrifice someone of value to him. Frankly, your death would be a matter of utter indifference to me, though I will of course make sure you follow her. Moreover, the sacrifice should be pure – a virgin – and I very much doubt that you, Mr Penhallow—'

'She's not a virgin,' said Kit. 'She won't do for your sacrifice.'

'What?' Marcus looked from Kit to Evie, then blanched. 'Oh, that is . . . preposterous! Not him!' he moaned, his chin quivering.

'We were together,' said Kit with a wolfish grin. 'This evening, in my hotel room.'

Sheer panic had blunted Evie's mind. She was drowning in a formless fog. Kit shot her a swift imploring look, and she couldn't comprehend why. For a second too long, she hesitated.

'That's right,' she said.

'You're lying!' shouted Marcus, foam flecking his mouth. He rounded on Kit, seeming about to strike him. 'You're not to defile her with your filthy allegations!'

Kit's lips curled in a smile of pure contempt.

Marcus lowered his fists and his gaze. 'It's beneath me to deal with this brute.' He turned away. 'Gag him!'

Kit broke into a torrent of abuse, using words Evie had never heard before. He offered to bribe the acolytes, if they would release Evie and himself and turn on Marcus Ellingham.

'You're wasting your breath,' said Marcus. 'They've come too far. They're all implicated.'

The figures crowded round Kit, screening him from Evie's sight in a sea of red. The sounds of an unequal struggle began – the smacking of fists connecting with flesh. When the figures moved away, Kit's eyes blazed in a battered face over a strip of cloth pulled tight across his mouth.

Marcus closed his eyes, wrapped in inward concentration. When he spoke, his voice had sharpened and risen an octave. 'The hour is approaching,' he called, lifting his head and flinging out his arms.

'What about Maltraver?' said Pomeroy. 'He's not here yet.'

'We can't wait for him,' Marcus snapped. 'He's drunk or drugged somewhere. We can do this without him.'

He held out his hands and an acolyte came forward with a jug to pour water over them. The acolyte offered Marcus a hood, but he spurned it. With a bow, the acolyte handed Marcus a dagger, its notched blade gleaming silver in the light from the lamps.

Marcus came to stand before Evie, holding the dagger in his right hand, point downwards. He was sweating despite the chill of the underground air, and Evie could see his jaw working. All the colour had left him, except for the red veins that stood out on his neck and in his red-rimmed, bloodshot eyes that blinked incessantly.

Could she use his fear against him? Maybe. But right now her own terror was too overwhelming, making it impossible to think.

'It is time,' said Marcus. His eyes shone like moons under dark water.

Two red figures came forward to untie Evie. The instant her arms were free, she struck out desperately, but they were stronger than her and seized her arms and half dragged, half carried her to the centre of the chamber, pushing her down near the well of black water. They knelt on her arms, pinioning them, and two more figures came over to hold her wildly kicking legs. She twisted frantically, but she was pinned like a butterfly on a board. Eventually, panting and exhausted, she stopped struggling and lay still, staring up into the shadowy darkness of the roof high above, her cheeks wet with tears she couldn't keep back. An acolyte raised a knife to cut away her outer clothes.

'Take your impure hands off her!' yelled Marcus, shoving the man away.

Using his dagger, Marcus cut away Evie's coat, pulled off her shoes, sheared away her stockings and sliced long slits in her dress so that her arms and legs were laid bare. Clinging to her pride, she didn't cry out, knowing her voice would betray the extremity of her terror. Instead, she stared at Marcus, filling her gaze with loathing, but he, perhaps guessing what he would see in her face, kept his own averted. He began to chant an invocation in Latin, and soon the acolytes lifted their voices to join in. The three who weren't holding Evie raised their arms so that their long sleeves fell back.

Over their voices came an outcry from Kit Hollins, who must have worked free of his gag. He screamed hoarsely at Marcus, pouring curses and threats upon him. It seemed to Evie that he was weeping.

'Which of you incompetent fools gagged him?' Marcus yelled. 'Shut his mouth!' Then, in a quieter tone: 'Evelyn can't abide raised voices. We need the still, quiet moment of the sacred.' He stood up, head lowered as though in prayer, and said to the watching acolytes, 'Raise the barrier.'

There came a whining screech of metal and Evie, craning to watch what was happening, saw three figures strain to push a massive iron-bound wooden wheel, taller than their heads, that stood against the far wall of the chamber. A distant roar of rushing water sounded under the floor and the flagstones under Evie's back shuddered and groaned. Somewhere near at hand came the slap of water against stone.

Marcus knelt alongside Evie, the point of the dagger flashing bright in his hand. Searing pain shot through her as he cut into her outer thigh, and a scream of agony she couldn't suppress burst from her lips. Four, five times, he cut her, pausing each time to judge, like an artist before a canvas, before making the cut; slashing the blade across her skin, not to the bone but deep enough to raise copious amounts of blood. She whimpered, turned her face away, and felt the bitter chill of water on her cheek.

She blinked away the tears blurring her vision. Water was gushing out of the flooded shaft, spilling in waves and rivulets across the floor. The light from the oil lamps picked out puddles forming in the uneven flooring. Streams of water bubbled up from the shaft, trickled across the flagstones, connecting the puddles. A primal, musky smell invaded Evie's nostrils. An odour she recognised.

Marcus wiped sweat from his brow with one long, trailing sleeve while his other hand held the blade – now dripping with Evie's blood – at arm's length. He seemed afraid of her blood. Might that be significant? If she could only *think*!

'With this sign of power,' Marcus intoned, 'I mark you, Evelyn Winstanley, as an offering to the immortal one. He will know you as his own. And now the rest . . .' He rose and walked round to her other side.

The agony of the cuts dispersed the cloud of terror in Evie's head, and suddenly her mind was clear again. She remembered her father's letter to Lorimer: *for this ritual must be done correctly; the spell must be spoken at the proper time, taking the right precautions.* If not . . .

Her mouth felt full of ashes. She swallowed repeatedly, trying to bring moisture back to her tongue. Could she remember? There could be no mistakes. She coughed spasmodically, trying to clear her throat.

Marcus knelt at her right side, the dagger raised, its tip pointing towards her flesh.

Evie looked him in the eyes and began to speak, at first in little more than a quavering whisper: '*Coniuro te, magne spiritus aquarum . . .*'

'What are you doing?' spluttered Marcus. 'It's not yet time. This has to be done properly or the spirit won't be bound. Stop!'

Evie felt the thread of her voice becoming stronger, resonating through her chest:

'*Veni ad locum istum . . .*'

'You can't do this!' Marcus's gaze snapped to the flooded shaft. Alerted by his panic, Evie's captors released their hold on her and began to back away.

Barely conscious of the pain now, Evie pulled herself upright, standing ankle-deep in water.

'Stop it, Evelyn! Right now!' Marcus screamed in her face.

She blinked at his proximity but kept intoning, '*Accipe hoc sacrificium sanguinis et liga te ad me . . .*'

'No!' Marcus shrieked. The dagger dropped from his nerveless hand and vanished beneath the rising tide. He clapped his hands to his ears to block out the spell.

Evie flung the final words in Marcus's face: '*Veni, veni, veni!*'

Shouts of dismay resounded as the acolytes broke ranks and bolted for the ladder, fighting to be the first to climb. In the centre of the chamber, the flooded shaft was now entirely submerged, but Evie saw something moving there, just beneath the surface, agitating the water. Marcus waded to the wheel, robes trailing through the tide, hauling at it, straining every muscle, but it wouldn't budge. He turned to the ladder and screamed at the acolytes who were swarming up it like a line of red spiders, robes flapping around their legs. 'Come back, you cowards!'

Evie looked back to the flooded shaft and clamped her hands across her mouth, forcing back the scream rising up through her throat. Something was emerging from it – cloaked in shadow. Blackness filled the air around it in a shimmering pulsating fog, blurring Evie's vision. The stench was overwhelming – the thick, primordial miasma of decaying matter from a stagnant pond. She wasn't certain what she saw, beyond an impression of curved claws, of lamplight glinting over scaled flanks encrusted with mud. She dreaded that the being would perceive her, yet she was unable to move, utterly transfixed by a dread she had never known, aware only that she was confronted by a being utterly alien to human-kind, that she and every other human were as nothing to it. She herself had summoned this apparition into the upper world, yet she could no more send it back than she could bring down a mountain.

The sting of her wounds suddenly became agonizing and she looked down to see the rising tide lapping at her lacerated thigh, her blood forming scarlet clouds in the water. Something like a colossal head swung in her direction, the two black pits of its eyes glowing with dark light. Slowly, unhurriedly, the apparition moved towards her as she stood, rooted to the ground in terror.

Then a strange movement beyond the dark cloud caught her eye. Kit lay slumped in his bonds, head flung back, throat exposed, only the whites of his eyes showing. From out of his chest, a form was rising – the shadowy figure of a young woman. Even as Evie stared, dumbfounded, the woman uncoiled herself upright, tangled hair clouding around her face. The sigils cut into her limbs trick-led fresh blood into the water. The four sigils that had been carved by Marcus, when it had been her turn to die.

The apparition stopped and inhaled. Then it turned and, with an eager whine, began shuffling towards the newcomer. The shadow-woman circled the outer edge of the chamber, drawing the creature after her, till she came to Marcus Ellingham as he cringed against the opposite wall, his arms upraised. Evie won-dered why he didn't try to run; then realised that he too was paralysed by terror.

The shadow-woman seized hold of Marcus and scrambled up him, wrapping her limbs around his body. With her right hand, she ripped apart his robes and shirt. Clinging to him with one arm and her entwined legs, she cupped her hand to her dripping wounds. Palm covered with her sacrificial blood, she wiped it over Marcus's arms and thighs. She took more blood, and drew her hand across his chest, his sweating forehead, the pale, hairy expanse of his belly, leaving scarlet smears on his quivering naked skin.

All the while, Marcus mewled and groaned in her embrace, squirming, trying to prise off her fingers, but she clung to him all the tighter, her nails digging into his flesh. She bent forward to breathe in his fear, gusts of soft rippling laughter breaking from her.

The apparition came on through the water, lured by the sacrificial blood. As it approached Marcus, the shadow-woman released her hold on him and sank beneath the surface, disappearing from sight.

The creature reared over Marcus, now cowering in abject terror. Its jaws opened, baring double rows of long, knifelike teeth.

There was a thin, high-pitched wail – Marcus screaming. For a moment his round, homely face, transfixed by shock, was illuminated in the dark light. He gave a muffled cry, abruptly cut off, as he was dragged down beneath the surface.

The water churned. A trail of bubbles reached the surface. Then nothing.

Evie and Kit were alone in the chamber.

Cold water lapped at Evie's waist, rising higher every moment.

Thirty-Seven

E VIE SHOOK KIT by the shoulder. When that had no effect, she yelled in his ear.

'Mr Hollins! Kit! Wake up! We're trapped!'

Groggily, he opened his eyes.

The water was at Evie's chest and still climbing.

Suddenly Kit was wide awake. He fought the ropes, but they held him tight. 'I can't get free,' he said at last. 'You have to get out. Now.' He jerked his chin towards the ladder, and the dim light through the trapdoor above their heads. 'Get help.'

She shook her head. 'The water's rising. There's no time.'

'Listen to me,' he said, ashen-faced and white-lipped. 'Don't be a fool. Get out of here. Save yourself.'

'It's you who's a fool. I'm not leaving you to drown.'

'No! Evie—'

She gave herself no time to think – afraid her resolve would waver. Ignoring his protests, she took a deep breath, held her nose and ducked under the ink-black water, feeling across the stone floor. She opened her eyes but could see nothing through the swirling murk. At last, her lungs screaming, she rose to the surface, gasping and spitting out gritty, muddy water.

Kit was a few feet away from her now. She could see his lips moving but couldn't hear what he was shouting through the water clogging her ears. He shook his head frantically and she realised he was begging her to get away, to save herself. She ignored his pleas. Filling her lungs again, she plunged back down, groped along the stone floor till her lungs were searing and black spots swam under her closed eyelids. As she kicked upwards, her foot slid over something that moved. She came up, spluttering for breath, pushing back her waterlogged hair and saw Kit struggling furiously against his bonds.

For a third time she sank under the water, fumbling in ever-widening circles. As bands of pain pulled tight across her chest, her fingers touched something, lost it, caught it again. She broke the surface, gasping but triumphant, holding the dagger that Marcus had used to cut her. Water filled her eyes, her ears, her mouth, stung the back of her throat and made a hampering carpet of her hair. She tried to stand, scrabbling with her toes, but she was no longer in her depth. She swam a few erratic strokes towards Kit. The water level had reached his chin.

He put his mouth close to her ear and yelled, 'They're pulling up the ladder. You have to go! Now!'

'I'm not leaving you!'

Once more, she filled her lungs. Propelling herself downwards from his shoulder, she felt along his body till she found the ropes binding him. Using the dagger to cut them was horribly awkward. Unable to see in the murky water, she had to find the right place by touch alone. Though the point of the dagger was sharp, the edges of the blade were blunt, ill-suited to sawing. The dagger kept skidding across the slippery, water-saturated ropes, and Evie feared she was cutting Kit's wrists and hands more often than his bonds. Twice more she came up for air, clutching onto Kit for support as she coughed and retched, then ducking beneath the water. Each time she rose, the water level had inched further up his face.

Then came a moment when Evie broke the surface to see only the top of his hair. She dived back down and sawed frenziedly at Kit's bonds, feeling his body jerk and thrash. At last, a rope gave way. She kept hacking. Another rope frayed, but the blade was blunted and useless so she dropped it and tore at the remaining strands with her bare hands. With a last convulsive effort, Kit broke free and they kicked for the surface, filling their lungs with blessed air.

From high above came a hollow boom, bouncing off the water. They looked up to see that the ladder had gone, the trapdoor was shut. The only light now came from the lamps in their niches, reflecting the water level just inches below. Above the lamps, the walls stretched upwards into gloom. Evie saw the horror in Kit's face that must have been reflected in her own. They were trapped, doomed to tread water like sewer rats till the moment when their strength failed and they sank beneath the surface.

Kit swam along the walls, searching for somewhere they could climb up, but the slabs of stone were smooth and slick with slime. As he returned, Evie saw his lips move but couldn't make out his words. She shook her head and slapped her ears, trying to clear them. Kit said something else, then pointed towards the centre of the flooded chamber, where water was still churning up through the shaft. As she stared uncomprehendingly, he turned his thumb to point downwards.

'What? No. It's not possible!' Already she was tiring, her limbs aching. The loss of blood from her wound, kept open by immersion in water, was weakening her. She shivered convulsively as the chill of the water took hold of her body. As they trod water, Kit put his arms around her, holding her up. She rubbed her ears and sank her head on his arm.

An oil lamp teetered as water lapped around it. With a hiss and a splash, it fell, its light extinguished.

'We could follow the water to its source,' said Kit, his voice clearer now in her ear. 'There must be some kind of outlet.' He didn't add: *If we can find it before we drown.*

A second oil lamp was swept away by the tide. Just one now remained, its light dimming every moment.

'I'm not much of a swimmer!' she warned him.

'I'll hold you up. The longer we stay here treading water, the more energy we use, the harder it'll get.'

'What about the afanc? What if it's still down there?'

'The *what?*'

'The creature that took Marcus Ellingham.'

Kit looked confused.

Of course – he'd been unconscious.

'It doesn't matter,' she said aloud. For if the afanc returned, there was nothing they could do.

She said no more. It was an effort to speak through the chattering of her teeth. Cold was seeping into her flesh, making her bones ache. She couldn't feel her legs or feet. Her arms were wrapped around Kit's neck, clinging to the warmth of him, but her strength was ebbing with every passing moment. *I suppose a quick death in the flooded shaft is better than a slow death through exhaustion, dragging Kit down with me.*

She pressed her lips against his ear. 'Let's do it', she said.

'Right then.'

She let go of Kit and swam shakily, her numbed limbs flailing, till she could tell she was over the place where the shaft emerged for she felt the stream of icy water coming up from the depths. Kit appeared close by. She caught a glimpse of his pale bruised face, his dark hair plastered against his head, just before the last oil lamp guttered out, leaving them in impenetrable darkness. For a sickening moment, Evie felt so entirely alone, it seemed as though she was already dead.

Their hands clasped.

'The shaft must change direction at some point,' came Kit's voice, right beside her. 'We keep swimming downwards till we find the outlet. Don't struggle; you'll waste your strength. I'll draw you with me. Whatever happens, don't let go. Are you ready? Three breaths, then we dive.'

She took three breaths, saturating her lungs with the stale air of the chamber. Kit pulled at her hand as he turned like a seal and kicked downwards. With a swift kick of her own, she followed him, down into the shaft.

CHAPTER

Thirty-Eight

A s THEY SWAM down into the icy depths, the pressure grew stronger, hurting Evie's ears, and the overwhelming force of the current hurled them back and forth against the side of the shaft. Evie's numb fingers slipped from Kit's and suddenly she was alone, unable to see or to hear, spiralling, whirling, turning, not sure if she was pointing downwards or upwards.

In the vortex of the water elemental.

An iron band of pain gripped her chest. Lights flashed across her closed eyelids. Her awareness of where she was, of her own body and its agony, fell away, and instead she saw her father reading the ancient spell, saw him realise too late that the spirit he had raised was coming to destroy him. She saw Sukey Hollins, Teddy Windle, Ethel Maddeley, lured down into the stronghold of the circle of shadows, following a path they hoped would take them to love but finding death instead. She saw Janet Rae, seeking escape from a dreary life. Fergus Lorimer, realising too late that his most brilliant pupil had betrayed him. Marcus Ellingham, ready to sacrifice love and honour for his dark ambitions, yet taken like her father by the very spirit he had raised in hubris. There were other faces, too, that she didn't recognise, floating in the vortex. Now it was her turn. They were waiting for her to join their ranks, to be borne away in the jaws of the afanc. She felt her consciousness disintegrating.

Something seized her wrist in an iron grip. *The afanc!* She tried to beat it off with her other hand, lashing out wildly, finding she was not, after all, ready to die – and felt not cold scales but warm skin. The arms about her were human, and they were holding her up . . . to a place where she could breathe. She drank in the precious air.

Her fingertips groped the space around her. She was side by side with Kit in a pocket of air just below the roof of a horizontal tunnel. Kit tried to keep her steady, but Evie bobbed like a cork, buffeted by the current, her head grazing the roof. It didn't matter. Nothing mattered except the need to keep breathing. They were not yet free. They had to move on through the tunnel, trust to luck that they would find more air further along. Kit conveyed as much with his touch. She squeezed his fingers to show she understood, and then they kicked off again, ricocheting and jolting against the sides of the tunnel.

Evie's lungs were already straining when they collided with a wall of bricks, blocking the tunnel. No time to return to the air pocket, even if they could find it again. Had they come so far, to end like this? She felt the fast flow of a current around her ankles and bent down to examine where it was coming from – a narrow gap at the bottom of the wall. Less than a foot high. Big enough to pass through? Perhaps. There was only one way to find out. She tugged Kit's arm, pulling him down so that he, too, could feel the space.

At once Kit seized her, pushing her through the gap. Evie jack-knifed, wriggled like an eel, and found herself in a waterlogged pipe; it fitted around her almost like a second skin, giving her only inches of space to manoeuvre. She hauled herself forwards frantically, hand over hand, knowing she was almost at the end of her endurance. Just as it seemed her lungs would implode, the pipe opened out, and the current tumbled her down a vertical chute. She fell helplessly, landing with a jolt, head-down underwater. She struggled to rise – and discovered the water was only waist-deep, and she could breathe again. The downpour from the outlet high above was falling all around her. She coughed and wheezed, as water streamed from her mouth and nose. As soon as she had control enough of her breathing to use her voice, she craned her head upwards, heedless of the deluge pounding onto her face. 'Kit!' she screamed.

Useless. He couldn't hear her, of course. Would he be able to squeeze his bigger frame through the narrow pipe? How long could he last without taking in air? She couldn't judge time down here but surely too much had passed. She pictured him, his body wedged into the confined space, his struggles weakening as water filled his lungs. Somewhere in the endless darkness up above her head the pipe had surely become his coffin. He was dying or already dead, hopelessly trapped and utterly alone.

Great shudders seized her. She bent double, clutching her knees, racked with horror and grief.

And then ... unmistakable ... came the sounds of someone sliding down the chute to land with a splash close by. Sobbing with relief, she groped for him – found him. They clung to one another, whilst they lay, half submerged, gasping, filling their lungs with air that was foul but, in that moment, the sweetest they'd ever tasted.

They scrambled to their feet. Evie had the sense that they were in a large tunnel, through the bottom of which ran a stream of sluggish water. They turned in the direction of the current and waded through the water, stumbling in the darkness like children, hand in hand.

Eventually, a glimmer of light showed in the distance. At first Evie wasn't sure whether she was imagining it, but soon it became brighter until it was unmistakable. They moved quicker despite their exhaustion and at last the patch of brightness resolved into the night sky, spangled with stars. They flung themselves forwards, emerging from the mouth of the tunnel and into the open.

Not far ahead, the stream bubbled briskly into a river, its dark water visible under the gleam of starlight. Just ahead of the point where stream and river joined, they scrambled up a steep sandy bank and flung themselves to the ground, panting. They lay side by side, not moving, content to rest with the night breeze on their faces, grass beneath them and fresh air moving freely through their aching lungs.

When at last Evie was able to sit up to take stock of her surroundings, she realised that they were not far from the spot where the
Cherwell flowed into the Isis. She remembered Marcus Ellingham
– what seemed like an eternity ago – telling her about an underground stream, the Trill Mill, that came out about here. They must
have been following it on the last leg of their escape.

They assessed their injuries. They were covered in bruises and
abrasions from having been flung against the walls of the shaft,
and their clothes were sodden rags. Kit's wrists and hands were
covered in cuts from Evie's inexpert wielding of the blunt dagger.
But the most serious wound was the one on Evie's thigh where
the sigil had been cut into it. Fear and the numbing effect of the
water had blotted out the pain, but now it struck her with full
force.

Kit ripped off a couple of strips from his sodden shirt, washed
them in the river, then used one to clean her wound and tied the
other round her thigh to stem the bleeding. 'We need to clean it
properly,' he said. She heard his bewilderment as he continued,
'Why did Ellingham do this to you?'

'It's an occult sigil, to summon the afanc, the water spirit. He
intended to cut three more.'

'Is that . . . what he did to Sukey?' His voice shook.

'Yes,' she whispered.

'What stopped him from completing it, with you?'

'You don't remember?'

'Not really. You started saying something in Latin. It terrified
Ellingham and those other lunatics in red capered about in a
panic. I must have fainted like a puny fool, no help to you at all.'

'You didn't faint. You went into a trance.'

He looked at her blankly.

'What happened down there . . . something like a door opened
inside you to another realm. Your sister, Sukey, came through it.
She lured the afanc to Marcus Ellingham. She saved us both,
through you. I think you must be some kind of shaman, Kit.'

'Do you mean like Madame Trent-L'Espoir?' he said, and actually laughed.

'Not like her, because she's a fraud, or at least mostly a fraud. She knew enough, though, about the occult to understand at the seance when she was in the presence of a genuine power. She tried to tell me about the opening door. I realise now that she meant you. Don't you see?'

'I don't see, no. I don't understand anything of what you're saying. Isn't it enough that we're alive?'

'Yes, it's enough.' Evie shivered, suddenly aware that her legs and arms were bare.

'You're frozen. Can I touch you?'

She nodded, teeth chattering, suddenly awkwardly aware that he was a man, and virtually a stranger. Still, there was nothing amorous in his touch as he swiftly rubbed her hands and feet, her arms and legs, now purple with cold.

'We need to get you to a doctor,' he said. 'The police will have someone they can call in.'

'No! Not the police.'

'Those madmen tried to murder you, Evie! We have to tell the police.'

'I went to them before, after Janet's body was found, and again when Lorimer was murdered. I told them about the occult sigils and the circle of shadows. Inspector Hammond thought it was all nonsense. He suspected me of killing Lorimer.'

'But . . . we have to tell them.'

'We don't have any evidence, Kit. It will be our word against men like Charles Pomeroy and Edgar Deverell-Drummond, with their money and their connections. Even if the police find the secret chamber, it's not proof that anything illegal happened. And besides, any investigation of the cellars will lead the police to Maltraver's body.'

'What of it?' He was watching her warily.

'You told me earlier tonight that you'd never killed anyone. Is that still true?'

Kit's hands tightened and his face contorted. 'He offered to pay me in vintage wine from the college. We went down to the cellars. I thought he might have Grace there, like you said. He'd put on this daft fancy dress. I confronted him, told him I was Sukey's brother, demanded to know the truth, whether he had murdered her the way Janet was murdered and what he'd done with Grace. He laughed at me, laughed about Sukey. That's when I went for him. He brought out a dagger, tried to surprise me with it, slip it through my ribs, but I managed to get it from him – and then I used it. I'm not sorry, Evie. I would do it again. He betrayed Sukey. Even if he didn't kill her himself, he was responsible for her death.'

Kit stared ahead, his mouth set in a grim line. 'I kept going, looking for Grace, until I went through a door into a round room lit by braziers. There was some kind of pattern burnt into the floor, I couldn't make it out. It seemed to be moving. And then . . .' He brushed his hand across his face. 'I don't remember. The next thing I knew, I was down in that chamber, trussed up like a chicken. I don't know about Grace. I let you down.'

'Marcus Ellingham gave me his word, my life for hers, when he burnt the kuroskato sigil,' Evie said. 'I hope that means she's safe. As for Maltraver, if anyone deserved to die, it was him. But the law wouldn't see it that way, nor would the police. If you once come to their attention, it won't take them long to find out who you really are. The fact that you created a false identity in order to get close to Maltraver will look suspicious in itself. It would only be our word that Sukey is dead, let alone how she died. Members of the circle of shadows could testify against you. If they convict you of killing a peer of the realm, they'll hang you for sure, Kit, whatever the extenuating circumstances. We can't risk that.'

He shrugged. 'At least that way I would have the chance to tell the world what Maltraver and Ellingham did to Sukey.'

'You wouldn't get that chance,' she told him. 'And if you're found guilty of murdering Maltraver, your parents would lose you as well as your sister. You've avenged Sukey, and Maltraver got what he deserved. Isn't that enough?'

He buried his face in his hands. Tentatively, she put an arm about him. They stayed that way for a while.

Then Kit shook himself. 'We need to rest. Have you a place in Oxford where you can stay safely?'

'No, nowhere.'

'Then I'll take you to my hotel room. If you're willing to trust me.'

Trust? Did she even know what trust was anymore? Marcus Ellingham's face swam across her vision, mocking her. But she and Kit had a bond now, forged out of water, darkness and the shadow of death, and she was so tired she was going to have to find a safe place to sleep soon or collapse on the ground.

'I trust you.'

He stood up, stretching his aching body. 'Do you know where we are?'

'Close by Folly Bridge. We can't go around by the road – it passes the police station.'

She wondered what the time was, guessing from the chill in the air that it was sometime in the dark hours before dawn. Her wrist-watch was gone, no doubt ripped off when she was hurled through the flooded shaft.

They left the riverbank and made their way barefoot through water meadows. The air was damp and a layer of mist hung waist-high above the ground, so that they seemed to be wading through a sea of swirling white. Evie limped, stumbling over uneven ground that was hidden by cloudy vapour and long grass, cutting her feet on stones; but worse by far was the stinging pain in her thigh. The wound was still bleeding, turning the improvised bandage crimson, and loss of blood was making her feel faint. With a proud shake of her head, she rejected Kit's offer to carry her, though she leant more and more on his arm. Ahead of them loomed a dark mass of college buildings.

Not much further now.

A barn owl flew overhead, a pale ghost on silent outstretched wings, sweeping across the meadows. A fence, topped by spikes, appeared abruptly out of the haze. Kit lifted her over, before scrambling over himself. They were at the edge of a playing field. Too tired to speak, she leant against him as she measured with her eyes the distance they still had to go.

Gradually, Evie became aware of a faint noise wafting across the quiet of the water meadows. She and Kit looked back at the strip of trees marking the riverbank they'd just left. Further down the river, several lights moved.

'It's them,' she croaked in terror. 'They must be looking for Marcus's body – for ours, too – to hide the evidence before dawn breaks.'

'They won't see us if we keep still,' said Kit. 'It's too dark. If we move, they may spot us.'

They stood motionless, hearing only the sound of their own shallow breathing, muffled by the low mist around them. Evie's heart fluttered like a trapped wild animal. She willed herself to stay unmoving, though every instinct cried out to her to run. Her hand found Kit's, their fingers clasped.

The new moon slid out from under a bank of cloud. Its light bathed the surface of the mist through which they had already passed, yet didn't reach the place where they stood, leaving them in shadowed obscurity. Evie started to breathe easier.

Then, like curtains swept back by a gigantic hand, the mist parted and rolled away to reveal the surface of the field where they stood. The long grass was marked by a trail of bright flecks, glittering like phosphorescence in the moonlight, disclosing a line that led from the river, across the grasslands, straight towards the place where they stood. Drops of her blood. The sigil had betrayed her.

Beside her, Kit stiffened. He'd seen it too.

Perhaps their hunters wouldn't notice . . .

A cry went up from the riverbank.

Kit's grasp tightened on Evie's hand and they ran, setting off across the playing field. Here at least the ground was more level, and Evie shot a look back over her shoulder to see that their pursuers had fanned out behind. With her panic helping her to push past the throbbing agony in her thigh, she ran faster than she would have thought possible just moments before, though aware she was holding Kit back. She gritted her teeth, tried to drive her legs faster, though pain shot across her chest and her breath came in heaving gasps.

At last they reached the boundary of the playing field, where high college buildings took on substance, bounded by unscalable walls. A path skirted the walls, cut off by another fence. Once more, Kit lifted Evie over and they raced along the path, past a metal gateway and doors set into the walls. They tried each one, but all were locked.

They came to another black metal gateway, towering over their heads and surmounted by spikes. Evie pushed at the wicket gate. It creaked open with a clank and whine of metal that signalled their location, and then they were running along a narrow path, bounded on one side by a thick high hedge and railings and on the other by tall buildings with barred windows. They rounded a curve in the path – and there ahead of them was a road, shrouded in the pre-dawn mist. Just before it, the path ended in another set of towering metal gates, topped by long pointed spikes.

The other gates had been unlocked, perhaps these would be too. Evie tried it.

It was locked.

'Can you climb it?' said Kit. Without waiting for an answer, he grabbed Evie, hoisting her up onto the gate. She scrabbled to get a grip on the vertical bars, clenching her teeth as she dragged herself upwards. The spikes surmounting the gates were still several feet above her. As she reached for the horizontal bar over her head, a searing cramp-like agony shot through her thigh, as though the dagger was being plunged in once more. Her hands, sweaty with pain, slipped over the smooth metal and she slid back down, stripping the skin from her palms. Kit caught her and lowered her, and she collapsed to her knees on the path.

'I can't,' she panted, struggling to breathe through the stabbing wound, trying not to scream aloud.

Kit positioned himself in front of her, turning to face the way they had come.

They didn't have to wait long. Soon, footsteps were echoing from the neighbouring buildings, and then around the bend in the path came seven dark figures. No longer wearing red robes and hoods, they were now dressed incongruously in what looked to be evening dress, their faces exposed, smooth-faced and strangely young-looking. Each held a dagger similar to the one that had wounded Evie.

Deverell-Drummond giggled. 'No way out for the little rats.'

Lamplight glinted on their blades.

'I'll kill you if you come any closer,' said Kit.

Pomeroy wavered. 'It's true. He killed Maltraver.'

'Don't be pathetic,' said an older man through his teeth. Pomeroy shot him a resentful look. Evie didn't recognise the man, but she caught the pitiless expression in his hard blue eyes. 'Look at them. They're finished.'

A murmur ran through the group. Slowly, they began to advance.

Over his shoulder, Kit said to Evie, 'I'll hold them off. Find a gap through the hedge, then run like hell.'

'And leave them to murder you? Not bloody likely!' She seized the gates, gasping as the icy metal scorched like fire against her raw palms. Fighting through the pain, she clung onto the bars, now slick with her blood, shaking them so that they rattled in their hinges, the din echoed and reverberated, shattering the still-ness of the street. Above the metallic clamour, her voice rose in a shout.

'Help us! Someone! Help us!'

'Shut her up!' someone shouted.

A dagger whistled past her ear, clanged as it struck the bars and ricocheted off. She bent and tried to grasp it, but it lay just out of her reach on the pavement beyond the gate.

Using the railings to haul herself upright she pounded them with her fists. 'Help! They're going to murder us!'

But beyond the gates, the street remained obstinately quiet.

Two men sprang at Kit, who moved like lightning, kicking back one, striking another and springing away out of reach. They eyed him warily, evidently not used to street fighting.

'You bloody cowards!' snarled the blue-eyed man. 'Bring him down!'

Kit backed away and crouched low, fists extended, keeping his body between the attackers and Evie.

'We rush him together,' said Charlie Pomeroy. 'On my count—'

Without warning, he lunged forward with a blade pointed at Kit's abdomen.

There was a loud crack followed by a cry of agony, and Pomeroy was cradling his shattered hand, his blood spattering the path.

'Seven against two. That's hardly sporting,' came a voice behind Evie.

Beyond the gates stood Pelham, his revolver pointing through the bars, smoke still drifting from the barrel.

'What the devil have we here?' said Deverell-Drummond, curling his lip as he stared at Pelham.

'What we have here,' said Pelham, 'if you don't scuttle off like the curs you are, is your deaths.' Slowly, deliberately, he pulled back the hammer.

For several heartbeats there was silence, broken by the song of a blackbird, heralding the dawn. More birds took up the salutation. The hunters wavered, their faces distorted by confusion and hatred. As Pelham raised his arm and took aim, his hold tightening on the trigger, they broke, scattered and raced back along the path, their retreating figures lit by the breaking dawn.

Deverell-Drummond called back over his shoulder, 'You won't get away with this, Evelyn, you bitch! This isn't the end. We'll be coming for you.'

Thirty-Nine

THE NEXT FEW hours blurred in Evie's mind. Afterwards, she recalled fragmentary flashes: how, as dawn broke, Pelham brought her to the Eastgate Hotel, reassuring her, in the face of her terror and disbelief, that Grace was there, safe with Harriet. She vaguely remembered a door opening, Harriet's jaw dropping in shock as she staggered in, kept upright only by Pelham's supporting arm. She had a dim recollection of Kit leaving them to return to his lodgings to sleep. But her clearest memory was of Grace, wrapped up warm under the bedclothes, her dark hair spread over the counterpane, and of herself breaking down in sobs that she stifled against Pelham's chest so as not to wake their sleeping sister. Then there had been the smell of antiseptic, followed by stinging pain as Pelham washed and dressed the wound in her leg, along with her other injuries. She had distracted herself by pouring out the whole fantastic tale to Pelham and Harriet, whose reactions veered between shock, horror and – when she spoke of the being that had appeared in response to her summons – stupefaction.

Then Pelham and Harriet had told her how they had raced to Oxford in pursuit of her and Grace. Their attempts to gain entry to Talbot College had been met with outraged refusals and threats to summon the police. They'd been hurrying to search the river-side when they came upon Grace in an alley off the High Street, swathed in a blanket amidst a group of streetwalkers. The women had spotted her wandering alone and disorientated, not knowing who or where she was, and had taken pity on her, seeing off the men who had tried to accost her.

In this, if in nothing else, Evie concluded that Marcus Ellingham had told her the truth: he had set Grace free.

Harriet had taken Grace to shelter at the Eastgate while Pelham combed the streets and the riverside for Evie until the moment when, just as he was returning to the hotel in despair, he'd heard her screams shatter the pre-dawn silence.

~

Around noon the following day, Evie sat with Pelham, Harriet and Grace for luncheon at the Eastgate. Grace was drowsy, dark rings circling her eyes, but the terrible compulsion had gone and she was free once more. The kuroskato embedded in her arm had vanished without a trace. She asked no questions and said she remembered nothing – seemingly unable or unwilling to relive all that had happened – and stayed close to Evie's side.

'I don't hear his voice anymore,' she told Evie.

'Don't fret, dearest. He won't be back. Ever.'

As she kept a wary eye on Grace, whose attention was taken up by Harriet's attempts to ply her with food, Pelham passed a newspaper onto her lap – an extra edition of the *Oxford Journal*, its front page carrying news of the discovery of the body of Alexander Crosbie, Viscount Maltraver, found in a back alley some distance from his college with a gaping hole in his chest. The murder weapon had not yet been found. Robbery had doubt-less been the motive, for the viscount's wallet, pocket watch, cufflinks and gold tiepin were missing. According to Inspector Hammond of the city's police, there was as yet no definite lead regarding who had slain the viscount, yet police thinking inclined to the view that the killer had been someone from the criminal underclasses. Investigations, declared Hammond, would focus on the urban poor and vagrants who blighted the serene streets of Oxford.

Evie leant towards Pelham and said, in a furious whisper so that Grace wouldn't hear, 'So, this is how it ends. They've covered up the murders of innocent people in a tissue of lies, and the only crime the police will investigate is the killing of a viscount – a man who thoroughly deserved his fate. They've got away with it.'

'For now, perhaps,' he murmured. 'But don't count on it being over. They know you may yet unmask them. You will have to be careful, Evie.'

His attention was caught by someone, and he waved to them, missing Evie's scowl. She followed his gaze and saw Kit Hollins approaching.

'How nice to see you again, Mr Penhallow,' said Grace sleepily. 'Would you like to share our luncheon? Harriet thinks Evie and I need feeding up.'

'It's good to see you too, Miss Winstanley,' said Kit. 'Good to see you looking yourself again.'

'His name isn't Penhallow, Gracie,' said Evie. 'It's Kit Hollins. He's an actor. Don't you remember me telling you?'

'I think so,' said Grace, drawing her brows together. 'But everything seems so confused in my head. No one is as they seem. It's like *Alice's Adventures in Wonderland*.'

'Does that make me the March Hare,' asked Kit with interest, 'or the Knave of Hearts?'

'The Cheshire Cat, I think,' said Evie, as Grace draped an arm tight around her. 'Because from here, all we can see of you is your grin.'

Obligingly, Kit grinned.

Harriet shook her head reprovingly at Evie.

'Won't you sit with us, Mr Hollins?' said Evie.

As Kit joined them, Harriet told him with some satisfaction, 'I thought you couldn't be the kind of man Evie took you for. When you recognised—'

'*The Masque of Anarchy?*'

A smile broke across both their faces.

'Why is that significant?' Evie asked, looking from one to the other. Pelham, too, looked blank.

'You should read more poetry, dear,' said Harriet. 'You might have solved your mystery sooner. And you might have had more confidence in Mr Hollins.'

Evie felt the colour rising in her cheeks. Kit shot one intense look at her, then he too flushed and looked away.

For a while they all talked of inconsequential, cheerful things. It seemed to Evie that everyone shrank from invoking the horrors of the last few days, conscious of the need to protect Grace especially against memory and pain.

At last Kit said to Evie, 'Could I speak with you, before I go?'

She nodded. As she rose, Grace took advantage of Kit saying goodbye to Harriet and Pelham to pull her downwards and whisper in her ear, 'He's so much nicer here than he was in Yorkshire. He seemed so stuck-up there. He likes you, Evie.'

'How can you tell?' Evie faltered.

'The way he looks at you, of course,' said Grace, with something of her old smile. 'Don't you know *anything*?'

Evie collected Grace's coat – for her own was gone beyond recall – and joined Kit at the hotel entrance. 'Let's go out,' she said. 'I need to feel the daylight.'

They walked slowly along the High Street, Kit keeping pace with Evie's limping gait.

'How's your injury?' he asked.

'Well enough, though Pel says I'll always bear the scar.'

Kit flinched. She saw that his hands shook. 'That man . . . that devil—' he started to say, then stopped, seeming to choke on his emotions. 'I'm sorry I didn't believe you when you warned me not to underestimate them. If we'd confronted them together, been better prepared—'

'We both made mistakes, Kit. Me more than anyone. I was an unutterable fool about so many things. What matters is that we're still here.'

They came to a towering stone archway.

'This must be the Botanic Gardens,' said Evie. 'Let's go in. I want to see green things under a living sky. I've had enough darkness. I thought we were going to die in the dark down there.' She tilted up her face, letting the light beat down on her closed eyelids.

They passed through into a walled garden, bordering the Cherwell, and walked to and fro in the dappled sunshine, among the May flowers. By unspoken agreement, they avoided the paths that led to the river.

As they walked, passers-by glanced at them curiously, and it wasn't hard to guess why. The impeccable lines of Kit's light grey suit hid the injuries to his body, but bruising shadowed his face, and below his cuffs the backs of his hands were covered in cuts. Evie, too, carried visible marks of the battering she'd received underwater, though the fact that she bore only a small resemblance to the bedraggled and bloodstained sewer rat of the previous night was due largely to the efforts of Harriet, who had gone out first thing and bought her a walking dress. Long-sleeved and high-necked, it hid the worst of the abrasions. Harriet had found boots too, though it had been hard for Evie to get her feet – cut to ribbons by their flight – into them. Gloves had been out of the question; Evie's palms were swathed in bandages.

'I think the worthies of Oxford disapprove of us,' said Evie.

'Do you care?'

'No,' she said. 'Though it's not very pleasant to resemble a prizefighter.'

'You, Evie?' He marvelled at her. 'I don't think anyone would take you for that.'

'Are you mocking me?'

'Not at all, lass.'

'I think,' she said reflectively, 'that I prefer your real voice.'

'Why, thank you, my lady.' He raised an eyebrow and tipped an imaginary cap.

'Now you're definitely laughing at me,' she retorted.

'Only a little.' He grew grave again. 'I didn't like Aubrey Penhallow either.'

They walked through an arch in the wall, past a pond and into a more remote part of the garden where no one was close enough to overhear them.

'Does Grace know what you were ready to do for her?' he asked.

'Of course not,' Evie said. 'She would be immeasurably distressed. Pel and Harriet have agreed – she will never know.'

'Grace has a loving sister.'

'And Sukey had a loving brother.'

His face contorted. 'I didn't save her.'

'You mustn't blame yourself. You had no notion she was in danger.'

He passed a hand across his eyes. *He's seeing what happened to Sukey*, she thought. *He'll always see it.* She raised an uncertain hand, then let it fall, not knowing what to say, what to do.

He cleared his throat and spoke again. 'Will you be in Oxford long?'

'We're leaving late this afternoon. My mother returns to England tomorrow and Grace is eager to be home.'

'And you, Evie? How are you?'

'I . . . never want to see Oxford again.'

'That I can understand.'

'What about you? When do you leave?'

'Soon. I'm taking the train to see my parents in Manchester. I have to tell them . . . about Sukey.'

She pressed her hands to her mouth. 'I'm so sorry, Kit.'

For a moment his eyes appeared too bright, but all he said was, 'Let's walk a little further.'

They strolled on, amidst a riot of sweet peas, peonies, irises and delphiniums. Industrious bees kept up a busy hum and butterflies chased one another through the daisies dotting the lawns, reminding Evie of the fritillaries on the hillside by the Sithwater. She heard the echo of Marcus Ellingham's voice whispering, 'Love is a weakness,' and felt suddenly sick, her stomach twisting.

Gradually she became aware that Kit was saying something. She asked him to repeat it.

'Can I see you again, in London?' he said. 'I want . . . very much, to see you. Can I call on you?'

Could he? She looked at him – the iridescent green eyes, the long planes of his face, the high cheekbones, the sweep of dark brown hair – but her vision seemed to blur. The eyes became golden brown, set in a homely rounded freckled face, topped with chestnut hair above a shy, friendly smile – Marcus Ellingham, blotting out Kit, blotting out trust, blotting out the bright day.

She turned away. 'I can't.' Her voice sounded muffled. 'All I can see is ... *him*. And *that place*.'

Darkness came into Kit's eyes. 'And I would remind you? I've been selfish, badgering you. I shouldn't have spoken.' He held out his arm, saying in quite a different tone, 'Come. I'll accompany you back to the hotel.'

'There's no need to escort me.'

'There's every need. I'm not leaving you alone here. You've made some mortal enemies and they'll be seeking their revenge.'

'In that case, they may follow me, and Oxford's no more dangerous than anywhere else.' Yet she took his arm and went with him, her bandaged hand resting on his sleeve. 'Pel gave me a similar warning just now.'

'And will you listen to either of us?'

'Of course. I intend to be on my guard.'

'And tomorrow? How will you feel then?'

'I don't know,' she admitted.

They walked on in silence. She was conscious of his proximity, of the texture of his sleeve beneath her fingertips, of the warmth of his arm beneath the cloth. There was something she needed to say, though she guessed he wouldn't want to hear it.

She took in a breath, and her words spilled out. 'Sukey,' she said. '*She really was there*. She came out of you. She saved you, and she saved me too. You could tell your parents, if you think it might help a little – unless you believe I'm completely mad, of course ...' Her words trailed away. With her disengaged hand she clutched the skirt of her dress, crumpling it into folds. 'Kit, you didn't see the afanc, did you?'

'I did not.'

She glanced up. He was looking not at her but straight ahead, his profile set, his expression unreadable.

'But ... you believe it was there?' she persisted.

He didn't answer.

'There is something within you,' she said. 'I mean, I think you have a power that—'

'I want nowt to do with it,' he said swiftly.

'All the same, a door opened inside you that might not be easy to close. Please, Kit, be careful.'

A rueful smile flashed across his face. 'So now *you* are warning *me*. Don't worry yourself. I'm always careful, Miss Winstanley.'

They had come back to the entrance to the Eastgate. As they halted, she withdrew her arm from his and they faced one another.

'When do you have to leave?' she asked. Now the moment had come, she was oddly reluctant to let him go. The feeling caught her by surprise.

'Now, I think,' he said. 'I mustn't miss my train. Goodbye, Miss Winstanley.' He strode off before she could reply.

Evie stood on the hotel steps, looking after him as he passed into the distance and was lost to sight among the crowds.

It's for the best, she told herself. *If we met again, it would only remind us of what we went through. He'll be glad, one day soon, that I've let him go out of my life.*

For some strange reason, there was a knot of pain in her chest. *Don't be weak, Evie. This will pass.*

With something like a sigh, she turned and walked up the steps to the hotel.

Three Weeks Later

E VIE WALKED ALONG the riverbed in the shadow of Hammersmith Bridge. The sky was thick with cloud and the threat of rain. There was no one else in sight; her only companion was the indefatigable D'Artagnan, nosing through drifts of flotsam and jetsam, tail waving like a banner. Round stones crunched and slid under her feet. Water swirled over her boots and she jumped back with a gasp, before she realised it was just the incoming tide. Pulling herself together, she threw a stick for D'Artagnan, who charged in pursuit, long ears sailing.

Evie watched the fast-flowing, slate-grey water as the seagulls wheeled and soared over the surface, emitting sharp, aching cries like lost spirits. The Thames was deep and wide here, the trees on the far bank barely visible through the haze. A breeze struck chill against her face and the air felt heavy with water.

Something caught her eye. She stared. Could there be something out there, moving just beneath the surface, against the flow of the current? She held her breath and watched for a minute, but the movement subsided, lost amidst the ever-shifting water.

Are you still there? Will you always be there?

She felt the ache from the sigil carved into her thigh, burning through her long, clinging skirts. Although it had begun to heal, she had noticed that it hurt afresh whenever she was near water. *Probably the damp*, she told herself, trying to be robust. She mustn't be timid about this, or she would never again be able to approach a river or a lake, let alone the sea. She understood now that she had a choice: she could give way to her fear and let anxiety over what the future might hold limit her life, or she could confront her terror head-on and become an expert in the very things that haunted her, in the stuff of her nightmares.

Papa had wanted to keep her away from the study of the occult, for her own safety. But Papa was gone, and she was still here. She had solved the mystery that had swallowed him up, and surely that had to count for something. She didn't want to give up on her studies – archaeology would always be close to her heart – but the investigation had woken something inside her, a new passion. She could take evening classes. Work by day, study by night. Surely she could do both, if she was determined enough.

Her mind now made up, she pulled a scrap of paper from her pocket on which she had written a draft of an advertisement.

E. A. Winstanley, occult consulting detective, offers expert, open-minded and rigorous investigation. Specialist in apparitions, spectral phenomena and supernatural occurrences of all kinds. Reasonable fees plus expenses. References available.

Frowning, she considered it, and then, with the stub of a pencil, added: *Discretion assured.*

Her advertisement would go out to *The Times*, though she couldn't send it until she had found a business premises to rent. She had no idea, as yet, how she would raise the necessary funds, but somehow she would find a way.

For a moment longer, Evie stood motionless. Then, with a defiant shake of her head, she returned the paper and pencil to her pocket. Calling to D'Artagnan, she scrambled up to the towpath as all around her the rain began to fall.

Acknowledgments

It's a pleasure and a privilege for me to acknowledge the people who have helped this book on its journey to publication.

To my terrific agent, Lucy Irvine. The first time we spoke, you told me how you had read two of my manuscripts within a week – *Circle of Shadows* being the second – and that you had loved them both. That's when I knew you were the perfect agent for me. And I was so right about that. Thank you for everything.

My heartfelt thanks to Calah Singleton who went all out to acquire Evie's story for Hodderscape. You have done so much to shape the final version. I enjoyed working with you so much, and hearing your vision for my books. Thanks too, for a memorable lunch with you and Lucy where we shared our mutual love of golden age detective fiction, especially the writing queens, Agatha Christie and Dorothy L. Sayers.

Thanks to the team at Hodderscape: especially Molly Powell, Marina Dominguez-Salgado, Laura Bartholomew, Rachel Southey, George Biggs and Katy Archer. Most of all, huge thanks to Delayna Spencer who joined Hodderscape to become my new editor at a late stage in the process. It has been a joy to see *Circle of Shadows* through to publication with you, and I'm looking forward to working with you on the next one.

My thanks to Daisy Woods for the gorgeous cover. It has the vibe of a traditional Edwardian novel, yet with a distinctly modern edge. It's so right for the story and enhances it in every way.

Grateful thanks to Alan Heal for the exemplary copy-editing, and for your message about how much you enjoyed reading my book. Also, to Rachel Eley for meticulous and thorough proof-reading. I felt my book was in safe hands with you both.

Thanks to Katie Blagden and Rufus Purdy, both of whom were wonderfully generous with their time, ideas, and appreciation for *Circle of Shadows*. And especially, Rufus, for our discovery of a shared love of the ghost stories of Algernon Blackwood. Julia Golding of the Oxford Centre for Fantasy gave me some inspirational feedback on chapters that she read.

Kit Nevile, who was then at Canelo Publishing, gave me an enthusiastic reception and lots of sage advice when *Circle of Shadows* won a prize in a competition run by the Iaminprint Team. Thanks to the judges at Canelo, and to Elane Retford and Sarah Post at Iaminprint for setting that up.

Paula Seager and Gavin Tangen read the entirety of *Circle of Shadows*, and both were generous with their advice and warm with their enthusiasm. Arthur Flay – another Algernon Blackwood enthusiast – also read the manuscript, and we shared many talks about the tradition of supernatural stories in books and cinema. Thanks especially for recommending William Somerset Maugham's *The Magician*. Its chilling depiction of an occult magician, based on the real-life figure of Aleister Crowley, was a major influence on how I imagined Robert Wenless.

Every writer needs writing buddies – for supportive critiques, for pooling advice, and most of all for friendship. They write too, so they get how much the writing matters to an author. I am lucky to have found some wonderful writing buddies. First and foremost, the Pinklings: Laura Caputo, Gillian Bentley-Richardson, Emily Randall-Jones, Sanam Akram, Lucille Abendanon, Sara Lilley and Carey Camburn. For years now we have sustained one another: reading each other's work, helping with outlines, synopses and tricky plot problems, and sharing information on tactics for dealing with the publishing industry. You have become my friends and allies throughout the writing of this book, as well as its predecessor, *The Binding Spell*. Your support has meant so much to me. Thank you all.

Usma Malik, Natalie Denny, Mandy Lovell, Jen Hicks, Iva Litova have been great writing buddies, ready to read, to share, to laugh, to congratulate and commiserate, and most of all to encourage one another. Anna Burtt set up the Westhill Writers Group in Brighton and provided much nurturing support and excellent advice for writers, along with a copious supply of tea and cakes. The Westhill Writers are a lovely group, and gave me generous feedback on a chapter from early on in the book. It's a great thing to find writing buddies who can help you navigate through the opaque channels of publishing. Frances Quinn, Anna Hayward and Ciar Byrne are all writers who know how challenging the industry can be, and have been hugely generous with their advice and support.

I am so thankful to have Sarah Garrett in my life. Whenever we met in various cafes, and shared the happenings in our lives, the good and the bad, you always found time to ask for the latest instalments in Evie and Kit's adventures. When I began to lose heart and to doubt that their story would ever get into print you kept me going with your unswerving belief in my stories. You never doubted it would happen for me one day – or if you did, you didn't admit it. Who would have thought I would get this far? *Well, you did, Sarah.* Which makes me so happy and proud to be able to dedicate the published version of *Circle of Shadows* to you.

To Elena and Sophia – what can I say here that you don't already know? I am so incredibly lucky to have the two of you in my life. You have learned the hard way over many years that a parent who's writing fiction can be even more trying to live with than when she's writing history. Yet through it all you have helped me in so many ways, even going with me on mysterious walks through Oxford to trace Evie's footsteps in 1904. And, of course, by tracking down nice places to eat in Oxford, reminding me that research trips should also leave time for having fun and refreshments. Thank you for your patience in putting up with me when I get distracted because my mind is busy with made-up characters. Most of all, thank you for your unfailing love.

About the Author

Marisa Linton is a Brighton-based professional historian, professor (Kingston University), writer and academic, specialising in the history of witchcraft and magical beliefs, revolution and terror. She has worked as a historical adviser, including for the TV series, Dangerous Liaisons (Starz/Lionsgate, 2022). Her previous published books have all been historical non-fiction, including *Choosing Terror* (Oxford University Press), about Terror in the French Revolution. She also writes for the popular history market such as BBC History Magazine. Marisa won the Times/Chicken House Prize in 2023 for her YA folk horror *The Binding Spell*.

RAISING READERS

Books Build Bright Futures

Dear Reader,

We'd love your attention for one more page to tell you about the crisis in children's reading, and what we can all do.

Studies have shown that reading for fun is the **single biggest predictor of a child's future life chances** – more than family circumstance, parents' educational background or income. It improves academic results, mental health, wealth, communication skills, ambition and happiness.[1]

The number of children reading for fun is in rapid decline. Young people have a lot of competition for their time. In 2024, 1 in 10 children and young people in the UK aged 5 to 18 did not own a single book at home.[2]

Hachette works extensively with schools, libraries and literacy charities, but here are some ways we can all raise more readers:

- Reading to children for just 10 minutes a day makes a difference
- Don't give up if children aren't regular readers – there will be books for them!
- Visit bookshops and libraries to get recommendations
- Encourage them to listen to audiobooks
- Support school libraries
- Give books as gifts

There's a lot more information about how to encourage children to read on our website: **www.RaisingReaders.co.uk**

Thank you for reading.

hachette
UK

---

[1] National Literacy Trust, Book Ownership in 2024, November 2024
https://nlt.cdn.ngo/media/documents/Book_ownership_in_2024

[2] OECD. 2021. 21st-century readers: developing literacy skills in a digital world. Paris, France: OECD Publishing.
https://www.oecd.org/en/publications/21st-century-readers_a83d84cb-en.html